PRAISE FOR LYNN AUSTIN

"[A] lovely stand-alone Christmas tale. . . . While fans of *If I Were You* will be eager to read the next chapter of Audrey's and Eve's lives, this charming book will also be a delight for inspirational readers looking for a feel-good Christmas story."

PUBLISHERS WEEKLY, starred review of *The Wish Book Christmas*

"Austin's latest novel has endearing characters with flaws that allow growth. . . . There's no putting down this nostalgic, appealing read."

LIBRARY JOURNAL on *The Wish Book Christmas*

"Austin shines in this excellent tale of three women who struggle to survive WWII in the Netherlands. . . . This is a must-read for fans of WWII inspirationals."

PUBLISHERS WEEKLY on *Chasing Shadows*

"Austin has written a powerful tale of domestic heroism and faith, with all three women questioning and then turning to God for strength."

BOOKLIST on *Chasing Shadows*

"As always, Austin has penned a moving, intricate, and lovely work of Christian fiction that is excellently researched with an underlying message of hope. Highly recommended."

HISTORICAL NOVEL SOCIETY on *Chasing Shadows*

"If you enjoy historical novels set during World War II, you will not want to miss the very moving portrayal of this time period, *Chasing Shadows* by Lynn Austin. . . . It shows the importance of faith during difficult times. It also emphasizes the importance of doing the right things, even when those things are not easy to do."

FRESH FICTION

"Austin transports readers into the lives of her characters, plunking them in the middle of a brutal war and giving them a unique take on the traditional World War II tale. Readers won't be able to turn the pages fast enough to find out how Eve and Audrey met and what could have gone so terribly wrong."

LIBRARY JOURNAL, starred review of *If I Were You*

"[A] tantalizing domestic drama. . . . Its message familiar and its world nostalgic and fragile, *If I Were You* looks for answers in changing identities and finds that it's priceless to remain true to oneself."

FOREWORD REVIEWS

"Lynn is a masterful storyteller. The characters become people you feel like you know and you truly care about. The plot has unexpected turns and keeps you riveted."

ECLA LIBRARIES on *If I Were You*

"Lynn Austin is a master at exploring the depths of human relationships. Set against the backdrop of war and its aftermath, *If I Were You* is a beautifully woven page-turner."

SUSAN MEISSNER, bestselling author of *Secrets of a Charmed Life* and *The Last Year of the War*

"I have long enjoyed Lynn Austin's novels, but *If I Were You* resonates above all others. Austin weaves the plot and characters together with sheer perfection, and the ending—oh, pure delight to a reader's heart!"

TAMERA ALEXANDER, bestselling author of *With This Pledge* and *A Note Yet Unsung*

"*If I Were You* is a page-turning, nail-biting, heart-stopping gem of a story. Once again, Lynn Austin has done her homework. Each detail rings true, pulling us into Audrey's and Eve's differing worlds of privilege and poverty, while we watch their friendship and their faith in God struggle to survive. I loved traveling along on their journey, with all its unexpected twists and turns, and sighed with satisfaction when I reached the final page. *So good.*"

LIZ CURTIS HIGGS, *New York Times* bestselling author of *Mine Is the Night*

"Lynn Austin has long been one of my favorite authors. With an intriguing premise and excellent writing, *If I Were You* is sure to garner accolades and appeal to fans of novels like *The Alice Network* and *The Nightingale.*"

JULIE KLASSEN, author of *The Bridge to Belle Island*

"With her signature attention to detail and unvarnished portrayal of the human heart, Lynn Austin weaves a tale of redemption that bears witness to Christ's power to make all things new."

SHARON GARLOUGH BROWN, author of the Sensible Shoes series and *Shades of Light,* on *If I Were You*

"Lynn Austin's tradition of masterful historical fiction continues in *If I Were You,* an impeccably researched look into the lives of two remarkable women. Her unparalleled skill at evoking the past . . . will appeal to fans of Ariel Lawhon and Lisa Wingate. While longtime fans will appreciate this introspective tale from a writer who deeply feels the nuances of human nature, those uninitiated will immediately recognize why her talented pen has led her to near-legendary status in the realm of inspirational fiction. An unforgettable read."

RACHEL MCMILLAN, author of *The London Restoration*

"Lynn Austin knows how to create conflict with her characters. *Par excellence.* Her latest novel is no exception. *If I Were You* tells the story of a *Downton Abbey*–like friendship between Audrey, from the nobility, and Eve, a servant at Audrey's manor house. . . . Bold and brilliant and clever, *If I Were You* will delight Lynn's multitude of fans and garner many new ones."

ELIZABETH MUSSER, author of *When I Close My Eyes*

ALSO BY LYNN AUSTIN

For Christine—
Blessings!
Lynn Ch. Austin
Psm 115:1

LONG WAY HOME

LYNN AUSTIN

Tyndale House Publishers
Carol Stream, Illinois

Visit Tyndale online at tyndale.com.

Visit Lynn Austin's website at lynnaustin.org.

Tyndale and Tyndale's quill logo are registered trademarks of Tyndale House Ministries.

Long Way Home

Cover designed by Faceout Studios, Amanda Hudson

Interior designed by Dean H. Renninger

Edited by Kathryn S. Olson

Published in association with the literary agency of Natasha Kern Literary Agency, Inc., P.O. Box 1069, White Salmon, WA 98672.

For information about special discounts for bulk purchases, please contact Tyndale House Publishers at csresponse@tyndale.com, or call 1-855-277-9400.

Library of Congress Cataloging-in-Publication Data

A catalog record for this book is available from the Library of Congress.

ISBN 978-1-4964-3739-6 (HC)
ISBN 978-1-4964-3740-2 (SC)

Printed in the United States of America

28	27	26	25	24	23	22
7	6	5	4	3	2	1

For Ken, always

And for our children:
Joshua, Sara, Benjamin, Maya, and Snir

And for our grandchildren:
Aiden, Lyla, and Ayla

With love and gratitude

1

Peggy

"I know it looks hopeless," I told Jimmy Barnett's father. "But we can't give up until Jimmy is better. Until he's home again." We stood side by side on Blue Fence Farms that summer afternoon, watching one of their brand-new thoroughbred colts get the feel of his legs. Mr. Barnett and I were comfortable with each other and never needed to say much when we were together. He looked at me and nodded, and the sadness I saw in his eyes made me feel like someone had stuck a knife in my chest. Mr. B. took me on his veterinary rounds sometimes, even though I was just the gal who lived across the road from his clinic in the apartment above the auto-repair garage. He said I had a way with animals and they calmed right down when they were around me. But Jimmy was the one who should have been helping his father now that the war was finally over. They should have been driving around the countryside together to all the dairy farms and horse breeders, treating cows with mastitis and horses with colic. Jimmy had been studying to be a veterinarian like his dad before that awful December day when the Japanese bombed Pearl Harbor.

"We can't let Jimmy give up on living," I said.

Mr. Barnett didn't reply right away. The new foal pranced around on the other side of the fence, his long, racehorse legs as thin as matchsticks. It made me smile to watch him. But Mr. B. wasn't looking at the colt. He was gazing into the distance, where the sun lit up the mountain's chalky cliffs. I thought of the psalm that says, "I look up to the mountains— does my help come from there? My help comes from the Lord, who made heaven and earth!" and I silently begged God to help us.

Mr. B. finally spoke. "Jim has to want our help, Peg. But he doesn't." He squinted his eyes as if the sun was shining in them, then added, "He doesn't even want to live." He turned and started walking back to his truck. His shoulders sagged, and I thought for the first time that he looked like an old man. He had always seemed so sturdy and strong to me, with a broad chest and arms that were brawny enough to wrestle a horse into a stall or hoist a baby calf into its pen. Yet he had a gentle smile and an easy laugh that made all of the lines in his face smile, too. How it must hurt Mr. and Mrs. Barnett to know that their only child tried to kill himself. Jimmy arrived home from the war more than a month ago, and in all that time he barely spoke to them. He wouldn't talk to anyone. He just sat in his room and stared at nothing, like he was sleeping with his eyes open. When I visited him, he looked right through me without seeing me. I ran home in tears because for as long as I had known him, Jimmy was one of the very few people who really saw me.

Mr. B. climbed into his truck, an old 1938 Ford that he'd been driving around on all sorts of back roads and across cow pastures since before the war. Nobody was making new trucks during the war, but he'd planned to go down to the Ford dealership with Jimmy and buy a new one as soon as he arrived home from the Army. Jimmy came home but he wouldn't go with his father. He wouldn't leave his room, not even to buy a brand-new truck.

I yanked open the door on the passenger side and climbed in. It closed with a rusty-sounding creak. We were supposed to head back to the veterinary clinic, but Mr. B. just sat there with his door open and one leg still hanging out. He was gazing at the mountains again, where cloud shadows moved across the slope below the cliffs.

"Mr. B.?" I said. "I'm sure Jimmy will get better again. He just needs more time."

"I hope so," he said with a sigh.

"He must have seen some horrible things during the war, and it will probably take him a while to get over them. But you fought in the first war, right? And you were okay afterwards." There was a picture of a much-younger Mr. Barnett on the mantel in their living room, wearing an Army uniform. They put Jimmy's picture beside it after he enlisted. Mr. Barnett had been a veterinarian in the Great War, back when they still used horses in the cavalry. Jimmy was a medic in this war and took care of soldiers, not horses. But I guessed he and his father witnessed many of the same things.

"Yes, some of the men I knew suffered from shell shock," Mr. B. said. "They call it battle fatigue now. We were all told to go home and put the war behind us."

"And you did that, right?"

"Jimmy and I are very different. He always did have a tender heart. Remember how he was with that dog of yours?"

"Yeah, I remember." The bedraggled stray showed up out of nowhere nine years ago when I was eleven, barely a week after Mama's funeral. It kept hanging around Pop's auto-repair garage, rummaging through our garbage every night. Pop waved a tire iron at him and shouted, "Hey! Get out of there, buster!" So I started calling him Buster. If you could have seen that dog back then, you wouldn't wonder why everyone in town chased away his mangy hide. But I cleaned him up, took care of him, and fed him, and he turned out to be a real nice dog, with short beige fur, oversize pointy ears that stick up, and a long tail that wagged with happiness whenever he saw me. Buster and I became best friends. He was all I had, really, in the way of friends. I liked to think Mama was looking down at me from heaven and that she sent Buster to me.

One terrible day, Buster chased after a rabbit and ran right out into the middle of the road. Mrs. Franklin couldn't stop her car in time and hit him. I saw it all happen, and I raced into the road where Buster was yelping and whining and trying to drag himself out of the way. I scooped him up, blood and crushed bones and all, and just kept running with him, straight across the street to the veterinary clinic. There were people in the waiting room with their pedigreed dogs and fancy cats, but I ran in, covered with Buster's blood, crying and hollering, "Help! Help! Somebody help my dog! Please!"

It was summertime, and Jimmy was working at the clinic, and it's a good thing he was, too, because Mr. B. took one look at Buster and said, "He'll need to be put down." At first I thought he meant I should put him down on the floor, but Mr. B. shook his head and said, "The dog won't live. He's suffering."

"No, no, please! Can't you do something? Can't you operate on him?"

"I don't think there's much I can do. I'm sorry."

"You have to try! Buster is my best friend!"

"Even if I did work on him, there's not much chance your dog will survive the surgery. He may have internal injuries."

I heard what he said but I couldn't stop crying and begging. Then Jimmy spoke up. "Can't we give it a try, Dad? I've seen how that dog follows her everywhere."

"The leg can't be saved. It's too badly mangled."

"Then he'll hobble around on three legs," Jimmy said. "It'll be good experience for me to see you do surgery like that." I saw Mr. B. shake his head as if he didn't want to do it, and I started losing hope. But Jimmy leaned close to him and said, "The girl just lost her mother, remember?" I held my breath, waiting to see what would happen. Jimmy took Buster from my arms. "What's his name?"

"Buster."

"And what's your name?"

"Peggy. Peggy Ann Serrano. Please try to save him! Please!"

"Okay, Peggety. Now I can't promise you that Buster will live through the operation, but I can promise that we'll try to save him. I won't give up on Buster until we've done everything we can possibly do." I still remembered Jimmy's words and how he said he wasn't going to give up. He always saw hope in places where there wasn't any.

I was over at the clinic every spare minute, taking care of Buster until we knew that he was going to live. Of course, I couldn't pay for an operation like that, so I told Mr. B. that I would clean the dog pens and the horse stalls for him—whatever he needed me to do. Jimmy became my hero for saving my dog. He nicknamed me Peggety that day and has called me that ever since.

"You operated on Buster nine years ago," I told Mr. B. now, "and he's running around on three legs just as good as you please."

"So he is." He gave me a small, sad smile and swung his leg inside the cab and slammed the door. A deep, wearying grief had settled over him ever since Decoration Day—the day that Jimmy tried to kill himself. I remembered the day because the village officials held a memorial service in the cemetery behind the church for all the fallen soldiers. I looked at Mr. Barnett's ashen face now and it seemed as if all hope had bled right out of him. I feared the sadness would be the death of him if Jimmy didn't get better. That was another reason why I couldn't give up—for Mr. Barnett's sake as much as for Jimmy's.

"Maybe the doctors will be able to figure out why he's so depressed," I said, "and they'll coax him into talking again. Maybe his battle fatigue will be better after he rests in the hospital for a while."

"Let's hope so." Mr. Barnett turned the key in the ignition and the truck growled to life.

The Barnetts lived beside the veterinary clinic in a comforting white farmhouse with bay windows in front and a frilly porch that wrapped around the front and sides. Before Jimmy went to war, that porch used to overflow with his friends on warm summer evenings. The music of the Andrews Sisters and Jimmy Dorsey's band would spill into the night from Jimmy's radio. I would gaze at the house from my bedroom window across the road and hum along to the music.

I went into the farmhouse when Mr. Barnett and I got back, calling to Mrs. Barnett from the kitchen door to tell her we were home. "I'm upstairs, Peggy," she called back. "Come on up." I found her in Jimmy's room. It needed cleaning after all the weeks he'd stayed in there with the window shades pulled down to block the sunlight as if he didn't want to see the view of the distant mountain ridge or the new yellow-green buds that were bursting from the trees. But I didn't think Mrs. Barnett was in there just to clean. She had been so excited when Jimmy wrote that he was coming home, and she'd made plans to cook all of his favorite meals, including the red velvet cake he always asked for on his birthday. Mrs. Barnett was my friend, too, and more of a mother to me than Pop's girlfriend, Donna, had ever been.

After we knew that Buster would live, years ago, and I'd been cleaning dog pens and sweeping up for a while, Mrs. Barnett came to me one day and said, "I have a little present for you, Peggy, for working so hard." It was a boxed set of bubble bath and talcum powder that smelled like roses. Then she filled up the tub for me in her own bathroom. She gave me a bottle of Halo shampoo that made my hair all shiny and nice and said I could keep that, too. When I turned thirteen, it was Mrs. Barnett who took me to buy my first bra and coached me through all the changes of womanhood. I made a regular pest of myself after Jimmy enlisted, running over to his house all the time, asking his mother if she'd heard from him. I knew how much she loved him and how she would suffer if the doctors couldn't figure out a way to save him. I wanted to help Jimmy for her sake, too.

"Can I give you a hand with his room, Mrs. B.?" I asked her now. She turned to look at me and I saw tears in her eyes. Jimmy's eyes were the same greenish-gray color as hers, like rainwater. They were kind eyes, filled with love and compassion the way I always imagined Jesus' eyes must have looked. But Mrs. Barnett seemed older than ever before, too, her curly brown hair fading to gray like an old photograph, her sweet, wrinkled face lined with worry.

"Imagine . . . our Jimmy lived all through that war, went through all those terrible battles in dangerous places with barely a scratch. And now this. I guess there are some wounds you just can't see."

"I'm going to find a way to help him." I carried the vacuum cleaner out of Jimmy's room and put it in the hall closet for her. "I'm not going to give up until he's better."

"Oh, Peggy—"

"I mean it. I know Mr. B. has work to do, but I can drive you over to the veterans' hospital once they let us visit him again. We'll talk to him and remind him of all the good reasons he has to live."

She sank down on his bed and ran her hand over the bedspread. "We waited so long for him to come home from the war and now . . . Well, we have to trust the doctors. They're the experts. But I can't bear to think of Jimmy all alone in that place."

"I'll go with you." She reached for my hands as I sat down beside her, and squeezed them. Tears slipped down her cheeks. I saw her throat working as if she was trying to talk but nothing would come out. She was the one who found Jimmy, barely alive, and I knew the memory still haunted her. She pulled me into her arms. "We won't give up, Mrs. B.," I said through my own tears. "We won't!"

She hugged me long and hard, then backed away to wipe her eyes on her apron. "Gordon and I tried so hard to get Jimmy to tell us what was wrong," she said. "We thought something terrible must have happened to make him so depressed. Something he just couldn't forget."

"Or maybe it was a lot of things all adding up."

"Yes . . . maybe."

"If we can figure out what made him so sad, we can all help carry part of that load for him. Maybe the answer is in there somewhere," I said, pointing to the duffel bag and rucksack Jimmy had dumped in the corner of his room. "Maybe we can piece the story together and figure out what went wrong."

"Do you really think so?" I saw hope in her eyes and the deep love she had for her son, and I wanted it to be true.

"Yes, I do believe it. Let's look through his things together." I lifted his rucksack from the floor and set it on the bed, watching as Mrs. Barnett reached inside and pulled out each item—a mess kit, a shaving set, his discharge papers. She found a pocket-size copy of the New Testament and Psalms, and I leafed through it, noticing that several verses had been underlined. On the back flyleaf, Jimmy had printed an address without any name: 573 S. Second Street, Brooklyn, NY.

"I wonder who this girl is," Mrs. B. said. She had taken out a photograph in a simple metal frame of a pretty, young woman wearing a nurse's cap. I turned it over and saw writing on the cardboard backing: *All my love, Gisela.* My pulse started doing the foxtrot. Maybe Gisela held the key that would unlock Jimmy's depression.

"Is she a girlfriend from college?" I asked.

"I don't think so. He didn't have a steady girlfriend before he enlisted."

"Gisela is an unusual name. Did Jimmy ever mention her in his letters?"

She got a faraway look on her face as if she were trying to peer back through time and across the vast Atlantic Ocean. "Not that I recall. But he wrote less frequently after the Nazis surrendered. He was working in a hospital . . ."

"Might she be one of the nurses he worked with? It looks like she's wearing a nurse's cap. Maybe that's where he met her."

"Maybe. But he didn't mention a woman in his letters. Or after he got home. But then he barely spoke two words to us." Mrs. Barnett and I searched all the way to the bottom of Jimmy's rucksack, but we didn't find anything else that told us who Gisela was. "I saved all the letters he sent home," she said when we finished. "You can read through them if you'd like."

"That's a great idea. Maybe we'll find another clue."

She went into her bedroom to fetch them for me but was interrupted by the telephone. I heard her hurrying downstairs to the front hallway to answer it and then her voice in the distance. "Yes . . . Yes, I see . . . Ten o'clock, then . . . Thank you."

She was out of breath after climbing the stairs again. "That was the veterans' hospital. They want us to go there tomorrow morning to talk about a treatment for Jimmy."

"Is he getting better? Can he come home soon?"

"They didn't say. But we'll be allowed to visit with him briefly after our appointment with the doctor." I didn't ask Mrs. Barnett if I could go with her, but I must have had a pleading look on my face because she asked, "Do you want to come with us, Peggy?"

"Oh yes, if you'll let me. If the hospital will let me."

"They said family only, but you're part of our family after all these years, aren't you?"

I wondered if Mrs. Barnett had any idea how happy her words made me. I loved Jimmy Barnett and I loved his parents, too. Their home once held so much life and joy, and I wanted it to be that way again, for my own sake as well as for theirs. During the war, I worked at the IBM plant across the river, building aircraft cannons. I believed that if I did my part, the Allies would win, and Jimmy and his family would be safe, and life would go on. The war was over, and my prayers were answered when Jimmy came home. But nothing was the same as it used to be.

Mrs. Barnett handed me the box of letters she had fetched and we sat down on Jimmy's bed again. He had enlisted in 1942, and his letters filled a shoebox that once held a pair of Mr. Barnett's work boots. We only had time to skim the most recent letters, sent from Germany in flimsy airmail envelopes. We didn't find Gisela's name in any of them. "You can take the letters home to read, if you'd like," Mrs. B. said, but I shook my head. Jimmy's letters belonged here, with his parents. His words were precious to them, especially since he no longer spoke to anyone.

"But may I take this?" I held up the small New Testament and Psalms we'd found in his pack. I wanted to read the verses Jimmy had under-lined, thinking they might have been important to him.

"Yes, of course," Mrs. Barnett replied. She drew me into her soft arms for a hug before I left, something we probably both needed.

I hurried across the road and ducked into Pop's garage before going upstairs to change out of my work clothes. "You need me for anything, Pop? Before I get changed?"

He was bent over a car engine and didn't even look up. "It's not like you're around if I did need you," he muttered. I handled all of Pop's paperwork and wrote up invoices for him. He was busy with a lot of car and tractor repairs these days and could have used more help, but I had returned to work at the veterinary clinic after my wartime job at the factory ended. I knew how to replace spark plugs and do oil changes, things I'd helped Pop do since I was a kid. He could have taught me more, but I enjoyed working with dogs and horses and even cows and pigs more than cars and trucks. There was nothing more amazing than watching a baby calf or a foal being born—that miracle of new life emerging into the world after a painful struggle. I never grew tired of it.

Over the years that I'd been working at Mr. Barnett's clinic, I not only cleaned the dog kennels and horse stalls, but Mr. Barnett showed me how to feed the animals and keep watch over the sick ones until they'd recovered enough to go home. The clinic also boarded animals for their owners, so there was always a dog or two to walk or a horse to groom. A month after Buster's surgery, I was feeding a newly spayed dog when Mr. Barnett asked, "How old are you, Peggy?"

"Eleven."

"So tell me. Do you like working here?"

"Oh yes, sir! It's the best part of my whole day."

"Well, then. I think it's time I started paying you for all the work you do around here." My heart did a little dance. I loved working in the clinic. I hoped he really meant it.

"But . . . aren't I still paying you for Buster's operation?"

"You've already paid that debt," he said with a wave of his hand. "If it's okay with your father, I'd like to pay you to continue helping me after school. You have a nice way with the animals. They like you."

I had nearly burst out bawling from his kind words. I had to swallow my tears and blink my eyes real fast. "I-I'll ask Pop when I go home. But I'm sure he won't mind." And he hadn't minded. The Great Depression still cast a shadow over the country, and many people were desperate to earn a little extra money. But I could tell that Pop was disappointed in me for not taking more interest in the garage that was his livelihood.

"I'll get to work and write up that invoice for you after I get changed," I told Pop now. "And let me know what parts you want me to order." Buster was waiting for me outside at the bottom of the steps to our apartment, his tail wagging in greeting. Pop's girlfriend, Donna, wouldn't let him come inside unless I was home, complaining that he stank up the place. I took a minute to greet him and let him know I was happy to see him, too, then told him to wait outside while I flew up the stairs to our apartment to change out of my barn clothes.

"You sound like a herd of elephants coming up those stairs!" Donna griped from her usual place on our sagging sofa. She was still in her housecoat and a haze of cigarette smoke hovered around her.

"Sorry. I'm wearing my work boots." I kicked them off near the door and opened one of the living room windows. It was nearly suppertime, but a quick peek into the kitchen told me she hadn't started anything for our dinner. My pop loved Donna, so I tried very hard to love her, too. But I suspected that Donna would be happier if I moved out and she could have Pop all to herself. He'd been lonely after Mama died and had started drinking every night at the Crow Bar, where Donna worked as a barmaid. By the time I was in high school, she had moved in with us. The whole town knew that she lived here and that they weren't married. And I'd been old enough to be embarrassed and ashamed about it.

Yet I understood Pop's loneliness and how he'd needed someone to talk to. Mama had been the one who would rub his shoulders after a long day of work and make sure there was a hot meal on our table, even when money was tight after paying the mortgage on his garage. Mama was the one who sewed clothes for me out of hand-me-downs and sent me off to school with my hair brushed and braided. But she had felt very tired on the last morning I saw her, too tired to fix my hair or my lunch. She sat in an armchair in our living room, her swollen ankles propped up on the footstool. "Can you pack your own lunch today like a big girl?" she'd asked.

"Okay, Mama." I smeared jelly on a leftover biscuit and added an apple to my lunch sack. Before I left for school, Mama took my hand and laid it on her stomach to let me feel our baby kicking inside her.

I never saw her again. Pop came upstairs for lunch at noon and found her sprawled on the floor. He carried her to the car and raced to St. Luke's Hospital, but it was too late. Mama and our baby both died a few hours later.

Tomorrow's trip to the veterans' hospital to see Jimmy was still heavy on my mind as I went downstairs to work in Pop's cluttered office. The familiar scents of engine oil and exhaust fumes saturated the space. Buster lay at my feet like my shadow as I wrote up invoices and ordered new fan belts and spark plugs. A few bills needed to be paid, but business at the garage was good, and we had more money coming in than going out. All the while I worked, writing checks and adding numbers on our adding machine, I kept reaching down to scratch behind Buster's ears, and I prayed that the doctors would tell us Jimmy was getting better and that he would be able to come home tomorrow.

Along with Buster, Jimmy had helped fill the hole in my life during those terrible, lonely years after Mama died and everything at home had started falling apart. Jimmy did chores alongside me at the clinic after I started working there, and even though he was four years older than me, he would still take time to say, "How are you doing today, Peggety?" He would always ask me about my day the way Mama used to do.

About a year after Mama died, Jimmy found me slumped in an empty horse stall one day, crying my eyes out. "Hey, hey! What's wrong, Peggety?" he'd asked.

"Nothing . . . nothing." I sniffed and wiped my nose on my sleeve, but when I tried to stand up, he made me sit down again.

"Let's just sit here a minute and you can tell me about it," he'd said. He sank down in the straw beside me and waited. He just waited, as if he had all the time in the world, braiding a few pieces of straw together while he did. His patience won me over. My story spilled out with my tears.

"Some kids pushed me down in the mud on my way home from school, then they laughed at me. They always make fun of me, saying that I have cooties. Sometimes they call me 'grease monkey,' and they make ape noises at me because of Pop's garage, and because I can never get the grease out from under my fingernails after I help him. But today they made fun of me because of Buster. They called me 'dog girl,' and they howled and barked at me all the way home." I felt beat up all over again as I told Jimmy my story.

"Who are these kids?" he said when I finished. He was roaring mad. "Tell me their names, and I'll take care of them for you." There were too many to name.

"It doesn't matter," I said.

"Of course it matters!"

"Pop says I have to learn to stand up for myself." He'd also said, *"Sticks and stones may break your bones, but names will never hurt you."* But that wasn't true. The names did hurt.

"Those other kids are wrong," Jimmy said. "You're a great kid, Peggety. And Buster is one of the bravest dogs I know." Tears filled my eyes again at his words. "You should tell your teacher about those bullies."

"Okay." I had nodded my head so he would believe that I would do it. But my teacher that year was Miss Hastings, and she looked at me the same way all the kids in my class did. I longed to stand close to her because she smelled nice, the way my mama had. I'd started to forget my mama, and I didn't want to. But whenever I got too close, Miss Hastings would back away a little bit.

I never told her about the bullies, of course. The kids still made fun of me, and Miss Hastings still kept her distance from me. But the fact that Jimmy had cared, that he would have stood up to all those other kids for me, meant everything. *"You're a great kid, Peggety. You're a great kid."* I repeated those words to myself again and again. And I kept the little straw braid he had made to remind me of them.

That was years ago, but oh, how I wished Jimmy would open his soul to me now the way I had with him that day. I would listen to him and do anything I could to make things right. It was a terrible feeling not to be able to help my best friend.

I took Buster up to my room after Donna left for work. That night, I read through all the New Testament verses Jimmy had underlined in his little Bible, trying to see a pattern, but I couldn't. I was ready to give up when I saw that the first verse of Psalm 22 had been underlined. "My God, my God, why hast thou forsaken me? why art thou so far from helping me, and from the words of my roaring?" In the margin beside it, he'd written *Gisela*.

I made up my mind that when we visited Jimmy tomorrow, I would bring his little Bible. I still had the braid of straw he'd made, and I used it to mark the page with Psalm 22. Jimmy used to believe in God and in prayer. I wondered if he still did.

I turned off the light, picturing the woman's face in the photograph. "Who are you, Gisela?" I asked the smiling girl. "What happened that Jimmy can't bear to talk about it?"

2

Gisela

On the day that the world came to an end for my family and me, it didn't happen through a flood the way it had for our ancestors in Noah's days. It ended with fire. That day was November 9, 1938, my sixteenth birthday. We'd had a quiet celebration in our apartment in the Jewish neighborhood in Berlin where Mutti's and Vati's families had lived for generations. But unlike past birthdays when our apartment overflowed with aunts and uncles and cousins, only Mutti and Vati and my ten-year-old sister, Ruthie, were there to celebrate with me.

Our family had sensed disaster five years earlier, when Adolf Hitler came to power, and my uncles had immediately begun looking for ways to flee Berlin. My father refused to run. "This storm will blow over," he insisted after the Reichstag burned in 1933. "Just like the tides at sea, the water may rise but it always recedes again. People will come to their senses. The Nazi Party won't remain in power very long."

The tide didn't recede. It continued to rise higher and higher until it became an overwhelming flood. Vati's two brothers planned to flee to the United States but learned there were immigration quotas and only a limited number of Jews were allowed to enter each year. Uncle Hermann went to Ecuador and Uncle Aaron to Cuba while they waited to enter the United States. Mutti's brother and his family moved to Paris, taking my beloved grandmother with them. My family was the only one left in Berlin.

On the gray November afternoon of my birthday, the tension in Berlin's streets resembled a beehive that had been poked with a stick, as Ruthie and I hurried home from our Jewish school. Vati arrived home early from work. He tried to make us believe it was for me, but I saw the worry and fear in his eyes. I rescued his newspaper from the rubbish bin and read the headlines. A German diplomat named Ernst vom Rath had been assassinated in Paris by a seventeen-year-old Jewish man. It seemed like a distant spark, miles away from Berlin, but it ignited a conflagration, unleashing a firestorm of hatred known as Kristallnacht—the night of broken glass. A night of terror.

Vati gave me a book of poems by the American poet Emily Dickinson for my birthday. It was a lovely volume with gold lettering on the leather cover. The poems were in English, a language I was studying. Mutti's birthday present to me was a pearl necklace that had belonged to her grandmother. I had put the pearls on and was delighting in their cool, silky feel against my skin when we heard shouts and screams in the street below our apartment. We ran to the window and watched in horror as young men from the Hitler Youth poured onto our street, smashing into the ground-floor shops and looting the contents. When the Jewish owners tried to stop them, the youths dragged them into the street and beat them mercilessly. The angry shouts and bloodcurdling screams were like something from a nightmare. Then Vati noticed smoke and flames billowing from the synagogue down the block, and he ran to fetch his coat.

"Daniel, no!" Mutti begged. "Please, don't go out there! Please!"

"I have to help rescue the holy books," he replied. "Turn off the lights, Elise, and don't answer the door."

The firemen arrived but used their hoses only to prevent the Gentile-owned buildings from burning, not to save our synagogue. My body trembled as terror overwhelmed me. Vati! My beloved Vati was out there! Mutti pulled me away from the window and made Ruthie and me hide in her bedroom. The stench of smoke filled the apartment as the night dragged on. The sound of shattering glass crashed continuously as if thousands of crystal chandeliers were plunging to the ground.

When Kristallnacht finally ended after two days, we learned that hundreds of Jewish buildings and businesses had been set on fire all across Berlin. Jewish homes and schools and hospitals had been ransacked and demolished with axes and clubs and sledgehammers. Hundreds of Jews had been beaten and slaughtered. When the last of the flames died away and the smoke cleared, I was no longer a child.

Vati never returned home. We waited in suspense for two months to find out what had happened to him. In January, we finally received a postcard from him and wept with relief to learn that he was still alive. He'd been arrested along with thousands of other Jewish men and sent to the Buchenwald concentration camp. He was never given a reason why or told what his crime was. The Nazis didn't need a reason. *Take the girls and leave Berlin without delay,* the postcard read. *Go to my brother Aaron. I love you more than words can ever say.* Mutti wept for three hours after reading it.

"We need to go to Cuba like Vati said," I told her when she finally calmed down. "Do you know if he was able to get our visas and landing permits?"

Tears filled Mutti's eyes again as she shook her head. "I don't know anything about it. He didn't want me to worry. I wouldn't even know where to begin." Mutti fell into such a pit of despair that I didn't think she would ever climb out. She had depended on Vati for everything, and he'd indulged and spoiled her. She'd never had to make plans beyond tomorrow, and she was incapable of doing it now. If my mother, my sister, and I were going to find refuge in Cuba, I was going to have to save the three of us myself.

I started by going to Vati's former law office, trudging alone through the snowy streets since Jews weren't allowed to take public transportation. One of Vati's law partners, Herr Kesler, had been a lifelong friend and had remained one even after it became forbidden to socialize with us. He looked shaken when I told him that Vati was in Buchenwald. "I am truly sorry to hear that," he said when he could speak.

"He wants us to escape to Havana, Herr Kesler, but Mutti doesn't know where our papers are."

He looked up, his expression brightening. "They're here. The Cuban landing permits are here, in our office safe. Your father completed the affidavits and other paperwork your family needs for your US visas, and you're on the waiting list."

My relief was so profound that I sank to the floor. Herr Kesler hurried around his desk and helped me to a chair, calling for his secretary to fetch me a cup of coffee.

"He also put money in the safe for your steamship tickets, but there wasn't quite enough yet. He had to pay an exorbitant amount for the landing permits. He'd planned to sell a few more things."

"We can sell these pearls," I said, fingering the necklace Mutti had given me for my birthday. I seldom took it off.

"No, my dear child," he said, his voice gentle. "Those are precious to you and your family. Keep them. I'll come to your apartment this evening after dark and talk to your mother. I'll do whatever I can to get your father released from Buchenwald, but the three of you need to escape to Cuba as soon as possible."

In the weeks that followed, Herr Kesler helped us sell our remaining possessions to raise money. He had to do it on the sly by claiming that Vati owed him money and he was confiscating our possessions in payment. We sent a package with food and warm socks to Vati in Buchenwald and lived like vagrants in our nearly empty apartment while we waited.

And then in May, a miracle! God parted the Red Sea for Vati, thanks, I suspected, to the behind-the-scenes efforts of Herr Kesler. My father sent a postcard saying that he and a handful of other Jewish prisoners would be released from Buchenwald provided they left Germany for good within two weeks. They would not, however, be allowed to take their families.

I raced across Berlin to Herr Kesler's office on a sunny spring day with Vati's postcard in hand. He was overjoyed for us. "I'll have my secretary check all the steamship lines," he said. "We'll book you on the first voyage to Cuba that we can find."

"But Vati isn't supposed to travel with us."

"I know. But perhaps if I book his ticket in tourist class, and your mother books yours in first class, we can get away with it. You can reunite on board."

I gave him a fervent hug. "How will we ever thank you for everything you've done?"

"There's no need. Your father is a good man. Your family doesn't deserve any of this."

Herr Kesler learned that the Hamburg-Amerika-Linie's luxury passenger ship *St. Louis* would be making a special voyage to Havana, Cuba, departing from Hamburg on May 13. It would be carrying more than 900 passengers, nearly all of us Jewish. The cost was 800 Reichsmarks for each first-class ticket and 600 Reichsmarks for tourist-class. The Nazis required us to pay an additional 230 Reichsmarks each for the return voyage, in spite of the fact that none of us planned to return. After purchasing the tickets and our train fare to Hamburg, our money was nearly depleted. It didn't matter. The government would allow us to leave with only ten Reichsmarks each in our pockets. Six months after Kristallnacht, our ordeal was almost over. Our family would be safe in Cuba while we waited for our turn to immigrate to the United States.

My stomach ached with apprehension on the train journey from Berlin to Hamburg. Would Vati really be waiting there for us? Would the Nazis really allow us to leave? I worried and fretted about a thousand things that might go wrong, but most of all, I feared that this would turn out to be a cruel, sadistic trick, and we would be left with nothing—no father, no money, no belongings, no home to return to in Berlin. But I prodded Mutti and Ruthie forward in spite of my fears. That was my job now.

When we arrived at the port in Hamburg that evening, the line of passengers waiting to board stretched down the wharf to the gangway. I halted in amazement to view the immense ship. It was impossible to see all of it from where I stood, but the sight of its great black hull, its pristine white upper structure with dangling lifeboats, and its two steaming smokestacks painted red, white, and black renewed my courage. A brass band from the steamship company played lively music to see us off on our journey. It felt to me like the Nazis were celebrating our departure, saying "good riddance," especially when I saw flags with swastikas flying on board the *St. Louis*. For a moment, I had the terrifying thought that we were boarding a floating prison.

"Where's Daniel?" Mutti whispered, glancing around as we took our place in line. "Do you see him anywhere?" I didn't. We inched forward, closer and closer to the gangway. Water heaved and slapped against the pier and the ship's hull. The ropes tying the ship to the dock were thicker than my legs.

"We shouldn't be departing on the Sabbath," I heard a woman behind me say. "And today is also the thirteenth. Those are very bad omens."

"Superstitious nonsense," a man replied.

"Even if it is nonsense," she said, "we shouldn't be breaking the Sabbath."

When it was finally our turn to board, my mother halted as if she had decided to go no farther. She still hadn't seen Vati and she'd been insisting for months that she wouldn't go to Cuba without him. "Maybe he's already on board," I whispered to her. "Come on, and don't make a fuss. He isn't supposed to travel with us, remember?"

A steward escorted us to our wood-paneled stateroom. I'd never been on a ship before, and I was the last person to go inside, unable to stop gawking at the splendid interior. It resembled one of the grand hotels where we used to stay on holidays. After the steward left, I was about to close the door when I noticed a sudden movement in the shadows outside our stateroom. It was Vati! I let out a cry and ran into his arms. Mutti and Ruthie heard me and ran out to hug him, too.

"Daniel! Oh, Daniel! I thought I'd never see you again," Mutti wept. She clung to him as if she'd never let go. I heard voices approaching in the corridor and quickly pushed everyone into our room, closing the door.

"I'm not supposed to be on this deck," Vati said, "but I had to see you, Elise. I had to know that you and our girls were here. That you were safe."

"Stay with us, Daniel. Who's to know?"

"The stewards down below know who all of the former prisoners from Buchenwald are. They'll know if one of us goes missing. We have nice living quarters down there, a deck, common rooms, and our own dining room, separate from first class. I'll be fine, Elise. Once we're out at sea, we'll find a place to meet every day. The voyage only takes two weeks."

I wiped my tears of joy and relief. Vati was with us again. I didn't have to hold our family together anymore. Ever since Kristallnacht, I'd felt as though I was lugging a huge steamer trunk on my back as I carried the weight of responsibility for my mother and sister. Now I could finally set it down again. I could relax and enjoy the voyage, and I wanted to savor every moment of our journey to freedom, including our departure. "It must be almost time to set sail," I said. "I'm going up on deck to watch us shove off, if that's all right. Come with me, Ruthie." I grabbed her hand and opened the door, not waiting for my parents to reply. They needed a few minutes alone after all these months apart.

The crowd of somber passengers that had already gathered at the rail seemed strangely subdued to me. I wondered if they had the same mixed feelings that I did—relief at finally escaping the fires of persecution, yet sorrow at leaving our homeland, our ancestors' homeland. Would we ever see Germany again? Some of the passengers were waving to people on the wharf below, but we didn't have anyone to wave to. The band continued to play, oblivious to the shouted commands of the sailors and dockworkers as they raised the gangway and untied ropes. The sudden blast of the ship's whistle made me jump and cover my ears. Ruthie let out a startled yelp too, then we looked at each other and laughed. The band stopped playing below. The ship trembled beneath me. We were moving. The gap of water separating us from shore grew wider. I wanted to watch the city of Hamburg grow smaller and smaller until it disappeared from sight. My old life was ending and a new one beginning.

"Right on time," a voice behind me said. I turned to see a young man about my age studying his pocket watch. "Germans are always on time." He closed the lid and returned the watch to his pant pocket. He was as handsome as a film star, with hair the color of honey and eyes the same greenish-blue color as the water. I wondered if he was a Gentile and if he would dare to speak to me if he knew I was Jewish. He smiled and held out his hand. "*Guten Abend*. I'm Sam Shapiro." A Jewish name. I smiled in return and released Ruthie's hand to shake his. That was the very first time I held Sam's strong, warm hand in mine.

"I'm Gisela," I told him. "Gisela Wolff."

"You can take that off now," he said, pointing to the yellow star we were required to wear on our clothing. "We're no longer in Germany. We're free."

3

Peggy

JUNE 1946

I rode into Newburgh with Mr. and Mrs. Barnett the following morning, and we took the car ferry across the Hudson River to the veterans' hospital in Wappingers Falls. We were a little early and more than a little nervous, so we spent a few minutes walking around outside the hospital. The peaceful grounds offered a sweeping view of the river and of the distant mountains that had surrounded me and grounded me since childhood. I hoped Jimmy could see the mountains from his hospital room and that they would remind him of home and the people who loved him.

I had remembered Jimmy's Bible and I pulled it from my pocket to show his parents. "I brought this along to give to Jimmy, if that's okay with you."

His mother caressed my shoulder. "Of course, Peggy. That's a wonderful idea."

"And look—I found the name Gisela, the woman in the photograph, written in the margin beside this psalm."

I showed Mr. Barnett the marked page and he shook his head in bewilderment. "Martha showed me the photograph but neither of us can recall Jim ever mentioning her."

"There's an address in Brooklyn written on the back page. See? Does Jimmy know someone who lives there?"

Mr. B. studied it for a moment. "Not that I know of. Maybe it's one of his Army buddies."

"Maybe we'll get a chance to ask him today." I put the Bible back in my pocket as we walked up the stairs to go inside. The hospital was a square brick building three stories tall, with an odd white-pillared replica of a Greek temple pasted onto the second floor like an afterthought. It was as if someone had decided that the institution's dull facade needed to be taken more seriously, so they added a completely useless miniature version of the Parthenon. It did nothing to inspire my confidence in the VA. The waiting room was stark and institutional, with drab linoleum floors, a row of uncomfortable metal chairs, and an antiseptic odor that made my nose tingle. A soldier at the information desk led us up a flight of stairs to Dr. Morgan's office for our appointment.

I disliked the doctor almost immediately, even before he began speaking to us as if we were barely worth his time. He ordered us to sit, then lit a cigarette.

"Corporal Barnett is suffering from combat exhaustion," he said, exhaling smoke with his words. "It's my considered opinion that he could benefit from a course of insulin therapy."

"What's that?" Mrs. Barnett asked.

The doctor ignored her question, tapping ash into his ashtray as he consulted the papers in his file folder. "It says here that he served as a combat medic."

"That's right," Mr. Barnett replied. He reached to take his wife's hand.

"Because of the nature of their work, medics often suffer from compassion fatigue as well as combat stress. Their condition can sometimes be relieved by therapeutic rest. With insulin therapy, patients are administered large doses of insulin each day over a period of weeks in order to induce a coma. The goal is to shock the system out of psychoneurosis."

I nearly cried out in protest. I hated the way he talked about Jimmy as if he were a case to be solved instead of the living, breathing man we loved. But Mr. Barnett interrupted first. "An insulin coma? Is that even safe?"

"Of course." Dr. Morgan drew on his cigarette again, then waved his hand dismissively as he exhaled. "Why else would I prescribe it?" I had seen Mr. Barnett approach his four-legged patients with more concern and compassion than Dr. Morgan showed us. "Insulin therapy has been in use for some time. The deep, induced coma gives patients' brains relief from anxiety and the nightmares which often plague them."

"And you believe this will cure our son's depression?" Mr. Barnett asked.

"We prefer the word *relieve* rather than *cure*. Psychoneurosis isn't some ordinary disease with an instant cure. It will require time and expertise to ameliorate the patient's symptoms so we can dig down to the root cause."

"I would think it's fairly obvious what the root cause is," Mr. Barnett said. "Our son, Jim, just witnessed the horrors of modern warfare. He went away healthy and whole and came home a broken man."

"Yet millions of other soldiers have been able to resume their former lives, haven't they? Unfortunately, for the handful like Corporal Barnett, the war has acted as a catalyst, exacerbating the patient's underlying childhood neuroses."

I wanted to punch the smug doctor right in his cigarette-smoking mouth. How dare he accuse Jimmy of being ill as a child, before the war! He'd grown up in a happy, loving home with two devoted parents. The Barnetts seemed to have been shocked speechless.

Dr. Morgan held up his hand as if to stop our protests before we spoke them. "The purpose of this appointment is to explain the treatment—which I have just done—and to inform you that the treatments will begin tomorrow morning."

I wanted to beg the Barnetts to refuse and to bring Jimmy home with us right now. But I had no right to interfere.

"How is Jimmy?" Mrs. Barnett asked. "He's been here for a week now. Is there any improvement at all?"

"We've been observing him all week before deciding which course of therapy he might benefit from. Once the insulin therapy begins, it may take several weeks or even months to see an improvement."

There was little more for anyone to say. The Barnetts were desperate to help their son and would do anything the experts said. And I was eager to get out of the stifling office. The doctor's cold, impersonal words along with his arrogance and his clouds of cigarette smoke made me feel as though I couldn't breathe. I wanted to see Jimmy for myself.

Dr. Morgan crushed out his cigarette. "Any questions?"

"How often may we visit?" Mrs. Barnett asked.

"Not at all for the first two weeks of therapy. Reminders of family and home may only confuse and upset him. After that, visiting hours are on Sunday afternoons." He pushed a little button on his desk. The door opened behind us and the soldier reappeared. "Show them the way out, Private." The meeting was over. It had lasted as long as it took the doctor to smoke one cigarette.

We followed the soldier down a different flight of stairs to a nurses' station. "Patient's name?" one of the nurses asked.

"James Barnett," his mother replied. She took her husband's hand again.

"He's in the common area. This way." We followed her to a large, sunny room at the rear of the building, facing the river. Patients in hospital pajamas sat around the room, some reading books, some sitting at tables playing cards, some talking to the orderlies, and some simply staring outside at a group of patients playing baseball on a distant field. "You'll have to keep this visit short," the nurse said. "Twenty minutes at the most, please." She gestured to a pale, thin man seated by the door.

I didn't recognize Jimmy. He had always been robust and vigorous, a country boy who'd grown up in the outdoors, but now he resembled the concentration camp survivors I'd seen in newsreels. He rose like an old man as we approached and let his parents embrace him. "Hey, it's me—Peggety," I said when it was my turn. His face showed no emotion.

The Barnetts each took one of his arms and led him outside through the open door. He seemed to like being outside, where the grounds resembled a park with trees and benches and winding walkways. Mrs. Barnett talked about the spring garden she was planting, and I told him about the new racehorses that had been born on Blue Fence Farms. Mr. Barnett described the pickup truck he was still thinking of buying. Jimmy didn't respond to any of us. He walked like a weary soldier carrying an overloaded pack. I wished he would talk to us and let us carry some of his burden. He suddenly halted in the middle of the path.

"I'm tired," he said with a soul-weary sigh.

"Do you want to go back inside?" his father asked. Jimmy nodded, and we slowly led him back to the common room. We found a grouping of empty chairs and sat there with him. None of us could take our eyes off him, knowing our time together was quickly slipping away. Would Jimmy even know who we were the next time we came? I remembered his Bible and pulled it from my pocket.

"Here. This is yours. I thought you might want it." I had to lift one of Jimmy's hands and fold his fingers around the book.

"He can't have that," a voice from behind me said. I turned to see one of the orderlies glaring down at me. "He isn't allowed to have any possessions until his treatments are finished."

"It's just a Bible," I said.

"Dr. Morgan's orders."

Our time was up. The Barnetts bent to hug Jimmy again and we followed the soldier back to the building's entrance. I could barely see where I was going through my tears. If only we could take Jimmy out of this terrible place. He needed to come home, to the people who loved him. Yet I knew his parents feared he would try to kill himself again if they did.

Mr. Barnett halted when we reached the car and held his wife in his arms for a long time. I heard her sobbing against his chest. "It's all right, Martha. Everything will be all right," he soothed. "We have to trust the doctors." I turned away to gaze down at the shining river, praying that he was right.

None of us spoke until we were on the ferry again. Mrs. Barnett stayed in the car as we crossed the Hudson River, but I got out and stood at the rail with Mr. Barnett, the wind blowing my hair, the boat plowing across the dark, fish-scented river. I had forgotten to ask Jimmy who Gisela was, but maybe it was for the better.

"Do you really trust Dr. Morgan?" I asked, breaking the silence. "Do you think he knows what he's doing?"

"I honestly don't know," he said softly. "But we don't have a choice, do we? He's the expert."

I made lunch for Pop and myself when I arrived home, careful not to rattle too many dishes and wake up Donna. The Crow Bar stayed open until 2 a.m. every night except Sunday, and she had worked last night. I brought the sandwiches and a cup of coffee down to Pop's garage along with a dog biscuit for Buster so we could all eat together. I told Pop about visiting Jimmy at the VA hospital and how he didn't seem to be any better. "Poor fella," Pop mumbled. He drained his coffee and returned to the muffler he was replacing.

I changed into my work clothes and walked back across the road to the clinic. Tears rolled down my face as I worked in the barn. I couldn't forget how ill Jimmy had looked and how we'd had to leave him in that terrible place. "We need Your help, Lord," I prayed. "Please show us how to help him." God seemed very far away. My tears fell harder when I remembered that Jimmy had been the one who first taught me about prayer.

We had been feeding the horses in the little corral outside the barn one day when I looked up at him and said, "Can I ask you a question?" Jimmy was sixteen at the time and I was twelve.

"Sure, Peggety."

"It's about praying."

He'd looked surprised. He'd probably been expecting a question about horses. "Praying? You mean like . . . to God?"

I nodded. He gave me a sheepish grin before shrugging and saying, "Well, okay."

"The minister prays for sick people every Sunday and asks God to heal them, right? But some of them die anyway. My mama went to Mass every week and lit candles when she prayed, yet she and our baby both died. Why do people pray if God doesn't answer them?"

Jimmy let out a long whistle. He took off his cap and scratched his head. "I'm not sure I'm qualified to answer that," he'd replied, "but I'll tell you what I do know." He settled his cap on his head again. "Praying isn't only about asking for a bunch of things on a list. It's about talking to God the same way you talk to someone you love, telling Him what's bothering you and thanking Him for the good things He gives us. God really likes hearing what we have to say. And we feel better after talking with Him."

"But the pastor prays for a whole list of sick people."

"Yeah, I guess he does. I don't know, Peggety. But my dad once told me that God knows a lot more about every situation than we do. We have to trust Him and believe that if He doesn't answer our prayers exactly the way we want, then He must have a good reason for it."

I couldn't imagine any good reasons for my mother to die.

When I'd returned home after talking with Jimmy that day, I'd remembered that Mama used to have a wooden crucifix hanging in her bedroom. Pop must have put it away after she died because it wasn't there anymore. I searched through all of her drawers until I found it. That cross was still hanging on my bedroom wall to remind me to talk to God every day and tell Him the things that were bothering me. I'd learned more about prayer in the years that had followed, but Jimmy's words came back to me during the war when Mrs. Barnett and I prayed so hard together for it to end and for Jimmy to come home safely. And now I was praying for God to show me how to help Jimmy be whole again. *If He doesn't answer our prayers exactly the way we want, He has a good reason.*

I was shaken from my thoughts by the roar of a motorcycle coming up the road. The sound grew louder and louder until it finally halted in front of the veterinary clinic. Mr. Barnett had gone out on a call, so I hurried over to see who it was before he bothered Mrs. Barnett. A man dressed in black had climbed off the cycle and set the kickstand. He was removing his helmet. "Can I help you with something?" I asked.

"Oh, hey! Yeah, I came to see Corporal Barnett. Jim and I were in the Army together. Is this his place?"

I was normally wary of strangers, but I had the crazy thought that maybe God had sent this stranger to help us figure out what had happened to Jimmy. "Yes! Yes, it is. But he isn't here. He's . . . um . . . at the VA hospital."

The man grinned and ran his fingers through his curly black hair, matted and sweaty from his helmet. "Well, hey. I'm not at all surprised that they gave him a job there. Best darn medic in the whole Army." I simply stared at him, unable to form any words. "That's why I came here all the way from Ohio. To thank him for saving me. Not just physically, you know? But up here." He tapped his forehead. "What time does he get home from work?" He must have seen the tears that filled my eyes because he said, "Hey, hey . . . what's wrong? Jim isn't sick, is he?"

I nodded. "He tried to kill himself."

"No! I don't believe that for a minute! Not Jim! He's the one who always cheered everyone up when we were down. He was always telling us that God had some sort of grand plan for the world." He started to put his helmet on again. "I gotta go see him."

"Wait! They won't let you in. They're not letting any visitors in to see him for the next two weeks."

"Well, what are they doing to him in that hospital?" His thick black eyebrows drew together in a frown above his olive-dark eyes. He was a good-looking man—or would be once he bathed and shaved off the shadow of stubble on his face.

"They want to put him into a coma using insulin," I said. I knew I shouldn't be telling a stranger such personal things, but I couldn't shake the feeling that he'd been sent here in answer to my prayers. Maybe he knew who Gisela was.

"You gotta get him out of that place right away! Believe me, I know what they'll do to him in there!"

"We do want to get him out, but he has to get better first."

"Whatever you do, don't let them give him the water treatment. It's torture! They fire a high-pressure hose at you—first hot water, then cold, then hot. I thought I was going to die!"

"Why did they do that?"

"They called it 'therapy' to help me get over my shell shock or battle fatigue or whatever crazy name they've decided to call it nowadays. I convinced them that the water had worked. I told them hey, no more nightmares, no more shakes. Then I got out of there as fast as I could. Listen, I could use a cold beer. Is there a bar around here?"

"The Crow Bar is a few blocks back that way," I said, waving in the direction of town. "But it isn't open yet. My pop has some beer in our refrigerator, though. I live right over there, across the street. Come on." This stranger who knew Jimmy had also suffered from battle fatigue, and I wanted to hear more about how he had gotten well enough to leave the hospital. And I wanted to show him Gisela's picture.

"Okay, thanks. I've been riding all day to get here. Slept in a park in Pennsylvania last night." He raised the kickstand on his motorcycle and wheeled it across the road as I led the way.

"I'm Peggy Serrano by the way," I said as we walked.

"Hey, Italian, like me. We got the same hair. I'm Joe Fiore."

"I'm only half-Italian. My mother's family was Irish."

"So are you his girlfriend? You in love with Jim or something?"

"No, nothing like that." In truth, I was in love with Jimmy and with his whole family. But I wasn't his girlfriend and I never would be. How could I explain what Jimmy and his parents meant to me? All my life, I had stood on the outside looking in at their warm, loving home—something I never really had. Even before Mama died, ours wasn't a close family like theirs. The Barnetts were an ideal to me, something I wanted for myself someday. If I could have wished for anything, it would be to live in a house like theirs with a husband like Jimmy who would be a good father to our children. A husband who would pray before meals like Mr. B. did and sit beside me in church. And I would wish that I could work with animals all day, the way Jimmy had planned to do. Pop accused me of living my life through the Barnetts instead of getting on with my own, and he was probably right. I used to imagine that Jimmy would fall in love with me and marry me, but it was just a girlish fantasy. Jimmy cared about me, but in a pitying sort of way. He always had lots of friends and girlfriends hanging around him.

Buster came from our backyard as we approached, barking at Joe. He was very protective of me, and he didn't seem to like Joe's motorcycle. I grabbed Buster's collar, saying, "Shh, it's all right. Joe is a friend."

"Hey!" Joe suddenly shouted. "That's the famous three-legged dog!" He quickly parked his motorcycle and held out his hand to Buster. "Jim told us all about you, fella!"

"He did? What did he say?"

"Well, it's kind of funny. Some of us had lost an arm or a leg, you know? And that was a pretty big thing. Hard to get used to, right? Felt like our life was over and done with. Jim said there was this dog back home that had gotten run over by a car, and his dad, who was a veterinarian, didn't think it would live. But he did the surgery anyway, and now that dog was leading a happy life just like any other dog, except with only three legs." I was very surprised when Buster finally sniffed Joe's hand, then let him scratch behind his ears. "Jim said the pretty, young gal who owned that dog loved him just the same as before, when he had four legs. The story gave us all hope, you know?"

His words startled me. Had Jimmy really called me pretty?

"We laughed and made a lot of jokes about it. Someone said the dog's name should be 'Tripod,' so we all started calling him that. Jim would tell stories about all the crazy things that dog could do—save damsels in distress, catch bank robbers, save drowning kids—like he was Lassie. Jim even had the three-legged dog saving the world from Hitler. Made us laugh, hey? And now I get to meet the real Tripod in person."

I watched in amazement as Buster cozied up to this stranger as if he were an old friend. "You should be honored, Joe. Buster usually doesn't make friends with strangers so quickly."

"We understand each other, don't we, boy? See? My leg is gone, too." Joe lifted his pant leg and let Buster sniff his prosthetic leg. I'd seen prosthetic limbs on soldiers before, but the sight of one on this young, gregarious man shocked me.

"I'm so sorry, Joe. I had no idea."

"Hey! We should take Tripod with us when we visit Jim. I think he'd get a kick out of seeing him."

It was a great idea. I started imagining ways I could sneak Buster onto the hospital grounds on visiting day. I would need help, though. I hadn't even been able to sneak in a little Bible.

"Hey, how about that beer you promised?" Joe said.

"Oh, sorry." I led him around to our backyard, which grew smaller every year because of all the junk cars Pop parked there for spare parts. "Come on, we live upstairs."

Joe halted when he saw the steep wooden steps leading up to our apartment. How could I have forgotten about his leg so quickly? I was about to apologize when he said, "How about if I wait here and you bring it down. If it's not too much trouble."

"Not at all. Have a seat." I gestured to the rickety wooden chair I had dragged outside to escape from Donna's cigarettes. I hurried up the steps and went straight to the refrigerator for the beer. I was about to race downstairs again when I remembered the photograph of Gisela and fetched it from my bedroom.

"Ah! That's what I'm talking about!" Joe said when I handed him the beer. I noticed a tremor in his hand as he reached for it, just like the one Jimmy had. I watched him guzzle the beer, wondering if he always drank beer so early on a weekday afternoon.

"Joe, how long ago was it that Jimmy was joking around about Buster? How close to the end of the war?" In Joe's story, Jimmy had sounded so much like the man I once knew, trying to cheer everybody up and encourage them. It would help me to know how long ago he'd begun to change.

"Well, let's see . . . I was wounded over in France, trying to take back one of those little towns—Saint Something or Other—from the Jerries. One minute we were on the move and the next thing I knew, *kaboom!* The whole world exploded. When I came to, I was ten feet from where I'd been walking, and there was a giant hole in the street. I was covered with so much dirt and dust I had to spit it from my mouth and wipe it out of my eyes. All my buddies had disappeared. I yelled for them but I couldn't even hear myself yelling because my hearing was gone. I tried to sit up and the first thing I saw was that my leg had been blown off. You can't imagine what it's like to see part of yourself laying there, no longer attached to the rest of you. I had the crazy thought that I could just reach down and stick my leg back on." His hand trembled harder now, and when he lifted the bottle to his mouth to drain it, he spilled beer on himself.

I didn't know what to say. I had no idea if it helped Joe to talk about his experiences or made them worse. He didn't give me time to decide. "Then the pain kicked in," he said. "But our man Jim showed up right about then and wrapped a tourniquet around what was left of my leg and gave me a shot of morphine. I was never so happy to see a living person in my life. Bullets and bombs were still flying everywhere, and here's Jim, crawling around through all the rubble and bricks saving people . . . Hey, you got another one of these?" he asked, lifting the empty beer bottle.

"Sure. I'll go get it." I took my time climbing the stairs, shaken by his story. I felt like we both needed time to recover. I gave him the second beer and watched him take a few swallows. "Can I show you something?" I asked after Joe paused and smacked his lips. I handed him the picture of Gisela. "Do you know who this woman is? The name Gisela is written on the back."

"Hey, she's a real looker!"

"We found the picture in Jimmy's rucksack. I was hoping you might know who she is. It looks like she's wearing a nurse's cap, so I wondered if she might be one of the Army nurses."

"Sorry. I don't remember her." He handed back the picture.

"Thanks anyway." I needed to finish feeding the horses, but I didn't want to leave Joe alone when he was still so shaken up. "Where are you headed next, Joe? Back home?"

"No," he said quickly. "No, not for a while. I need to get out on the open road and clear my head." He sipped his beer and scratched Buster, who lay at his feet like an adoring servant. I let the silence linger until he broke it. "There was this girl back home I was gonna marry. Barbara wrote to me all through the war. She even took the train to the VA hospital in DC when I was there and said she didn't mind at all about my leg being gone, she was just glad I was alive. But when I finally got home, everything was different. She complained that I spent too much time at the bar and nagged on and on about me not looking for a job. We started arguing all the time. Barb said I'd changed. Maybe it's true, I don't know. Probably is. But I finally said we were through, and I spent my Army pay on a motorcycle and got out of there. I got a whole list of Army buddies I'm planning to visit."

Joe's words sparked an idea. He had provided a glimpse of the war and Jimmy's part in it, so maybe some of Jimmy's other friends could supply a few more pieces of the puzzle. Maybe one of them knew who Gisela was and could tell me why Jimmy carried her picture. "How long are you planning to stay here in town?" I asked. "I would love to talk with you some more, but I have to finish feeding the animals over at the clinic first."

"Hey, I'm not in a hurry. Is there a park around here someplace where I can sleep tonight?"

"You don't have to sleep in a park. Why don't you have dinner with Pop and me—and Buster, of course." The dog smiled up at Joe as if he'd understood and was endorsing the invitation. "There's a daybed in Pop's office that you're welcome to sleep on. There's a bathroom in there, too." Pop used both whenever Donna got mad at him or he was too drunk to climb the apartment steps.

"Well, hey. That's very nice of you, Penny."

"It's Peggy. I'm going to head back to work now, but you're welcome to visit with Buster while I'm gone. Pop's repairing a car in his garage if you want someone to talk to. I'll be back in about an hour."

"Can you get me another beer before you go?"

"Sure."

I was surprised by how quickly Pop warmed to Joe over dinner. He listened as Joe shared more of his war stories, and didn't seem to mind that Joe drank all his beer. The two of them set off for the Crow Bar after dinner that evening like old pals. I didn't know what time they finally got home, but I was startled out of bed at five in the morning by a bloodcurdling scream, coming from Pop's office below my bedroom.

It took me a moment to remember that I'd told Joe Fiore, the stranger on the motorcycle, that he could sleep down there. And hadn't he said he used to have nightmares? I leaped out of bed and grabbed my robe. Buster, who was barking loud enough to wake the whole world, scrambled toward the door ahead of me. I passed Pop, who stood swaying in his bedroom doorway looking woozy and red-eyed. "What's all the racket?"

"I think Joe might be having a bad dream."

"Well, somebody shut him up!" Donna called out from inside their bedroom. "And that blasted dog, too! I'm trying to sleep."

I flew down the stairs and into Pop's office. It was dark, but I knew my way around the junk-filled space. Joe lay writhing on the bed, eyes closed tight, wailing and moaning. Sweat covered his face and dampened his hair as he thrashed in the twisted bedcovers. He wore only his undershirt and boxers, and I glimpsed the red stump of his leg that ended at his knee. I should have let Pop come down.

Buster whined as I called Joe's name and shook his shoulder. "Joe! Wake up, Joe. You're having a nightmare. Wake up." He gave a startled gasp and opened his eyes. Then Buster licked his face and Joe seemed to relax.

"Hey . . . hey, there. Sorry about that, Tripod. Thanks, boy." I was starting to see that even though Joe smiled and laughed a lot and seemed easygoing, he was still hurting inside just like Jimmy. Joe's pain was understandable since he had endured the trauma of losing his leg. Jimmy had no visible wounds, but maybe they were all on the inside where we couldn't see them. He finished scratching Buster's head as his breathing returned to normal, then looked up at me. "Sorry I woke you up. You can go back to bed now. I won't be sleeping anymore tonight." He slurred his words a little, as if still feeling the effects of all the alcohol he'd drunk.

I pulled out the wooden desk chair and sat down, my heart rate finally slowing. "I'll stay up with you for a while."

"Suit yourself," he said with a shrug. He sat with his back against the wall, the blanket wrapped around himself. He patted the bed, inviting Buster to jump up beside him. Buster glanced at me before leaping onto the daybed. He knew he wasn't allowed on the furniture, but I decided to make an exception tonight. Joe's hands slowly stopped their violent trembling as he stroked the dog.

"Would it help if you talked about your nightmare?" I asked.

"Nah, I can never remember what they're about. Just the feeling they leave."

"Which is . . . ?" I prompted.

He shrugged again. "I don't know. The same feeling I had after I'd been hit and I realized that my leg was gone and I thought I was going to die. I was scared and mad at the entire universe. And the pain was like nothing I'd ever . . ." He paused, swallowing. "I saw what was left of my buddy Hank . . . His head was gone and—" Joe must have seen me shudder. He stopped. "Sorry . . . sorry."

"You don't have to apologize. I did ask you to tell me about your nightmare. But let's talk about something else. Tell me about your motorcycle. How long have you had it?"

Joe relaxed as he talked about his new ride and the feeling it gave him to speed down the open road, passing cars and trucks as if they were standing still. He confessed to ignoring all the speed limits, then laughed at my shocked expression.

"Hey, I already cheated death once before, remember? They say cats have nine lives, so maybe I do too."

He was impressed that I understood terms like "red-lining" the tachometer. "I've been helping Pop in his garage for years," I explained. "Pop was lost for a while after Mama died, and the bank nearly foreclosed on this place. It was up to me to hold everything together until he found his way again. That's when I started taking care of the bills and doing the accounting and all that. Pop is a great mechanic when he's sober."

"How old were you when she died?"

"Eleven. But I'd been helping Pop fix cars since I was old enough to stand up. He used to like teaching me things."

"So Donna isn't your mother?"

I shook my head. "And she isn't Pop's wife, either. Not legally, anyway."

"She was a lot of fun at the bar last night. You should come with us tonight."

"It's Sunday. The Crow Bar is closed on Sundays." I looked up at the window, high on the wall, and saw that the sun was beginning to rise, slanting its rays through the dingy venetian blinds, creating a shadow like prison bars on the floor. "You're welcome to come to church with me in a few hours, Joe. You can meet Jimmy's parents. I always sit with them."

"Nah, I got nothing to wear."

"I don't think it matters what you wear. At least not to God."

"I don't belong in a church any more than Tripod does. Right, buddy?"

I didn't push him. I knew very well how it felt not to belong. Around the same time that I was trying to get Pop to sober up, Mrs. Barnett invited me to go to Sunday school and church with her. Jimmy had a record of perfect Sunday school attendance, and his mother showed me a string of little enamel medals that he'd earned, like something a soldier would wear on his uniform. She was proud of Jimmy for all those pins, and I longed to earn that many so she would be proud of me, too.

Sunday school was divided up by grades, the boys separated from the girls, and we sat around tables with the teachers for the lessons. I knew all the other girls from school and they knew me. They acted sweet when the teacher, Mrs. Dayton, introduced me to the class, but whenever she wasn't looking, they would glance at me and whisper and giggle behind their hands. I heard the word *cooties*.

"What's so amusing?" Mrs. Dayton asked innocently after she caught them giggling.

"Nothing, Mrs. Dayton," Joanie Edmonds said sweetly. Her father owned the pharmacy in town, so she was rich. The other girls flocked around her and teased me unmercifully. I decided the string of perfect attendance pins wasn't worth going back every week and being laughed at. But whenever I needed to escape from my life for a while, I would meet Mrs. Barnett in the church lobby and she would let me sit with her and Mr. Barnett during the service, even though I didn't have a hat and white gloves like everyone else. I would pretend that the Barnetts were my family, and I would feel happy for an hour or so, especially when she would put her arm around me. As soon as the service ended, I would say, "I gotta get home and fix lunch for Pop."

Mrs. Barnett would nod and say, "All right, dear," as she talked with her friends, and I would squeeze through the crowd and run home. I supposed it was a lie because Pop would still be in bed on Sunday mornings after staying out late the night before, but I knew I was different from all those church people. I didn't belong. They were just letting me visit because Jesus told them they should. If Joe Fiore went to church with me, people would act polite to him, too. But nobody would invite him home for Sunday dinner.

"Hey, I'm taking off," Joe said when I returned from church at noon. He had his helmet on and was standing beside his motorcycle, waiting for me. Disappointment made me halt in my tracks, fumbling for words.

"What? You're leaving? Right now?"

"Yeah, but I wanted to say goodbye, you know? Thanks for taking me in and feeding me and everything."

"But where are you going? I thought you wanted to visit Jimmy in the hospital."

"We can't visit him for two more weeks, right? I'm gonna look up a couple of guys Jim and I knew in the Army in the meantime."

"Will you do me a favor and ask if they know what happened to Jimmy? When he started to change and get depressed?"

"Sure. Got it. And I'll ask them about that girl in the picture, too—what's her name again?"

"Gisela." I retrieved a pen from my purse and quickly scribbled *Gisela* on my church bulletin, then tore it off and handed it to him. I wondered if I should write down my name, too. Did he even remember it?

I watched his motorcycle roar away and wondered if I would ever see Joe Fiore again.

4

Gisela

MAY 1939

Our first day aboard the luxury liner *St. Louis* turned out to be a beautiful, sunny one. I slept well for the first time in months, even though I was still getting used to the motion of the waves and the constant thrum of the ship's engines. After breakfast, which was served by waiters wearing white jackets, I wanted to explore every inch of the ship. According to the information packet, there were decks where we could stroll or lounge in the sunshine, a gymnastic hall, a cinema, several dining rooms to choose from, a dance hall, and much, much more—including a swimming pool that would be set up once we reached a warmer climate. What I had seen of the public rooms so far had impressed me. They really were "first-class," with lush carpets, sparkling chandeliers, and polished woodwork. I could hardly believe that we were being allowed to enjoy such luxuries again. When I'd first entered our stateroom last night and saw how beautifully made up it was, it stunned me to think that people would go to all that trouble for Jews. I still feared this voyage would turn out to be a cruel trick.

"Let's explore the ship, Ruthie," I said as soon as we'd returned from breakfast. "Want to?"

She shook her head and slumped down on her bed. My sister was a thin, wispy eleven-year-old with Mutti's raven hair and Vati's sad, dark eyes. She had lived under Hitler's cruel shadow for as long as she could remember, and it had transformed her into a skittish, fearful child.

"We'll get lost," she replied. I suspected that she'd been frightened by all the reminders of our Nazi tormenters, like the swastika flags and the portrait of Hitler in the social hall where we'd just eaten. We'd been confined to our apartment for the past six months, barely venturing out after our Jewish school burned down. But even before Kristallnacht, we'd gradually been denied all the pleasures we'd once enjoyed, like attending a concert or walking in the park or visiting the Berlin Zoo, simply because we were Jewish. The luxurious *St. Louis* seemed like an alien world to all of us.

"Fine, I'll go by myself," I replied. I opened the door to leave, and there was Vati hovering in the shadows again. I started to say his name, but he held a finger to his lips, warning me to be quiet. We slipped inside our stateroom together. I had been so overjoyed to see my father last night that I hadn't taken a good look at him in the dimly lit cabin. But today, with sunlight streaming through the porthole, it was clear how much he had suffered in prison. His skin was a sickly gray, and he sat down shakily after we all hugged him.

"Are you ill, Daniel?" Mutti asked. She pressed her palm to his forehead.

"I was ill in the camp," he replied. "Dysentery, I believe. But I haven't had a fever for a week now. Just a lingering cough." I stayed to visit for a while before growing restless again. Neither Ruthie nor Mutti was going to let my father out of her sight anytime soon, and I still wanted to explore the ship.

"I'm going off by myself, then," I told everyone. "I'll be back in time for lunch."

My excitement grew as I wandered through the narrow corridors, running my hands along the metal railings that we would need if the seas grew rough. The passageways were pristine and clean and smelled of fresh enamel paint. I climbed a set of steep metal stairs, following the sound of distant laughter and voices, and reached the sports deck, where a game of shuffleboard was in progress and squealing children played tag. The sky was the glorious blue of a sapphire, and I tasted salt on my lips. I made my way to the ship's rail, holding my jacket closed against the wind, the breeze snarling my hair. I felt so alive and free that I thought I might never go back to my stateroom.

"Gisela!" I turned at the sound of my name and saw Sam Shapiro walking toward me, holding his kippah on his head so it wouldn't blow away. I was amazed that he'd remembered my name. "Hello again," he said with a little bow. "How did you enjoy your first night on the *St. Louis*?"

"I slept better than I have in months," I replied. I raked my blowing hair from my eyes, wishing I had put on a nicer dress and taken more time with my hair. "How about you?"

"I enjoyed it very much. And after that wonderful breakfast, I'm off to explore the ship. Would you like to come with me? Or maybe you are waiting for someone?"

"I'm on my own. And I had the same idea. I would love to go exploring with you, Sam. Where shall we start?"

"I thought I'd go up to the very top deck and work my way down." Sam had a natural instinct for finding his way, and we wandered all over the *St. Louis* that morning, talking about our families and getting to know each other. He was eighteen, two years older than me, and had grown up in Frankfurt. "My father escaped a year ago and is waiting for us in Cuba," Sam explained. "My grandmother was very ill at the time and my mother wouldn't leave her behind. I've been responsible for Mutti and my two younger brothers ever since. Oma died last month, and now we're finally on our way to join my father."

"I know what you mean about being responsible. My father was arrested on Kristallnacht and my mother fell to pieces. It's been up to me all these months to keep her and my sister going and to get us all out of Germany."

"I'm sorry to hear about your father. Mine barely escaped arrest."

We had been walking and talking and exploring for more than an hour by then, and I already liked and trusted Sam Shapiro. I told him the truth about how Vati suddenly had been released from Buchenwald and that he was aboard this ship. "So maybe there will be a happy ending for all of us in Cuba," Sam said. We reached the stern, and I stared down at the ship's wake, churning far below us.

"I can't imagine a happy ending yet," I replied. "Not until our quota number is called and we can immigrate to the United States."

"It's the same with my family. But for now, it's wonderful to be able to stop worrying for a while and to get away from my brothers for an hour and to spend time with a pretty girl."

I was flattered but suddenly shy. My experience with boys had been very limited, and I didn't know how to respond to his compliment. I decided to change the subject by asking a flood of questions. "What will Havana be like, do you think? What will you do there? Will you miss Germany?" We walked and talked until lunchtime and still hadn't finished exploring the ship, but Sam needed to get back to his family. Since my father wasn't allowed to eat with us in first class, Sam and I conspired to sit at the same table for dinner that evening so our mothers and siblings could meet.

Dining in the first-class social hall was like eating in a magnificent restaurant with crystal glasses and silverware, white linen tablecloths, and even an orchestra that performed while we ate. The ceiling of the huge space soared two stories above us, with a gallery around the second floor and a sweeping double staircase that made me feel like royalty as I descended to the main level. We could even choose our own meals from the menu. Mutti and Sam's mother seemed to enjoy each other's company but Ruthie and Sam's brothers, who were twelve and ten, were shy with each other.

I sat beside Sam and we talked nonstop. I'd had crushes on boys in the past, and I would giggle with my girlfriends about what it would be like to hold hands with a handsome boy or even kiss him. But the fear and degradation we'd endured for the past few years had dashed any dreams I might have had about meeting and dating a boy. My growing friendship with Sam seemed like something from a fairy tale. "Did you know there's a cinema on board?" Sam asked. "They're screening a movie tonight, and I promised to take my brothers. Want to go with us?"

"I'd love to! It's been years since we were allowed to go to the movies." We made arrangements to meet outside the theater, and while it wasn't exactly a real date since Ruthie and Sam's brothers tagged along, I was excited and thrilled to be seated in the darkened theater beside handsome Sam Shapiro. The film was billed as a light romance, but when the lights dimmed and the screen came to life, a newsreel of Adolf Hitler began to play.

"The day of reckoning for Jews is at hand," the Führer bellowed. A shock wave reverberated through the theater like an electrical current. The fear I'd felt for the past five years came rushing back. I looked away from the goose-stepping soldiers on the screen, feeling sick to my stomach. Ruthie began to sob. All around me, people rose to leave.

"Let's go," Sam said. "We don't have to listen to this." I could tell that he was livid. I was glad to get out of there, too, and so was my sister. "This is no different from home," Sam said. "The Nazis enjoy toying with us, giving us hope and then snatching it away again."

As other people left the theater along with us, I overheard a distinguished-looking gentleman say, "I'm going to speak with the captain immediately about this insult."

"Let's take Ruthie and your brothers up on deck," I suggested, "and we'll look at the stars." We had a view from the promenade deck of billions of stars sparkling in the sky and the giant swath of the Milky Way high above the ink-black water. We stayed until the children complained of the cold.

"Do you want to finish exploring with me tomorrow?" Sam asked. "I may have to bring my brothers along, though."

"I don't mind. I'll ask if Ruthie wants to come, too."

Shortly after breakfast Monday morning, the ship docked in the French port of Cherbourg to take on more passengers. The sky was sunny and clear once again, and as Sam and I stood at the rail with our siblings, we had a clear view of the streets along the waterfront. "Look!" he said, pointing. "No Nazi flags or swastikas anywhere." The streets of Hamburg had been plastered with the hated symbols on the day we left as the city prepared to celebrate its 750th anniversary. "See, Gisela? The rest of the world really is free. And now we will be, too."

The *St. Louis* didn't remain in port for very long, and soon we were steaming out into the ocean again. Sam and I spent most of Monday together, trying to take advantage of all the amenities that were offered to first-class passengers like us, including language classes. While most people opted for Spanish lessons to prepare for life in Cuba, Sam and I were eager to improve our English skills, anticipating a more permanent future. Before parting ways at the end of the day, we made plans to meet again tomorrow.

On Tuesday morning the swelling waves and tossing seas were so ferocious that most people stayed inside. At breakfast, the waiters had to raise the little wooden sides on all the tables to keep the dishes from sliding off. After eating, I hurried to our meeting place to be with Sam. "We're crossing the Bay of Biscay," he explained. "The seas can get pretty rough here." He offered me his arm and we linked them tightly to steady ourselves in the wind and rough waves. We laughed as we staggered against each other like a pair of drunkards. The delicious thrill of his nearness, our bodies touching, canceled any fear I might have had of the roaring ocean. "We're west of France and north of the Spanish coast," Sam shouted above the wind. "The Bay of Biscay is notorious for harsh weather and dangerous sailing."

"And shipwrecks?"

"Sometimes." He wrapped his arm around my waist and pulled me close. We stood in the stern, looking down at the ship's wake. After watching for a few minutes, we could see and feel that the ship was changing course. My stomach rolled over.

"We're not turning back, are we, Sam?" As frightening as it was to be sailing through such turbulent seas, the thought of returning to Hamburg was even more terrifying.

"We're a long way from Hamburg now. We won't turn back. You're shivering. Do you want to go inside?"

"Not unless you do." I felt safe by Sam's side, journeying through the storm with him. It was as if we were the only two people in the world and had only each other to think about.

A few minutes later, we noticed that the ship was changing course again. When it happened a third time, Sam said, "I think I know what the captain is doing. He's tacking—deliberately zigzagging so we don't face the swells head-on."

"How did you learn so much about ships?"

"My grandfather had a sailboat on the Bodensee, and he taught me how to navigate and sail it. That seems like a lifetime ago now. You would make a good sailor, Gisela. You don't seem at all seasick."

I smiled up at him. "Well, not yet, anyway."

By the time we reached calmer seas and the clouds began to thin, Sam and I had peered into every corner of the ship, as well as into every corner of each other's lives. We eventually veered onto the topic of our faith. We were sitting very close to each other on folding deck chairs, covered with thick blankets, when Sam's blue-green eyes grew serious. "I want to ask you a question, Gisela. Are you a Jew because you were born to Jewish parents or by true belief?" I frowned, not sure I understood. "In other words, all of the laws given in the Torah, the stories of Abraham and Moses, the Exodus from Egypt—do you believe they're all true or simply traditions carried over from the past?"

I took a moment to ponder his question, shutting out the noisy conversations around me as other passengers emerged from below to come up on deck. I focused only on Sam. I was learning every inch of his handsome face, from his square jaw with its golden stubble to his thick, sandy hair and dark brows. I loved his eyes most of all and the laughter that would appear in them but also the intensity I sometimes saw there. I would never be able to look at the sea again without thinking of Sam's eyes and how they changed from green to blue to gray like the waters of the ocean.

"I'm a Jew by belief," I told him. "For as long as I can remember, our family has celebrated the Sabbath and all the yearly feasts and festivals, and I believe in the truths they teach us. I believe in God and that He parted the seas to rescue us, the same God King David sings about in the Psalms."

"I love the Psalms," Sam said softly. "They cover the entire range of human emotions, from fear and grief to joy and love, in such an honest and forthright way."

"When our lives began to change in Germany," I said, "my father insisted God had a reason for everything that happened and we could trust Him. We celebrated Passover even when Vati was in Buchenwald— and we saw a true miracle when he was released. Vati believes God allowed him to be arrested and to suffer in the camp so he could tell the world what the Nazis are doing to us. He believes that when the freedom-loving Americans hear about it, they'll come to our rescue." I could tell by Sam's intent expression and the way he hung on my every word that he believed as I did, but I asked anyway. "What about you? Are you glad to be Jewish, in spite of Herr Hitler?"

"I am. And I agree with your father about God's purposes. The fact that we're no longer welcome in Germany—just as Jews have been unwelcome in so many other places, many times before—emphasizes the need for our people to find a homeland of our own."

"Where would that be? Wouldn't we have found a homeland by now if there was a nation that wanted us?"

"Our true homeland is Eretz Israel. God promised it to us in the Torah, and that's our true home. I believe our people will live there again, someday."

"Really? When we close the Passover seder with the words 'Next year in Jerusalem,' it seems like something you'd only wish for on a star, not something that could really happen."

"God told the prophet Isaiah that He would bring us back to our homeland a second time. The first return was in the days of Ezra and Nehemiah. Maybe the second time is coming soon."

"Vati says the British are in control of Palestine, and they're against the idea of a Jewish homeland."

"I know. But imagine a country where everyone is Jewish and we get to make our own rules and laws. A place where people who hate us aren't allowed to live—or even to visit."

"I can't imagine it," I said with a sigh. The sun was growing warmer and I pushed the wool blanket aside. "But I also can't imagine what it will be like to live in Cuba. Or the United States for that matter."

"If we're going to start all over again," Sam said, "if thousands of us are fleeing persecution in Germany and other places, why not give us a real home?" His passion for the subject was clear, his excitement infectious. "Would you go to Palestine, Gisela? Would your family?"

"I've never thought about it before. There were Zionists in our congregation who talked about returning there. But I've heard it's very primitive compared to Europe. And my family is used to nice things. These past few months have been very hard on Mutti, living in our nearly empty apartment."

"My mother is the same. But would you be willing to go when we're old enough to make our own decisions?"

"I don't know. I'll have to think about it some more. All I've thought about for the longest time was taking care of Mutti and Ruthie and getting out of Germany."

Sam suddenly sat up in his lounge chair and leaned close to face me. "What if one of God's purposes in all we've been through was so you and I could meet? What if our futures are going to entwine from now on?"

My heart raced. I knew how fond I was growing of Samuel Shapiro, and it amazed me to think he might feel the same way about me.

"That . . . that would be wonderful," I stammered. I hoped my smile told him just how wonderful it would be.

The weather cleared, and later, Sam and I listened to a small orchestra perform on the upper deck. That evening, we went to the cinema again. The captain had apologized for the insensitive newsreel and promised it would not happen again on this voyage. As Sam and I settled into our seats and the lights dimmed, he took my hand in his. I knew it belonged there, warm and snug and safe. We smiled at each other in the darkness.

By Friday, we were inseparable. The *St. Louis* was almost halfway to Cuba, and at one point, we were called up on deck to catch a glimpse of the Azores in the distance. We could see windmill blades through the drizzling mist. It was a welcome change from seeing nothing but endless water all around us every day. In a way, I would be sad to have our journey end. Spending time with Sam had been a precious gift to both of us. We were suspended in time between our past and our future, free from family responsibilities, free from the threat of violence and persecution. The crew members treated us with dignity and respect, something that had been missing from our lives for a very long time. As sundown approached on Friday, we prepared to celebrate Shabbat. Nearly all of the 937 passengers were Jewish, and the crew had set aside three separate "synagogues" where we could pray. The Orthodox congregation assembled in the first-class social hall. Reform Jews used the dance floor. And Conservative Jews met in the gymnastic hall. The fact that we were offered this much consideration and effort seemed like a small miracle, too. The captain even ordered that the portrait of Hitler in the social hall be covered during services.

As the days passed and the second week of our voyage began, Sam and I noticed that the mood of the passengers on board the *St. Louis* began to change from worried wariness to cautious hope. And our feelings for each other continued to blossom and bloom. Memories of all the conversations we'd had and the fun things we'd done together on board the ship gradually replaced the tragic memories of the past few years.

Then on Tuesday, Sam led me to our secret place behind the row of lifeboats where we would hide from his brothers when we wanted to be alone. But the light had gone out of his eyes and he seemed uneasy. "I have some very sad news to share with you, Gisela. It has upset me a great deal. I found out today that Moritz Weiler, the kind, elderly professor in the cabin next door to ours, has died."

"Oh no! What happened?"

"He has been ill for some time, but Mrs. Weiler said that he died from a broken heart."

"Oh, Sam. He was so close to freedom in Cuba."

"I know. But what's even worse is that we won't arrive in Cuba for four more days, so Professor Weiler will have to be buried at sea."

"His poor wife. Is there anything we can do?"

"The rabbi is with her now. They're having the burial service tonight, after 10 p.m., so the rest of the passengers won't be distressed by it. But Mother and I are going."

"I'd like to go with you."

Sam knocked softly on my cabin door later that night, and we held hands as we made our way up to deck A, near the swimming pool, with a handful of other passengers. I recognized Captain Schroeder and the ship's first officer, Herr Ostermeyer, their hats removed in respect. "The ship has come to a stop," Sam whispered. "Can you feel it?" I did, and it left me strangely unbalanced. After a few moments, the men bearing the stretcher approached, followed by the rabbi and Mrs. Weiler. A gate in the ship's railing stood open, and Mr. Weiler's body, which had been wrapped in a special canvas shroud, was placed on a plank in the rail's opening. The rabbi spoke a brief service in Hebrew. Then, in a moment I would never forget, one of the crew members tilted the wooden plank and the body slid down into the sea. We heard a distant splash a moment later. "Remember, God, that we are dust," Sam murmured with the other mourners.

I didn't know why the death and burial of a gentleman I'd never met moved me so deeply, but it did. Sam saw my tears and, without a word, took my hand and led me to our quiet place beneath the lifeboats. We sat on the cold, hard deck, our backs against the wall, our arms wrapped around each other for comfort.

"I feel so sorry for his wife," I said. "She has no family here to grieve with her. And she doesn't even have a plot of land or a grave that she can visit and mourn for her husband. It just isn't fair that she has nothing— that we have nothing! None of us has a place to live or a home to call our own. We're separated from our families and our friends. It just isn't fair! Why is this happening to us, Sam?"

"Only God knows," he whispered. Sam looked into my eyes for a long moment, then leaned close and kissed me for the first time. It began as a gentle meeting of our lips—once, twice, three times. Then we surrendered to our feelings with all the passion two young people in love had to give. I knew with a certainty I would never doubt that I was in love with Sam Shapiro. And he loved me.

Some people might say we were much too young for such a deep love, that it was only a teenage infatuation. But after everything Sam and I had survived, and the responsibilities that we'd been forced to shoulder for our mothers and siblings, we both had aged well beyond our years. We were adults, not children. While other young people our age might have experienced the loss of a grandparent or a beloved pet, Sam and I had tallied more losses than either of us could count, including our childhood, our home, and our freedom. We'd seen people beaten and lying dead in the street, killed for no other reason than that they were Jewish—like us. We knew how short and fragile life was, and we were determined to savor all the little blessings God sent every day, like the sunlight sparkling on the open sea and the moon playing hide-and-seek with the clouds at night as we sat in each other's arms beneath the lifeboats. We were headed for a new life, a new beginning in Cuba, and I wanted my new life to include Samuel Shapiro.

We remained in the shadows, holding each other closely and kissing until the distant commotion we heard on a deck below ours grew quiet. We heard three short blasts of the ship's horn and felt the ship begin to move forward once again. We learned the following morning that a despondent crew member had jumped overboard to commit suicide after Professor Weiler's funeral. The *St. Louis* had halted and a rescue boat had been launched, but the search for the missing crewman had ended unsuccessfully. I recalled the conversation I'd overheard before the ship set sail—how departing on the Sabbath and on the thirteenth day were bad omens—and I shivered to shake away the thought.

On Wednesday, the Jewish Feast of Shavuot began. The crew transformed the social hall for the celebration, with flowers and bowls of fruit and two palm trees that were borrowed from the dance hall. The traditional shipboard party to celebrate the end of the voyage would fall on the second day of Shavuot, Thursday evening. It was to be a fancy costume ball. Some passengers wore elegant evening attire. Others fashioned costumes from bedsheets and miscellaneous articles of clothing. Sam and I didn't dress up, but after the elegant meal ended and the tables were pushed aside to create a dance floor, we danced until our feet ached—and then we danced some more. I would never grow tired of being held in Sam's arms and resting my cheek against his chest to hear his heartbeat. We stayed up until the last song ended at 3 a.m. Then one of the stewards announced that the beam from the Bahamas' lighthouse was visible in the distance. Before saying good night, we went out on the deck to see it.

"That's a symbol of our future together, Gisela. It's shining off in the distance for now, but it will grow brighter and brighter in the days to come. We will get there one day. We'll be together forever, I promise you."

"I love you, Sam."

"And I love you. We'll be together no matter what. We're part of each other's lives, now and forever."

"Some people might try to tell us this is just a shipboard romance."

"No, this is real, Gisela. Can't you feel it?"

"I can."

Sam had brought his family's prayer book with him, and we placed our joined hands on top of it as we pledged our love to each other, sealing it with a kiss.

We were thousands of miles from the Nazis' reign of terror. We were free. And Samuel Shapiro and I were helplessly in love.

5

Peggy

JUNE 1946

The next two weeks dragged by as we waited for Jimmy's insulin treatments to end so we could visit him again. Every morning, Mrs. Barnett and I prayed that the treatments would help him. Work in the veterinary clinic slowed, with TB testing all finished and another spring birthing season over. June hadn't ended yet, but summery weather arrived early, bringing long, sweltering days. I sat in Jimmy's hot upstairs bedroom for a few minutes every afternoon, looking around at the mementos of his boyhood and slowly rereading all of his letters. When I compared his early letters, written when he was still in basic training, to the letters he wrote from the battlefield in Europe, I thought I detected a change. In the beginning, he talked about the friends he'd made and how the Army was forging them into a team. By the time their training ended, Jimmy and his fellow recruits had formed a brotherhood, able to work together for the common goal of defeating the enemy.

I fanned myself with my notebook in the stifling bedroom as Jimmy came alive again through the words of his letters. I felt like I was with him as he described life aboard a troop ship on the way to Great Britain. It was overcrowded, and they'd slept in bunks a foot apart from each other, wondering how many Nazi U-boats were shadowing them. He frequently mentioned two friends in particular, Mitch O'Hara and Frank Cishek. Mitch had been Jimmy's college roommate, and Frank Cishek was also a medic.

His letters grew shorter and more somber as time went on and his company became engaged in the thick of battle. I had learned more about the D-Day invasion from reading the newspapers than from Jimmy's letters. It was only when reinforcements relieved him and his men for a short R and R that he'd had time to write. *Just to let you know I'm okay . . . Sorry I've been too busy to write . . . Thanks for your letters. Please keep them coming . . .* I thought I'd found the letter he'd written after Joe Fiore and dozens of others from their company had been wounded in battle. Jimmy had stayed behind at the field hospital where the soldiers from his company had been taken, making sure their conditions had stabilized and arrangements had been made to ship them to a military hospital in England. But the war wasn't over for him yet. I checked the date of his letter and knew that nearly a year of hard fighting remained before victory in Europe was declared.

That sense of belonging and camaraderie that Jimmy described was something I had never really experienced for myself until I'd worked in the IBM plant during the war. The factory job offered me a brand-new beginning in life. Nobody knew my past or that I was the "dog girl" with "cooties" who lived above her father's garage. I had graduated from high school near the top of my class, and my school counselor had encouraged me to apply for a nursing scholarship. The demand for nurses was great during the war and he thought I would easily qualify. Mr. Barnett offered to write a letter of recommendation for me, but Pop was firmly against the idea because it would mean leaving home and living in the nurses' dormitory in New York City during my training.

I still remember the night Pop and I stood talking about it in his garage, and he looked up at me from behind the engine he was repairing and said, "You don't belong in that great big city, Peggy Ann. Especially during a war, with thousands of soldiers running around. You're too naive. You've never even been away from home overnight."

It was true. There had been no giggling pajama parties with friends, no trips to summer camp, no weeklong visits with doting grandparents. To be honest, I had been a little nervous about leaving home all alone for the first time, so I tore up the application to nursing school and took the job across the river as a Rosie the Riveter, instead. It was at the IBM plant that the exciting world of friendship opened up to me, like the friendships Jimmy had described with his pals during basic training. I was surprised and pleased when the other girls wanted to befriend me. When one of them said, "Golly, you're pretty," I actually looked over my shoulder to see who she was talking to. As we ate our lunches together, worked side by side all day, and shared our aches and pains on the bus rides home after a long day, I was included as part of the group for the first time in my life. The work was boring and monotonous and exhausting, but I looked forward to going each day just to see my friends. They even invited me to go to dances with them on the weekends, but I was too shy.

The two years I worked there had flown by—and then the war ended. I was overjoyed, of course. But oh, how I missed my friends! We all promised to stay in touch and vowed to never forget each other. But all the other girls had boyfriends or husbands who were returning home from the war, and I didn't. I had my job at the veterinary clinic, which I loved and had missed. And I had Pop to take care of. Donna lived with us by then, but she didn't know how to cook or how to make sure Pop wasn't drinking too much or how to pay his bills and order auto parts for him the way I did.

As I remembered how lonely I'd been those first weeks after my job ended, I wondered if part of Jimmy's depression stemmed from missing his friends and from the loss of a shared mission. If I ever saw Joe Fiore again, I would ask if any of Jimmy's closest friends, like Mitch O'Hara and Frank Cishek, had been killed. Jimmy might have suffered unbearable grief, not to mention guilt as a medic, if he'd been unable to save the buddies he'd lived with and served alongside for so long.

I closed my notebook and put the letters back into the shoebox for the day. The temperature was probably close to ninety degrees, much too hot to sit in a closed-up bedroom. I walked back across the street to Pop's office, which wasn't much cooler, and switched on the little desk fan, quickly grabbing all the loose papers as they began to flutter all over the desktop. I had just gotten everything anchored down when Pop came in. Donna was with him.

"Got a minute to talk?" he asked.

"Sure."

They sank down on the daybed and I swiveled my wooden desk chair around to face them. Donna wore a determined expression, her shoulders squared and her chin raised as if she were about to enter a boxing ring. Pop looked as though he'd rather be any place else but here. They made me uneasy. Something was coming, but I couldn't guess what. Donna nudged Pop as if prompting him to begin, and he gave a nervous cough. "Um . . . the Crow Bar is cutting Donna's hours," he said.

I waited, but when he didn't continue, I said, "That's surprising. With all the local GIs returning home and coming to the bar to play pool and drink with their friends, I would think business would be good. Joe Fiore said it was packed the night he went there with you."

"Yeah, well . . ." Pop coughed again.

"They want a younger barmaid," Donna blurted out in her cigarette-raspy voice. "After all the years I worked at that dump, you'd think they'd show a little more gratitude instead of insulting me! I told them I quit!" She was spitting mad and her eyes were watery.

"I'm so sorry," I told her. And I meant it. "That was cruel of them." Donna was on the wrong side of forty years old, and her years of heavy smoking and hard drinking had taken their toll. I could see how her orange-red dyed hair, low-cut blouses, and sagging bosom would no longer be attractive to a younger generation of bar patrons.

"Good riddance to that firetrap," she spat.

Pop cleared his throat and wiped his palms on his coveralls. "I . . . um . . . that is, Donna and me wondered if . . . well . . . if you could show her how to do the books for me. She wants to take over."

The air suddenly felt very close. "You want *my* job?" I asked.

Donna nodded. She didn't seem the least bit embarrassed to face me. "Don't you think it's time you moved on?" she asked. "Instead of hanging around here and mooning over that poor, godforsaken boy from across the street? He didn't want you before the war and he ain't in any shape to want you now. You're a smart girl. You gotta see that."

I couldn't reply. I had seen wounded animals in the clinic lash out at anyone who came close, so I sort of understood Donna's reaction. But I still was left speechless. Pop reached across the narrow space and rested his hand on my knee as if trying to soften the blow. "You don't really want to hang around here forever, do you, Peggy Ann? Stuck in this one-horse town all your life? You could do anything."

My heart began to race. "Are you going to kick me out of my home, too?"

"No one is kicking you out," Pop said. "You done a good job taking care of me, Peggy Ann, cooking for me and things all these years. But Donna wants to take over now that she's not working until all hours of the night. We're thinking about making it legal—her and me."

It was what Donna had long wanted. I would hear them fighting about it sometimes when they'd been drinking too much. *"It's just a piece of paper,"* Pop would say. *"What do we need that for?"* Donna had been married once before and divorced. She wanted the security that a husband would provide. Pop's garage and our apartment would be hers once they married. I longed to ask if she was going to continue sleeping until noon every day, and if she even knew how to cook, but it would be wrong to spew my hurt feelings all over her. This had been Pop's decision, too.

I struggled to pull myself together. As calmly as I could, I asked, "Move on to what? Where am I supposed to go?"

"Like your pop said, you could do anything you wanted," Donna replied. "You're a pretty girl and you did real good in school, as I recall. I never did finish, you know." In all the years Donna had lived with us, she'd never once told me I was pretty or encouraged me in school. I had the bitter thought that she was only being nice to me now because she wanted to get rid of me.

"You're right," I said, standing. "Why don't you start showing Donna around the office and the garage, Pop. I can answer her questions when I get back. I need to run across the street and tend to one of the horses and I'm already late." It wasn't true. I was running away to hide my tears from them. I was unwanted. I didn't belong here. I felt like the "dog girl" all over again. I hurried into the barn where a new horse named Pedro was being boarded, and busied myself by giving his coat a good brushing. My tears fell as my thoughts swirled like dirty dishwater down a drain. Since when had Pop ever cared about my education or my future? The only people who had taken an interest in me had been Jimmy and his parents—not Pop and certainly not Donna. I wouldn't have gone to high school at all if it hadn't been for Jimmy.

I had just finished the eighth grade in the summer of 1939, and Jimmy was getting ready to start college at Cornell. We were working here in the barn together and talking about all kinds of things when he asked, "Are you excited about starting at the regional high school this fall, Peggety?" I shook my head. "You aren't? Why not?"

I was embarrassed to say why, but he coaxed the truth out of me. He was an expert at digging deep and getting me to share my feelings. I told him how I didn't have the right clothes to wear and how I would feel out-of-place in such a big school. "And besides," I added, "Pop doesn't see any reason for me to go. He never went past the eighth grade, and he owns his own garage."

Jimmy showed up at my apartment a few days later with his girl-friend, Tina, and her best friend, Cathy. They sat me down on the rickety chair in our backyard, then Cathy wrapped a towel around my neck and gave me a real beauty-parlor haircut. She'd been studying how to do it in the high school's vocational program. Tina gave me some movie-star magazines to look at while Cathy was cutting, just like in a real beauty parlor. Jimmy disappeared into the garage, where Pop was replacing an alternator, leaving us to our "girlie stuff," as he called it. When Cathy was finished, Tina squealed and oohed and aahed over me and made me feel pretty. Then Jimmy came back, and he carried on like he didn't recognize me, saying, "Who is this pretty young lady? I don't believe we've ever met." I barely recognized myself when I looked in the mirror.

"I'm going to be working in Flo's Salon on Main Street," Cathy told me before she left. "You come on in whenever you need a trim." Tina said I could keep the magazines. Later, I found three grocery sacks on my bed, filled with used clothes that the girls must have outgrown. Jimmy never said a thing about the clothes, but I knew he was behind it. And when Pop told me that he'd changed his mind about me going to high school, I knew who had talked him into it.

I returned to my present dilemma when Pedro nudged me with his muzzle as if trying to soothe my hurt feelings. I was being cut adrift, asked to give up my job and leave my home, and I had no idea where to turn or what to do. If I took another factory job somewhere, I might make new friends and recover the sense of belonging that I'd lost when the war ended. But who was I kidding? A few million soldiers had just returned home from the war and every available job would go to one of them. I heard someone enter the barn and oh, how I wished it could have been Jimmy, coming to rescue me again. But it was Mr. Barnett.

"I was just coming to look in on Pedro," he said. "I thought you'd gone home."

The word *home* touched a nerve, and I maneuvered to Pedro's other side to hide my tears. I didn't want to bother the Barnetts with my problems or ask for their advice about my future. They had enough heartache dealing with their son's future right now. They didn't need me to unload my problems on their shoulders, too. "I don't mind checking up on Pedro," I said. "He's a great horse."

"Well, I'm glad you're still here. I forgot to mention it earlier, but Dr. Morgan's office called. He wants to talk to us again before we visit

Jim on Sunday. Would you be able to come with us to our appointment tomorrow? You were a great comfort to Martha and me the last time."

My tears flowed but I didn't have to hide them. "I would be happy to, Mr. Barnett."

*　　*　　*

Dr. Morgan wasn't one degree warmer or friendlier than he'd been the last time. Once again, he lit up a cigarette as soon as we were seated and delivered his news through clouds of smoke, looking at the file folder in front of him, not at us. "Corporal Barnett has finished the prescribed course of insulin treatments with little noticeable improvement," he began. I felt like he'd punched me in the gut and knocked all the wind out of me. He could have at least paused for a moment to let us digest the bad news, but he plowed on. "The orderlies reported that he did react to the last few injections, becoming upset and trying to push the needle away—"

"For heaven's sake, why didn't they stop?" Mr. Barnett asked. "Especially if the comas weren't doing any good?"

Dr. Morgan seemed irritated by the interruption. "As I was about to say, the corporal's reaction was a positive sign. His emotional affect had been flat up to that point." I remembered Joe Fiore's description of the water treatment as torture and wanted to point out that anger is a natural response to inhumane treatment.

"When will our son be able to come home?" Mrs. Barnett asked.

"I don't recommend that he leave the hospital until there is some improvement."

"Not even for a day? For a visit?"

"No. The corporal suffers from severe depression and is still uncommunicative. He doesn't interact with the other patients or participate in group therapy."

"So what's next?" Mr. B. asked.

"I've scheduled him to begin a course of electroshock therapy next week."

I bit my tongue to remain silent, hoping this treatment wasn't as bad as it sounded. But as the doctor went on to explain, it turned out to be even worse than it sounded. "Electrical currents are applied to the patient's brain to disorder the mind and jolt the patient out of his emotional distress. It can be quite effective in cases of severe depression like the corporal's. The shock treatments are applied three times a week for a period of two to six weeks."

"Is it dangerous? Are there risks we should know about?" Mr. B. asked.

"No procedure is without risk. In this case, we will deliberately try to induce a seizure or a convulsion. This temporary disordering of the mind can halt the cycle of depressing thoughts and suicidal ideation. One side effect may be memory impairment. The patient may forget names or seem confused—"

"Don't let them do it!" I begged Mr. Barnett. "There must be some other way!"

The doctor pinned me with a stern look. "If there were, I would have prescribed it."

"But you don't even know if it will work on Jimmy."

"There are never any guarantees, young lady." He stubbed out his cigarette, signaling that the meeting was over.

"Wait. What positive results might we expect?" Mr. Barnett asked.

"Electroshock therapy can have a calming effect on patients suffering from battle fatigue. They report fewer nightmares and angry outbursts afterwards. Many experience varying degrees of memory loss, as I said, but that can be a positive thing if any troubling, traumatic experiences are also erased. Our goal is for the patient to reach the point where he'll interact in group sessions with other patients."

Mr. Barnett closed his eyes and sighed. "We'll have to trust your judgment, Doctor."

We went downstairs, expecting to be able to visit with Jimmy as we had the last time, but we were turned away. "Visiting hours are on Sundays only," we were told.

"I'm sorry I spoke up in Dr. Morgan's office," I told the Barnetts on the drive home. "I had no right to butt in and tell you not to do the electric shocks."

"That's okay, Peggy." Mr. Barnett offered me a weak smile in the rearview mirror. "To be honest, it sounded horrifying to me, too. But we would do anything to help Jim, and there just doesn't seem to be any other alternative."

We would have to trust that the doctors knew what they were doing.

* * *

I sat with the Barnetts in church Sunday morning, and I knew the three of us were praying the same prayer we'd been praying for the past four years—that Jimmy would come home safe and sound. I was also praying that God would send me a sign to tell me where I should go now that Donna and Pop were kicking me out, and what I should do with the rest of my life. I would have to find a new job since I only worked at the clinic part time. And I would have to find an apartment that allowed dogs because Donna hated Buster.

I walked home from church by myself, brooding about my life, and when I looked up, there was Joe Fiore's motorcycle parked in front of Pop's garage. He had returned after all. I hurried around to the backyard and found him sitting in the wooden chair with Buster by his side. "Joe! You came back!"

He smiled and looked me up and down. It was the way any red-blooded man would look at a woman, and I felt my cheeks warm with embarrassment. I hadn't been around very many young men because they'd all been off fighting the war, so I wasn't used to being appraised that way. "I told you I'd come back," Joe said, pulling himself to his feet. "Hey, you ready to go see Jim? I've been talking to Tripod about it and he's all set to go."

"You mean you're willing to help me sneak Buster in to see Jimmy?"

"Sure! Why not? Hey, we're gonna need a car, though. Tripod doesn't want to ride on the back of my cycle."

"We can take Pop's car. But let's have lunch first. Have you eaten? Visiting hours don't start until one." The weather was nice, so we ate our baloney sandwiches outside. Then I ran across the street to tell the Barnetts that I planned to drive myself and that I was bringing an old Army buddy of Jimmy's with me. I didn't mention that we were bringing Buster. If I was going to get into trouble for this stunt, I didn't want Jimmy's parents to suffer for it.

Joe gave a low whistle when we arrived at the hospital, taking in the view of the distant mountains and the wide, dark river below us. "Nice view!" he said. "The VA hospital in Ohio wasn't half this nice."

I fastened Buster's leash to his collar and explained to Joe how he could make a wide circuit around the edge of the grounds, staying mostly out of sight, then end up in the little park behind the visiting room where we'd taken Jimmy the last time. I had no idea if Joe could walk that far across the grass with his prosthetic leg, but he didn't seem fazed by the plan.

"You can take your time," I told him. "I'll need a few minutes to find Jimmy and help him walk outside to meet up with you. He couldn't walk very fast the last time."

"Got it." Joe set off across the grounds, limping only slightly, with Buster loping happily alongside him.

The Barnetts hadn't arrived yet, and I was shocked to find Jimmy seated in a wheelchair this time. I crouched in front of him. His body was still much too thin, yet his pale face had an unhealthy puffiness to it that reminded me of a loaf of Wonder Bread. "Hi, Jimmy. It's me, Peggety. I thought we could go outside again, okay? I have a surprise for you." It turned out that the wheelchair made it easy to maneuver Jimmy to the rear of the little park by myself. I spotted Joe and Buster sneaking their way along the edge of the hospital grounds and hoped that none of the orderlies did. I parked Jimmy's chair at the very end of the sidewalk and turned it so Jimmy could see them coming, then crouched beside him. He might not remember Joe, but how could he ever forget Buster, the famous three-legged dog?

"Hey, Corporal Jim!" Joe called when he was a dozen yards away. "Remember me? Joe Fiore?" He let go of Buster's leash and the dog bounded toward us in his lopsided, zigzagging run. He went straight to Jimmy, planted his front paws on his chest, and licked his face as if it was covered with ice cream. Jimmy made an odd, strangled sound and I tried to pull Buster away—then realized it was laughter! Jimmy was laughing!

"Down, boy. That's enough," I said after a few moments. Buster calmed down enough to sit at Jimmy's feet with his head on his knees, while Jimmy stroked him and scratched behind his huge ears. Joe was grinning when he caught up with the dog.

"So hey, Jim! I thought you were making up all those stories about Tripod," he said. "Turns out he's real! You really did save this dog, and then you saved me. I don't know if you remember, but the last time we saw each other was in Normandy, France, and I only had one leg. Now I have two and I'm as good as new, see? You saved my life, Jim. And you gave me hope. I just wanted to come here today and say thank you." He reached to shake hands and Jimmy shook Joe's in return. My tears of joy fell faster than I could wipe them away.

Suddenly I heard a shout and hurried footsteps coming down the path toward us. "You there! What do you think you're doing? Get that dog off this property! Now!"

"We're visiting our friend," I replied. "He loves this dog." I tried to block the orderly's way, but he brushed me aside to confront Joe.

"You and that dog need to leave. Now!"

"Hey, can't you give us another minute?" Joe asked. "The corporal hasn't seen his dog in a while, you know?"

"I'm going to count to three, and you and that mutt had better be on your way out of here or I'll call security!"

Joe lifted his chin and clenched his fists. My heart began to race as he took a mean stance, ready for a fistfight. "Go ahead! I fought bullies just like you during the war," Joe said. "They were called Nazis, and we wiped out the whole pack of them! You want to try taking me on, too? Hey? Do you?" Buster barked as if eager to join the fight.

I stepped between the orderly and Joe, who was as bristly as a barn cat with its hackles raised. "I'm sorry, sir. My friend and I will take the dog home now. Could you please wheel Corporal Barnett back inside for me? His parents will be coming to visit him shortly." I bent to squeeze Jimmy's hand and said, "Bye for now. I'll visit again soon." Then I found the end of Buster's leash and gave it a tug. My tears started falling again when I saw Jimmy reach out to pat Buster's head one last time.

6

Gisela

I had never experienced anything like the hot, humid tropical air that greeted us on Friday morning, May 26. We had been at sea for two weeks, and today would be our last full day aboard the *St. Louis*. Sam and I were twitching with excitement and anticipation, barely able to stand still let alone sit down to wait. In spite of the merciless sun and unaccustomed heat, we stood outside at the ship's rail with our fellow passengers, watching as we sailed down the coast of Florida. It was visible in the distance, offering our first glimpse of the United States. "We'd better start getting used to this climate," Sam said. "My father says Havana has two seasons—hot and hotter."

We passed the city of Miami in the early afternoon, shimmering like a glowing mirage in the distance. Although the United States was still miles away in our dreams, seeing its shoreline renewed our hope that we would be allowed to immigrate there one day. We were thousands of miles from the Nazis and within sight of our future home. Sam and I talked about our future all that day, able to dream of one at last after the Nazis had closed and locked every door to us back home. Sam had once considered becoming a pharmacist like his father, but a whole world of new possibilities would be open to him once we settled in the United States. I had enjoyed science classes in school before being barred from attending and had thought of becoming a nurse. But now I had no other thoughts for my future except spending it with Sam.

We took a break from the relentless sun later that afternoon, and I stood in line with Sam outside the purser's office so he could send a telegram to his father in Havana saying we would be arriving tomorrow morning. My father waited right behind us to send one to Uncle Aaron. Vati looked happier than I had seen him in years. Everyone's hopes were so high, we could have flown the rest of the way to Cuba. At sundown, Sam and I ate our last Shabbat meal on board the ship with our mothers and siblings. "I'm so excited I could stay up all night!" I told him as we said good night.

"I know, but we'd better get a good night's sleep. Tomorrow will be a big day for us—our first one in Cuba."

"Do you think we'll live near each other?"

"I'll insist on it! I know my father will help your family get settled." He held me tightly and kissed me good night, then murmured, "We're another day closer, Gisela." It had become our private motto at the close of each day. We were another day closer to spending a lifetime together.

The blast of the ship's horn jolted me from sleep early Saturday morning. I pulled back the curtain that covered the porthole and saw that it was still dark outside with stars shining in the sky. But as I continued to stare, I was able to distinguish a few faint white buildings onshore. "I think I see Havana!" I shouted. "Mutti! Ruthie! We're there! We're in Havana!" The three of us hugged each other, bouncing with excitement.

The breakfast gong sounded at 4:30 a.m. but I was almost too excited to eat. I went to the social hall with Mutti and Ruthie anyway, hoping that Sam would be there. On the way, we passed people in the passageways, hauling their suitcases up to the deck in preparation. Sam and his family were already eating breakfast, and we sat down at a table next to theirs. The portrait of Hitler glowered down at us from the wall again, and I wanted to stick out my tongue at him and say, *"You have no power over us!"* I had sensed that the ship was slowing for the past several minutes, and suddenly there was a rumbling vibration beneath our feet. "What's that?" I asked.

The waiter who was serving coffee to Mutti replied, "The ship's anchor is being lowered, Fräulein." We were there!

Sam and I and our three siblings rushed to the window on the starboard side of the dining room to peer out. We could see buildings and the city's skyline in the distance in the early morning light.

"But we aren't in the harbor. Why is the ship anchored so far from the harbor?"

"I don't know," Sam replied. "Waiting for permission, maybe? Or a berth? But look, see that tall dome in the middle? I think that's Havana Cathedral. I recognize it from the postcards my father sent us. And those high walls must be El Morro, the old fort that guards the entrance to the harbor."

We sat down again and quickly finished our breakfast, then hurried back to our staterooms to finish packing so we could leave the moment they anchored at the dock and lowered the gangway. The sun was already broiling, but we all wanted to go up on deck and watch everything that was happening as we prepared to step foot on Cuban soil at last. The ship's orchestra performed on the deck, putting us in a festive mood. "Do you think our legs will be all wobbly when we get back on land?" I asked Sam. We had our arms around each other, not caring who saw us.

"I wouldn't be surprised," he said, laughing. "Although you took to the waves pretty fast for a girl who'd never sailed before." We watched as a launch approached from shore and a man in a white suit came aboard. We soon learned the reason why when the loudspeaker announced that all passengers were required to assemble in the social hall for a medical inspection. Sam hurried below to get his mother and brothers, and I found Mutti and Ruthie in our stateroom, talking with Vati. He still looked pale and unwell from his imprisonment, and he still had his nagging cough after two weeks at sea.

"I'm worried about how thorough this exam is going to be," he said.

"We'll all go together," I told him. "The rest of us look healthy enough. Maybe the doctor won't notice." I felt Vati's forehead the way Mutti always felt ours when we were ill. He didn't have a fever. I kissed his cheek and hugged him to reassure him. There wasn't a worry in the world that could diminish the joy I felt. "Just remember to smile and don't look so worried, Vati. The Nazis are far away now. No one can stop you from being with our family again." We joined the long line in the social hall to file past the Cuban doctor, and it turned out to be a swift inspection. "See? Nothing to worry about," I whispered. "Just a little hurdle, and now we can land." The doctor left. The ship's quarantine flag was lowered. Sam and I went back up on deck, taking Ruthie and his brothers with us.

Soon, another launch arrived, filled with Cuban police and immigration and customs officials. Their uniforms weren't Nazi ones, but experience had made me uneasy around uniformed men. Sam's brothers wanted to see where they were going, so he told them they could follow them on their own. The boys returned a few minutes later to report that the officials had gone into the dining hall and were eating breakfast. Sam had noticed my nervousness and said, "Don't worry. This will all be over in no time."

By midmorning a flotilla of small rowboats and motorboats had crossed the harbor to greet the ship. Some were fruit vendors selling fresh pineapples and bananas. But most of them were relatives of the passengers who waved and shouted up to us from seventy-five feet below. Many of the women and children on board had husbands and fathers waiting for them in Cuba, like Sam did. We raced below to fetch our mothers. Vati was still in our stateroom and he came up on deck with us, too. Sam had just returned with his family when one of his brothers spotted their father. They waved wildly to each other, shouting with joy. "You did it, Sam," I whispered, squeezing his hand. "You got your family here safely." Vati and I searched for Uncle Aaron and called out his name, but we didn't see him.

The Cuban immigration officials had started processing passports, and the few fortunate souls who'd had their landing permits stamped were already standing at the top of ladder with their luggage, waiting for the launch to return and take them to land. "How I envy them," I sighed. "They're going to be the first people to get off the ship." The launch returned, but only the immigration officials were allowed to board it. They had inexplicably stopped working and were returning to Havana. "Why are they leaving?" I asked aloud. "They haven't finished processing everyone's passports." It was the question everyone seemed to be asking. The launch motored toward Havana, leaving the Cuban police behind and my fellow passengers and me bewildered.

Hours passed. Sam's father and the people in the other little boats returned to shore. Everyone grew irritable and impatient. Most people decided it was too hot to wait on deck and went below, but Sam and I stayed, unwilling to be separated for a single moment. After lunch, a British passenger ship steamed past us and docked at the pier. Why were they being allowed to land and we weren't? Midafternoon, another launch tied up to our ship; another uniformed official boarded the landing ladder. The purser broadcast the names of a woman, her two children, and four other passengers, asking them to come to his office. Before long, the group descended the ladder, their suitcases were handed down to the launch, and off they went toward shore.

Sam exhaled in frustration and wiped the sweat from his brow with his handkerchief. "This will take weeks if they're only going to let us off a few at a time."

"But people *are* getting off, Sam. Let's not lose hope. Your father must be doing everything he can to help you."

"I know one of the men on the passenger committee," Sam said. "Let's go ask if he has any information."

It took us more than an hour to find the man. The ship that Sam and I had explored with such glee now seemed like a hot, oppressive maze of dead ends. "There is a mix-up of some sort concerning our landing permits," the gentleman from the passenger committee told us.

"You mean the permits we bought in Germany?"

"Yes. It should be straightened out soon."

But it wasn't. We were still waiting with no news long after the sun set. We returned to our staterooms at the end of the day, pulled our nightclothes from our packed suitcases, and prepared to spend another night on board the *St. Louis*. "We're another day closer," Sam and I whispered to each other before we parted. I refused to allow this delay to discourage me.

Sunday morning found us still anchored in the bay. We heard the sound of guns being fired and later learned that an American warship had arrived and had been greeted with a military salute. A new passenger ship was now tied up in the harbor where the first one had been. Sam and I and our families gathered in the social hall with the other passengers to demand answers from the committee. "Other ships are landing and letting off passengers," someone said. "Why can't we land?"

"Those were English and French ships. This one is German."

"What difference does that make?"

"We aren't sure. We've also been told that a religious holiday in Cuba may be adding to the delay. It's the Feast of Pentecost, and many offices are closed. Perhaps more customs officials will be available to process our papers after the weekend." The sun set on Sunday night, a fiery red ball in the tropical sky.

There was a small ray of hope on Monday when Max Aber, a Jewish doctor who'd been living in Cuba, arrived in a launch to pick up his two little daughters. The girls had traveled from Hamburg without their mother, under the guardianship of another passenger. Everyone gathered around him, showering him with questions as he waited near the ladder for his girls to collect their belongings. "What's going on? Do you know when we will be allowed to leave? Can you help us?" He couldn't. All he knew was that the delay seemed to involve our landing permits. Late that afternoon, fifteen more passengers were allowed to leave. We demanded to know why and learned that they had boarded in Cherbourg, France, and weren't German.

We tried to be patient, but we all longed to be off the ship, out from under the swastika flag and Hitler's glowering portrait. Our initial joy on arriving in Havana evaporated in the humid heat. Our despair climbed with the temperature as our questions went unanswered. What was causing the delay now? Why weren't we being allowed off? We had all purchased Cuban landing permits, hadn't we? Everywhere Sam and I went, we saw people weeping. Boatloads of anxious relatives continued to surround our ship. We saw Sam's father again, and Vati finally spotted Uncle Aaron, who shouted up to us that there was no explanation onshore for the delay, either.

Vati knocked on our stateroom door as we were preparing for bed and Mutti quickly let him inside. His eyes were wide with fright and he couldn't catch his breath. "Daniel, what's wrong? What happened?" Mutti cried.

"They ransacked our cabins! Tore the place apart! They know which of us were in Buchenwald and they went after us."

"Who did, Vati?"

"Crew members from this ship."

The bottom seemed to drop out of my stomach. We had believed we were safe from the persecution we'd experienced back home. "You need to report this to someone," I said.

"We can't. Those crewmen are all Nazis. We can hear them playing the piano in our dining room in the evenings and singing Nazi songs."

"But the captain isn't a Nazi. He allowed us to cover Hitler's portrait during Shabbat, remember? We need to tell him about this."

"No, no, Gisela, no. Look out the window. They have us surrounded." I went to the porthole and looked out. Cuban police boats encircled the ship. Sam and I had seen them earlier that evening before saying good night. Now those boats were sweeping the *St. Louis* with their searchlights. "It's just like it was in Buchenwald. We're on a prison ship," Vati said. He spent the night in our stateroom. None of us got much sleep. We were trapped once again.

Tuesday, May 30, dawned and nothing had changed. We'd been

anchored here since early Saturday. Four days with land in sight and no way to get to it. Four days with few answers. I felt the way I had on Kristallnacht when we'd been trapped in our apartment, wondering if we would ever be able to leave it again. When the passenger committee finally gave us an explanation, the news was devastating. The Cuban president had passed a new immigration law in Cuba, and the landing permits we'd purchased in Germany were no longer valid.

"Representatives from the Jewish Joint Distribution Committee are meeting with the Cuban president today," we were told. "They're asking that he at least honor the permits that were issued before the new law was passed." His words were met with murmurs of alarm as we all wondered when our permits were dated and when the law had been passed. "Even if we aren't allowed to land in Cuba," the leader continued above the anxious voices, "we have Captain Schroeder's promise that he will make every effort to land us somewhere outside of Germany."

"I don't know where in the world that would be," Sam said when we were alone again. "If there was a place outside of Germany that wanted us, we would be there already." We'd gone up on deck again to see if we could spot his father in one of the boats and tell him the news. It was the same deck where the burial at sea had taken place. Suddenly we heard an agonized scream and, a moment later, a distant splash. The gate in the ship's railing hung open, and the area all around it was splattered with blood.

"Max Loewe just slit his wrists and jumped overboard!" someone shouted. We looked over the rail and saw him thrashing below us, the water around him turning red. His wife began to scream. A long blast of the ship's whistle signaled "man overboard," and more passengers raced to the side of the ship to see.

"Murderers!" Loewe screamed from far below. "They'll never get me!" We heard another splash as one of the crew members jumped in to save him. He swam toward Herr Loewe. Several police boats sped toward him, too. Loewe kicked and fought with the sailor who'd reached him, crying, "Let me die! Let me die!" The police pulled both men into their boat. The ship's siren finally stopped wailing as the police hurried toward shore with the two men. Many of the passengers watching with us were weeping.

"I need to go be with my father," I told Sam. "I know he'll be upset by this. Mutti, too. I need to be strong for them."

"I'll go with you. Your father and I can say afternoon prayers together."

The passengers cheered when the heroic sailor returned to the ship later that day. We were told that Max Loewe was in the hospital and would live. But his distraught wife would not be allowed off the ship to go to him. Rumors were whispered all around that another passenger, Dr. Fritz Herrmann, a physician from Munich, had also attempted suicide today by taking an overdose of sleeping pills. "It goes to show how hopeless we all feel," Vati said. "And desperate. There will be more suicides if they try to take us back to Hamburg. Many of us would rather die than let the Nazis kill us." His words made me shiver with fear. Would those be our only options if we returned to Germany—kill ourselves or let the Nazis do it? There were more police boats with searchlights after dark, making sure that none of us escaped. Vati was right—we'd become a floating prison.

On Wednesday, Sam and I went up on deck to watch for his father and Uncle Aaron again, anxious for news of what was happening onshore. We didn't see them. The sun was too hot for us to stay on deck for very long, and the dining room was stuffy and airless. Few of us felt like eating. We wandered aimlessly, trying to reassure each other that this stalemate couldn't possibly last much longer. We were near the purser's office when we overheard a woman pleading with him. "Don't take us back to Hamburg! Please! I would rather die!" Later that evening, someone from the passenger committee quietly asked Sam to be part of a suicide patrol, watching the decks all night in two-hour shifts so no one else would jump overboard.

I awoke on Thursday morning feeling numb and drained of emotion. How much longer would we be held in suspense this way? Surely the Cuban officials would have pity on us, wouldn't they? Sam raised my spirits and revived my hopes whenever we were together, but we spent less time with each other as the days dragged by, both of us obligated to comfort our families. We happened to be outside together near the landing ladder when a small boat approached and an official from the shipping company shouted up, asking for a representative from the passenger committee. His message when the representative arrived devastated us. The *St. Louis* had been ordered to leave Havana within three hours. I leaned my head on Sam's chest and wept. We heard weeping coming from all over the ship as word spread.

A little while later, we saw the crew preparing to lower the ship's launch. "Look," Sam said. "That's Captain Schroeder getting into the boat." He had changed into civilian clothes and was going ashore. Was he abandoning us or going for help? Around three o'clock we heard a rumbling sound as the ship's engines started up. The deck vibrated beneath our feet.

"Oh, Sam, no! No!" I cried. I was convinced that the Nazi sailors who had ransacked Vati's room had taken over the ship and were heading back to Germany. Sam and I were still on the deck, wondering what we should do, when suddenly a group of women whose husbands were waiting onshore stormed the Cuban police who were guarding the landing ladder, desperate to get off. The police fought back, knocking a pregnant woman to the deck. Sam and I ran to help her.

"She needs a doctor," Sam said when he saw that she was unconscious. He and another passenger scooped her up and carried her to the infirmary. I stood again, my legs trembling. The police had drawn their guns. I couldn't move, frozen with fear. I was terrified that my father would join the mob and do something rash. He knew firsthand what awaited us in the Nazi prison camps. By the time Sam returned, the standoff with the police had swelled to a large crowd. I didn't see my father among them. We waited, afraid to leave and yet afraid to go below. Our feeling of being trapped was too overwhelming whenever we went below.

At last, we saw the ship's launch returning with Captain Schroeder. He immediately ordered the police to stand down, saying that this was still his ship. "I deeply regret that this had to happen," he told the crowd. "Now you need to disperse please."

"Is it true that we're going back to Hamburg?" someone asked.

"I will meet with the passenger committee, and then they will inform you."

Sam and I went to find our families and waited with everyone else in the stuffy dining hall. It was hard to believe that we had danced at a fancy ball here barely a week ago, and Sam and I had made plans for our future as we'd glimpsed the beam of the Bahamas' lighthouse in the distance. Now, as we waited for Herr Joseph, the committee spokesman, to tell us our fate, I wished that my heart held even a glimmer of the joy and hope I'd felt that night. The room grew very still after Herr Joseph arrived and began to speak.

"After hours of negotiation, the Cuban government still refuses to accept our landing permits." Moans and weeping greeted his words. "We have been ordered to leave Havana by 10 a.m. tomorrow morning." I huddled with my family in despair. Sam was trying to comfort his mother. "Wait, listen," Herr Joseph continued. "The shipping company has given Captain Schroeder permission to sail the *St. Louis* to any port that will allow us to land."

"They're lying to us!" someone shouted. "This ship is flying a Nazi flag! If we leave Havana, we'll end up back in Hamburg!"

"No, I promise you that's out of the question. Once we set sail, the captain will travel slowly along the US coastline as we wait to hear from the Americans. We're hoping their government or perhaps the Canadian government will provide sanctuary for us. Our story is in all of the newspapers. The whole world knows of our plight."

That evening, dozens of relatives arrived in boats again, saying the news was all over Havana that we were leaving tomorrow. People sobbed and stretched out their arms to each other as they shouted their good-byes, including Sam's mother, who sobbed with grief. I could already see the huge weight of responsibility Sam was forced to carry again. Vati and Mutti wept as well, as they told Uncle Aaron goodbye for now. I wondered if Vati still believed God had a reason for everything that happened. I was too frightened to ask him. If he lost his faith, how would I ever hang on to mine?

The committee asked Sam to be on suicide watch again after dark. Despair hung over the ship like fog. I lay awake long after midnight, watching the strobe of police searchlights through the porthole of our floating prison.

When Sam and I went up on deck on Friday morning, we saw that the police were no longer allowing the flotilla of small boats to approach. Our last connection with our relatives onshore had been cut off. We had been on this ship for three weeks now, two at sea and one in the harbor, and it was clear that the crew was preparing to set sail. One last police launch arrived with a civilian on board, and the ship's loudspeaker summoned everyone to the social hall. He introduced himself as Milton Goldsmith, the American representative from the Jewish Joint Distribution Committee. "Don't give up hope," he told us. "You are not returning to Hamburg. Our committees around the world are working to ensure that you can land somewhere outside of Germany. We're waiting at this moment to hear from the US government. The world is watching."

Someone in the hall began to chant, *"We must not sail. We must not die,"* and hundreds of us quickly joined him. *"We must not sail. We must not die."* The chant was still ringing out as Mr. Goldsmith left. The Cuban policemen who'd been stationed on board all left, as well. The rumble of the engines increased as the ship finally began to steam toward the open sea. Passengers lined the rails, some weeping, some standing in stunned silence as Havana's skyline faded in the distance.

"We have no place to go," I said to Sam. It was a devastatingly hopeless feeling.

We sailed all night and all day Saturday, heading slowly north toward Miami. Sam and I could only steal short snatches of time together, as his mother and both of my parents grew increasingly depressed. "My mother keeps asking, 'What are we going to do? Where are we going to go?'" Sam told me. "I don't know what to tell her. It's up to me to take care of everyone, and . . . and I don't know what to do." Holding each other for a few minutes each day gave both of us comfort.

When we awoke on Sunday morning, I looked out the porthole and was relieved to see that we were still off the coast of Florida. We were so near and yet so far. Not long after breakfast, a US Coast Guard cutter approached. "Maybe this is good news," Sam said as we watched the cutter circle our ship. Everyone waved to the Americans, and for a few minutes, I dared to hope for a rescue. But then the Coast Guard captain called out to us through a loudspeaker, and I understood enough English to know that the Americans weren't going to come to our rescue or offer us refuge.

"Do not approach any closer. You will not be allowed to land," the loudspeaker blared. The cutter was circling us to prevent people from jumping overboard and trying to swim to shore.

"I don't understand why the Americans won't help us," Sam said. "Isn't it called the land of freedom?" None of us understood it.

That evening, the *St. Louis* turned south again, back toward Cuba. The passenger committee announced that we would be allowed to disembark on the Isle of Pines, off the Cuban coast. The news was met with applause and relief. Once again, we brought our suitcases up on deck in anticipation. Late that night, we were told to go to bed. We wouldn't arrive until tomorrow morning.

Morning came and went. We spent all day Tuesday in limbo as negotiations to land on the Isle of Pines or possibly the Dominican Republic continued. In the end, all of those negotiations fell through. On Tuesday night, we sensed the ship changing course, heading north once again. Vati was convinced that the Nazis were deliberately playing with our emotions, offering hope, then snatching it away, simply to torture us. If that was their plan, it was succeeding. We were Jews. We were hated and rejected by the entire world. Nobody wanted us. Our only certain welcome was in a Nazi concentration camp.

We sailed all day Wednesday with no idea where we were headed. On Thursday, the loudspeakers summoned everyone to the social hall. Herr Joseph from the passenger committee made the announcement we'd all been dreading to hear: "The captain has been ordered to return the ship to Europe." A gasp swept the room. Vati looked as though he might faint. I began to shiver from head to toe, remembering the beatings and killings in the streets, the fires, the relentless fear that awaited us.

"Are we going back to Germany?" someone called out.

"Not necessarily. Please, remain calm. We have a long voyage ahead of us, recrossing the Atlantic. In the meantime, the Joint Committee and many other friends are working on our behalf to find sanctuary. The world is watching."

"Does the world know that the Gestapo is waiting to arrest us? Do they know about the camps?" someone shouted. There was no reply.

Once again, everyone began to chant: "We will not return. We must not die. We will not return. We must not die." I couldn't draw a breath deep enough to join in. We were sailing back to Europe.

7

Peggy

"Hey, what are we going to do about Jim?" Joe Fiore asked me. "We gotta spring him out of that place."

"I know. If it was up to me, I would, believe me." I didn't want to return to Pop's apartment after visiting the VA hospital with Joe and Buster, so I drove up the hairpin turn to the lookout point and got out of the car. Whenever I was upset, it always helped me regain my perspective to gaze down at the broad valley and see villages and green fields below and rows of purple hills in the distance. It was a God's-eye view of this beautiful valley that was my home. Too late, I remembered that it might not be my home much longer, and a dark emptiness filled me.

Joe barely looked at the view. He was agitated, pacing back and forth in the parking lot, running his hand through his curly black hair, kicking gravel against the guardrail. "Jim hardly looked like himself, you know?"

"I do. Listen, I didn't have a chance to tell you before, but the doctors plan to try electrical shocks next."

"Don't let them do it! The guys I knew who went through those shock treatments barely knew who they were afterwards! There was this one guy—he and I had been playing gin rummy all week. He'd been beating the pants off me. After they shocked him, I sat down with him at our usual table and started shuffling the cards. He said, 'I don't know how to play that game.' Can you believe it? I had to teach him how to play all over again. Another guy broke down in tears because he couldn't remember if he was married or not, and he was afraid he wouldn't recognize his wife when she visited. Now, you tell me what good something like that does?"

His words filled me with dread. Dr. Morgan had mentioned memory loss. One way or another, we were losing Jimmy. Who would he be without all of his memories? I felt helpless. "His parents are afraid to bring him home, Joe. His mother found him after he tried to kill himself and they're terrified that he'll try again—and that they won't find him next time."

"But the doctors are killing him in that place!"

I didn't know what to do. Buster finished sniffing all the bushes and came to sit at my feet, nudging me with his head as if to remind me that he needed to be petted. I remembered how Jimmy had reacted to Buster and felt a smidgen of hope. "But you know what, Joe? It worked today, seeing you and Buster. Jimmy laughed! Did you hear him? He was petting Buster and he shook your hand. He wouldn't have done those things the last time I saw him. Do you think more of his old buddies would be willing to come and visit him?"

"Sure! Everyone thought the world of him. They'd be as upset as I am to see him this way."

"I could use your help finding some of Jimmy's friends and asking if they'd come to visit him. I've been reading through all the letters he sent home during the war, and he mentioned two men in particular who seemed to be his friends since basic training." I pulled my notebook from my purse and paged through it. "Let's see. Mitch O'Hara and . . . Frank Cishek. Do you know them?"

"Yeah, I remember Mitch. And Frank was a medic, like Jim."

"Do you know what happened to them?"

He looked up at the clouds, scratching the stubble on his chin as if trying to remember. "They were both still in the fight the day I was wounded. Frank was, anyway. I know that for sure because he helped Jim carry me to the aid station."

"What about the chaplain?" I flipped my notes to search for his name. "Bill Ashburn. Jimmy said he enjoyed talking with him when things slowed down."

"Oh yeah. Chaplain Bill. He came to see me before I got evacuated, but I wasn't in any mood to hear his God talk, you know? Tell you the truth, if any of us wanted to talk about God or pray or something, we'd sooner go to Jim than the chaplain. Jim was one of us, you know? He was real, not all up in the clouds."

"I do know. Jimmy was always very good at listening and saying the right thing."

"Exactly!" Joe pointed his finger as if firing a pistol and hitting the bull's-eye. "Hey, I'm working up a thirst. Let's head back to town and I'll buy you a beer. You like beer?"

"The bar is closed on Sunday," I reminded him. "Maybe Pop will let you have one of his." We climbed into the car, the seats broiling from the sun. Buster stuck his head out the window on the drive down into the valley, his mouth open and tongue hanging out as if he was laughing with delight. How I loved that dog! But what in the world would I do with him now that Donna wanted me out?

"The countryside sure is nice around here," Joe said. I swallowed the knot in my throat at the thought of leaving this beautiful valley and steered down the winding road. I couldn't see around the next corner in my life any more than I could see what was around the next curve. I decided to turn my thoughts back to Jimmy.

"So how can I get in touch with some of his old friends, Joe? How did you know where to find Jimmy?"

"Oh, you know, just from shooting the breeze over a beer or playing poker or killing time on guard duty. We'd talk about our girlfriends and what it was like back home, what we planned to do when the war ended . . . things like that. I have a good memory, you know?" He tapped his forehead. "I remembered that Jim's dad was a veterinarian and that he lived in a little town in the Hudson Valley, sixtysome miles from New York City. It wasn't hard."

"What about the others—the chaplain or Mitch what's-his-name or Frank the medic? Do you remember where they're from?"

"Hmm, not offhand. But maybe if I thought about it for a while over a cold beer . . ."

When we reached home, I saw the Barnetts' car parked in their driveway and wondered how their visit with Jimmy went. "Say, Joe, I need to talk with Jimmy's parents and tell them about you and Buster. You want to come with me? I think they'd enjoy meeting one of Jimmy's friends."

Joe climbed out of the car and set Buster free from the back seat. He shut both doors and started walking backwards, away from me. "Another time maybe." He turned and shuffled toward the backyard, calling for "Tripod" to come with him. I walked over to the Barnetts' house by myself and accepted the coffee and apple cake Mrs. Barnett offered me. We sat around their kitchen table, and I could tell by their faces that their visit had been disappointing.

"I have exciting news," I told them. "One of Jimmy's Army friends, Joe Fiore, came to the hospital with me and we snuck Buster in to see him. Jimmy laughed out loud when Buster started licking his face!"

"Really?" Mrs. Barnett asked. Her hands fluttered to her face as if trying to hold in her joy. "He really laughed?"

"Yes! And he was petting Buster the whole time until the orderly chased us away. Jimmy seemed to remember Joe, too, and shook hands with him."

"I wish I had been there to see it," Mr. Barnett murmured.

"So do I. But it's a good sign, don't you think, Gordon? We should tell Dr. Morgan about it the next time we see him."

"Yes, although I doubt if he'll approve of Peggy's canine therapy." We all smiled, and it felt so good to smile.

"So now I have a plan," I said. "If you'll allow me to try it, that is.

Jimmy's buddy Joe lost his leg in battle and Jimmy got him to an aid station and saved his life. I'd like to find more of Jimmy's pals from the war and ask them to visit, too. Maybe one of them can tell us what happened to Jimmy and when he started to change and why he became so depressed. Maybe they know who Gisela is and why he carries her picture. I'd like to remind him of all the good memories from his past—like saving Buster—and maybe sneak photographs and things into the hospital so he'll remember how happy he once was. Joe and Dr. Morgan both said the electric shocks will take away Jimmy's memories, so we need to help him get those memories back."

Mr. Barnett took my hand for a moment and squeezed it. "I think those are very good ideas, Peggy. They're certainly worth trying."

"I'm a little afraid to show Gisela's picture to Jimmy until we learn more about her," I said. "I'm afraid it might bring back a terrible memory. But can you think of something else we can bring to him?"

"I'll help you dig around in his room," Jimmy's mother said. "You can bring him anything you think will help—perhaps his photo album? The hospital probably won't let him keep anything, but we can show him, can't we? Oh, Peggy, I'm just so happy to think that our Jimmy laughed again."

We went upstairs to his room as soon as we finished our coffee and cake. Mrs. Barnett showed me a wooden box Jimmy had made in Boy Scouts to earn a woodworking badge. He'd filled it with mementos—baseball cards, his string of perfect Sunday school attendance medals, a model airplane he'd glued together from a kit—nothing a grown man would want, but things that once held special meaning for him. Mrs. Barnett left me there to search by myself, and I lost all track of time as I sorted through the box.

I still hadn't reached the bottom when I found a manila envelope filled with newspaper clippings. They were from May of 1939 and told about a passenger liner called the *St. Louis*. It seemed like a funny thing for a kid in high school to keep, but as I skimmed through the articles, I remembered how obsessed Jimmy had been with the story at the time. A steamship filled with Jewish refugees had been fleeing Nazi persecution but couldn't find a nation that would take them in. Their plight had made headlines in all the newspapers as the world watched and waited to see what would happen. One of the articles showed a grainy picture of the ship in Havana Harbor, surrounded by rowboats filled with distraught relatives calling out to their families on board. One passenger became so depressed at the thought of returning to Germany that he had jumped overboard to kill himself.

The story made me pause for a moment. How had Jimmy reached the same point as this Jewish man, who had felt so hopeless that death seemed like the only solution? Jimmy had a home and a family to return to, a future as a veterinarian with his dad, and a hundred other things to look forward to. He must have known there were plenty of people he could turn to for help, unlike the man in the story. So why had Jimmy done it?

I continued reading. The United States government had turned down the passengers' request for sanctuary and had sent the *St. Louis* away. The Canadian government did the same thing. I remembered how upset Jimmy had been by that news. "A lot of Americans are prejudiced against Jewish people," he'd told me. According to the newspaper, our government decided that if they made an exception to their immigration quotas and let these refugees into the country, then multitudes of people would be jumping on ships and trying to get into the States. I shook my head in disbelief. If these refugees had no home and no country that wanted them, what were they supposed to do? I understood from my childhood a little of how those poor people must have felt—being disliked and unwanted and tormented for no reason at all. If Donna had her way, I might not have a home for much longer, either.

Along with all the newspaper articles was a carbon copy of a letter that Jimmy had sent to President Roosevelt, asking him to intervene on behalf of the passengers. That was just like Jimmy—always trying to right wrongs and fix things, standing up for people the same way he'd offered to confront the bullies for me. The last article in the envelope told how the ship's captain had no choice in the end but to turn the ship around and return to Europe. I wondered what had become of those nine hundred passengers. The tragedy of the *St. Louis* seemed even more poignant now that the world knew the horrible truth about the Nazi atrocities—the concentration camps, the gas chambers, the crematoriums. Six million Jews had been murdered. Had the *St. Louis*'s passengers become victims of the Nazis, too?

Even now, a year after the war ended, the nations still seemed to be arguing about what to do with the Jewish people. They filled displaced persons camps all across Europe, still looking for a permanent home. I had just read a newspaper article last week that told how President Truman was urging the British government to allow 100,000 Jewish refugees to immigrate to Palestine. The British foreign minister had replied that the Americans wanted them to move to Palestine because they didn't want them in the United States. Where were all these people supposed to go?

I put everything back into the wooden box and went home, feeling discouraged.

Joe was sitting upstairs in our living room, laughing and drinking highballs with Donna and Pop. A Yankees' game blared from the radio. The apartment was steaming hot and Pop had set up two rotating fans to blow the warm air around on high speed. "Hey! I remembered where Chaplain Bill was from!" Joe said when I walked in. "Danbury, Connecticut!"

"That isn't far from here," I said. "Just across the New York State border."

"Told you I had a good memory." Joe tapped his forehead with the empty highball glass he was holding.

"We could search for his name in the Danbury telephone book and—"

"Let's go! We'll take my motorcycle." He rose to his feet, swaying slightly. Even if I had the courage to ride on the back of his motorcycle, I certainly wasn't going to do it after he'd been drinking.

"How about tomorrow instead?" I asked. "We'll get an early start."

"What's all this?" Pop mumbled. "Where're you going?"

"Nowhere today, Pop."

"Oh, go on, you two," Donna said. "Why not take off and have a little fun?" She wore a sly smile and I realized what she was up to. If she could kindle a spark between Joe Fiore and me, he might take me off her hands.

"We'll go tomorrow, Joe. Bright and early," I said. *And in my car.* I went into my bedroom and closed the door.

I was up early the next day so I could do my chores at the clinic and explain to Mr. Barnett where I was going. Pop had let Joe sleep overnight in the office again, and waking him up at nine o'clock in the morning wasn't something I relished doing. But it had to be done. I was much too shy with strangers to drive to Danbury, Connecticut, and talk to the chaplain by myself. Where on earth would I start? What would I say? Joe Fiore already knew the man, and besides, Joe was talkative and outgoing enough for both of us. I scrounged through my bedroom for all the spare change I could find for the pay telephone. Meanwhile, Joe got dressed and swallowed a fistful of aspirin and a cup of strong coffee. I talked him out of taking his motorcycle. "It will only make your headache worse. Maybe next time." If there was a next time. Who knew when Joe would take off again?

We found two listings for William Ashburn in the Danbury telephone directory. The first was the chaplain's father, who kindly gave us directions to Chaplain Bill's parsonage. The former Army chaplain turned out to be older than I'd imagined, in his forties I guessed, with a worried-looking face, rounded shoulders, and thinning brown hair. He invited us into his kitchen for coffee. His wife apologized for the state of her house, blaming their three children. "Please don't fuss," I told her. "It's our fault for showing up unannounced."

He asked us to call him Bill, and he seemed to remember Joe, although Joe admitted he never attended any of the religious services that the chaplain led. I explained that I was an old friend of Jim Barnett and he said, "Oh yes! I remember Jim very well. We had a lot of interesting conversations. In fact, Jim was one of the few people who enjoyed talking about God with me." His voice trailed off and he was quiet for a moment before adding, "He had a very mature faith for a man his age. I hope nothing has happened to him."

"Well, he's in the VA hospital, I'm sorry to say, suffering from battle fatigue and depression. He, um . . . he tried to end his life."

The chaplain looked shaken. Coffee sloshed onto his hand as he returned his cup to its saucer. "Oh no . . . no, not Jim. I can't believe that. He was one of the most courageous men I ever met. He would crawl around in the thick of battle, taking care of his wounded men even though mortar rounds were coming in and shrapnel and bullets were flying all over. I couldn't have done what Jim did."

"I guess it finally got to him, you know?" Joe said quietly.

"But that's just it," Bill said. "He didn't let anything get to him. Not when I knew him, anyway. He was convinced that nothing could harm him unless God willed it. He used to quote that psalm to me . . . How does it go? Something about all our days being written in God's big black book? No, I find it very hard to believe that Jim would try to take his own life."

"That's not the Jimmy I know, either," I said. "That's why I'm trying to piece his story together and figure out what happened to change him so much. Something must have."

"The war was—" Bill stopped and I saw him swallow hard. "None of us are the same after what we saw. And did."

"Hey, we did what we had to, you know?" Joe said. He was getting restless and fidgety, jiggling his foot and tapping his knuckles against the table. He probably wanted a beer, but it was much too early in the day to start drinking.

I turned back to Chaplain Bill. "Can you remember when you last saw Jimmy and if he seemed like himself?"

"Let me think. It must have been in the late fall of '44. We were fighting our way toward the Rhine, and Jim and I worked together in the battalion aid stations. I offered comfort and he helped the overworked doctors." He ran his hand through his thinning hair. "I-I confess that I would freeze sometimes, if someone was badly hurt and was afraid of dying. Jim often did a better job of praying with them than I did, I'm ashamed to admit. I told him he should be the chaplain, not me." Bill gave a nervous laugh, but I could see that the memories haunted him. He looked at me as if pleading with me to understand. "I mean, what do you say when someone asks, 'Am I going to die?' and you know they probably are. What do you say?"

"That must have been terrible," I murmured. "I'm so sorry." The words felt meaningless, even to me.

"Hey, I could use a smoke," Joe said. "I think I'll step outside, if you don't mind." The kitchen was quiet for a moment after the door closed. I could hear a vacuum cleaner running upstairs.

"Anyway," the chaplain said, gathering himself. "The Nazis made their big counteroffensive that winter, and every available man was called in to fight them. Jim and I got separated, and I don't recall running into him again after that."

"I have the letters he sent home," I said. "He fought in what the newspapers called the Battle of the Bulge, I think."

Chaplain Bill stared off into the distance as if lost in his thoughts. Then he sighed and turned to me again. "Can I be honest with you, Miss Serrano? I don't think I will be much help to Jim. Oh, I'll be more than happy to drive over and visit him, but as far as offering spiritual help? I'm not your man. I mean, where was God when the world was burning and millions of innocent people were suffering and dying? How could He—?" Bill stopped and tugged at his clerical collar as if it was choking him. I waited, like Jimmy always did, in case he wanted to say more. "I've decided to set aside this collar for a while. I'm not the spiritual leader my church needs. I guess you could say I have a lot of questions for God right now, and so I've written my resignation. My wife isn't very happy with my decision. She says I'm not the same man she married, and I guess she's right." He gave a nervous laugh, and I felt so sorry for him that I wanted to hug him. "Did you have any more questions for me? I don't think I've been much help."

"You've been a huge help. I know now that Jimmy was still his old self before that last winter of the war. But listen, do you think you can help me get in touch with some of the other men he fought alongside? I'm hoping that they'll supply a few more pieces of his story. If I knew their addresses, I could write to them."

He brightened. "Sure, I could help you with that. I'll contact our company commander."

"That would be wonderful! Jimmy's two closest friends were Mitch O'Hara and another medic named Frank Cishek."

"Frank Cishek. That name seems familiar for some reason. Let me write this down."

"I would especially like to contact those two men. And also, any soldiers like Joe Fiore who give Jimmy credit for saving their lives. I think it would encourage Jimmy if they wrote to him and sent pictures of their families so he would know how many people he helped."

Chaplain Bill fetched a pen and notepad from the telephone stand to copy down the names. I told him where the VA hospital was and that visiting hours were on Sunday. He promised to come next Sunday after his church service. I got out my little camera—a graduation present from Mr. and Mrs. Barnett—and asked Chaplain Bill if he would let me take his picture for the album I wanted to make for Jimmy. Then I wrote my name, address, and telephone number on the pad for him. "One more thing," I said, pulling Gisela's picture from my bag. "Do you know anything about this woman? Her name is Gisela. Was she one of the nurses Jimmy worked with, maybe?"

He studied the photo, rubbing his forehead as if concentrating. "I don't think I've ever seen her before. Her name sounds foreign though, doesn't it?" He handed back the picture.

I left feeling hopeful that he would do whatever he could to help Jimmy. But I also left Connecticut with a deep ache in my heart for Chaplain Bill.

8

Gisela

Sam and I spent much of our time gazing out at the endless expanse of ocean every day and wondering what would become of us. There were no signs of life beyond our ship, not even a bird in the sky, and the emptiness emphasized how abandoned and homeless we felt. We sailed for nearly a week after learning that the *St. Louis* was headed back to Europe, without any idea where we were going to land. Sam said prayers with his brothers, Vati, and the other men every day at sunrise and sunset, pleading with God for help. The passenger committee asked all of us for donations to help pay for the countless telegrams they were sending around the world from the ship's radio room, pleading for help. The strain wore everyone down until we were drowning in despair. Captain Schroeder tried to toss us a life ring, addressing us in the social hall on Friday afternoon before Shabbat. "Whatever happens, you will not be returned to Germany," he promised. It was enough to keep most of us treading water for a few more days. Saturday would mark exactly four weeks to the day since we'd set sail from Hamburg. Four weeks! And now we were nearing Europe once again.

Four more long, stressful days passed. On Wednesday, June 14, we were summoned into the social hall at 10 a.m. for a meeting. Captain Schroeder watched in silence as Herr Joseph from the passenger committee read the telegram that they had received:

```
Final arrangements for disembarkation
all passengers complete. Governments
of Belgium, Holland, France, and England
cooperated magnificently with American
Joint Distribution Committee to effect
this possibility.
```

Our ship could land at last! We would be welcome in those four countries. Cheers and cries of joy erupted all over the hall. I huddled with my family as we wept and laughed and hugged each other. Sam's family did the same. Herr Joseph waited for silence, then thanked Captain Schroeder on our behalf for keeping his promise. The *St. Louis* would be landing in Antwerp, Belgium, on Saturday, June 17, and we would be disembarking at last to be dispersed to our new host nations. We celebrated with a huge party in the social hall that night. Everyone rejoiced. I danced in Sam's arms until the band finally put away their instruments and went to bed. Our prayers had been answered.

My father spent the next few days with Sam and his mother as we tried to decide which of the four countries we would choose. Our mothers had become friends, Sam and I were inseparable, and Vati had offered to help Sam take care of his family while his father remained in Cuba. We decided against Holland because it was too close to Germany. Belgium and France weren't much more distant, but at least Mutti had a brother in Paris. Eventually we chose Great Britain because it was an isolated island, even though none of us knew a soul there. It felt safer. "Sam and I already speak a little English," I reasoned. "And if we all improve our skills while we're waiting, we'll have an advantage when our US quota numbers are called."

On Saturday morning, the American Jewish committee representative, Morris Troper, sailed out to us on a tugboat from the Dutch port of Flushing, along with relief workers from the four host countries. Everyone on board strained for a glimpse of the man who had worked so hard to save our lives. Children formed a reception line to greet him. As the *St. Louis* sailed the remaining miles to Antwerp, Belgium, Mr. Troper and the four relief workers took their places behind a table in the social hall to decide our fates. "We will do our best to keep families together," they announced.

But Sam and I weren't a family, not yet. I clung tightly to his hand as we waited in a long line in the social hall with our parents to speak with the representative from England. I happened to glance up, and a chill came over me when I saw the portrait of Hitler glowering down on us from above. I felt like a mouse under the watchful eye of a hawk.

Vati presented our case to the British representative, as did Sam, and we learned that the most important factor in deciding our fate was the quota number on our US immigration applications. Passengers with the lowest numbers received preferential treatment because they would be out of their host country the soonest. Sam's number was lower than mine by thousands. The final decisions would be announced by five o'clock, after the workers conferred with each other.

Soon after two that afternoon, Sam and I stood on the deck of the *St. Louis* as it docked at the pier in Antwerp. It was the first time we'd tied up on land since leaving Hamburg on May 13. Now it was June 17. We were so close to freedom, and yet I feared that something still could go wrong. Hadn't we all cheered and rejoiced when we'd arrived in Havana? "To be honest," I told Sam, "I'm still not quite willing to believe that our ordeal is over. And what will we do if you and I end up in different countries?"

He pulled me close and kissed the top of my head. "We'll find a way to be together, Gisela. I promise."

We returned to the social hall at five o'clock to learn our fates. The representative from Great Britain read his list of names first, and neither

Sam's family nor mine was on it. I barely had time to recover from my disappointment when they started reading the list for Belgium. Near the end of the list of 214 names was Shapiro. Sam and his family would be staying in Belgium. I held my breath until they reached *W* and said, "Wolff," then I could breathe again. We hadn't gotten our first choice of England, but thank God we would remain together. "And at least we'll be free from the Nazis in Belgium," Sam said.

We ate dinner aboard the ship for the very last time, and we were the envy of all the others when we were the first ones allowed off the *St. Louis*. I couldn't believe the moment had finally arrived. At seven o'clock that evening, my feet touched land once again. As we were walking down the pier away from the ship, I heard a passenger behind me say, "We've sailed ten thousand miles without ever stepping foot on land, and now we're back in Europe, three hundred miles from where we started."

As it turned out, we had little time to celebrate our freedom once we disembarked. We were met by an escort of Belgian policemen and taken to a special train that was waiting for us on a nearby siding. An iron barrier blocked it off from the public streets. Our luggage was collected and we were quickly shuttled into the rail coaches. They were third-class coaches with hard, wooden seats, like the ones designated "for Jews only" in Germany. The coach windows were barred and had been nailed shut. We were locked inside and watched over by the police all the way to Brussels. "It's for your own safety," we were told. It didn't feel that way. I sat with my head on Sam's shoulder, clutching his hand for the two-hour ride.

Everything was in a state of confusion when we arrived in Brussels that night. Names were read off and families scrambled to find their luggage before being shuttled off to spend Saturday night in various hotels around Brussels. We were told we'd be moved once again in the morning. I needed to remain close to my family, so I barely had a chance to say goodbye to Sam before he and his family were whisked off to a different hotel. I was terrified that we would remain separated when morning came and I would never see him again. As it turned out, we were all reunited in the morning and were met by officials from the Jewish Joint Distribution Committee, welcoming us to our new home in Belgium.

My family and Sam's would settle in Antwerp, where there was a large Jewish community comprised mostly of refugees like us. We would live in a Jewish neighborhood near the city's elegant train station. "Our stay in Belgium is only temporary, my dear ones," Vati assured us. "But for now, let's settle in and wait patiently until we're allowed to immigrate to the United States." America felt real to me now that I had glimpsed it from a distance, even if my opinion of that country had been tainted by their cruel rejection of us.

The Joint Committee paid for our support, providing enough money for us to rent a small apartment. Sam's family moved into the same building, right across the hall from us. We owned nothing except the contents of the suitcases we'd brought with us on the *St. Louis*, and we spent the remainder of June trying to set up housekeeping again. Little by little, throughout the month of July, we began to reclaim the lives we'd lost when the Nazis came to power. Sam and I explored Antwerp together, drinking coffee in the cafés in the Grote Markt or strolling through the city's lovely parks or even going to the cinema to help us learn Flemish. It was a new experience for us to be able to roam freely without fear of being accosted and beaten by Hitler Youth. There were no restrictions against Jewish people, no hateful propaganda posters or signs that said *No dogs or Jews*. And yet I felt as though I was moving forward on thin ice, testing each step, afraid to put on skates and glide effortlessly, unable to believe we were truly free.

Throughout the pleasant summer months, Sam's father wrote countless letters to his wife as they debated whether or not he should leave Cuba to join his family in Belgium. Mr. Shapiro told us that while we'd been waiting on board the ship in Havana Harbor, the Nazi Party in Cuba had flooded the island with propaganda against Jews, arousing public opinion against allowing us to land. And after the United States and Canada refused us entry, the Nazis had bragged to the world that they had been right about us—nobody wanted dirty Jews in his country. In the end, the question of moving to Belgium was settled for Sam's father when he was denied entrance because of the deluge of immigrants already flooding the small country. Sam would continue to be responsible for his mother and brothers. He found a part-time job delivering furniture for a Jewish-owned store to help support them and applied to study at a school in Antwerp in the fall.

In August, Sam and I were returning home from the English classes we attended together in the synagogue when my parents and Sam's mother asked us to sit down in our tiny kitchen for a conversation. "My dear children," Vati began, "Mutti and I and Mrs. Shapiro have been talking, and we all agree that it isn't wise for you two to spend all of your free time together the way you've been doing and as you did on the ship."

A cold dread filled my heart. I was holding Sam's hand and I gripped it tighter beneath the table. "We know you love each other," Vati continued. "And we believe your love is genuine. But you're much too young for such an intense relationship and certainly for marriage. Now that we're all free again, we want to urge you to make some new friends and spend time with other young people your age. Gisela, you need to finish your education—and didn't you once think of becoming a nurse? Sam, you will be enrolling in the university when that becomes possible, so you both have many years of study ahead. You're so young, and you'll have the rest of your lives to be together and be responsible for each other. Why not enjoy these last few years of your youth instead of suffocating each other?"

Neither of us replied right away. The kitchen faucet dripped like a ticking clock. I couldn't look at Sam. My insides squeezed as if gripped by a fist, as I fought a surge of panic. It was the same panic I'd felt after we were sent to different hotels on our first night in Belgium. The anxiety returned whenever we were apart for too long, and the fear would arise inside me that I would never see Sam again. *Suffocating?* It was the opposite. I couldn't breathe when we were apart. And now our parents wanted us to spend less time together? Did Sam share their opinion?

Did he think we were suffocating each other? I swallowed my tears as I waited for him to reply.

"May I ask you a question, Mr. Wolff?" Sam said at last. "How did you meet Gisela's mother? Was it arranged by a matchmaker?"

"No, we met at a wedding. Her cousin was marrying my best friend. I saw Elise across the room and thought she was the most beautiful woman I'd ever seen." He looked at Mutti and she seemed to glow as he reached to take her hand. As a child, I'd seen their deep love for each other, and I had watched it grow even stronger under all the pressure we'd endured.

"And how long was it," Sam asked, "before you knew that you wanted her beside you for the rest of your life?"

Vati nodded and held up his hand. "I understand what you're saying, Sam—and it was, in fact, only a matter of months. But I was seven years older than you are right now, and my wife was four years older than Gisela is. We both had completed our educations. All we're saying is that for the next few years you need to have interests in life aside from each other."

"Are you going to forbid us to be together?"

"Not at all. But will you at least consider what we're asking? Spend time with other friends. You don't need to see each other every day. Especially once Gisela starts classes in the fall."

Sam and I loved our parents. We knew we had a duty to obey them. As hard as it would be to spend time apart, we reluctantly agreed. Vati helped Sam find a study partner at the synagogue, a young man his age named Aaron Goldberg, and they began learning Gemara with the rabbi. It was through Aaron that Sam was introduced to the Zionist organization in Antwerp. They attended meetings together, and afterwards I would sit outside with them on the steps of our apartment and listen to their long discussions on warm summer nights. I watched Sam's growing interest in the movement to resettle in the ancient land of Israel.

"We should all make plans to immigrate to Palestine instead of the United States," Aaron insisted. "It's our ancestors' homeland."

"I thought the British White Paper restricted Jewish immigration after the Arab Revolt?"

"There are other ways to get into Palestine for those who are determined. We could go there on student visas, for instance."

"Aren't most of the settlements farming communities?" Sam asked. "I know nothing about farming."

"We would join the other pioneers, Sam, and build a nation. We'd be preparing the way for more immigrants to come in the future. They'll need engineers to drain the swamps and set up irrigation systems—the land has been wasting away for a thousand years. And medical professionals to fight malaria and other diseases."

"And weapons and military fighters?" Sam asked.

"Yes. To protect ourselves. We need a homeland where no one can ever persecute us again."

A group of children were playing ball in the street as we talked, and Sam tossed the ball back to them when it landed at his feet. I was slowly growing accustomed to seeing Jewish children playing safely outdoors again, young couples walking hand in hand to the cinema, mothers pushing babies in carriages, and elderly people sitting in the park in the sunshine—things that we'd been forbidden to do after the Nazis came to power.

"I'll never forget how it felt to be on that ship with no place to land," Sam told Aaron. "There wasn't a country in the world where we were welcome, and we feared that we'd have to return to Hamburg. That should never happen to any of our people again."

"I'm just saying give Palestine some thought. It may be years before we're allowed into the United States."

Later, Sam asked me what I thought about establishing a homeland in the ancient land of Israel. "It sounds like life there would be a constant struggle," I replied. "With hostile neighbors and barren land and ruined cities. I just want to live our lives, Sam, don't you? I want to have a home and children and just live in peace. Haven't we already gone through enough turmoil for one lifetime?"

"I agree. I don't feel much like a pioneer or a freedom fighter. All I want is a safe home and a future with you. Starting all over again will be enough of a challenge without trying to do it in a desolate country with warring neighbors."

"Then let's be patient and wait until the United States lets us immigrate there."

As September approached, Ruthie and I and Sam's two brothers prepared to attend school in Antwerp's Jewish community. I was excited about finishing my last year of secondary school and had enrolled in a program to complete a nursing certificate two years after graduating. We were settling into our new lives in Belgium, even if they were only temporary. And even though it was difficult, Sam and I obeyed our parents' wishes and spent a little less time with each other. For a few brief months, we were all happy.

Then, on September 1, 1939, two and a half months after Sam and I and our families had arrived safely in Belgium, our future dreams were shattered once again. The Nazis staged a brutal, lightning-quick invasion of Poland. In response, Great Britain and France declared war on Germany. Europe was at war again. And tiny, neutral Belgium, our new homeland, stood directly in the path of the warring nations.

9

Peggy

It was past noon by the time Joe and I returned home from visiting Chaplain Bill in Connecticut. Joe had spent the first part of the drive talking nonstop about his favorite baseball team, the Cleveland Indians, comparing them to the New York Yankees, and the remainder of it asleep. I had hoped we could talk about Chaplain Bill. I wanted to ask Joe what he thought of our visit, but I was afraid he would become upset again. Bill's comment about the war haunted me. *"None of us are the same after what we saw. And did."* Clearly he and Joe Fiore and Jimmy Barnett had been deeply affected by their experiences, and I didn't see how insulin comas and electrical shocks and jets of hot and cold water were going to erase four years of seeing the world burning and millions of innocent people suffering and dying, as Bill had described it. His faith had been shaken, and I wondered if Jimmy's had, too.

I changed into my work clothes as soon as I got home and hurried across the road to the clinic. I was working in the dog kennels when Mr. Barnett found me. "I'm heading out to Blue Fence Farms, Peggy. Do you have time to come along?"

"Sure, I'd love to." I was supposed to be teaching Donna how to take over Pop's bookkeeping this afternoon, but I was feeling stubborn and a little sorry for myself. Donna had waited all these years to take an interest in Pop's business, so she could just wait a few hours longer. As Mr. Barnett's truck rattled down the country roads toward the thoroughbred ranch, I told him about my trip to Danbury to see Chaplain Bill. "He isn't depressed like Jimmy is," I said, "but his faith has been shaken and he's questioning God. He's going to resign from his church."

"That's a shame."

"The chaplain remembered Jimmy as having a lot of faith for a young man. He said that Jimmy was courageous under fire, crawling around to take care of his wounded men while the bullets were flying. When the chaplain asked him why he was so fearless, Jimmy had quoted a Bible verse that said all of his days were written in God's book."

Mr. Barnett didn't reply, and when I glanced at him, he was wiping his eyes. "We talked before Jim went overseas," he finally said. "Jim was afraid of being afraid. That's the verse I told him to remember. I reminded him that even the hairs of his head were numbered. And that God would never forsake him."

"If Jimmy still believed those things, then it doesn't make sense that he would try to kill himself, does it?"

"That's true," Mr. Barnett murmured. "I guess the question is, what happened that made Jim stop believing them?"

"I'm hoping I can talk with more of his Army buddies and try to find out. The chaplain promised to send me the addresses of some of the men who served with Jimmy so I can write letters to them. I just wish it didn't take so long. I hate thinking of him getting electrical shocks to his brain."

"I know," Mr. B. said softly. "Let me know if I can do anything to help you, Peggy. I think you may be on the right track."

We arrived at Blue Fence Farms, one of my favorite places to be, and parked the truck outside one of the stables. I loved the fragrant fields out here in the country, the green, gently rolling pastures dotted with graceful, long-legged horses. And always in the distance, the familiar mountains standing guard over our valley.

The farm manager had hired a new horse trainer named Paul Dixon, and Mr. Barnett wanted to meet him since they would be caring for the horses together. Mr. Dixon seemed young for such an important job, probably no more than thirty, and as long-legged as one of the thoroughbreds. He had worked with a renowned trainer in the horse-racing world before the war and came highly recommended. I could have guessed by the slow, easy way he stretched out his words that he'd grown up in the South even before he told us he was from Kentucky. As we walked through the stables with him, talking about each of the horses and their peculiarities, I saw his affection and admiration for the animals in his care. I liked him right away, and I could tell that Mr. Barnett did, too.

"Can you take a look at Persephone while you're here, Mr. Barnett?" he asked. He removed his cap to wipe his brow, unleashing a mop of reddish-brown hair. "She isn't used to me yet, and I don't want to spook her." The mare was expecting her first foal in a few weeks, sired by a famous thoroughbred named Best Chance. But today Persephone was skittish with Mr. B., too.

"Let me try," I said. She was my favorite horse on the farm because she was shy, like me. I had worked hard to win her trust, which came slowly. I edged up beside her now, talking to her, then stroked her neck and her shoulder until she calmed down and allowed Mr. Barnett to examine her.

"Everything looks fine," he said when he finished. "Thanks, Peggy."

My afternoon at Blue Fence Farms gave me a welcome reprieve from worrying about Jimmy and all the other broken soldiers like Joe and Bill. I could forget, for a little while, that Donna was determined to push me out and send me off on my own. My heart felt lighter by the time we climbed into the truck again to head back to the clinic.

I was surprised to see Joe's motorcycle still parked outside Pop's garage when we arrived. I'd figured he would probably take off now that we'd visited Chaplain Bill. I was even more surprised to find Joe inside the garage, helping Pop work on a car. "So Pop has you working now?" I asked.

Joe looked up with a grin, his handsome face smudged with grease. "Hey, it's about time I did something around here to pay for my beer, you know?"

I wanted to ask how long he planned to stay, but Pop tilted his head toward the office and said, "Donna's waitin' on you."

She was already seated at my desk, smoking a cigarette and paging through a catalog of automotive parts. The ashtray she'd brought with her overflowed with butts, and the room stank of cigarette smoke in spite of the whirling fan and the open window. Joe's saddlebags lay open on the floor, his clothes strewn all over, the blankets on the daybed in a rumpled heap. I resisted the urge to tidy up since it was no longer my office.

"Oh no you don't," Donna said when Buster tried to walk in behind me. "I don't want that dog in here. He'll stink up the place. Out!" Buster was my second shadow whenever I was home, and he had trotted into the office with me like he always did, ready to nap in his usual place beneath the desk with his head on my feet. He didn't know that this was Donna's office now. I knelt down to scratch his ears and give him a hug so I wouldn't say something nasty to Donna, then gently pushed him out and closed the door.

"So Joe is on the payroll now?" I asked. "Whose idea was that?"

"I don't know," Donna said with a shrug. "All of ours, I guess. He's going to be a great help to your father. We've been so busy lately."

We've been so busy. In her mind, Pop's business was already hers. I pulled up a folding stool and sat down beside Donna to teach her my accounting system. I showed her how to write up invoices and fill out order forms. I gave her the stack of monthly bills that needed to be paid and showed her where to file them for tax purposes. I handed over the checkbook and banking information. Donna turned out to be good with numbers—a skill I supposed she'd learned by tallying patrons' tabs in her head all these years. She was not the least bit apologetic about taking over my job, as if she assumed this was her right. At one point, when the sound of Joe's laughter carried into the office from the garage, she said, "Your young man certainly is handsome, isn't he?"

"He isn't my young man."

"I can tell he's taken a shine to you."

"What makes you say that?"

"Why else is he sticking around?"

I opened my mouth to explain that we were trying to help Jimmy get well, then closed it again. Why bother? Donna was writing her own version of this story and probably envisioned us riding off into the sunset on Joe's motorcycle. I wanted to tell her that Joe Fiore might be charming and good-looking, but he drank too much. And I'd spent a lifetime with people who drank too much. I'd been so busy trying to help Jimmy that I hadn't had time to think about my own life, but I knew it wasn't going to include Joe. Yet whenever I tried to imagine myself as a waitress or a store clerk, I couldn't do that, either. I was awkward around strangers and terrible at engaging in conversation with them or smiling and being friendly and flirtatious like Donna. I had always gotten along best with animals. Give me a kennel full of dogs or a stable filled with horses, and I'd make friends with all of them.

Joe ended up staying all week and working in Pop's garage every day. Twice, he woke us up in the middle of the night with nightmares, and I had to go downstairs to awaken him. I had trouble falling back asleep after returning to my room, so I looked up the Bible verses that Chaplain Bill and Jimmy's father had mentioned and saw that they were already underlined in Jimmy's Bible. Maybe I could read them to him when I visited on Sunday. I found the Psalms strangely comforting as I worried about my own future. On my darkest nights, I pictured Donna's face every time one of the Psalms mentioned "mine enemies," and I wondered if I dared to hope for God's deliverance. I wanted my life to go back to the way it used to be, with Donna selling drinks at the Crow Bar and Jimmy helping his father at the veterinary clinic, but that wasn't going to happen. A month had passed since Jimmy had tried to kill himself and he wasn't getting any better.

I went looking for Joe on Saturday evening so we could plan our trip to the hospital the following day. I found him in our backyard, preparing to leave. He had cleaned himself up for a night out on the town—although not at the Crow Bar, he said, to show support for Donna. "Hey, why don't you come with me?" he asked. "We could have a real good time."

"Thanks, but I don't drink much."

"So? We can find a place that has a band or a jukebox, and we can dance, you know?"

"I don't know how to dance."

"I'll teach you. Come on. You'll be the prettiest girl in the place." I shook my head. His magnetic smile disappeared, replaced by an angry frown. "Hey, why're you giving me such a hard time? I thought we were friends." Joe's temper seemed to be easily triggered. I needed to appease him.

"We are friends, Joe. But I know I wouldn't enjoy myself, and it would have nothing to do with you. I'm sure you'd be a charming companion and a lot of fun to be with, but I don't really like going out to bars. Listen—about tomorrow. If you're still planning to go to the hospital with me to see Jimmy, I think we should leave as soon as I get home from church. Chaplain Bill is going to drive over after his own church services."

"We can take my motorcycle."

"I was thinking we would take the car again. I don't mind driving."

We'd been talking out in the backyard all this time, and Donna must have been eavesdropping from the kitchen window because the screen door opened and she shouted down to us from the top of the apartment stairs. "I'm going to need the car tomorrow, Peg. Didn't your father tell you?"

I wondered when Donna had decided that the car I'd been driving ever since gasoline rationing ended was now hers.

Joe gave me a happy grin. "Guess it's my motorcycle, then."

* * *

I was restless all through the church service, my anxiety building over the upcoming motorcycle ride. I headed for the door as soon as the service ended and was surprised when a man who looked vaguely familiar greeted me at the end of the aisle. "Good morning, Miss Serrano. Nice to see you again." It took me a moment to realize that he was the new horse trainer from Blue Fence Farms. His tousled auburn hair looked darker after being tamed into submission with Brylcreem.

"Oh! Good morning, Mr. Dixon. I . . . um . . . It's nice to see you, too." I knew I should take time to greet him properly and welcome him to our church. After all, Mr. Dixon was new in town. But I was so clumsy at making small talk. And I was in a hurry to get to the hospital. "I-I . . . Please excuse me, but I'm running a little late today." He gave me a baffled look as I hurried away.

Of course, Joe was still sound asleep when I returned home from church. I had to wake him up and pump him full of aspirin and coffee before he was ready to go. I could have hitched a ride to the hospital with the Barnetts, but I was afraid that Joe would be angry with me for leaving him behind, especially after I'd refused to go out with him last night. I needed his help. He was friends with the other soldiers I would be trying to contact.

My knees were knocking as I got ready to climb onto the back of his motorcycle. "I've never been on one of these before, Joe. Promise you'll take it slow until I get used to it, okay?"

He just laughed. "Now, you gotta hang on to me unless you want to fall off," he coached. "Just wrap your arms around me like we're in love." I did as he said, then cried out and gripped him tighter as the motorcycle roared to life. I couldn't tell if I was trembling or if it was the machine rumbling beneath me. Probably both. I had never clung so tightly to a man before. It felt strange yet somehow kind of nice to be so close. Then Donna ruined it by calling out to us. She had walked down to the mailbox in her robe and slippers to fetch the Sunday newspaper.

"Have fun, you two!"

Fun? In a hospital? Joe revved the engine and we roared off. My ears were ringing by the time we boarded the ferry to cross the river. For most of the way, I had rested my forehead against Joe's back and closed my eyes. I wondered if he'd be mad at me if I asked the Barnetts for a ride home.

"This place gives me the heebie-jeebies," Joe said as we dismounted in front of the hospital. "Talk about bad memories! Hey, they aren't going to give Jim the water-torture treatment, are they?"

"The doctor hasn't mentioned it." *Yet.*

"Well, if they do, we gotta bust him out of there right away, you know?" Joe was getting nervous and agitated just looking at the building. I felt sorry for him. Buster had been with him the last time to bolster his courage.

"You don't have to go inside, Joe. Why don't you walk the long way around and meet us out back again?"

"Yeah. I think I will."

I hurried inside and found Jimmy in the common room, sitting in a regular chair, not a wheelchair. "Hi, Jimmy, it's me—Peggety." I crouched down and took his hand. He held mine in return, but I could tell from his expression that he was struggling to place who I was. "I'm your friend from across the street back home. We used to work together in your father's veterinary clinic." I didn't want to frustrate him by expecting a response, so I released his hand and asked, "Do you feel like taking a walk outside? Your buddy Joe Fiore is here to see you again, but we had to leave Buster home this time." He stood and I linked arms with him as we walked outside. His shoulder was level with the top of my head. He seemed stronger and not as shaky as before. We sat down on an empty bench with a view of the wide gray river below us and the mountains in the distance. I had been thinking about what I wanted to say all week, and I hurried to get the words out before Joe made his way to us.

"You have a lot of friends, Jimmy. You always did. But for as long as

I can remember, you've been my best friend. Sometimes my only friend. You always listened when I needed someone to talk to, and you knew just what to say to make me feel better. I know you must have a lot on your heart, and it must be breaking in two or you wouldn't be in this place. You can tell me anything and I'll listen. I want to help you the way you helped me so many, many times."

I reached up to wipe away a tear, and Jimmy turned his head to look at me. "Thanks, Peggety," he said. His voice was so soft I barely heard it, then he looked away again. My tears fell faster. I stood as Joe sauntered up with his limping stride and cocky grin.

"Hey, Jim. Joe Fiore. How're you doing?" He didn't wait for a reply but shook hands and then just kept talking in his cheerful, rambling way as he stood in front of Jimmy. "I need to thank you again for saving my life. And not just me, you know? Plenty of guys owe their lives to you. That's why we want to help you get out of this place and back home again. I know we saw a lot of terrible things over there and our lives were on the line plenty of times. I was pretty messed up by it all, you know? And not just because of my leg. But you told me to hang on, that I was going to be okay, and that's how I know you're gonna be okay, too. You told me life will always have some rough spots, remember? But you said the good Lord was hanging on to me. I'll never forget that. And you were right. I'm okay, now—well, most days, anyway." He gave a shaky laugh. "I'm getting a little better every day, and you will, too. Just let me know what I can do for you and I'll do it, you know? I mean it. Hey, I owe you my life." Joe had stuffed his hands into his pockets to control their trembling. He was getting choked up and fidgety. I was scrambling for something to say when Joe looked away and said, "Hey, here's another old pal you might remember—Chaplain Bill."

Joe's relief was apparent. Bill offered his hand and Jimmy shook it. I couldn't tell if he remembered Bill or not, but as Bill sat down on the bench beside Jimmy and started talking, Joe got out his cigarettes and moved away to smoke one. I decided to let Bill and Jimmy speak in private, and I moved away, too. I stood beside Joe while he smoked, watching a ship on the river below us. Fifteen minutes later, the Barnetts arrived.

"It's wonderful of you to come all this way to visit Jim," Mr. Barnett said after I introduced him to Joe and Bill. "His mother and I appreciate your concern and I'm sure Jim does, too."

"It's the least we can do," Bill said. Joe was restless and I could tell he wanted to leave.

"I can ride home with Jimmy's parents if you want to go," I told him.

He pulled me away from the others and said, "Yeah, sorry. It's just that seeing those guys in the white coats and all the messed-up soldiers like Jimmy and me . . . it brings back some bad memories, you know? I escaped from a place just like this one. Sorry."

"You don't need to apologize. I thought what you said to Jimmy was wonderful. I'm sure he's grateful that you came. Do you know how to get back to our apartment?"

"Yeah, sure. See you later." He strode off across the grass toward the parking lot.

Chaplain Bill was getting ready to leave too, and he looked so weary and sad that I just had to say something to him. I walked with him to the hospital doors, searching for words. "I-I know it's not my place to say anything, and you don't really know me at all, but I've been thinking about you all week, Chaplain Bill, and I just want to say, please don't stop being a pastor. People need you." Two orderlies pushing patients in wheelchairs were waiting to get through the doors, and we took a moment to hold them open for them. Then Bill gestured to some chairs just inside and we sat down.

"A pastor is supposed to speak for God," he said. "And to God. I can't seem to do either."

"I can see how much the war affected you. You and Joe and Jimmy— it seems like your souls are filled with grief. I felt that way once, after my mama died. I was eleven years old and my pop started drinking a lot, and I felt all alone. I could have used somebody to talk to who understood my grief. I'll bet there are kids in your church who've lost their fathers in the war. Maybe some wives who've lost their husbands, too. And parents like Jimmy's who are all torn up inside. Everyone is hurting in big ways and small ways, and we need someone who understands and who will pray with us and cry with us. Please don't desert them, Bill. They need you now more than ever."

"But that's the problem, Miss Serrano. People come to me every day asking how God could have allowed so much death and sorrow and destruction, and I don't have any answers for them."

"Maybe you don't need to have answers. I mean, I'm no expert with things like this, but . . . maybe you could just listen to people and cry with them and admit that you're hurting, too. That's what Jimmy always did best—he just listened. And that helped me more than anything else."

Bill was quiet for a long moment, staring at his shiny black shoes. "You're right about Jim," he finally said, his voice soft. "That's why everyone always turned to him. He listened to them."

I pulled a handkerchief from my purse and wiped my eyes. I missed Jimmy so much! If only I could talk to him about Donna and Pop and ask him to help me figure out what I was supposed to do with the rest of my life and where Buster and I were supposed to live. Jimmy was my best friend and I wanted him back. And more than anything else, I wanted to listen to him talk about what was tearing him up inside.

"I think I'm still really angry with God," Bill said.

"Me, too." It was the first time I admitted it. I cleared my throat. "But that's okay. All the people who've lost loved ones are probably mad at Him, too, if they're honest. I've been reading the Psalms at night when I can't sleep, and it sounds like some of those writers were also pretty mad. But they had it out with God and shouted their heads off. Even Jesus felt like God had forsaken Him, remember?"

Bill took my hand and squeezed it for a moment, then stood. "Thank you. You've been an enormous help to me."

The Barnetts and I stayed until visiting hours ended. When we hugged Jimmy goodbye, he embraced us in return. It seemed like a good sign. We were all encouraged when I told them on the way home how Jimmy had thanked me and said my name. But we had also noticed that Jimmy seemed confused and disconnected from us some of the time as if he were sleeping with his eyes open. When his mother talked about home, he'd gazed into the distance as if trying to remember a place he'd once visited a long time ago.

Joe's motorcycle wasn't in front of Pop's garage when we arrived. I hoped he hadn't gotten lost along the way. I trudged upstairs, my heart heavy with grief for Jimmy and Joe and Chaplain Bill. Donna was getting a beer out of the fridge, and the first thing she said to me was "Did you two have a fight or something?"

"What?" It took me a moment to figure out what she meant. "You mean Joe and me? No. He wanted to leave the hospital before I did, so I rode back with the Barnetts."

"Well, it sure looks like a fight to me. He came tearing in here without you, packed his bags, said thanks for the beer and everything, then tore out of here before I could blink."

"So Joe is gone?"

"That's what I just said, isn't it? Looks like you missed your chance, Peg."

Maybe I had, but not in the way Donna meant. Joe seemed like a broken man to me, and I had hoped that by helping Jimmy, he would be able to heal, too. I took Buster into my room and closed the door. It was a long time before I could stop crying.

10

Gisela

The May morning was still dark when I awoke to an explosion that rattled the windows and shook the room. It was followed by another and another. In between the blasts, I heard a roaring, growling sound that I couldn't quite place at first. It grew louder, closer. When I realized what it was, my heart seemed to stop beating—the drone of airplanes. Hundreds of them.

Belgium was under attack.

"Oh, God, please . . . no," I whispered.

Months had passed after France and Britain declared war on Germany last September, and not much had changed for our Jewish community in Belgium, aside from a growing uneasiness about the world situation. We observed Rosh Hashanah, Yom Kippur, and then Sukkot. My family had celebrated my seventeenth birthday in November, but we didn't speak of the horror of Kristallnacht just one year earlier. In December, every Jewish home lit candles for Hanukkah, brightening the cold, winter nights for eight days.

Then in early April, a month ago, the Nazis surprised the world by invading and occupying Norway and Denmark with the same lightning warfare they'd used when invading Poland. Their tanks and planes had been unstoppable. The Nazis seemed determined to swallow up all of Europe. Even so, Passover brought us the reminder of God's deliverance from slavery.

We understood firsthand what freedom meant after escaping from Nazi rule, although we would all breathe easier once we were allowed to immigrate to the United States. We were still waiting. In the meantime, I was looking forward to starting nursing school. Sam hadn't been able to enroll in the university, but he was deep into his Torah and Gemara studies at the synagogue and worked part-time.

Our adopted nation of Belgium had declared neutrality and had posted troops to protect our borders, but neutrality hadn't prevented Belgium from being invaded during the last war. With Germany to the east and France to the west, Belgium had become a blood-soaked battlefield back then. I had wanted to ignore all these things and continue to believe that Sam and I were safe, that our families were safe, that the Nazis couldn't touch us here. But the unmistakable sounds of distant warfare no longer allowed me to do it.

The noise had awakened Ruthie, too, and she sat up beside me in the bed we shared, her eyes wide with fear. We gripped hands as flashes like lightning shone from behind the window shades in bright bursts, followed by more rumbling booms. "That's not thunder, is it, Gisela?" she said. I shook my head and pulled her into my arms.

"Is it the Nazis?" Ruthie asked. "Are they coming here, too? Are they going to find us again?"

I saw no point in lying to her. "It does sound like we're being attacked. Let's see if Vati and Mutti are awake."

Vati was sitting in the dark at the kitchen table, still in his pajamas. Mutti was making coffee, and when she turned to us, I saw that she had been crying. "Come here, dear one," Vati said, pulling Ruthie onto his lap.

"Is there going to be a war here, too?" she asked.

"Well, I'm afraid it looks that way."

She buried her head against his shoulder and sobbed. "I don't want them to come here, Vati! I don't want them to find us again!"

"Shh . . . shh . . . ," he soothed. "Belgium sided with the Allies in the last war, and they defeated the enemy in the end. The Americans joined the fight, and they changed the course of the war. It will be the same this time—you'll see. The Americans will come to our defense."

I wanted to believe my father, but bitter disappointment made me reluctant to trust the Americans to rescue us. We huddled in our kitchen, feeling the apartment building shudder and listening to the sound of our lives changing once again. If we were all about to die, I wanted to be with Sam at the end. "May I invite Sam and his family to come over?" I asked. "Please? They shouldn't be all alone."

"Yes, of course," Vati replied. "Let's all get dressed and I'll go see if they want to join us."

They did, and our two families sat in our living room, trying to find a news report on the radio as the distant explosions continued and sirens wailed. "Does this building have a basement?" Sam asked. "Maybe we should move down there if the air raid gets worse."

"The Nazis will probably attack the Belgian military installations and airfields first," Vati replied. "But it wouldn't hurt to gather some blankets and food and flashlights and take them down there, just in case."

"What if they win, Vati?" Ruthie asked. "What if the Nazis win and they take over Belgium, and they come after us again?"

"We'll figure out a way to escape from them. We escaped once before."

But had we? I was beginning to understand why Max Loewe had jumped overboard in Havana Harbor. He had exhausted all hope of ever finding refuge and safety.

More than a week passed as the war raged throughout Belgium. We spent each night with our neighbors in the building's dark, damp basement, watching the cobwebs sway on the rafters above our heads as bombs shook the foundations. The British and French offered the

Belgian military no help. We learned on the radio that the Nazis had invaded the neighboring Netherlands on the same day they'd invaded us and forced its government to surrender. There seemed to be little hope for us. The stress took a huge toll on Vati. He had never fully recovered his health after being imprisoned, and his nagging cough left him too weak to eat most days. He remained much too thin. Sam seemed overwhelmed as well, with his mother and brothers depending on him. There were no letters from his father advising him what to do. We all felt so helpless.

"I don't have anyone I can confide in but you, Gisela," Sam told me in one of our few moments alone. There had been a lull in the fighting, so we sat on the front steps of our apartment building as we had so often before the invasion. But children no longer played in the street, and a haze of smoke dimmed the spring sunlight. The air smelled of burnt metal. Our Jewish community was a ghost town. Everyone huddled inside around their radios, desperate for good news. "I have to remain strong for my mother and brothers," Sam said. "I keep assuring them that everything will be all right, but I don't think it will be. The Nazis are going to win. And then what?"

"Vati says the men at the synagogue are discussing what to do. You aren't alone. They'll figure something out."

"The Nazis hate us. If they win, they'll persecute us here the same way they did back home in Germany."

"Then we'll have to pray that they don't win. The British and French will fight them off. And Vati says the Americans will help us again."

"But will help come in time? The Nazis bombed Rotterdam in order to force the Netherlands to surrender, killing hundreds of innocent civilians. They'll do the same thing here. If they bomb Antwerp . . . We're so close to the train station that we're certain to be a target." His words sent a shiver of fear through me. I wanted to lift his spirits but didn't know how. Instead, I spoke words that I didn't really believe.

"We'll figure out a way to escape from Belgium. There must be some place we can—"

"There's no place to go, Gisela. My father and I worked so hard for so long to get US visas and landing permits for Cuba. That was my only goal for months, and when I finally was able to get my family on board that ship, it seemed like an answer to prayer. And now here we are again. The Nazis surround us on all sides. They patrol the seas with their U-boats. We're trapped. We didn't even have one year of freedom together!" His voice broke and he took a moment to recover. "Just when we've adjusted to a new life, all of the rules are going to change again when the Nazis occupy our city. I don't have the energy to start all over again."

"I know, I know," I murmured. "But in spite of all that we've been through, we met each other and fell in love." I rested my head on Sam's shoulder as I tightened my hold on him. A smoke-scented breeze blew loose debris down the street, remnants of someone's home or business that had been blasted to pieces. My instinct was to gather everything up and return it to the owners, as if that would somehow make a difference. I struggled for something to say that would give both of us hope. "It's natural to want to see what's coming around the corner and make plans for the future, especially with your mother and brothers to take care of. Having a plan seems like the only way to keep hope alive. But none of us can see the future any longer. We'll make ourselves crazy if we keep imagining the worst and trying to prepare for it." I lifted my head from his shoulder and kissed Sam's whiskered cheek before resting it on his shoulder again.

"All we have is today, Sam. That's true whether there's a war or not. We have our families and each other and we're together. We have enough food to eat and a roof over our heads, and that's all that we need for now. It isn't up to you or Vati or anyone else to figure out a way to save us. God was the One who parted the Red Sea, not Moses and not us."

"I just wish He would do it soon."

"Me, too."

While we waited, Sam and Vati continued to pray at the synagogue down the street with the other men. Our mothers scurried out to shop whenever they could, buying whatever they could find on the increasingly empty store shelves. Other than that, we remained in our apartment, listening to the sounds of war and the depressing news broadcasts.

Near the end of May, we heard devastating news from London. "That can't be right!" I said with tears streaming down my cheeks. "Have I misunderstood?" I gripped Sam's sleeve, hoping I had translated incorrectly. He held up his hand for silence as he continued to listen, then slumped forward with his head lowered.

"What is it, son?" Vati asked.

It was a moment before Sam lifted his head and cleared his throat. "The Nazis have surrounded the British and French armies. The Allies are trapped on the French coast with their backs to the English Channel. It looks like both armies will be forced to surrender."

"Surrender? Then all is lost? Europe is defeated?" None of us wanted to believe it.

Then the news we'd all dreaded and feared was announced. The Belgian military forces, which had held out against the far-superior Nazi forces for eighteen long days, had been forced to surrender. Since Antwerp was an important shipping port, the Wehrmacht quickly occupied our city. The newspaper and radio broadcasts fell under Nazi control, but we were able to get occasional news broadcasts from England, which Sam and I translated for everyone.

Sam and I barely slept for the next few days, waiting beside the radio for the latest news bulletins and speeches from Britain's prime minister. Between the two of us with our limited English skills, we learned that Britain had called for every available fishing boat and civilian craft to help the Royal Navy rescue their Expeditionary Force and evacuate them to Great Britain. Some of France's soldiers were evacuated with them, but thousands more French troops had been forced to surrender.

We were listening to a German radio station a week and a half later when we learned that Hitler and his victorious troops had arrived in Paris. Mutti burst into tears, knowing that her brother and mother lived there. France signed an armistice on June 22. In a mere forty-three days, nearly all of Europe had become captives of the Nazis or their allies.

Vati switched off the radio after hearing the news and said what we had all been thinking. "It's over. It seems the Americans have refused to become involved in Europe's war. There's no longer any hope of a rescue."

Neither Sam's family nor mine moved from where we sat. Our eyes were dry. We had long since run out of tears. Now that my father had turned off the staticky radio, we could hear the floors creaking in the old building as our neighbors moved around upstairs. Vati seemed to be gathering his thoughts as if he had something more to say. We all waited. "I'll tell you what we are going to do," he said. "We're going to return to our jobs and our schools and live our lives as best we can for as long as we can. And may God help us all."

July and August were hot, airless months. We remained inside our apartments except to dash to the store or the synagogue, fearful of the Nazi soldiers that had taken up residence in Antwerp. Seeing swastikas and hearing my native language spoken in the streets of our adopted home filled me with fear. The Jewish Joint Distribution Committee, which had been supporting us and the other refugees from the *St. Louis*, left Belgium when the Nazis arrived. Sam worried about how we would survive. "The Belgian government is going to take over our support," Vati told us after coming home from the synagogue one evening. "They've promised not to betray us to the new authorities."

I started nursing school in September as planned, riding the streetcar to my classes near the hospital. The school was run by Catholic nuns, and two girls from my synagogue named Esther and Rachel also studied there. We rode together to school and back every day. I loved nursing school from the very first day and found my studies exciting and challenging, a welcome diversion from our impossible situation. Sometimes, when I shared what I'd learned with Sam at the end of the day, we could almost forget that we were hated Jews with no place to call home.

Then, just as everyone feared, the dreaded Nazi persecution began all over again. In October, the Nazi-run newspapers announced the first of their anti-Jewish laws, declaring us "undesirable" and restricting our freedom. We knew our lives would get increasingly worse. I turned eighteen in November, and although two years had passed since Kristallnacht, the only thing that had changed for my family and me was that we were living in Antwerp instead of Berlin.

By December, it was too cold for Sam and me to sit outside on the front steps, so he asked me to sit with him on the drafty second-floor landing instead, saying he had news. Cooking odors wafted from behind apartment doors, along with the occasional sounds of pots rattling and babies crying. We had to move aside from time to time as our neighbors came and went. My school was on a break because the Christians were celebrating Christmas, and tonight was the first night of Hanukkah. We should have been lighting candles, but even if we could have afforded them, no one wanted to advertise the fact that we were Jewish.

"I got a letter from my father today," Sam told me as we nestled against each other on the hard wooden steps. His honey-brown hair was tousled from being outside in the wind, and I reached up to smooth it into place. Sam had grown a beard since we'd arrived in Antwerp a year and a half ago, and it was darker than his hair, the same dark color that his eyebrows were. I loved the soft feel of his beard against my cheek. "My father has been to every foreign consulate in Havana, begging the officials from every country in South America to take us. But the doors keep slamming shut."

"Doesn't the world know what's happening to us?"

"If they did, wouldn't they be trying harder to help us?"

"I would hope so." I wanted to believe that the nations' silence and seeming lack of concern for us was from ignorance, not indifference. But hadn't the world known of our plight aboard the *St. Louis* and refused to help? "So we really are trapped now," I murmured as the truth sank in. "We can't escape from the Nazis."

"Well, there are still some underground organizations that will help Jews escape to Switzerland, or even Spain, for a hefty fee. And Aaron Goldberg and I are still meeting with a Zionist organization that is trying to help us. The British closed Palestine to immigration, but I looked into getting my brothers there on student visas. In the end, my mother thought Palestine was too dangerous—as if it's any safer here in Belgium with the Nazis!" He gave a bitter laugh.

"Would you have gone to Palestine with them? Your brothers are only—how old now? Twelve and fourteen? I can see why she might be hesitant."

"She didn't want our family to be separated any more than we already are. She wouldn't have been allowed to go with them, and she would be left here all alone if I went with them." The creases in Sam's forehead told me how frustrated and worried he was. He spent much of his time while I was in school trying to take care of his family and looking for a way to help us all escape from Belgium. As grim as his father's news from Cuba was, I suspected there was something more that he was hesitant to tell me.

"What else is going on, Sam? What aren't you telling me?"

He gave a crooked smile that didn't reach his gray-green eyes. "You know me too well," he said. "We just learned the Nazis rounded up a group of Jews here in Antwerp and shipped them out by train to forced-labor camps."

"Are they people we know?"

"None of them were families from the *St. Louis*. They all came to Belgium as refugees before we did. But some of the men went to our synagogue." He paused for a long moment, then said, "I have to fight back, Gisela. I'm going to start working with the Belgian Resistance."

"Sam, no!" His words sent a chill through me that was colder than the December night.

"I may be out of touch with everyone at times, so I'll need you to look after my mother and brothers for me while I'm gone."

I gripped him tighter than ever. "Please don't do it, Sam. Please don't put your life in danger."

"Our lives already are in danger. They could conscript me for forced labor anytime."

"Your family needs you! I need you!"

He pulled me close and rested his cheek on my hair. "That's who

I'm doing this for, Gisela. For you and for my family. If we don't start fighting back, none of us will survive. The Nazis are singling us out to destroy us. The sooner we start pushing them out of Belgium, the sooner we'll all be safe again."

"How long will you be away? Where will you stay? What will you be doing?"

"I can't tell you any details because I don't know them yet. The Resistance is still loosely organized right now. But I suppose we'll be doing the usual things—collecting information about enemy movements and equipment and fortifications, then radioing it to the Allies in Britain. I speak some English, so I can help with that. Antwerp is an important seaport, and the Allies need to know about the defenses that the Nazis are constructing. The Resistance also rescues downed British pilots whenever they can, and I can help as an interpreter." I could see his excitement at being able to do something to fight back. I would go crazy, too, if I didn't have my nursing studies. But I didn't want the man I loved to go underground and risk his life.

Three children who lived on the first floor came out of their apartment just then and started playing a game of tag on the steps, running up and down and jostling us as they passed. "We have no privacy anymore," I lamented. "Remember our special place beneath the lifeboats on board the *St. Louis*? And now with you being gone . . . I don't want us to grow apart."

"That will never happen, Gisela. We may not be together as much as we'd like, and we may even become separated in the future—"

"God forbid!" I said, holding him tighter.

"But no matter what happens, our hearts are one. Your soul and mine are fused together, and nothing and no one will ever keep us apart."

"My parents' families have all been scattered," I said, remembering my aunts and uncles, "and yours has been, too. That's what I fear the most, Sam—that we'll become separated and we won't be able to find each other again. The world is such a huge place, and it seems like everywhere we turn for help, people hate us."

He released me and took my face in his hands, our foreheads touching, his breath skimming my skin. "I'll find you, Gisela. If it takes the rest of my life, I'll find you. Let's promise that we'll never stop searching for each other. Promise?"

"I promise," I whispered. Sam ignored the squealing children and sealed our pledge with a kiss.

11

Peggy

The week stretching ahead of me, until I would be able to visit Jimmy again on Sunday, seemed very long. Donna didn't want my help or advice in Pop's office, so I spent a lot of time across the street with the animals or visiting with Jimmy's mother or sometimes sitting alone in my room with Buster, talking to God the way Jimmy taught me to do. I told Him that it seemed like Jimmy would take tiny steps forward each week, responding to people and to Buster, but then he would forget all about us a week later after his shock treatments. I worried that the electric shocks were hurting him, not helping him. Dr. Morgan said he was no closer to coming home. Chaplain Bill had promised to send me the addresses of Jimmy's friends, but I hadn't heard from him. I had counted on Joe Fiore for help, but he'd vanished, and I was beginning to think that my crazy idea of writing to Jimmy's friends was a dumb one. What made me think I could do any good if the doctors couldn't? And on top of all that, I was no closer to figuring out my own future. "I could really use some help here, God," I muttered aloud.

I decided to take Buster for a ride into the countryside to cool off on Wednesday afternoon. Maybe we'd stop by the bridge on the way home so he could splash in the river's rocky shallows. I checked the mailbox one last time before leaving—and there was a letter from Chaplain Bill! I hurried around to the backyard, tearing open the envelope as I went, and sat down on the rickety chair to read it.

> *Dear Miss Serrano,*
>
> *I've been thinking about your wise words to me when we spoke at the hospital last Sunday, and I was reminded of the book of Job in the Bible. Job suffered unimaginable losses, and the friends who came to visit him thought they had to have answers for him. They tried to explain why God had allowed Job to suffer, but all of their pious explanations were flat-out wrong. The best thing they could have done—the only thing they should have done—was sit with him and mourn with him. God's reply to all of their wrong-minded reasoning was that we can't possibly understand what God is doing. His ways are beyond understanding. But we do know that He loves us and that we can trust Him. I have a meeting with the church consistory this afternoon, and I've decided to rethink my resignation. Thank you for helping me reach this decision. You were a godsend.*
>
> *Enclosed is the address for one of the men you mentioned, Frank Cishek, who lives in Milford, Pennsylvania. He gave his address to me right after we were discharged and said that since we didn't live very far away from each other, we should get together sometime. We haven't managed to do that yet, but maybe he and I can visit Jim together one of these days.*
>
> *I've contacted the Army asking for the addresses you requested, and I'll be in touch again as soon as they send them to me. I would like to help you write letters to all of these men, if you'll allow me to. I think your idea is a wonderful one and that it will be a great encouragement to Jim. Perhaps we can also ask the men who live*

far away to send photographs to help jog Jim's memory. Let me
know what you think.

Thank you again, Miss Serrano, for helping me get back
on track.

Sincerely,
Reverend Bill

I read Bill's letter a second time and then a third, unable to stop smiling. I couldn't decide which was the best news—that Chaplain Bill wasn't quitting after all or that he thought my idea was wonderful and was going to help me or that Frank Cishek lived only fifty miles or so away from me. I was trying to decide when I heard the rumble of a motorcycle coming up the road. It stopped out front, revving the engine twice before shutting off. I leaped up and hurried around to the front of the garage with Buster. And there was Joe. I didn't know what to say. I wanted to hug him and tell him how happy I was to see him because now I wouldn't have to visit Frank Cishek by myself, but Joe spoke first.

"Hey, sorry for taking off without saying goodbye, but I had to clear my head, you know? I hope your pop isn't mad at me or anything."

"I can't speak for Pop, but I'm sure glad to see you! Chaplain Bill sent me Frank Cishek's address, and guess what? He lives in Milford, Pennsylvania, just across the New York State border from here. Tomorrow is the Fourth of July, and we could easily drive over there together. You knew Frank, right?"

"He helped Jim carry me to the aid station. I owe him my life."

I cooked spaghetti and meatballs for dinner and the four of us ate it together in our tiny, stifling kitchen. Every fan we owned was blowing, but they made little difference. "I'm glad you two made up," Donna whispered as I was washing the dishes afterwards. "Don't let him slip away this time." She tried to talk me into joining them for a night out on the town, then got angry with me for refusing, slamming the door behind her on the way out.

Joe slept until one o'clock on Thursday afternoon, missing our village's brief Fourth of July parade, comprised of kids on bicycles, the high school marching band, and lots of flags. I had hoped Joe would be too hungover to want to ride his noisy motorcycle, but he started it up and we rode up into the lovely Pocono Mountains in Pennsylvania. The sunny day made for a beautiful ride, and it felt good to get out of the rut of worry I'd been stuck in. We stopped on a mountaintop along the way for a spectacular view of the Delaware River valley.

"Look at that view!" Joe said. He turned in a circle with his arms outstretched.

"You can see three states from here," I told him. "New York, New Jersey, and Pennsylvania."

"It's great to be out on the open road, isn't it? You should come with me next time I go. You'd love it." When I didn't reply, he added, "Donna says there's nothing keeping you tied down back home." My good mood vanished like the sun behind a cloud.

"Donna must have forgotten that I work at the veterinary clinic."

"So? They're friends of yours, aren't they? They'd give you some time off."

"Let's get going, okay? We don't want to ride home in the dark."

The village of Milford was nestled in the river valley with views of mountains in every direction. Flags fluttered from nearly every public building and storefront and most of the houses. The aroma of charcoal grills and sizzling hamburgers filled the air. The address turned out to be Frank's parents' home. His mother, who was making potato salad, told us that Frank and his girlfriend were watching a baseball game over at the Milford ball field. "It's just a few blocks away. You can easily walk there."

The wooden stands were packed, the game in full swing with lots of enthusiastic cheering and shouting. It took Joe a minute or two to spot Frank. He had wavy reddish-blond hair that he wore slicked back from his high forehead, and ears that stuck out just a little too far. He was sitting a few rows up in the bleachers with his arm around a dark-haired girl. Beside them were two other men who resembled Frank and had to be his brothers. They were all cheering and laughing and drinking Coca-Cola. When the inning ended, Joe called up to him. "Hey, Frank! Remember me? Joe Fiore?"

It took a moment, but then a lopsided grin spread across Frank's face. "Joe! Of course! How are you?"

"A lot better than last time you saw me, right?" When Frank's grin faltered, Joe quickly added, "Hey, that's okay. They fixed me up with a brand-new leg and I'm good as new. Hey, you got time to grab a beer and talk?"

"Well . . ." He turned to his girlfriend.

"This here is a friend of mine," Joe said before she could respond. "Peggy . . ."

"Serrano," I supplied.

"Peggy is a good friend of Jim Barnett's. I know you remember Jim."

"Yes, of course."

"Well, he's in the VA hospital, and Peggy and I are trying to get him out of there. We could use your help."

"What? In the hospital? Jim?"

"Go ahead, Frankie. I don't mind," his girlfriend said. "Bring me a hot dog on your way back."

"Okay. Sure. I have plenty of time for a friend of Jim's." Frank stood, then carefully stepped down between the other spectators. There was a concession stand and some picnic tables behind the bleachers. The smell of hot grease, french fries, and popcorn filled the air. "Want to grab a hot dog or a Coke or something?" Frank asked. "There's a picnic table over here where we can sit."

"Do they sell beer?" Joe asked.

"Nah, it's a kid's ball game. So how do you know Jim?" he asked me as we sat down at the weathered table.

"I've lived across the street from Jimmy all my life. I work in his father's veterinary clinic part-time."

Frank's face lit up with recognition. "Say, are you the girl who owns the three-legged dog?"

"Yes, I—"

Frank clapped his hands and burst out laughing. Joe joined in.

"Jim told us all about that dog, right, Joe?"

"Yeah, we called him Tripod, remember?"

"I sure do!"

"Hey, I met that three-legged dog, Frank. He's real! Jim didn't make him up after all—although I haven't seen him save any orphans yet." They both had a good laugh about Buster before getting serious again, and I caught a glimpse of the close friendship Jimmy and his pals must have shared during the long, harrowing years of the war.

"So you say Jim's in the VA hospital? What happened?"

"He's been very depressed ever since he got home," I replied. "Then, a little over a month ago, he tried to kill himself."

Frank's head jerked back in shock. "What! Not Jim! That's . . . that's hard to believe!"

"He won't tell anyone what's wrong, so I'm trying to talk to some of his friends from the Army. If we can figure out what happened and when he started getting depressed, I'm hoping we can help him. Joe says he seemed fine the last time he saw him in France, after he was wounded. And we talked with Chaplain Bill, who said Jimmy's faith in God made him seem fearless."

"That's true. Jim was fearless. Not in a reckless way, but he would put the needs of the wounded men ahead of his fears."

"I've read the letters Jimmy sent home to his parents, and he spoke a lot about you and another friend, Mitch O'Hara. I know that the three of you were friends ever since basic training, so I'm hoping you and Mitch can tell me more. I'd like to figure out when Jimmy changed and why."

"Um, Mitch is gone," Frank said quietly. His Adam's apple bobbed as he swallowed hard. "Mitch died in Belgium, four months before the war ended."

"Was Jimmy there? Does he know?"

Frank nodded. "Jim knows. He was there." I wondered why Jimmy hadn't said anything in his letters home about losing Mitch. Frank looked away for a moment before turning to us again. "I-I never talk about the war. It's better for me that way. I've never told my parents or my girlfriend or anyone else what we saw and did. Nobody. You understand that, right, Joe?"

"Yeah."

Frank drew a deep breath. "But if you think it will help Jim, I'll try to answer your questions." The occasional pop of fireworks cracked in the distance as we'd talked, but a sudden burst of firecrackers nearby echoed like machine-gun fire, startling both men. Frank ducked as if about to take cover beneath the picnic table before catching himself. Joe, who had been standing, hit the ground, his arms raised to shield his head until the explosions stopped. When he stood again, brushing dirt and grass from his clothes, I feared he would be embarrassed. Instead, he was furious.

"Stupid fools! They ought to know better! We've heard enough fireworks to last a lifetime!"

"It bothers me too, Joe." I could see that both men were shaken.

"I'm gonna go grab a Coke," Joe said. He sauntered away, and I watched him light a cigarette and flirt with the two teenage girls at the concession stand while Frank regathered himself to tell his story.

"Jim and Mitch and I became friends in boot camp. We went through the Normandy invasion and the very worst that the enemy could throw at us as we pushed the Nazis back toward the Rhine. But Mitch was wounded during that long, terrible winter before the war ended, in what they're calling the Battle of the Bulge."

"I remember reading about that last winter in the newspapers—the freezing temperatures and all the snow. It was around Christmas, wasn't it?"

Frank nodded. "The Nazis had been on the run, and the war seemed to be nearing the end. But then they turned around and made a deadly assault on the Allied forces in the Ardennes Forest. We were outnumbered, and the Nazis demanded that we surrender. The bad weather meant we couldn't get ammunition or supplies or air support. Mitch was wounded in a mortar attack, and Jim and I carried him to the aid station in Bastogne. It was set up in a house in the middle of town and was jam-packed with casualties. Jim went back to check on Mitch whenever he could because he was worried about him. I mean, we'd gotten him to the aid station and he might have recovered if we'd been able to evacuate him to a field hospital for surgery. But Bastogne was surrounded by Nazi troops and under siege. The aid station wasn't equipped to do surgery and they were running out of medical supplies. Then on Christmas Eve, the foul weather cleared and the Luftwaffe bombed Bastogne. The aid station took a direct hit. There were about thirty wounded men inside and all but two or three of them died, including Mitch. Jim took it very hard. We both did. Mitch had his whole life ahead of him, and it didn't seem fair. I remember Jim crying his eyes out and shaking his fist at the sky and just raging."

"At the Nazis? Or at God?"

"I don't know. Maybe both." Frank took a moment to collect himself. I could tell by his shaking voice and trembling hands how much it was costing him to remember. He drew a breath and let it out with a sigh. "Jim seemed to have it all together as far as his faith was concerned. He carried a little Bible in his pack and we'd see him reading it whenever he had free time. He was always willing to talk about God with anyone, anytime, but not in a pushy way, if you know what I mean. But he wasn't the same after Mitch died."

"Did he seem depressed?"

"Not exactly. Just quieter. More determined than ever to save every single wounded soldier. If there wasn't any fighting, he would help out at the nearest aid station or field hospital. Wouldn't take any time off. We were offered a leave after the siege was finally lifted and reinforcements came in, but Jim wouldn't take it. He just kept working."

"The doctor at the VA hospital told us that a lot of medics suffered from battle fatigue."

Frank nodded absently as he stared at the rear of the bleachers. "From the time we landed in France until the war ended, Jim and I saw a lot of men blown to pieces. You can't help thinking that it's going to be you one of these days. We were both close to Mitch, and after he died, there were many times when Jim and I wondered why Mitch was gone and we were still alive. But the war doesn't pause to give you time to grieve. You need to keep going, and so you learn to reach deep inside and find that steel. You close yourself off to what you see and just do your job. But no matter how tough you are, sooner or later, in one way or another, it's going to get to you. Especially when the men who are wounded and dying are your friends."

"Do you think that's what happened to Jimmy?"

"Maybe. Who knows? He was tough when he needed to be. Being a medic means having to make split-second decisions, life-and-death choices, who can be saved and who can't. You have to keep your head and try to calm the patients down, stop the bleeding, give them morphine, get them off the field to an aid station. If you know there's no hope, you have to leave them behind and move on. That's a tough decision to make. And in the last weeks that I worked with Jim, he was finding it harder and harder to do it. It was as if he didn't want to give up on anyone, no matter how badly wounded they were. He'd say, 'We have to try to save them,' even when it was obvious from the severity of their wounds that they couldn't live."

Frank paused again and closed his eyes for a moment. Knowing Jimmy, I understood how impossible it must have been for him to leave anyone behind. I heard cheers from the ball game in the distance, along with more firecrackers. I waited until Frank opened his eyes again before asking, "When did you last see Jimmy?"

"As I say, they offered us leave later that winter, after reinforcements came and we were pushing back the Nazis again. I took the leave and Jim didn't. I couldn't talk him into going no matter how hard I tried. He said he hadn't been able to save Mitch but maybe he could save someone else. It ended up that they shuffled men around in a couple of companies to make up for all the casualties, and Jim and I got separated for the remainder of the war. I think, in a way, it might have been easier for him to work with men he hadn't known since boot camp."

"So that was the last time you saw him?"

He started to nod, then said, "No, wait. I did see him one more time. After the Nazis surrendered, he came looking for me and the other guys from our old company. Wanted to see which ones of us made it, he said. He was working at a hospital near Weimar, I believe it was, taking care of patients from the concentration camps. He didn't visit for very long."

"Did he seem the same?"

"Hard to tell. We were all numb by then—giddy that the war in Europe was over but worried sick that we'd be sent to the Pacific to fight the Japanese and we'd have to go through that hell all over again. Jim and I talked, but . . ." He gave a shrug. "We weren't the same idealistic guys we'd been in basic."

"Jimmy had this photograph in his pack," I said, reaching into my bag. "The name Gisela is written on the back. Do you know who she is?"

Frank took it from me and studied it. "She's very pretty. Sorry, but I don't think I've seen her before. Jim never showed this photograph to me, and the guys always showed pictures of their wives and girlfriends. She would have been someone to brag about for sure."

"So Jimmy must have met her after Bastogne? Might she be an Army nurse?"

"Wait a minute. There were two nurses who worked in the aid station in Bastogne. They were both from Belgium. Civilians. Not part of the US Army, just volunteers. Jim spent more time there than I did, so he would have gotten to know the nurses better. The aid station was set up in a house in the center of town, and he'd go whenever things were quiet to check up on Mitch and the others."

"Do you think she might have been one of those two nurses?"

"Well, maybe." He gazed into the distance, concentrating. "One of the nurses had dark skin and hair, as I recall. I remember hearing a story about a couple of our wounded soldiers, obnoxious guys, who refused to let a colored nurse take care of them. The physician at the aid station just shrugged his shoulders and said, 'Then die.' They got the message pretty quickly. The other Belgian nurse . . . I can't remember her name, but the men all loved her. They called her an angel. Jimmy told me the guys promised to bring her a parachute when the weather cleared and the airdrops began, to repay her for all her hard work and devotion to our soldiers. She had a fiancé, and she wanted to make a wedding dress from the silk. But she was killed inside the aid station when it was bombed. They had to use the parachute for her shroud."

"What a heartbreaking story," I murmured. If that nurse was Gisela, I was glad, now, that I hadn't shown her picture to Jimmy. "Thank you for talking with me, Frank. I know how hard it must be to remember."

"I'll do anything I can to help Jim."

"I think it would mean a lot to him if you paid him a visit. He may not remember you at first because the electrical shocks erase some of his memories. But he seemed to remember Joe. And we even managed to sneak my three-legged dog in for a visit. That really cheered Jimmy up."

"What should I say to him?"

"I don't know. Just let him know he has a good friend standing by him. Remind him of happier times in basic training. Tell him about your life now, how you're coping. Give him hope that there can be a happy ending after the war. You don't need to stay long."

"I'll be there. I promise." Frank invited us to stay and join his family for a picnic, saying, "Ma always makes enough potato salad and baked beans to feed Patton's Army." But Joe shook his head. I snapped Frank's photograph for Jimmy's album and gave him directions to the VA hospital. "Jimmy is lucky to have you," he said before we parted. "I can tell that you care about him a lot."

Joe didn't speak again until we had walked back to fetch his motorcycle. "Sorry I left you and Frank. I hate talking about the war. It brings it all back like in my nightmares. The fireworks do, too. I just want to forget everything, you know? The earsplitting explosions, the never-ending battles, seeing your friends blown to bits . . ."

"It's okay, Joe. I understand."

"Maybe that's what's wrong with Jim. Maybe he thinks the only way he can keep it all from coming back is to end his life."

I climbed onto Joe's motorcycle, wishing I could think of a way to "keep it all from coming back" for Joe as well as for Jimmy.

I wasn't surprised when Joe left as soon as we reached home. The sound of firecrackers was growing more frequent as the sun began to set, and Buster didn't like the noise any more than Joe did. I took Buster upstairs to my bedroom after Joe roared away, and I couldn't stop wondering if the Belgian nurse who had died in the aid station was Gisela. I heard a knock on my bedroom door, and Donna let herself in. She had one hand on her hip, the other holding a cigarette, and she wore an angry look on her face. "Look, I don't know what kind of game you're playing with Joe," she said, "leading him on one minute and then pushing him away, but that's a surefire way to lose a good man like him. If you're waiting for that fella across the street, you'll be waiting forever. I saw the kind of girls he used to take to dances and things—cheerleaders and college coeds. Nothing at all like you."

"Please stop," I said softly. "You have no idea what you're talking about." Tears filled my eyes when I recalled how Joe had hit the dirt, and I remembered Frank's grief as he'd forced himself to relive the horrors for Jimmy's sake. And here was Donna, going on and on with her nonsense.

"I have eyes to see, don't I?" she huffed. "And I've been around the block a few more times than you have, especially since you spend your days with dogs and cows instead of with real people or with a real boyfriend."

"You don't know anything about me or my life," I said. I was growing angry, too. "You've never bothered to ask, Donna, after all these years. You've never given me the time of day until now—now, when you've decided you want to get rid of me."

"I'm telling you this is for your own good. You're a grown woman, and it's time you got on with your life. Joe is here and he's available. What would it hurt for you to go out with him? You have plenty of time to go trotting off to church like you're holier than everyone else, and what good is that doing you? Joe told me he likes you, but you're going to let him slip right through your fingers if you don't wake up."

I didn't bother to reply. I stood and walked past her through the door, grabbing a flashlight so I could take Buster outside for a walk. He couldn't roam very far without getting tired, and I knew that the boom of firework displays from the surrounding towns would make him nervous. We walked to the rusty bridge on the edge of town that spanned the shallow, rock-strewn river. I took the footpath down to the riverbank and sat on a rock, dipping my feet in the icy water while Buster sniffed around in the bushes and splashed in the gurgling stream. If I waited long enough, maybe Donna and Pop would go out drinking with their friends and leave me in peace.

12

Gisela

APRIL 1941

Spring arrived, bringing milder weather, longer days, and Passover. The nursing school closed for a few days in April for the Christian holiday of Easter, so I was home from my classes and able to help Mutti clean every corner of our apartment to prepare for the Passover seder. Food shortages and sky-high prices meant that our meal would be a simple one, but we scrounged enough ingredients to make a pot of chicken soup. Our apartment smelled heavenly. Mutti and Sam's mother had moved our two kitchen tables into our living room, and we set them with plates and utensils for the meal that began at sundown.

I was putting on the last-minute touches when I heard the front door open and close and voices and footsteps coming up the stairs. "I think Vati and the others are back," I called into the kitchen. He had gone to the synagogue to pray with Sam and his brothers before the seder. Suddenly I heard a cry and then a rumbling boom as if someone had tumbled down the stairs. I set down the plate of bitter herbs I was holding and ran to the landing. Vati lay crumpled with Sam bending over him, trying to help him up.

"Just a minute, give me a minute," Vati breathed. "I'm okay. Just a little dizzy." Sam slung his arm around Vati and helped him the rest of the way into the apartment and onto a chair. My father's appearance shocked me. He was out of breath and his skin looked deathly white. I had been studying nursing long enough to recognize that he was seriously ill.

"Are you all right, Vati?" I asked, crouching in front of him. I tried not to let on how frightened I was.

He pulled me close and I could feel all of his bones as I hugged him. "I'm fine, Gisela. Just a little tumble. Nothing's broken. Not to worry." But I was worried. How had I lived in the same apartment with him these past months and not noticed how sick he was? I had been too preoccupied with my studies and my precious minutes alone with Sam to take a really good look at my father or to notice that he coughed incessantly.

"Come," Vati said, pulling himself up from the chair. "Let's all sit down at the table and celebrate our freedom this night with the people we love."

I decided not to say anything about his health for now, but I noticed that he sat as if his ribs were hurting him, and he barely ate any food. My sister, Ruthie, hovered close to Vati, not leaving his side. I might not have taken note of our father's condition, but I could tell by Ruthie's worried expression that she had. I took a good look at her, too, and my sister seemed as thin and pale as a ghost, more like a young child than a growing thirteen-year-old. She chewed her nails while Vati read the Passover Haggadah and seemed to jump and flinch at every little noise outside the apartment. We had all lost weight because of the food shortages, but fear seemed to be nibbling away at Ruthie from the inside. I chided myself for not paying closer attention to my own family. We were all suffering from the suspense of waiting, just as we had on board the *St. Louis*, never knowing what tomorrow would bring and always fearing the worst.

As the evening wore on and we relived our miraculous deliverance from slavery in Egypt, I remembered our seder tables in Berlin, set with a white tablecloth, Oma's silver candlesticks and serving pieces, and Mutti's special china with the gold trim. Tonight's improvised celebration, with only a taste of wine for each of us and a few pieces of matzah, seemed sad and shabby in comparison. Once again, we were slaves, held in bondage by Pharaoh Hitler, who wouldn't allow us to go free. I wondered if God still heard our groaning. How much longer would we have to suffer before He came to our rescue?

I cornered Mutti alone in the kitchen the next morning while Vati was at prayers and demanded she tell me what was wrong with him. "Has he seen a doctor? It's obvious he's very sick." She could see I wasn't going to let it drop, so she told me.

"The doctor says it's tuberculosis. He has prescribed rest. There's not much they can do for him outside of a sanitarium, and we're not allowed to use any of them."

"Do you want me to speak with one of the doctors at the hospital where I'm training? Maybe I can get someone there to help him."

Mutti's gentle face looked careworn and weary. Her hands felt chapped as she smoothed my hair from my forehead. "It won't do any good, Gisela. He insists he's fine."

The school remained closed for Easter Monday, but I was in my bedroom reviewing my notes that afternoon, preparing to return to school the next day, when I heard shouting and the sound of a commotion outside in the street.

"What's that noise? What's going on?" Ruthie asked. She liked to sit beside me on the bed we shared and read while I studied.

"Let's go see." I took her hand and we went into the living room, which faced the main street. What I saw made me draw in my breath in horror. The scene below looked exactly as it had two years ago on Kristallnacht. An angry mob, armed with clubs and iron bars, was rampaging through our Jewish neighborhood, attacking and beating anyone unfortunate enough to be in the street. The rioters were pillaging all the neighborhood businesses, looting and ransacking the Jewish-owned shops. They were easy targets because the Nazis had required them to display special markings designating them as Jewish. Our apartment door flew open. Sam stood in the doorway.

"Is everyone home? Are you all inside?" He looked wild-eyed. I did a quick tally and nodded.

"What's all that noise?" Mutti asked, coming out of her bedroom. She and Vati had been resting.

"It's a pogrom," Sam replied. The sound of shattering glass carried up from below, the sound that had haunted my nightmares. Now the nightmare had returned. Before I could blink, Sam turned and ran down the stairs.

"Sam! No!" I screamed, racing behind him. "Don't go out there! Please! Please!" But he was only making sure the outside door to our building was locked. He hurried upstairs again, taking them two at a time. He herded his family into our apartment and locked our apartment door behind them. We all knew that our enemies could easily smash through both of those doors if they decided to.

Vati stumbled into the living room, holding on to the furniture and doorframes to steady himself. "Not again," he murmured.

Outside in the streets, the mob grew by the hundreds. They seemed to be mostly Belgian citizens, with Nazi soldiers and policemen standing on the sidelines, doing nothing to halt the rioting. As the chaos grew, thick black smoke began to rise above the treetops, coming from the direction of our synagogue down the block. Bright flames leaped into the air, lighting up the sky. The fire brigade arrived with clanging bells, but the mob refused to move, preventing them from dousing the fire. A dark column of smoke billowed a few blocks away where another synagogue stood. The acrid smell of smoke drifted up to us, even with our windows closed.

Mutti and Ruthie clung to Vati as if afraid he would try to rush outside to save the Torah scrolls again as he had on Kristallnacht, even though he was much too weak to do it. "I never imagined we would have to live through this a second time," he said. "Is there no place on earth where we're safe?"

I closed my eyes against my tears, and for a brief moment I remembered standing on the deck of the *St. Louis* with the port of Havana in the distance. We had been within reach of safety and refuge once. Only a narrow ribbon of water had separated us from it. We had seen it, smelled it, tasted it, before it had vanished like a mirage along with our hope.

My hand ached from gripping Sam's hand so tightly. My stomach had knotted into a ball of fear and anger. I wanted to scream and rage at our helplessness. I glanced at the others and knew by their tears and mute sorrow that they felt the same. During the Passover seder, we had dipped bitter herbs into salt water to remember our sorrow and tears in Egypt. We had sipped wine and sung songs like the people God had once freed from slavery. But it had been a lie. We weren't free.

The looting and vandalism continued throughout the night. The entire Jewish community remained locked inside as sporadic attacks continued for a second day. Another long night of rioting came three days later. I stayed home from school for the remainder of the week, hoping the officials at my school would hear about what was happening and excuse my absence. By the time the terror finally ended, two nearby synagogues had been badly damaged, and hundreds of prayer books and priceless Torah scrolls were torched in what people were calling the Antwerp Pogrom. The home of Antwerp's chief rabbi had been destroyed, the rabbi himself attacked. Encouraged by the occupying forces, Belgian pro-Nazi groups had initiated the attacks after movie theaters had screened a fiercely anti-Semitic propaganda film called *The Eternal Jew.*

I felt so trapped I wanted to scream. I had felt the same way aboard the *St. Louis*, floating on the endless sea with no place to land. "We have nowhere to hide, no one to turn to for help," I told Sam as he tried to console me. "We're at the mercy of our enemies who are becoming more brutal and hate-filled every day." I didn't want to return to school, afraid of being attacked in the streets. I wanted to stay close to my loved ones.

"You have to finish your nursing course," Sam insisted. He sat on the bed I shared with my sister, watching as I reluctantly packed my satchel. "It's what your parents want and what I also want for you, Gisela. You're halfway there. Only another year until you graduate."

"And then what? You know that we're never going to have a normal life again. The Nazis won't let us."

"It seems that way for now, but you have no idea how God might want to use your nursing skills in the future."

I wasn't listening. "You're going off to work with the Resistance again, aren't you? This could be the last time I ever see you or hold you or tell you how much I love you."

He took my face in his hands. His breath warmed my skin as our foreheads touched. "Gisela, listen. You know that I have to fight back. I'm doing it for you so you can have a future someday."

"I don't want a future without you in it! And you can't promise me that you won't be killed in this fight, can you?" I hated saying the words, as if talking about Sam's death might cause it to happen.

"Life has no guarantees, Gisela." He silenced me with a kiss before I could say more.

In the end, I conceded to everyone's wishes and returned to finish the school year. I poured myself into my studies and my hospital rounds to help take my mind off the hopeless situation my loved ones and I faced. I concentrated on making beds with perfect hospital corners, taking accurate temperature and blood pressure readings, and recording the results on patients' charts with precision.

At the end of May, the Nazis announced a new set of anti-Jewish laws. Among them was a law that forbade Jews to own property. Our Jewish landlord was forced to sell our apartment building, and of course higher rental rates soon followed. In June we were stunned to learn that the Nazis had invaded the Soviet Union. The war would now be fought on two fronts. Members of the Communist Party in Belgium immediately stirred up unrest with protests and riots. Sam was away from the apartment often throughout those months and he warned us to stay as close to home as possible.

More laws were issued in July. Jews were required to carry identity cards stamped with the word *Jew*. We were prohibited from riding on public transportation. When my classes started again in September, Esther, Rachel, and I were forced to walk across the city to school and back, taking care to avoid the main streets. I wondered how we would manage once winter came and the daylight hours grew shorter. Antwerp was under a curfew from dusk until dawn.

But when winter came, my worries no longer mattered. In December, I learned that I was no longer allowed to attend school at all. A new Nazi declaration made it illegal for Jews to attend public schools, universities, and trade schools in Belgium. And even if I did become a nurse, I would be forbidden to work in a Gentile hospital. Our community began arranging our own Jewish schools, just as we'd been forced to do in Germany. Ruthie and Sam's two brothers now attended classes in a synagogue a few blocks away. Our old synagogue down the street had been too badly damaged during the pogrom to use.

After the school restriction was announced and Sam returned from wherever he had been, we sat at the kitchen table with Vati and Mutti one evening, bundled in coats to save fuel. Sam had turned twenty this year, but he seemed a decade older, forced into maturity by the weight of responsibility he carried. "I have more upsetting news," he said. "The underground has learned that the Nazis have started deporting German, Austrian, and Czechoslovakian Jews from their homelands and taking them to concentration camps in Poland. You know what those people will face, Mr. Wolff."

Vati simply nodded. Talking often started one of his coughing fits. He sat with his elbows on the table, his hands on his forehead. For the past few months, he had absorbed each blow to the Jewish community as a personal assault and it had weakened him further. I wondered how much more it would take before my beloved father would be knocked to his knees for good, unable to rise.

"It's only a matter of time before they start doing the same thing here," Sam continued. "We have to be ready. We need an escape plan and a place to hide. We can't let them take us."

"I agree, but how? Where?" Vati asked.

"I think the answer has to be different for each one of us. It will be impossible for all of us to hide or escape together. Gisela, I think you should talk to the authorities at your school and see if they'll let you sit for your exams and get your degree six months early."

"But it's against the law for me to even attend. Besides, what good will it do to finish my degree?"

"Just ask them, Gisela. It doesn't hurt to ask. See what they recommend." I decided Sam was right. I wouldn't stay in our apartment and wait for the Nazis to knock on our door. I walked to school alone the next day—my friends were too fearful of defying the edict to attend any more classes—and I asked to speak with Sister Veronica, the school's headmistress.

"I'm very glad you came to see me, Miss Wolff," she said after she'd seated me at a small table in her office and served me tea. "You are one of our top nursing students, and it would be a travesty if you weren't allowed to continue your studies."

"Thank you, Sister Veronica. To be honest, I want very much to continue. But this new law makes it impossible. Back home in Germany, the laws against us came in stages, just like they're doing now, and each one made our situation worse. I know I'll have to drop out of school now, but I wondered if I could still take my exams and get credit for this semester."

The nun's eyes looked sad as she listened. It was hard to tell how old Sister Veronica was because only her face and hands were visible outside the black robes and headpiece she wore. But she had a kind face, and I saw a warmth in her pale-blue eyes that had convinced me I could trust her. "An idea has been coming to me as you were speaking just now, and perhaps—" She stopped, then said, "Let me back up a bit. I agree that the Nazis aren't going to stop issuing these terrible laws. I was talking with Father Francis, the hospital administrator, the other day, and we both believe the time has come for Christians to do whatever we can to help the Jewish community. I would like to encourage you to continue to attend classes so you can graduate in June."

"But would it be legal for me to stay in school? Won't you get into trouble if they find out I'm Jewish?"

"We're a private institution, Miss Wolff, not a public one, so that will be our defense if we need one. But I know Father Francis is determined to do whatever he can to help, and so am I. You'll blend in with all of the other girls in your student uniform. No one needs to know that you're Jewish." She smiled and patted my hand. Her kindness amazed and humbled me.

"Thank you, Sister. That's very generous and courageous of you. But it's a very long walk from my home, and I can no longer take public transportation. Our rabbi believes it's too dangerous for Jews to venture into the streets beyond our neighborhood. Jews have been attacked and beaten in broad daylight."

"Then here's another idea," she said. "You could live in the nurses' dormitory until you graduate so you won't have to travel back and forth to your home and be exposed to danger."

My first reaction was to say no. How could I leave my home, my family, and most of all, Sam? Yet I knew it would cheer Vati and give him hope if I were able to continue my studies without the fear he endured each morning when I left home to walk to school. I wanted to ease some of the strain from his shoulders, and this plan might do it. Then another obstacle occurred to me and my hope teetered. "How much extra would it cost for my room and board? My father is unable to work, and I already rely on a scholarship to study here."

"We could work something out." Her black robes rustled as she reached across the little table to lay a reassuring hand on mine. "In the past, our scholarship students have agreed to continue working at the hospital after graduation to help repay their costs. With a war raging, the need for nurses is only going to increase. But that's for a future discussion. Right now, I want to assure you that I'll do whatever I can to help you, Miss Wolff."

Her kindness brought tears to my eyes. "Thank you. Thank you so much. I will tell my parents about your generous offer and let you know what they say."

"Good. In the meantime, I will pray for your safety as you travel."

I decided to tell Sam about Sister Veronica's offer before I told my family. In a way, I wanted Sam to talk me out of it so we wouldn't have to be separated. Yet his answer didn't surprise me at all. "That's wonderful news, Gisela!" He squeezed me tightly and lifted my feet off the ground. We were standing on the landing outside our apartments, and when a door closed upstairs and someone started down the steps, he released me again. "You must accept the school's offer. You must!"

"But we'll have even less time together than we already have and—"

"Gisela, listen." He waited for our neighbor to brush past us and hurry down to the foyer before holding my shoulders and looking into my eyes. "There are two things I want for you, my love, and they are more important to me than anything else. First, that you finish your education. I've seen how much you've enjoyed your classes, and I know you'll make an outstanding nurse. And second, I want you to be safe. The Nazis could burst into our apartments at any time and do whatever they want with us. You're being offered a safe place to live and study, and I want you to take it. I'm sure your parents will want that for you, too."

"But you and I have never been apart for more than a week since we first met on the *St. Louis* and—"

He pulled me into his embrace. "We'll figure out a way to see each other, I promise. Accept their offer, Gisela."

We were still talking on the landing when another neighbor burst through the front door bringing a gust of wintry wind with him. "Have you heard the news?" he asked breathlessly as he hurried up the stairs.

"What news?" Sam asked.

"The Japanese attacked the United States. They destroyed one of their military bases in Hawaii and sank all their ships. The Americans have declared war. They're joining our fight at last!"

Could it really be true? Sam and I hurried inside to tell Vati the terrible, wonderful news.

13

Peggy

Before church on Sunday, I picked a handful of the wild daisies that were blooming among the weeds and rusted cars in our backyard and laid the bouquet on my mother's grave in the churchyard. I hadn't seen Pop visit the grave since Mama's funeral, nor had he purchased a headstone. A flat iron marker, nearly buried in the wiry grass, told me where Mama and our baby had been laid to rest. Maybe Pop, like a lot of other people, didn't like visiting cemeteries because they raised so many questions about life and what happened after death. And maybe that was why this cemetery and so many others were in churchyards—so we'd have a nearby reminder of heaven and God and the promised afterlife.

This church, which I'd been attending ever since Mrs. Barnett invited me years ago, was a neat white clapboard building that seemed to point to heaven like a beacon. Arched stained-glass windows in the front and along both sides curved to a point on top like an invitation to look up. Smaller arched windows above the doors also pointed up. Even the steep, peaked roof gestured to the sky. And the glorious bell tower, housing bells that were now clanging their Sunday morning invitation, was topped with a tall, central spire along with two smaller spires for good measure. Every week, the architecture reminded parishioners of the promise of heaven.

I remembered how hard it had been to carry my grief after Mama and our baby died. I had stumbled through the flat, lonely days all alone until Buster came along to console me. Jimmy probably mourned for Mitch and countless other friends who had died in the war, but who had consoled him? I could come to the cemetery to grieve and lay flowers, but he had no place to lay his grief. It suddenly occurred to me that Jimmy had tried to kill himself on May 30—Decoration Day. Several young men who had died in the war had been honored with a small ceremony in this cemetery that day. Jimmy might have known them.

Decoration Day had been mild enough for me to open our windows. I'd heard the drum cadence, carried on a breeze as mourners walked to the cemetery. A bugler had played taps. There'd been a military salute with gunfire. And less than an hour later, I'd heard sirens as the volunteer ambulance corps arrived across the street.

Now, all of these thoughts distracted me from the Sunday service. I couldn't have said what the sermon had been about. I nearly walked straight past the horse trainer from Blue Fence Farms, standing alone outside the church. It would be rude to ignore him a second time, especially since no one else seemed to have noticed him. I pushed past my shyness and greeted him, knowing it was what Jimmy would have done. "Good morning, Mr. Dixon."

"It is a great morning, isn't it? How are you today, Miss Serrano?"

"You can call me Peggy. And . . . and I'm fine, thank you." But obviously terrible at making small talk.

"I hope you'll call me Paul. Mr. Dixon is my father, who, by the way, doesn't know the front end of a horse from the rear." He grinned and so did I, but my smile didn't last long as my thoughts returned to Jimmy. I didn't know what else to say, so I waited to see if Mr. Dixon—Paul— could think of something. He was gazing out at the view of the distant mountains, turning the brim of his Sunday hat around and around in his hands. "This is such a pretty little valley," he finally said. "I could look at those mountains all day. But I suppose people who've lived here all their lives don't even notice them anymore."

"I do. I notice them. And I've lived here all my life."

"Someone told me I should drive up to the hairpin turn and the lookout to see the view from the top."

"You should. I love it up there." Did that sound like I wanted him to invite me along? Why hadn't I just kept quiet? "I-I'm sorry to rush off again, Mr. Dixon—"

"Paul."

"Yes. Paul. But I'm on my way to visit a friend in the hospital and . . ."

"I understand. It was nice seeing you."

I was heartened to see Joe's motorcycle parked outside Pop's garage when I returned home from church. Joe had disappeared again after our visit with Frank Cishek three days ago. Now he was upstairs in our apartment, standing at our stove flipping pancakes and having a laugh with Donna and Pop. Donna shot me a stern look as I came inside, one that clearly said, *"Now, don't mess this up again!"* I rolled my eyes and went into my bedroom to change my clothes.

Joe and I left on his motorcycle after lunch. Chaplain Bill and Frank Cishek were already waiting in the hospital's parking lot when we arrived, talking quietly. The two men couldn't have been more different: Frank tall and robust and earnest, the balding chaplain slumped and worried-looking. The four of us went inside together and found Jimmy sitting alone in the common room.

"Hi, Jim. Remember me? Frank Cishek?" he asked. He offered his hand and Jimmy shook it weakly in return. He seemed confused and wary as he looked us over, like a child facing four strangers, so I quickly introduced everyone as if he were meeting us for the first time.

"I told you those electric shocks are torture," Joe muttered. There were enough chairs for all of us, so we stayed inside the building this time, sitting in a circle around a coffee table like campers around a bonfire.

Jimmy listened without responding as Joe and Frank and sometimes Chaplain Bill chatted with him, recalling some of the men they'd known and laughing over incidents that had occurred in basic training or on the voyage across the Atlantic or during their training in Wales. The men tiptoed very carefully over to France, not mentioning the horrors of D-Day. I watched Jimmy's face for his reaction, but there was none. His three friends might have been describing a film they'd watched that Jimmy had never seen. I wondered if the shock treatments had erased all of those memories. At last, Frank grew serious.

"Those were hard years, I won't deny it. We saw some pretty terrible things, Jim, things that I don't think any of us will ever forget. Even now, the nightmares and bad memories keep coming back and it's hard to shake them off sometimes. I'll hear an airplane overhead or the sound of a car backfiring and my heart starts pounding and I break out in a sweat."

"I know what you mean," Joe mumbled. His growing uneasiness was apparent in the way he jiggled his foot and drummed his fingers on the arms of the chair. I sensed that any moment now, he would spring to his feet and bolt from the hospital. I knew that only his deep gratitude to Jimmy and Frank for saving his life kept him from doing it.

"But I'm learning to push those bad memories away with different pictures," Frank continued. "It's like turning to a different page in a photo album. In those pictures I see the people in France and Belgium and the Netherlands streaming out into the streets to greet us. I remember how they cheered and waved and thanked us—old people with white hair and canes, children who'd never lived in a world without war and famine and bloodshed. I remember how the pretty young gals would run up and kiss our cheeks and tuck flowers in our buttonholes and hop on the front of our tanks and trucks. Those are the people we fought to rescue, Jim. We gave them back their freedom. And whenever my mind flashes to the destroyed cities with nothing left but rubble, I remind myself that our families here at home didn't have to suffer through bombing raids and artillery fire because of what we did. My hometown is intact and the people I love are free—and so are yours—because of our friends who gave everything."

We were all looking at Jimmy, and I wanted so badly for him to nod his head and agree that Frank was right. But he didn't. He had stared at Frank while he'd been speaking but his face wore no expression at all. He might have been looking straight through him.

"I'm finishing school on the GI bill and getting married in another month," Frank continued. "I'd love to have you there, Jim. You and I were together through the good times and through the very worst that the war could throw at us. I thank God that we can all heal now and get on with our lives—"

"Mitch O'Hara can't." Jimmy's voice was barely a whisper, but we all heard him. My heart began to thud as I held my breath.

"No, Mitch O'Hara can't," Frank said after a moment. We were all quiet.

Then Chaplain Bill spoke. "All of Mitch's days were written in God's book before one of them came to be. You used to tell me that, remember, Jim? And you were right. People die every day in all sorts of ways when it's their time. But as Frank just reminded us, Mitch's life and his death meant something. It wasn't in vain. He helped bring victory and freedom to a warring world." The chaplain leaned closer to face Jimmy. "And life in this world isn't all that there is, Jim. Death isn't the end of Mitch's story."

Jimmy closed his eyes, and he seemed to shrink back inside himself until it was as if he no longer heard us or was aware that we were even there. Buster had once found a land tortoise in our backyard, and when it retreated inside its shell, pulling its legs and head inside, it seemed impervious to Buster's frantic barking and growling. I had lifted the tortoise with a shovel and carried it back into the weeds, afraid that Buster's poking paws and nose would cause the tortoise to lash out and bite him. Now I sensed we all felt wary of Jimmy's bite if we poked him again.

"I'm sorry," Frank told us later as we walked back to the parking lot. Jimmy's parents had arrived and we went outside so they could be alone with him. "I shouldn't have brought up the war. I shouldn't have said what I did."

I had been thinking that Jimmy's reaction had been my fault and that my plan to contact more of Jimmy's Army friends was a terrible one. But then Chaplain Bill spoke. "No, what you said was good, Frank, and exactly right. And Jim must have heard it because it provoked a reaction. Jim's parents told me that he barely spoke to anyone after he came home. The doctors can't get him to talk, either. But now we know that he's listening and he's aware of what's going on around him. And that he remembers things. None of us mentioned Mitch O'Hara's name, did we?"

We looked at each other and agreed that we hadn't. Jimmy had conjured up Mitch's name from the recesses of his memory in spite of all the attempts to erase it with insulin comas and electric shocks. And Jimmy still grieved for his friend. It made me even more determined to find out who Gisela was and what she meant to him.

Bill smoothed back his thinning hair, ruffled by a breeze from the river. "I think you're on the right track with what you're doing, Miss Serrano. Jim needs to face the memories that are causing him so much pain. If he hears from friends like Joe who were wounded, and finds out that they're okay now, maybe he can let go of the load he's been carrying. As for the friends like Mitch who are gone, I think Jim's angry with God for taking them."

I thought of how I had laid daisies on Mama's grave this morning and said, "Maybe we could do something with Jimmy to honor Mitch and the others. A ceremony or celebration of some kind."

"That's a great idea," Bill said. "Do any of you remember where Mitch was from and what work he did before the war?"

"I think he was from here in New York State, like Jim," Joe said.

"That's right," Frank said. "He and Jim were college roommates. They enlisted together."

"Good, good," Bill said. "I'll find out his address and talk to Mitch's parents about having a little memorial service for him. Maybe we can take up a collection for a scholarship in his name or help his family in some way if they need it. I'll look into it. But we should honor him and his life and make sure Jim has a part in it."

As Joe and Frank were saying goodbye, Chaplain Bill pulled me aside. "Before you go, Miss Serrano, I have something for you in my car."

"Please, call me Peggy."

He unlocked his car and handed me a file folder. "I've been working on a letter to send to Jim's fellow soldiers. My wife typed it up for me and I borrowed the church's mimeograph machine to make copies. I hope it's all right." I read Bill's letter and thought it was perfect:

> *Dear fellow soldiers,*
>
> *I think you will be as shocked as I was to learn that our friend and brother-in-arms Corporal Jim Barnett is in the VA hospital, suffering from battle fatigue and depression. I'm writing to ask you to please send him a word of greeting and encouragement. Tell him how you're doing, especially if you were wounded and he took care of you. Remind him of some of the good memories you shared with him.*
>
> *If you have a picture of yourself and maybe one of your family, please send that, too. We need to remind him of the lives he saved and the good work that he did. He needs to know that his work during the war wasn't in vain.*
>
> *Peggy Serrano, a longtime friend from Jim's hometown, is coordinating this project with Jim's mother, and they will put all of your letters and photographs into an album to share with him. Please send your letters and pictures to Jim's home address, below.*
>
> *With my sincere thanks,*
> *Chaplain Bill Ashburn*

Bill also handed me a paper bag. "Here are some envelopes and stamps. And this is the list of addresses that I have so far. I'll send more when I get them."

I thanked him for his help and climbed onto Joe's motorcycle for the ride home.

Joe left again after bringing me home that afternoon and didn't return. Early Monday morning before Donna was out of bed, I went down to Pop's office to type addresses onto the envelopes Bill had given me. I would mail the first batch today and wait for more addresses to come. I tensed when I heard footsteps outside the office. I would have to gather everything up quickly if it was Donna. This was her office now. But when the door opened, it was Pop. He stared as if surprised to see me.

"I hope it's okay to use your typewriter," I said. "I'll scram if Donna wants to work."

He picked up the stack of envelopes and ruffled the edges with his fingers. "What's all this? What are you doing?"

"I'm contacting some of Jimmy Barnett's Army buddies and asking them to write letters to him."

Pop set down the envelopes and gestured to the cluttered desk. "So all this has nothing to do with getting a job?" I struggled not to let him see how much his question hurt. Pop had let me go my own way all these years with barely a word of advice or encouragement, and now he made me feel like a stray dog that he wanted to be rid of. I swallowed my sorrow and shook my head, waiting for him to speak again. "Donna says she hasn't seen you make any effort at all to find a job."

"I already have a job. In the clinic across the street."

"Part-time, though."

"Yes, part-time."

He looked at the floor, shuffling his feet. "Donna told me about a Help Wanted sign in the grocery store in New Paltz. I told her I thought you could do better."

"Thanks for sticking up for me, Pop." I heard the sarcasm in my voice and wondered if he did.

"Listen, Donna wants the apartment all to herself. You can understand that, right? She says it's hard for two women to live in such a small space."

"It was my home first, Pop. She's the one who moved in with us. But I won't stay where I'm obviously not wanted. I just need a little more time."

"Okay, okay. I'll tell her."

"And even when I do find a job, it's going to be hard to find a place to live where they'll let me keep Buster. I know he can't stay here. Donna hates him."

"Can't your friends across the street find a new home for him?" His question stunned me. Give away Buster? After all these years and all that he meant to me? How could Pop even think about coldly giving him away? Buster was my shadow, my friend, my closest companion. I loved him and he loved me. As I stood and gathered up the letters and envelopes, preparing to leave, Buster emerged from beneath the desk and scrambled to his feet, making his tags jingle as he shook himself.

"I would rather sleep in the park than give up Buster," I told my father with cold fury.

He put his hand on my arm to keep me from brushing past him. "I know you think I'm being mean and that Donna and I are pushing you out—"

"Yes! Because that's exactly what you're doing."

"I want a better life for you, Peg. I've been stuck in this dump all my life, but you don't have to be. And you shouldn't let a stray dog hold you back from moving on."

It was the longest conversation I'd had with my father in years. I hadn't known that he could talk in whole paragraphs. But his heartlessness in wanting to give away Buster and push me out nearly broke my heart.

Pop stopped me again as I reached the door. "Let me know if you need my help with anything."

I had never heard those words before, either. I was about to shake my head, my thoughts reeling with anger and sorrow, when I did think of something. "I'll need a good used car. I have some money saved up from working at IBM during the war."

"Okay, okay." He nodded, staring at the floor, not at me. "I'll keep my eye out for one." I left him there.

Joe's screams woke me up again that night. He must have returned after I went to bed. Buster and I hurried downstairs to awaken him from his nightmare. Buster jumped onto the bed beside him, and Joe stroked his fur as he struggled to calm down. "I'm so sorry, Joe," I said. "I'm trying to help Jimmy, but I know I'm bringing back terrible memories for you, too."

"You're not bringing them back. They never left. Every little thing reminds me of the war."

How horrible that must be. To never leave the war behind? To relive it every day? I swallowed and asked, "Would it help to try to do what Frank does? Turn the page and remember the good?"

"I wasn't there for the liberation. I didn't get to see the parades." He stopped stroking Buster and clenched his fists. His expression changed from sleepy confusion after his nightmare to rage. "I hate my weakness! Hate that you have to see it! It makes me so furious—and it's never going to change! Only when I get drunk enough."

"Tell me what makes you angry, Joe. Losing your leg?"

"What do you think? I'll never be the same!" Buster lifted his head at Joe's shouts, then rested his head on his lap as Joe began petting him again. "The truth is, I was angry long before that happened."

"Can you tell me why?"

"Because you have no choice and no control over your life when you're in the Army. They order you to march into battle and you have to do it. You go into danger with bombs falling—and they don't care. Our lives weren't our own. We were just troops to them. They could move us around the way a kid plays with tin soldiers. They know a bunch of us are going to die in order to take some 'military objective,' but they just throw us at the enemy, and whichever side still has men standing when the shooting stops, that's who wins. They didn't know me or care about my life. I was just a number to them."

I could see the truth in what he was saying and didn't know how to reply. I remembered the drawings in the newspapers with our advancing men represented by arrows and shaded rectangles. I waited quietly for Joe to continue.

"After every battle, more of my friends would be lying dead and wounded all around me. Ever see what's left of a deer along the road after it's been hit by a car? The mangled, bloody mess of bones and hair? Imagine if that was someone you knew. Imagine wondering every morning if it was going to be you today. That's what we lived with. And if we complained, they told us to shut up and keep fighting. It was almost a relief when I was hit, except for the pain and thinking I was going to die. They told me I almost did die."

"I'm glad you didn't, Joe. And I'm glad we won the war. Remember what Frank talked about the other day? How your sacrifice brought freedom to the world? Suppose Hitler or Emperor Hirohito ruled over us?"

"Yeah, I know, I know. We fought for freedom. But where's my freedom? I know what Jim meant when he said that Mitch O'Hara isn't celebrating any victories. I suppose I should be grateful to be alive when he and so many others aren't. But I'll be a cripple for the rest of my life. I still feel pain in a foot that's no longer there. What's left of my leg is rubbed raw by that stupid contraption at the end of the day. There are so many things I'll never be able to do again. At least when I'm on my motorcycle, I'm my own man, making my own choices. You should come on the road with me. We could see the country, have some laughs."

"I can't leave Buster here all alone. Donna hates him."

"You're a good dog, aren't you, Tripod?" Joe said, scratching his huge ears. "Yeah, you're a good dog." Buster lapped up the attention like honey. Joe was quiet for a long moment before saying, "I don't think I can visit Jim with you again. Not for a while, anyway."

"I understand. You don't have to go back."

"It's just that I hate VA hospitals. I was sitting where Jim is not very long ago, and I kinda walked out without telling anyone. I keep thinking they're gonna grab me and make me stay."

"You really don't need to feel obligated to hang around here. I know you're probably eager to get out on the road again."

Joe looked up at me and gave a sheepish grin. "The thing is, I'm out of money. I think I bought drinks for everybody in the bar last night. I was wondering if I could stay and work here for a while. Just until I earn enough gas money to get back to Ohio. There should be some government checks waiting there for me. Do you think your pop or Donna would mind?"

I was pretty sure Donna wouldn't mind. She would imagine that Joe was hanging around because of me and hoping that I would leave with him. I wasn't in love with Joe Fiore. But he'd become a friend in the month that I'd known him, and I longed to help him heal his unseen wounds. I would miss him when he finally left.

"I don't know what Pop will say," I replied with a shrug. "You'll have to ask him. But I hope you know how grateful I am for all your help this past month. I couldn't have done it without you."

14

Gisela

I parted the blackout curtain an inch and gazed out the window of my dormitory, my longing for Sam and for my family a raw ache in my heart. The weather had turned bitterly cold, and with fuel shortages across the city, the other student nurses and I studied in the common room after supper where there was a small coal-burning fireplace. I would wrap myself in layers of donated sweaters and socks and drape a blanket around my shoulders as I pored over my notes, worried that my family was freezing in our tiny apartment. Nearly three months had passed since I'd left home and I had last seen my loved ones. At times, I became so homesick that I wanted to quit school and walk home. Now I reminded myself there were only a few more months until graduation.

The hospital loomed in the darkness across the street, its windows also shaded by blackout curtains that obscured every window. Smoke curled from the chimneys, and my gaze was drawn to a star shining brightly above the rooftop. Vati would know which one it was. He used to take Ruthie and me outside on warm summer nights in Berlin and we would look up at the stars together. "Make a wish on the brightest one," he'd say, "and then watch the sky. If you see a falling star, your wish will come true." My wish was for the war to end and for the Nazis to be defeated so we could all resume our lives, but that wish was too big. So instead, I wished that I could see Sam, just for a few minutes, just to feel his arms around me and know he was safe. I wished that he would tell me my family was safe and Vati was feeling better. I waited and watched the dark skies, but I didn't see any falling stars.

I closed the curtain again and turned away from the window to finish my schoolwork. We no longer had a radio and couldn't listen to music in the evenings or hear the latest news of the war. Radios had been banned by the Nazis since January.

The following afternoon, I was leaving the hospital after class and was about to cross the street to my dormitory when I heard someone calling my name. "Gisela! Gisela, over here." It was Sam, calling to me from behind the bushes. I ran to him. I didn't know how long he'd been waiting for me, but his bare hands felt like two blocks of ice as he held my face and kissed me. "Is there someplace we can go and talk?" he asked. "It's freezing out here." I couldn't bring him inside the all-girl nursing school, but one of the other student nurses had told me of a place where she secretly met with her boyfriend. It was where the garbage was collected, so the door was kept unlocked. Sam and I circled around to the rear of the building and slipped inside. He was shivering, and his hands and lips were blue with cold. I held him close to offer some of my warmth, then took his hands in mine and breathed on them to warm them.

"How long have you been waiting for me?"

"I don't know. But it's been so long since I've seen you, I just had to come."

"Tell me all the news, Sam. How are our families? How is Vati?"

"About the same. It's hard for him to walk to the synagogue when the weather is so cold, so we pray at home when I'm there."

"Can you tell me about the work you're doing? Is it dangerous?"

"I haven't had time to be involved with the Resistance this winter.

It takes every spare moment I have just to find work and earn extra money to survive. Between the cost of food and all the shortages, it's been difficult to do. But we're coping. Are you staying warm, Gisela? And eating well?"

"Yes. The food is simple but adequate. And I feel safe here."

"I miss you so much," he said before kissing me again. "But I'm happy to know that you're safe and well cared for."

"I wish you and my family had a safe place to hide."

"I know. My brothers are growing into young men and I'm worried that the Nazis will grab them on their way to school one of these days and use them for forced labor to help build their Atlantic Wall." I suddenly pictured Sam and his brothers standing on the deck of the *St. Louis*, young and lean and strong, their blond hair tousled by the wind and glowing in the sunshine. How long ago and far away that vision seemed.

"What about you, Sam? Is there a danger that the Nazis will take you?"

"There is, but I'm getting good at staying out of sight." He sighed and I realized how weary he was. He would have a long walk home in the cold. "The last time I heard from my father, he was still trying to get temporary visas for us in South America. I haven't received any letters since December, and now we just found out that it's too late. The Nazis passed a law in January saying Jews are forbidden to leave the country. And of course, going to the United States is out of the question, even if our immigration numbers were called, now that the Nazis are at war with them."

"I thought the Nazis wanted to be rid of us."

"They do. But I think they're worried that if we flee to other countries, we'll tell the world what they're doing to us here."

"What about the war? Have you heard any news? Are the Allies winning?"

"I don't know. We had to give up our radio. And you can't believe anything that the Nazi-run newspapers say."

"That's been the hardest thing for me, Sam—to keep going day after day, never knowing when or how this war will end. Or if it ever will. It's so hard to keep clinging to hope when there doesn't seem to be any."

"I know. But each day that passes means that we're another day closer, Gisela. We have to keep believing that, or we'll lose our minds." Sam kissed me, then pulled away and wiped the steam off the little window in the back door. The sun sat on the western rooftops like a fiery-orange ball. "I need to get home before curfew," he said, "but I had to see you, Gisela. I love you so much!"

* * *

I didn't see Sam again for the rest of the winter, and the agony of not knowing where he was and if he was safe made it difficult for me to concentrate on my studies. In March, rumors raced through the hospital that, just as Sam had feared, the Nazis were rounding up able-bodied men for forced-labor gangs to build their Atlantic Wall. A group of Jewish men were snatched after leaving their synagogue on Purim. I worried that the Nazis had taken Sam and his brothers, or maybe even Vati, and I waited anxiously to hear that they were safe. Why wasn't God helping us? Why didn't He save us from the Nazis the way He'd saved us from Haman's evil scheme in the time of Esther? I wondered if Vati still insisted that God had a reason for what was happening to us.

In early June, shortly before my graduation from nursing school, the Nazis announced that all Jews would be required to wear a yellow star on their clothing that said *Jew*. I asked Sister Veronica what I should do.

She fingered the large cross that she wore around her neck and I could tell she was giving my dilemma serious thought. "You probably won't need to wear a star here at school or in the hospital. But if you leave the campus—and especially if you go home—I think it would be wise to wear one." That evening, I sewed a yellow star onto one of my sweaters and carried it with me wherever I went, just in case. I had heard one or two of my fellow students and occasionally a patient at the hospital utter anti-Semitic remarks, but for the most part, no one seemed to know or care that I was Jewish.

On the morning of graduation, Sister Veronica sent me a message, asking me to come to her office. The little table was set for tea, and it struck me that this simple room was as serene and peaceful as Sister Veronica herself, as if untouched by the Nazi terror that flooded all of Europe. Emblems of her faith surrounded her—statues and crucifixes and paintings, images that were forbidden to us. I wondered if she drew faith and hope from them.

"First of all, I want to congratulate you, Miss Wolff, for being our top nursing student," she said as she poured the tea. "You're graduating at the very head of your class."

"Thank you." I had heard this surprising news from my instructors, who had all praised my accomplishment.

"I invited you here because I would like to ask you about your future plans."

"Well, I agreed to work at the hospital to repay what I owe for room and board, and I have every intention of doing that. That is, if the authorities will still allow a Jew to work here."

She set down her teacup and leaned toward me. "Gisela, we know how your people are being treated by the Nazis, and the administration here at the nursing school as well as the authorities in the church are all refusing to yield to their pressure. You are welcome to continue working here—and living here—for as long as you like."

"Thank you. I can't tell you how reassuring it is to know that we aren't alone."

"As for next fall," she continued, "I would like you to consider continuing your studies with more advanced nurse's training. You're capable of doing so much more than bedpans and sponge baths. The war has created a need for surgical assistants and wound-care specialists and nurse practitioners who can assist with triage. I believe you would excel in any specialty."

"Won't I need to work to repay my room and board fees first?"

"You can do that by filling in for nursing shifts part-time, whenever you're needed. We won't overwork you while you're studying, I promise. But tell me, might you be interested in continuing your training?"

I stared down at my hands, folded on my lap, as hundreds of thoughts and feelings raced through my mind. I loved nursing, and the idea of further studies excited and challenged me. Yet it seemed absurd to continue studying for a career and a life that I probably would never have. My life here at school with classes and hospital duties was completely different from the one my fellow Jews lived, huddled inside their apartments in a foreign land, waiting for the next Nazi pogrom to begin. Yet hadn't Sam said that God might want to use my nurse's training someday?

I looked up at Sister Veronica. "Yes, I think I would like to study more," I told her. "Thank you for giving me a chance to do that. But first, would it be possible for me to visit my father? The last time I was home, he was very ill. My mother has been caring for him this spring and I would like to spend some time at home to help her."

"Of course, Miss Wolff. I'm so sorry to hear about your father. Take as long as you need. I'll wait until you return before asking the head nurse at the hospital to assign you to the day shift." It was settled. For now, I had a future, of sorts.

I graduated with my nursing certificate that afternoon. The ceremony took place in the Catholic school's chapel. The other students' parents and loved ones watched with pride as we earned our nurses' caps. Antwerp was still too dangerous for my parents to risk attending, even if they had a way to get here. I heard the other girls chattering about their plans afterwards, some starting new jobs, others marrying their sweethearts or returning to their hometowns, and I felt very sorry for myself, envying their freedom. I had lived through two pogroms and feared there would be more. Yet my conversation with Sister Veronica this morning and the possibility of studying to be a surgical nurse were reasons enough to celebrate.

I had started to weave through the happy crowd to return to my room in the dormitory when I heard one of my roommates calling to me. "Gisela! Gisela, come here and pose with us!" Her father had a camera, and she and a group of our classmates were posing for photographs. I put my sweater and diploma on a chair and joined them, and we took several group photos with our arms around each other, all wearing our new nurses' caps. My roommate did an amusing imitation of one of the stodgier doctors at the hospital, and when I couldn't help laughing, her father chose that moment to snap a picture of me. "That was perfect, Gisela," my friend said. "You look so beautiful when you smile. I'll give you a copy when the roll is developed." I thanked her. I would frame the picture and give it to Sam.

I went back to retrieve my things and saw that my diploma and sweater had slid to the floor and were lying in a heap. The yellow star was clearly visible. I hurried over to scoop them up, but a girl from my class named Lina Renard reached them before I did. She had a look of surprise on her face as she held up the sweater, examining the star. "That's mine," I said quickly. "Thank you for picking it up for me." But Lina wouldn't let go of it.

"Well, well," she said with a sly smile. "It looks like you've been keeping a little secret from us, Gisela." My stomach rolled as I struggled for a reply. Lina seemed different from the other girls and had never been friendly toward me. She was very competitive and had made it clear that she had hoped to graduate as the top nursing student.

"I-I didn't think it was a secret," I finally said. "I thought everyone knew."

"Then why not wear it openly, for everyone to see?" she asked, holding it high. She had everyone's attention now as she displayed the star. I felt my face grow warm.

My roommate snatched the sweater from her. "Shut up, Lina," she said. She handed it to me and I hurried away.

I packed a small suitcase after my classes ended, prepared to walk home wearing the sweater with a yellow star sewn onto it. I had just emerged through the front door when Sam called to me from the bushes. "Gisela! Over here!"

I ran to him, my purse flopping off my shoulder, my suitcase banging against my leg in my haste to be in his arms. "Oh, it's so wonderful to see you!" I said as I dropped everything.

He lifted me off my feet and spun me around. "I'm here to take you home. I remembered that you graduated from school today. Hop on my bike."

Sam steadied the rusty used bicycle that he had scrounged and helped me climb on. I perched on the bar in front of his seat, hanging on tightly to the handlebars with one hand and balancing my suitcase on my knees with the other. I wondered how he would ever manage to steer the rickety old bicycle, but it only wobbled a little bit before Sam found his balance and pedaled off. He had learned his way around Antwerp during the past three years and had figured out how to avoid the Nazis' patrols and their favorite gathering places.

And soon we were home. It was wonderful to see my family again, but the changes that had occurred since I'd seen them six months ago shocked me. Everyone was noticeably thinner, their clothes hanging on them like they belonged to someone else. Vati was as pale as death and coughing more than ever. Mutti and Ruthie resembled frail, worried sparrows who startled at every sound in the streets outside as if expecting another pogrom. But the biggest change was that Sam's family had given up their apartment and moved in with my family to save money on expenses. Mrs. Shapiro now shared the bedroom with Ruthie, and Sam slept on a mattress in the living room with his brothers when he was home. Both of our families had been comfortably well-to-do back home in Germany, and to see them reduced to near squalor enraged me. I longed for God's vengeance on the Nazis for what they had done to us. But I swallowed my outrage and sat down with these loved ones to celebrate Shabbat and my return home.

"We're so proud of you, Gisela," Vati said when I told him about graduating at the top of my class. Then I told them about Sister Veronica's offer to study for an advanced degree, and his happiness seemed to overflow. "I would dance for joy at this news if I was strong enough," he said. "You have to accept her offer, Gisela."

"But it's going to mean living away from everyone for even longer, and I'm so lonely there. I miss all of you."

"And we miss you, darling girl," Vati said. "But it gives me great pleasure to hear of your success in spite of Herr Hitler's efforts to degrade and diminish us. You would be doing this for all of us."

After dinner, Sam and I offered to clear the table and wash the dishes, giving us a chance to talk alone in the kitchen. "I'll be starting work in the hospital when I return," I told him, "and earning a small salary, minus what I owe for my room and board. I want to send you as much as I can to help pay for food and expenses. But how should I send it? By mail?"

"No, don't trust the mail. Let me give it some thought."

"I feel like a traitor, living in relative ease with food and freedom while everyone is crammed into one tiny apartment."

"Gisela, I know you remember the story of Queen Esther. There's a reason why God has placed you where you are." I hoped he was right.

I stayed home and nursed Vati for a week and tried to cheer Mutti and Ruthie and give them hope. When my week was over, Sam took me back on his bicycle. We stood in the alley by the rear door of the nurses' residence to say goodbye. I would remove my sweater with the telltale yellow star before going inside.

"Now that I'll be living in the nurses' residence, you can visit with me in the lobby anytime you want," I told Sam. "Maybe I can even go home with you now and then. And I can give you all the money I've saved up."

He looked into my eyes and traced his fingers down my jaw. "I love you, Gisela." He sighed and held me close, and I sensed he was about to say things I didn't want to hear. Now would be the time for him to say, *"We're another day closer . . ."* but he didn't. "Tomorrow comes with no guarantees," he said instead. "For now, we need to hold any plans we make very lightly."

"But we'll see each other again, won't we?"

He kissed me and said, "God willing."

I spent the rest of June and July working in the hospital, doing what I had trained for two years to do, while waiting for my advanced nursing classes to begin in the fall. I loved my job, even the dull, messy parts of it, because it kept my mind occupied from thoughts of Sam and home. He showed up on his bicycle on a broiling day in late July to take me home for a brief visit, and I could tell that something had upset him. "We'll talk about it when we're all together," he said as we sped through the streets. Every store we passed had long lines of people waiting out front. I noticed that Sam took a winding route home to avoid the area around the train station.

Sam hadn't told my family I was coming and they were surprised and overjoyed to see me. "I would have cooked something special for you, if I had known," Mutti fretted, but I assured her that I wasn't hungry. Vati was sitting at a table in the living room when I arrived, teaching a mathematics lesson to Ruthie and Sam's brothers. It was summer, and it seemed absurd for them to be doing schoolwork when we faced such an uncertain future. But what else could they do to provide a distraction?

After all of our greetings, Sam quickly grew serious. "We've all heard about the arrests and deportations of Jews in other Nazi-occupied countries, but now they're starting to do the same thing here in Antwerp. The security police arrested a few hundred Jews at the Central Station as they arrived from Brussels. There was no reason and no recourse. There were more sudden arrests on nearby Pelikaanstraat."

"Where are they taking all these people?" Vati asked.

"To a temporary transit camp, for now, in a former Army barracks in the town of Mechelin. The camp is near a rail hub, and according to my sources, the plan is to deport every Jew in Belgium to camps in Germany and the east, maybe as far as Poland."

I saw my father shudder. "What should we do?" he asked.

"Everyone needs to go into hiding. We can't wait for them to come for us. The people I know in the Resistance are going to help. They can supply fake ID cards that aren't stamped 'Jew.' Gisela, I brought you home so we could all say our goodbyes—"

"No!" I cried out. "Please, no!" I was sitting beside Mutti and I clutched her arm, unwilling to be separated from her.

"You're already in a very safe place, Gisela, working and hiding among the Christians."

"But I don't want to be separated from any of you! We can all go to the work camps together."

"No, Sam is right," Vati said. "It's much better that we're apart for a little while than that we end up in a camp like Buchenwald."

Saying goodbye felt like tearing off both of my arms. But it had to be done quickly so Sam could take me back to my residence and return home before the curfew. I clung to him in despair in our private place behind the hospital, but he gently pried away my arms. "We don't have to say goodbye just yet. I won't go into hiding until I've found places for all of the others. I'll come back to you in the meantime so you'll know what's happening."

"Please don't put yourself in danger, Sam!"

"We already are in danger. All of us. Give me your identity card, Gisela, so I can have it altered or a fake one made. As long as you don't leave the nurses' residence or the hospital grounds, you won't be asked to show it." I marveled at this strong, brave man who was working so hard to save all of us.

Three weeks later, in mid-August, I returned from my nursing shift to find Sam waiting for me in the residence lounge. In spite of the summer heat, he was wearing an ill-fitting suit and tie—and no yellow star. He had shaved his beard, and if he hadn't spoken my name, I wouldn't have recognized him. My heart raced as we moved to a corner of the lounge away from the door to talk. "I don't have much time," he said, "but I need your help." My hands were trembling, and he took them in his.

"Nazi officers and the local police raided our neighborhood last night. They cordoned off several streets, dragged people from their homes, and loaded them onto military trucks. Thousands of us, Gisela. Not just men, but women and children, too."

"Not our families! Please, Sam—tell me that our families are safe!"

"They are for now. But we don't know when or where the next raid will be. I've been working with a Christian man in the Resistance named

Lukas Wouters. He owns a hotel in central Antwerp called the Hotel Centraal. He arranged hiding places for my brothers on farms outside of Antwerp, and my mother is going to live with him and his wife, posing as their maid. Remember that name, Gisela—Hotel Centraal."

"Yes, yes. And my family?" I couldn't breathe, praying they were safe, too.

Sam gripped my hands tightly and said, "I need you to be strong, Gisela, and to listen to me. Promise?"

"Just tell me," I whispered.

"Your father is dying. He knows it and your mother knows it. He is too weak and too ill to be moved, but he accepts this as the will of God."

My tears spilled over and rolled down my cheeks. "No. Why would God will such a thing?"

"Your parents have decided to stay in the apartment until the end. I couldn't convince them to change their minds. Your father said that as long as his two girls are safe, nothing else matters."

"But . . . but . . . maybe I can get him admitted to this hospital or . . . or—"

"He'll never agree because it would put you in danger. But listen, please. Ruthie doesn't want to leave your parents. That's why I need your help."

"I-I have a roommate, but maybe if I explain to her what's happening, she'll let Ruthie hide here and—"

"That's too dangerous. The Flemish National Union is pro-Nazi and they have many supporters here in Antwerp. It would only take one informant to go to the authorities and you and Ruthie would both be arrested." He paused and scanned the lounge as if worried he might be overheard. "I've also learned that some Catholic organizations are secretly hiding Jewish children in their orphanages. Do you trust the people at your school? Can you talk with someone and ask if they'll arrange a place for your sister?"

"I trust Sister Veronica, the headmistress of my school. I'll speak with her."

"Good. The only way Ruthie will agree to leave your parents is if she thinks she's staying with you."

"I don't want to lie to her, Sam. She'll hate me for it."

"Right now, it's the only way." He released my hands and reached into the inner pocket of his suit jacket. "Here's your new identity card. Your name is now Ella Maes, and you're a Belgian citizen. You were raised in Switzerland before the war, which explains your accent. Do you think the headmistress will help you change to this new identity?"

"I'll ask her. I'll go right away."

"Ask her to hurry. We don't know if our street and our apartment building will be next. I have to go," he said. "I'll come back tomorrow for your answer, and if they'll help us, we'll have to get Ruthie out of the Jewish neighborhood as quickly as possible."

"Sam, wait! Don't you need a place to hide? I could ask her to help you, too."

"I have a place." I could tell that he wanted to embrace me, and I longed to hold him, too, but the lounge was busy with nurses changing shifts. "I'll see you tomorrow," he said.

I went straight to Sister Veronica's office after Sam left and asked to see her. "She isn't here at the moment," Sister Mary Margaret said. "But if you'd like to wait, she should be back shortly." I sat in the chair she offered me, anxiously drumming my fingers on the armrest and trying to remain calm. And strong. Sam had hit me with so much devasting news that I hadn't had time to absorb it all. Vati was dying. I would probably never see him and Mutti again. That alone was enough to drop me to my knees in grief. But I had promised Sam I would be strong. Ruthie and I had to hide. We had to become different people.

"Hello, Gisela. You wanted to see me?"

I jumped to my feet at the sound of Sister Veronica's voice. I had been so deep in thought that I hadn't heard her coming. "I need your help!" I blurted. She smiled her gentle smile and gestured for me to follow her into her office. As soon as she closed the door, I quickly explained everything Sam had told her. When I told her that my father was dying,

I could no longer hold back my tears. She drew me into her arms, surprising me, and held me tightly.

"Of course we'll help you and your sister," she murmured as she allowed me to cry. It took several minutes for me to stop sobbing and pull myself together.

"I'm sorry . . . I'm sorry," I said, blowing my nose.

"You have no reason to be sorry. Now, how old is your sister?"

"Ruthie is fourteen, but she's small for her age and looks much younger."

"And I imagine you would like to stay as close to each other as possible?"

"Yes. My boyfriend said you sometimes hide Jewish children in your orphanages, and I would be willing to work as a nurse in a hospital nearby, and—"

"That's precisely what I was thinking. I'll start making the arrangements to get both of you out of Antwerp straightaway. Bring your sister here as soon as you can, and we'll take her to the convent. I don't think she should be seen with you in your room. I'm sorry to say that no one knows who they can trust during these trying times. Use the rear entrance where deliveries are made so you won't draw too much attention. Sister Mary Margaret can direct you there."

Sam arrived early the next morning and I told him the plan. I told him how to find the convent, and we arranged to meet by the service entrance.

"Sam, please tell Vati and Mutti I love them and I—" Tears choked my throat. I couldn't finish.

"They know, Gisela. All that matters to them is that you and Ruthie are safe. You're giving them peace of mind in an unbearable situation."

He left to fetch Ruthie, returning with her on his bicycle. She was wearing three dresses and a pair of trousers, layered on top of each other because Sam feared they'd be stopped if she carried a suitcase. My sister looked numb and pale. The dark circles beneath her eyes looked like bruises. She clung to me for several moments without saying a word. I was afraid we would both fall apart if I asked her about Vati. Then we all went inside, where Sister Veronica was waiting.

"Arrangements are well underway," she told us. "We'll need another day or so to print a nursing certificate with your new name, Gisela, but we've already secured a position for you at another hospital. You'll have time to pack your things and tell your friends that you've accepted a new job. We're also working on a birth certificate and the other necessary paperwork to show that Ruthie is an orphan. There's a room here in the convent where you can sleep in the meantime, Ruthie." My sister nodded and wrapped her thin arms around herself.

"If there's anything else we can do to help you," Sister Veronica told Sam, "I hope you won't hesitate to ask."

"I don't have words to tell you how deeply grateful I am," Sam replied. "I don't know anything about the Christian faith, but the Christians I've met have been unfailingly kind to us in our time of crisis, taking great risks to hide us, giving us money and food, even when both have been scarce."

"It's what our Savior taught us to do," the nun said with a smile. "You can come to me anytime. I'll know where Gisela is—or should I say Ella—and you can contact her through me whenever you need to." Sam seemed unable to reply. I knew he needed to leave soon.

"I'll be right back," I told Ruthie. I took Sam's hand and we stepped outside to say goodbye. As my tears fell, I prayed that I wasn't kissing him for the last time.

Later, I said goodbye to my roommate. She didn't seem surprised to hear that I was leaving so suddenly. "I know the secret you're keeping, Gisela," she told me, "and I'll be praying for you and your people." She pulled out the envelope of photographs her father had taken on graduation day and said, "Here, take one of these pictures so you'll always remember us."

"May I have a copy of this one, too? To give to my boyfriend?" It was the photo her father had snapped when he'd caught me laughing. I couldn't imagine ever laughing that way again.

"Of course! I'm just sorry I never got to meet your mystery man."

Two days later, Ruthie and I boarded a train to our new home in a town south of Antwerp. Sister Veronica advised me to wear my nurse's uniform as we traveled as if I was escorting a sick child. Ruthie did indeed look ill. I hoped she hadn't contracted tuberculosis from our father. She was told to memorize her new name, Ruth Anne Mertens. Sister Mary Margaret also came with us, presumably to make introductions and help us get settled in our new hiding places. But she opened her satchel when we were alone in the train compartment and explained another reason why she had come.

"I hope you won't feel that we're insulting your faith or your religion, but to safeguard your new identities, Sister Veronica believes it would be best if you attended Mass with the other nurses and pretended to be Catholic. And, Ruthie, the orphanage and girls' school where you'll be hiding is run by Catholic sisters, like me."

Ruthie looked up at me and I saw her alarm. "She's right, Ruthie," I said. "We have to do whatever we can to blend in."

Sister Mary Margaret gave me a prayer book and a set of rosary beads and spent a few minutes teaching us how to make the sign of the cross and other things we would need to know. "I'm sorry to say that your survival depends on your ability to look and act like Christians. You won't need to go to confession or partake of the sacraments," she said. "Just kneel quietly and pray. You should probably memorize our Lord's Prayer, too. It's here in the prayer book."

She showed me where to find it and I read the words silently: *"Our Father which art in heaven . . . Thy will be done . . . Give us this day our daily bread . . . Deliver us from evil . . ."* They were words that a Jew could pray—and perhaps I would have, if I hadn't been so upset and confused by what God was doing. And not doing.

"It may also help you to know," Sister Mary Margaret said as we neared our destination, "that Jesus, the man you see dying on the crucifix, is Jewish like you. He was also persecuted, even though He was innocent."

The orphanage seemed like a lively place, with girls in clean uniforms laughing and skipping in the hallways. The head nun showed Ruthie her bed in the dormitory and the matron found a uniform that would fit her.

When it was time for me to go, Ruthie clung to me, sobbing her heart out. "Don't leave me here all alone! Please, Gisela!"

I thought my own heart would break. "You know I would never leave you if there was any other way to keep you safe," I told her. "I'll figure out a way to visit you whenever I can. In the meantime, I need you to keep this for me. It belonged to Mutti's grandmother." I took off the string of pearls that Mutti had given me for my sixteenth birthday—the day our world began unraveling—and gave them to her. "They'll remind you of Oma and Mutti and me. We owe it to them to stay alive."

Ruthie looked so forlorn as she stood on the orphanage's steps, weeping and waving goodbye, that I nearly changed my mind about leaving her. We were both alone now.

*   *   *

On a November day soon after I had turned twenty years old, I happened to notice the newspaper headlines on my way to the hospital. The Nazis had captured and executed eight members of the Resistance movement in Antwerp.

I stumbled into the hospital chapel and knelt to pray for these eight men. And for Sam. I couldn't pray, *"Thy will be done."* But my unending prayer for all of us was *"Deliver us from evil . . ."*

15

Peggy

The letters and pictures from Jimmy's Army buddies started arriving in the mail. Mrs. Barnett and I read them together every day as we sat at her kitchen table and drank coffee. Some of the letters made us cry. "Is this too hard for you, Mrs. B.?" I asked.

She pulled a hankie from her apron pocket and wiped her eyes. "It is hard. But at the same time, it helps to hear how much good Jimmy did during the war. How much he meant to all of these men. It's just that . . . I want my son back."

"I know. We all do."

I chose portions of three letters that I wanted to read to him when I visited on Sunday, and hoped he would read the others himself. I had purchased a photograph album when I got my roll of film developed, and I stayed up late on Saturday night to create a scrapbook, using little black corners to hold the pictures in place and writing captions on the black pages with white ink.

It was raining when I woke up on Sunday morning, and that gave me an idea. After church, I knocked on the door of Pop's office where Joe was sleeping. I hated to wake him, but I figured he owed me for all the times he woke me up with his nightmares. Buster solved the problem by squeezing past me through the door and licking Joe's face. Joe groaned and wiped his cheek, then opened his eyes as I grabbed Buster's collar and pulled him away.

"I'm sorry for waking you up, Joe, but—"

"What time is it?" He sounded groggy. The office smelled terrible, with the combined stench of Donna's cigarettes and Joe's sweat and alcohol. It was hot in the office, and Joe had been sleeping in his clothes.

"It's past noon. Listen, I'm going to visit Jimmy today and I need your help. I know it's hard for you to go back to the hospital, but you won't have to go inside. I promise."

He sat up and ran his fingers through his dark hair, then scratched the shadow of dark stubble on his face. "What do you need me to do?"

"I want to take Buster to visit Jimmy again. He was so happy to see Buster the last time, remember? Anyway, it's raining today, so I'm hoping that none of the orderlies will want to go outside. I'll take Jimmy out to one of the benches with an umbrella. Meanwhile, you can sneak around the long way with Buster. Hopefully, no one will see us."

I made coffee while Joe shaved and changed his clothes and swallowed some aspirin. I listened to the sound of the wipers swishing and Joe's gentle snores as I drove, all the while doubting myself. Was I doing the right thing? Was I really helping Jimmy? Or would reliving the war through his friends' letters make matters worse?

We both stayed in the car on the ferry ride across the Hudson, the river as gray as the sky, the mountains hidden in the mist. I clipped Buster's leash to his collar when we arrived and went inside the hospital alone. Joe knew what to do.

"Jimmy, it's me, Peggety," I said when I found him. "I need you to come outside with me. Joe and I have a surprise for you. You remember Joe, don't you?" He didn't reply, but he allowed me to take his arm and lead him toward the rear doors.

I chose the bench farthest from the door and laid my plastic raincoat on it before we sat down. For some reason, I felt nervous as I waited for Joe and Buster. They eventually came along, and as soon as Buster spotted Jimmy, he strained against the leash to run to him. Joe limped as fast as he could to keep up. Buster planted his wet front paws on Jimmy's chest and licked his face like a lollipop, his tail wagging enthusiastically. Jimmy didn't laugh this time, but he wore a faint smile as he encircled the wet dog with his arms. Buster finally settled against Jimmy's legs with his head in his lap. Joe and I sat down beside him, our backs to the door, our umbrellas open to hide Buster from view. Jimmy stroked the dog's head as I opened the album.

"I brought some pictures to show you. I took them myself with the camera your parents gave me for graduation. Look, the mountains are so majestic, aren't they? And here are some pictures of the horses out at Blue Fence Farms. I love it out there this time of year when the new foals are grazing with their mothers." Jimmy was looking down at the page, but whether or not he was seeing anything, I couldn't tell. I waited a few more moments before turning the page. Next were pictures of his house and the clinic, his mother's zinnias and petunias growing along the front porch. The mountains looked like a stage backdrop behind the house. "We're looking forward to having you home again. We miss you, Jimmy."

He closed his eyes and his hand stilled on Buster's head. I turned the page.

"These next pictures are of some of your friends. I took this one of Chaplain Bill outside his church in Connecticut. And remember Frank Cishek? He came to see you last week? Joe and I went to visit him in Milford on the Fourth of July. And here's Joe with his motorcycle. And Joe with Buster."

"I've been working at the garage for Peggy's dad," Joe said. "Trying to earn some gas money. Hey, her pop knows an awful lot about fixing cars, let me tell you."

"Chaplain Bill and your mother and I wrote to some of your buddies who live farther away and asked them to send you their greetings," I said, turning the page. "They sent you these pictures of themselves and their families, along with letters to tell you what they're up to. Steve Thompson sent this picture."

"Remember him?" Joe asked. "The guy who was always whistling, especially when he was nervous? We used to tell him to shut up or the Nazis would hear him."

I saw Jimmy nod slightly and took that as an encouraging sign. "I'll read part of Steve's letter to you:

"I'm back home with my wife now and my little daughter, who I got to see again, thanks to you. I was away for so long that she didn't remember me. Anita and I have another baby on the way . . . I owe you my life, Jim. I'm still trying to forget the war, and with Anita's help, I'm slowly doing that. I hope we'll all be able to leave the war behind for good, one of these days, but in the meantime, if you do think back on those days, remember me and all the other men who are still able to enjoy life because of you."

I glanced at Jimmy and didn't see a reaction. I waited a moment, then pointed to the next photograph. "Chuck Lawson wrote to you, too."

"Hey, wasn't he the mooch who was always bumming cigarettes from everyone?" Joe asked. Jimmy stared at the picture and nodded.

"Anyway, here's what Chuck said:

"We went through the very worst together, Jim. I'll never forget you and the others because I'll never be as close to another group of buddies as I was to all of you guys. I have you and Frank to thank for getting me off the field after I was hit by sniper fire. You are true heroes. They tell me you're feeling pretty low, and I admit that I was, too, for about a year after I was wounded. There are still a lot of things I can't talk about. But life gets better, Jim—I promise. The war will always be with us, but the farther forward you go from it, the smaller it will seem in the rearview mirror."

Jimmy shifted on the bench as if the stone was starting to feel uncomfortable. I could tell he was growing agitated, and I hurried on. "I saved this letter for last," I told him, "because I thought his advice was really good. It's from Dave Moyers.

"Give my regards to Tripod when you see him. Your stories about that dog gave us all a good laugh, along with hope. It's been hard to go from being on the high alert of warfare to being back in my hometown where nothing much ever happens. I want to forget everything, yet sometimes it seems like I'm dishonoring the guys who gave so much if I simply return to the life I had before the war. At the same time, I owe it to them to be happy and to live at my very best because they can't.

I hear you're not doing too well, Jim, and I'm sorry. My advice to you and our other friends who are having a rough time is to remember the good things we learned and let go of the rest. We grew up fast and became men over there. Remember the value of working together as a team. Remember how we battled against a great evil and helped defeat it. Keep the positive things from the past, savor the present, and look forward to the future. That's what we did during the war, remember? If we hadn't been able to put yesterday's defeats behind us and picture tomorrow's victory, we never could have endured the present.

Last of all, be sure to let the people who love you help you out. Don't be afraid to ask for or accept their help. We couldn't have fought the war alone, Jim, and we certainly can't recover from it alone, either."

There were more pictures in the album, but Jimmy closed it after I read Dave's letter as if he'd seen enough. I was glad that he'd allowed me to read as much as he had.

Joe cleared his throat. "That's good advice, Jim. I guess I needed to hear it, too, you know?" He seemed as restless as Jimmy.

I summoned my courage to say the words that I had practiced last night. "You've always had a huge heart, Jimmy. You were always helping other people. I can't even count the ways you helped me. And Buster is living proof that you won't give up until you've tried everything. These letters say the same thing. You did more than carry stretchers. You carried the responsibility for your friends on your shoulders, too, and I think the weight got too heavy for you. It wore you out."

I took a deep breath and released it before continuing. "I'm worried that you're still carrying that load. That's why I wrote to your friends. So you'd see that they're okay now and you don't have to carry their wounds and their pain anymore. You can take it off your shoulders and lay it down. And then, like your friend Dave said, you can start imagining your future." I reopened the album to the first page. "That's why I took these pictures of the clinic and Blue Fence Farms. That was the life you'd planned before the war. You wanted to be a veterinarian and work with your father. You can dream of that future again."

Joe stood abruptly and glanced around. The rain had stopped, and other patients and visitors were starting to come outside. "I think I'd better take off with Tripod before somebody sees him," he said. "It was good seeing you again, Jim. You take care now."

I wondered if it was something I'd said that had disturbed him. I stood as well. I had promised Joe that we wouldn't stay very long, and he obviously wanted to leave. I walked inside with Jimmy, leaving the photo album and letters with him as he waited for his parents.

The sun peeked from behind the clouds as I joined the line of cars to board the ferry. Dave Moyer's advice about looking toward the future made me wonder about my own future. What did I want for it, besides seeing Jimmy get well? I realized that I didn't have any dreams. I listened to Joe's snores after we crossed the river, and it occurred to me that as far as I knew, Joe didn't have any dreams for the future, either. Sleeping and getting drunk were his ways of escaping the past and enduring the present.

* * *

I was exercising the dogs in the boarding kennels on Monday when Mrs. Barnett came hurrying outside, calling to me. "Peggy, I just got a call from Paul Dixon out at Blue Fence Farms. They have an emergency with one of their horses and Gordon is already out at Halfpenny Farm with another emergency. Would you be able to go out and help until he comes?"

"Me?" I felt a surge of panic. I had accompanied Mr. Barnett on emergencies, but I'd never handled one by myself. "Are . . . are you sure?"

"Yes. Gordon says to please hurry. He'll get there as soon as he can."

My legs felt wobbly as I ran home to get the car I always drove, not sure I could carry the weight of this new responsibility. But the car was gone. I found Pop and Joe in the garage, working on a truck. "I need the car for an emergency, and it's gone, Pop!"

He barely glanced up. "Donna has it. When do you need it?"

"Right now! Mr. Barnett asked me to go out to Blue Fence Farms for an emergency. I need to leave right away! When will Donna be back?" Pop shrugged and shook his head. I huffed in frustration. Mr. B. was counting on me.

Joe must have seen how desperate I was. "Hey, I can take you on my motorcycle." He wiped his hands on the coveralls Pop had loaned him and hurried into the office to fetch his keys. I climbed onto the seat behind him, and for once I didn't complain about how fast he drove. I needed to get there in a hurry, but at the same time, I hoped and prayed that Mr. Barnett's truck would already be there. He'd gone ahead and bought the new one that he had hoped Jimmy would pick out with him.

The truck wasn't there. My fear threatened to take over as a stable boy led me into the barn. Paul Dixon was waiting outside Persephone's stall. The young mare looked nervous and weary. This was her first foal. "Mr. Barnett said he would send for you," Paul said. "Thanks for coming."

"I-I'm happy to help." I wiped my sweaty palms on my overalls. "What can I do?"

"Well, Persephone is having contractions, but they aren't producing any results. The foal must not be positioned right, but she won't let anyone get close enough to help her. I've seen you work with her before. She likes you. You calmed her right down that time Mr. Barnett needed to have a look at her."

"I-I'll do my best." Persephone was one of my favorite horses, and my concern for her helped overshadow my nervousness. She needed me.

The stable boy brought me soap and a bucket of water and I scrubbed my arms and hands. Then I stood where Persephone could see me and started talking to her in a soothing voice. I took my time in spite of the urgency of the situation, moving slowly until she let me get close enough to stroke her neck. I was no longer thinking about needing Mr. Barnett but about what I needed to do and about calming the horse in her fear and pain. I had seen Mr. Barnett reposition animals in the uterus before, and he'd once coached me through the process with twin lambs. He'd said I was better able to do it because my hands were smaller.

I continued soothing Persephone and stroking her. Then I waited until a contraction ended and quickly slipped my hand inside. I groped around, and once I figured out where the foal's legs and head were, I could tell that it was lying sideways. I felt for the head again and made my way down its neck and shoulder, looking for a good place to grab and turn it into a better position. Each contraction squeezed my arm so tightly that I grimaced in pain.

"You can do it, girl. It's going to be okay," I murmured to the horse— and maybe to myself. Sweat poured into my eyes as I pushed and tugged. Then, just like that, everything fell into place. The foal's head and front legs moved into a position to be born, and nature could take its course. I removed my arm and a moment later, Persephone lay down on her side in the straw, grunting softly. Before long, the foal's head and front legs began to emerge. Within minutes, the new little filly was born. Tears filled my eyes, as they always did when I watched the miracle of birth. I stepped back to let Persephone tend her new baby.

"Great job, Peggy!" Paul breathed. I looked up in surprise. I had been so intent on my work that I'd forgotten anyone else was there. "You just saved two very expensive thoroughbreds," he said. I looked around and saw that Joe had also been watching from the doorway. I washed in the bucket and dried off with the towel the stable boy handed me.

Mr. Barnett came in just then to check on the new arrival, and Paul praised my work. "She calmed Persephone right down and repositioned the foal."

Mr. Barnett surprised me with a hug. "I couldn't have done it better myself, Peggy. Thanks."

I was amazed by what I'd done when I thought about it. I'd been so focused that I hadn't had time to get nervous.

"You were amazing," Joe said as we walked back to where he'd parked his motorcycle. "I've never seen anything like it before."

"It never gets old, you know? Watching babies being born." I was still feeling emotional, and my adrenaline was soaring.

"Hey, you said you needed a job, so why don't you do this for a living? You're good at it. And you seem to like it. I don't know very many people who'd want to stick their arm where you just did."

"I'm not a licensed veterinarian. It takes years of study and a lot of money to become one. And how would I support Buster and myself in the meantime? It's just not possible."

"You didn't seem to need a license to help that horse."

"Jimmy's father has taught me a lot in the years I've been working for him. He always explained what he was doing so I could learn."

"Well, I've never seen anything like that."

Joe went straight into the garage when we got back, bursting with excitement. He wouldn't let me leave and go upstairs until he'd told Pop in great detail what he'd just witnessed. "I've never seen anything like it," he said again. Pop looked at us as if Joe was making it all up. I couldn't help smiling.

Then Donna, who'd been working in Pop's office, joined us. "Oh, good. You're back," she said. "I have news. I just put in a good word for you with Mr. Edmonds down at the drugstore. His daughter is getting married and he's hiring someone to replace her."

I knew Joanie Edmonds. She was one of the girls who used to torment me in school and insist that I had cooties.

"It's full-time, waiting on customers and things like that. And the pay is good. I told him all about you, and he said to come in right away. The job is as good as yours."

I felt a rising panic. I'd learned to avoid the townspeople as much as possible after suffering years of ridicule as the "dog girl." Even worse, I lived beneath a shadow of shame because Pop and Donna were living together without being married. Everyone in the village knew about their sin, which was probably why I was never invited to the other girls' parties and sleepovers. The thought of facing my neighbors with a cheerful smile in the pharmacy every day made my stomach squeeze. Besides, I would have to quit working at the clinic, and after experiencing the rush of delivering a foal today, I didn't want to quit. I had missed it terribly during the years I'd worked at the IBM plant.

"I'll look into it," I told Donna. I wanted to go upstairs but she was blocking the way.

She put her hands on her hips and lifted her chin. "Why that face? Don't tell me you're going to let this perfectly good job slip away!"

"I said I'd look into it."

She held out the car keys. "Go today. Before he hires someone else."

I ignored her outstretched hand and gestured to the work clothes I was still wearing. "I need to get cleaned up first. And I can walk there."

I cried as I soaked in the bathtub and didn't know why. Was it remembering Joanie Edmonds's ridicule so soon after my success with Persephone? Was it the thought of giving up a job I loved? Or was it because Donna made me feel the same way that mean girls like Joanie always had—unwanted and rejected? Perhaps it was all of those things.

I went across the street to the Barnetts' house after my bath, telling myself it was only to see if more letters had arrived from Jimmy's friends. But in reality, it was because I craved the warmth and love that Mrs. Barnett always showed me. "Did everything go all right out at the horse farm?" she asked as she handed me two new letters. "I'm sorry we sprang it on you so suddenly."

"I didn't mind going. And yes, everything went fine. I was able to help one of the mares who was having a difficult labor."

She gave me the hug I'd been longing for, and we sat down at the kitchen table to open the letters. One of them was from Chaplain Bill, who'd sent a new batch of addresses. He also explained the plans for Mitch O'Hara's memorial service, which were taking shape. Mitch's family lived in a small town outside of Binghamton, only a few hours' drive from here. All we needed, Bill said, was permission for Jimmy to be released for a day so he could attend.

Another letter was from Dr. Morton Greenberg, who turned out to be one of the doctors Jimmy had worked alongside in Bastogne. In short, concise sentences, he wrote about their experiences there and how the tragedy had affected him. He urged Jimmy not to let the war destroy his faith in God or mankind. "Maybe Dr. Greenberg remembers the name of the Belgian nurse who was killed when the aid station was bombed," I said when I finished reading. "Maybe she was Gisela."

"The mystery woman in the photograph?" Mrs. Barnett asked.

"Yes. So far, none of Jimmy's friends has recognized her. But if Gisela is that nurse, maybe we can hold a memorial service for her at the same time that we honor Mitch."

According to the letterhead on the doctor's stationery, his medical practice was in Bergenfield, New Jersey. I wanted answers, and waiting to send and receive another letter from him would take too long. "Do you know where Bergenfield, New Jersey, is, Mrs. Barnett? Maybe Joe and I could drive there tomorrow."

"Gordon keeps some road maps here in the junk drawer," she replied. She stood to dig through it and found one for New Jersey. We unfolded it and spread it out on the table. Bergenfield was about seventy miles away.

"May I borrow this map?" I asked.

"Certainly." We were trying to refold it and laughing about how impossible it was to get it flat again, when Mr. Barnett arrived home.

"Thanks again for helping today, Peggy. Very well-done! Paul Dixon was impressed with your skill."

"I learned from the best," I said, smiling at him. "And I'm glad to help, anytime." We chatted for a few minutes and Mrs. Barnett told him about Chaplain Bill's plans for the memorial service.

"We need to get permission for Jimmy leave the hospital for a day," I added. "Do you think that's possible?"

"I'll call Dr. Morgan today and ask for an appointment. He never gave us a follow-up report after starting the shock treatments. If you're able to come with Martha and me, you can explain about the memorial service."

The thought of explaining anything to the fearsome Dr. Morgan gave me the willies, but I nodded and said, "I'll be happy to come."

I pulled Joe aside to talk in private when I got home, and he agreed to take me to New Jersey on his motorcycle tomorrow. We would sneak away early so I could avoid an argument with Donna. The job at the pharmacy could wait one more day.

* * *

Riding seventy miles on the back of Joe's motorcycle left me jangled and stressed. But I never would have gotten past the busy doctor's receptionist without Joe. He could talk the apples right off the tree with his charm and good looks, and he convinced the fluttery young schedule keeper to sneak us in for a quick chat between patients.

Dr. Greenberg was older than I'd expected, in his forties I guessed, with alert brown eyes and thick black hair that he combed straight back. He and Joe had never met, but as soon as I mentioned Corporal Jim Barnett, he gave us his full attention. "How is Jim doing?"

"He isn't any better, I'm afraid. Thank you for writing to him. We came today because you mentioned working with Jimmy in Bastogne.

Another medic told us there were two Belgian nurses who volunteered there and that one of them was killed."

"Yes. A terrible tragedy."

"I wondered if you remembered that nurse's name? The reason I'm asking is because Jimmy carried this picture in his rucksack and we're trying to figure out who she is and if she played a part in his breakdown." I took it from my bag and showed it to him. He put on a pair of dark-framed glasses and took his time studying it. I could tell he was searching his memory.

"I don't think I recognize her. I'm sorry. Those were long, desperate days, so it's hard to remember many details. But I don't think this is the nurse we worked with." He handed it back and removed his glasses.

"It says on the back that her name is Gisela."

He slowly shook his head as he thought about it some more, then suddenly said, "Renée! The Belgian nurse's name was Renée. I remember now. The soldiers gave her a parachute to use for a wedding gown."

I had reached another dead end in my search for Gisela. We thanked the doctor for his time, and he let me take his picture for Jimmy's scrapbook. I was about to leave when I turned back and said, "May I ask you one more question? You saw the same things that Jimmy did day after day—how were you able to get past the war and resume your life again? Because Jimmy hasn't been able to do that."

Again, he took a moment to reply. "It helped that I had a job and a family waiting for me back home. Both required my full attention and didn't leave me much time to contemplate the horrors I'd seen. I'd also had the unfortunate experience of losing patients before the war. It never gets easy, but it destroys any illusions one has about the permanence of life and the finality of death. Jim may not have been prepared for those lessons."

"Thanks again, Dr. Greenberg."

"You're welcome. Jim is a good man." I was almost through the door when the doctor called to me. "One more thing. Jim was a man of strong faith, able to see the larger, spiritual picture. Have you considered the idea that this might be a crisis of faith along with nervous exhaustion or battle fatigue?"

I realized that he might be right. "We haven't. Thank you." I was sure his psychiatrist hadn't considered it, either. I needed to talk with Chaplain Bill again.

* * *

I had every intention of dragging myself down to Edmonds' Drugstore the next day to apply for the job, but as I was doing my morning chores at the clinic, Mr. Barnett told me that he had arranged for an appointment with Dr. Morgan today, right after lunch. We were barely seated in the doctor's smoky office when he lit a cigarette and proceeded to berate us for trying to leave a photograph album and a pile of letters with Jimmy. "Patients in the corporal's condition are not allowed to have any personal items."

His stern lecture made my heart speed up. I was about to apologize and take full blame when Mr. Barnett said, "What is Jim's condition? That's what we've come here to find out." I could tell from his tone and the way he sat forward in his seat that he wanted answers and he wasn't going to let the doctor talk down to us. Most people, including the Barnetts and me, held doctors in very high esteem and we would never dare to question their decisions or expertise. But we were all losing faith in Dr. Morgan's treatments. They weren't helping Jimmy.

"Corporal Barnett suffers from extreme depression, emotional withdrawal, and suicidal ideation. His weakened physical condition is exacerbated by a lack of appetite and recurring nightmares that disrupt his sleep. They're apparently so bad that he forces himself to remain awake, causing sleep deprivation."

"And the shock treatments? Have they helped?"

Dr. Morgan inhaled on his cigarette and blew out a stream of smoke, making us wait. "We're still assessing the treatment's effectiveness, which is why I haven't notified you yet."

"It's been a few weeks. It seems to me that we should know if they're having an effect by now." I could tell that Dr. Morgan didn't like being put on the defensive. He tapped the ash from his cigarette. He was losing patience—but so were we.

"If you recall, I originally said that the electrotherapy treatments would last between two and six weeks. We don't see many patients as severely depressed as Corporal Barnett. He remains on suicide watch at all times."

"It's just that we haven't noticed much change in our son's condition, either, and it seems cruel to keep shocking his brain if—"

"I'll let you know when our team has completed our assessment and recommendations." He snuffed out his half-finished cigarette. Apparently our time was up. "Now, if there's nothing else—"

"There is," Mr. Barnett said. "Jim and his college roommate enlisted in the Army together, trained together, and fought alongside each other in Europe. Jim was there when Mitch was killed in Belgium. Their Army chaplain and some friends from their unit are planning a memorial service to honor Mitch. We'd like to check Jim out of the hospital for the day so he can attend."

The doctor started shaking his head before Mr. Barnett even finished his sentence. "I don't recommend you do that. Patients suffering from depression often find it difficult to adjust to new situations and environments."

"Well, the goal isn't for him to adjust to living in this hospital, is it? We hope to be able to bring him home for good."

"If that's your goal, and you don't want him to remain institutionalized or risk another suicide attempt, then I know of only one other treatment that would make it possible." I feared he was going to suggest the water torture Joe had described, and I was getting ready to protest. Instead, Dr. Morgan said, "Psychosurgery. It's a relatively simple surgical procedure, in which the patient's frontal lobes are severed and—"

"Are you suggesting a lobotomy?" Mr. Barnett nearly leaped from his chair.

"It's being done routinely and successfully in veterans' hospitals all across the country. By severing the connections between the patient's mind and his emotions, he is able to live the rest of his life calmly and at peace. You could bring him home with the expectation that he would be too docile to try to hurt himself again."

"We don't want him docile; we want him well!" Mr. Barnett shouted. Mrs. Barnett rested her hand on his arm as if trying to calm him.

"Then I suggest you be patient and give the electrotherapy treatments more time."

Mr. Barnett was still struggling with his anger. He stood, and when he spoke, his voice was quiet but still firm. "Let your staff know that we will be taking Jim away for a day to attend his friend's memorial service. And we will *never* give our consent to any surgical procedures. Good day." Mrs. Barnett and I rose with him. I wanted to applaud.

16

Gisela

MARCH 1943

I never felt fully settled in my new home or with my new nursing position after moving from Antwerp. My life had changed so many times since closing the door on our apartment in Berlin four years ago, with so many hopes and disappointments along the way, that this change didn't seem permanent, either. Not only was I separated from everyone I loved, I lived with the constant fear of being betrayed and arrested. The roundup of Jews continued, and as much as I longed to see Sam and my parents, I didn't want the generous people who were helping me to be discovered and arrested, too. I didn't visit Ruthie in the orphanage for the same reason. I would never forgive myself if I caused her to be arrested. Instead, I focused on my work at Hospital Sint-Augustinus and avoided making friends with the other nurses at work and in the rooming house where I lived.

The war continued to rage, but I didn't know many details of the battles and victories. No one trusted the Nazi-run newspapers to tell the truth. By listening to the conversations in the hospital lounge, I'd learned that the seemingly unstoppable Nazis had suffered a setback last fall when General Rommel was defeated in Egypt. And in February of this year, the Nazis were defeated by the Soviets in Stalingrad. By now, the war had spread across the entire globe, and I guessed from the amount of activity in the skies overhead and the ever-familiar sound of air-raid sirens that it was far from over.

Sam had promised to contact me through Sister Veronica, but he hadn't. And I had promised to visit my sister. In March, my longing to see someone I loved became so overwhelming that I set off from my boardinghouse on a Sunday afternoon to visit Ruthie, taking the trolley most of the way and walking the rest. The village of Mortsel, where the orphanage was located, looked as bedraggled and beaten down as the rest of Belgium, but at least the streets were peaceful on that chilly spring day. I was excited to see Ruthie and also a little nervous, hoping she would understand why I hadn't visited sooner, hoping she would forgive me. I was not prepared to be turned away on the orphanage's doorstep.

"Sorry, but you need official authorization in order to visit any of our orphans."

I stood my ground, and after explaining myself several times to various underlings who had come out to the front entrance to send me away, I insisted that Sister Marie, the orphanage's director, be told my name. After another long wait, I was finally taken inside and left to wait in the dark, narrow hallway outside her office like a penitent waiting to confess. I heard the sound of children at play in the distance. At last, Sister Marie invited me inside. She took a seat behind her desk and offered me a chair, but I was too upset to sit down. I told her why I'd come.

"I understand the reason for your request, Miss Maes," she replied. "But I'm afraid we cannot grant it."

A sudden dread filled me. "Why not? Where's Ruthie? Has something happened to her?"

"Not at all. Ruth Anne has had a difficult time adapting here, but in the last several weeks, she has finally settled in. I cannot allow your visit to disrupt her again."

"But I promised my sister that I would visit her! Sister Veronica arranged for me to work at Hospital Sint-Augustinus so I would be nearby and—"

"Sister Veronica runs the nursing school, not this orphanage. I'm sorry."

I battled to contain my outrage but it boiled over. "Is it any wonder my sister finds it hard to adjust? Ruthie and I are like hunted animals, living in constant fear, separated from our home and our family, hiding among strangers who we have to rely on for help! All we have left is each other! I need to let her know that I'm still here! That I love her!"

"You must calm down, Miss Maes," she said sternly. "I won't be shouted at." She waited a few moments until my breathing slowed before continuing. "Ruth Anne is supposed to be an orphan, remember? How will she explain who you are to the other children? Informants who betray Jews in hiding receive a bounty from the Nazis. If you're seen with her and someone contacts the authorities, we will all suffer the consequences. Your sister isn't the only Jewish child we're sheltering, you know."

I couldn't reply. I was so frustrated that I considered standing firm and refusing to leave until I saw her. Or if that failed, bursting into tears and appealing to her sense of compassion. But Sister Marie didn't have a sweet, kind face like Sister Veronica. In fact, she reminded me of the rottweiler our neighbors in Berlin once owned. I didn't know how she would react if I became stubborn. Or if she would make Ruthie suffer for my tantrum.

"Is there anything else?" she asked. She stood and gave me a look that clearly said I needed to leave, as she had work to do.

I thought of one more thing. "If I write my sister a note, will you give it to her? I want her to know I tried to keep my promise to visit her. Otherwise, she'll think I've abandoned her like everyone else has. The only thing that keeps me from giving in to despair some days is knowing I still have a sister. I still have a reason to keep living."

Sister Marie hesitated for so long that I thought she was going to refuse. But she finally opened her desk drawer and removed a pen and piece of stationery. She waited—impatiently, I thought—while I wrote the note. I folded it into a square when I finished and printed Ruthie's name on it. I wondered if she would ever get it.

"Change the name to Ruth Anne, please," Sister Marie said. "That's her name now. Ruth Anne Mertens."

"May I write to her again? Will you at least see that she gets my letters if I mail them to her? And maybe she can write back to me?"

"Try to understand, none of our other orphans receive mail. If they had relatives to exchange letters with, why would they be in our orphanage?"

* * *

The sadness I felt after my futile visit lingered for days. I felt cut off from everyone I loved. When I could no longer bear the silence, I wrote a letter to Sister Veronica. She surely must have heard the news that the Jews in Belgium were being transported to work camps in the east. She must be distressed by it, too. I asked her if there was any way she could check on my parents for me. Were they still in Antwerp? Had they gone into hiding? If they had been transported, could she find out where they'd been taken? I gave her my parents' address near the train station and added the name of the Gentile landlord who'd purchased the apartment building. He had been very kind to us. He might have answers. I also added a postscript, asking if she'd had any news from Sam. Weeks passed, and I was still waiting for her reply.

I was working in the women's ward in the hospital on a sunny afternoon in early April with an hour remaining on my shift when air-raid sirens began to sound. There wasn't much we could do when that happened except to brace ourselves and hope that the large red cross on the building's roof would prevent enemy airplanes from targeting us. Even so, I felt a shiver of panic each time the alarm sounded. I removed the blood pressure cuff from my patient's arm and waited, listening.

Then, above the wailing sirens, came the droning roar of aircraft. It grew louder, closer. I crossed to the window and looked out, and what

I saw made my heart stop. Airplanes filled the sky like an enormous flock of birds, too many to count. I'd never seen so many before. And so close! They didn't look like the Luftwaffe planes that I'd seen landing and taking off regularly at a local airstrip. The Nazis were using a former car factory in Mortsel to repair their planes.

The sudden rattle of antiaircraft fire from the ground confirmed that these were Allied planes. Then the first bombs began to fall, followed by thundering explosions that made the windows rattle. Not one or two bombs, but an endless chain of powerful explosions. The blasts boomed and rumbled and thundered on and on as if the entire world might explode. My pulse accelerated. Bombs had never fallen this close before. Plumes of black smoke billowed in the distance above Mortsel. Where Ruthie was.

"Oh, God, please! No!"

The hospital lights flickered and dimmed, then blinked off. Panicked patients called, "Nurse! Nurse!" as sirens continued to scream outside and bombs exploded and roared. My instincts told me to run, but there was no place to go. Why were the Americans bombing us?

I moved away from the window as the deafening explosions continued, my heart racing, my stomach heaving. The ward matron hurried from her station to assure the patients that all would be well, but she began herding any ambulatory patients who wanted to flee to safety down to the basement, just in case. They would have to use the stairs. The elevator was inoperable without electricity. The more seriously ill patients, like most of the ones I tended in this ward, had to stay where they were. The elderly woman whose vital signs I had just taken called me to her bedside. She had tears in her eyes as she asked me to pray with her. I held her hand while we recited the Lord's Prayer together. "Forgive us our debts . . . Deliver us from evil . . ."

It seemed like hours passed before the bombing raid ended and the roar of planes faded into the distance. The rattling antiaircraft fire and wailing sirens ceased. For a moment, the silence that fell seemed as deafening as the bombs. No one moved. Then a commotion started up in the hallway outside the ward. The lights were still off, but I heard telephones ringing and people running. I went to the door and saw doctors and nurses and nuns scurrying around. The matron beckoned to me and I joined a group that had gathered around her in the corridor. "Reports are coming in of catastrophic civilian casualties in Mortsel. At least two schools filled with children were hit. Every available doctor and nurse is needed."

Ruthie's school was in Mortsel.

There was no question that I would volunteer. But I felt such a rush of fear and dread that I wasn't sure how much help I would be. My hands trembled so violently I couldn't manage the buttons on my jacket as I prepared to go. I wobbled when I walked, my legs like jelly. I couldn't string two coherent thoughts together. I followed the others and did what I was told, quickly packing emergency kits and bandages and morphine, then crushing into the back of an ambulance with the other nurses and doctors.

One of the surgeons, Dr. Janssens, briefed us as we drove. "The Americans must have been targeting the Luftwaffe installation but something went terribly wrong. Hundreds of bombs fell on the center of Mortsel, in the area called Oude God. We have calls from four schools now, and the town's residential areas were also heavily hit."

I closed my eyes and prayed for my sister as we hurtled through the streets, alarm bells clanging. At last we halted. So much rubble clogged the streets that the ambulances couldn't get any closer. I struggled to push my dizziness and shock aside, grabbing my supplies and following the others, walking forward as if in a nightmare. I had seen Mortsel and the Oude God area a few months ago when I'd tried to visit Ruthie, but it was unrecognizable now. It resembled a scene from hell, bombed into oblivion. Bodies and parts of bodies lay scattered everywhere. Shouts from the workers along with pitiful screams and cries for help filled the air.

I struggled to concentrate as Dr. Janssens issued orders. He told us to do whatever we could to bring aid: apply tourniquets to stop bleeding, assess wounds, give injections of morphine, stabilize broken bones, perform triage to decide who needed surgery first. The medical personnel were told to spread out to the hardest-hit areas, and I was assigned to go with Dr. Janssens and three other nurses to St. Vincent School. We set off in that direction, dodging huge chunks of debris and downed trolley lines. Thick smoke from burning cars made my eyes water. I knew I needed to pull myself together, but all I could think about was Ruthie. Surely God wouldn't take her from me, too. Not after all we'd been through. Not in such a horrifying way.

We reached what was left of the school, and the sight of three small, lifeless bodies lying in the street overwhelmed me. I froze, paralyzed with horror. Workers were digging more bodies out of the rubble while teachers and distraught parents, blackened with soot and dust, screamed and wept. Someone grabbed my shoulders and shook me. "Nurse! Get ahold of yourself! You're needed over here." A group of children that the workers had rescued from the rubble were still alive. I prayed for strength and clarity of mind and went to work, applying all of my skill and training to help each child as if she were Ruthie.

Hours passed. I did what I could. We transported the most desperate cases to the hospital, with volunteers carrying them through the debris to the ambulances on stretchers. We set up a makeshift field hospital for those who didn't need immediate surgery or life support. We cleaned and stitched and bandaged thousands of wounds. But the image I knew would haunt my dreams for a long time was that of a mother sitting in the street, holding her lifeless child in her arms. "They were American planes," she wailed. "They were supposed to save us, not kill us!"

It was growing dark and there was no electricity. I was exhausted. Dr. Janssens offered to arrange a ride back to the hospital for me, but I couldn't leave until I found my sister. I asked one of the volunteers who had been digging in the rubble if the children from the orphanage attended this school. He nodded grimly and said, "Yes—poor little beggars."

I took my nurse's bag and what was left of my supplies and walked to the orphanage on the edge of town. It seemed undamaged from the outside but without electricity. A few flickering candles shone from inside. No one stopped me at the door this time. I was still wearing my uniform, filthy with dirt and blood, so I walked inside. The large, barren room that seemed to serve as a lounge was in chaos. There weren't nearly enough sisters to soothe the hysterical children. Those who weren't crying sat dazed with shock, staring straight ahead and shivering. Some held their hands over their ears. I scanned all the faces in the dim light for Ruthie's, but I didn't see her. One of the nuns hurried over to me, carrying a candle. "May I ask who you are and what you're doing here?"

"I-I'm looking for one of the orphans. Ruth . . . Ruth Anne . . ." I couldn't remember her phony surname.

"You'll need to speak with Sister Marie. This way please."

She was in the orphanage's infirmary where the most seriously injured students had been taken. Sister Marie turned to face me. "Did the hospital send you to help?" she asked brusquely. But then she recognized me. She marched out to the hallway, motioning for me to follow her. I spoke before she could.

"I will be very glad to help in any way I can. I've been treating casualties at St. Vincent School all afternoon, but I had to come and make sure Ruthie—"

"She's fine. She was with a group of older students who were on a nature hike today." I leaned against the wall, then slid all the way to the floor, thanking God. "But if you were at St. Vincent, Miss Maes, then you know that dozens of our children have been injured. Many are still missing. A few are confirmed dead. All of them have been traumatized. They saw their friends and teachers injured and dying. We're trying our best to calm them down." She said all of this in a voice tinged with anger, as if it would help me understand why I needed to leave.

I looked up at her from where I sat on the floor. "I'm not leaving until I see my sister. I need to see for myself that she's okay."

"Go into my office." She pointed down the hall. I crawled to my feet and waited in the office doorway, watching for Ruthie. I didn't recognize her at first. Her beautiful, dark hair had been chopped short and she hobbled toward me like an old woman, her legs so thin her knee socks wouldn't stay up. I pulled her into the office and she clung to me as if she'd never let go. She would turn fifteen in a few days, but she looked no more than twelve.

"Thank God. Thank God," I murmured. I couldn't remember thanking Him for anything in a very long time. "Are you okay?" I asked when we finally pulled apart. She nodded. Her eyes in the darkened room were large and filled with sorrow. She had Vati's eyes. His had looked this way when we'd said goodbye. "You weren't hurt when the bombs . . . ?"

"Our teacher took us on a nature walk," she said in a whispery voice. "We heard the planes and then the explosions . . ." Her eyes filled with tears.

I pulled her close again. "Oh, Ruthie!"

"Please don't leave me again, Gisela! Take me with you, please! I don't want to be alone again!"

"I know. I know." I waited for her sobs to die away and led her to the window seat behind Sister Marie's desk. The window was a huge, dark rectangle that showed our reflection, and I wondered how the night could have fallen so swiftly. Then I realized that the window had been painted for the blackout. "If there was any way I could take you with me and we could be together, I would do it, Ruthie. I swear! But we can't let anyone see us together."

"I can stay inside and hide. I don't mind. It's so cold and dark and crowded here."

"I share a room with two other nurses. It's just as dark and crowded there. The radiators don't work very well and the food isn't very good. Believe me, if I knew of another way . . ."

"I don't want to go back to school. I'm scared!"

I stroked her cropped hair the way Mutti used to do when she comforted us. "Your school was destroyed today," I said gently. "No one will be able to go back. It will be summer soon."

"What if they bomb us again?"

"It was a mistake. They meant to bomb the factory where the Nazis repair their airplanes, but something went wrong, and the bombs fell in the wrong place." I rocked her a little longer, rubbing her back.

"When will this war ever end?" she asked.

"We're all asking that question, Ruthie. Right now, no one knows the answer. But did you see all those airplanes the Americans sent today?" A shudder rocked through her as she nodded. "They are just as strong as the Nazis are. Everyone says that the Americans are going to defeat them soon. We just need to be patient."

She was quiet for a long moment as we sat holding each other. "Do you think we'll ever see Vati and Mutti again?" she asked in a tiny voice.

"Only God knows. But no matter what, we still have each other."

I ended up staying through the night. Ruthie and I talked and reminisced, and we both dozed for a bit, curled up on the broad window seat together. Whether Sister Marie forgot about us or whether she was giving us a few hours together, I would never know. But I was grateful. A different nun came in the morning and told Ruthie it was time for breakfast. We hugged and said goodbye, and I left. I needed to go home, bathe, and change my uniform for my day shift at the hospital. My rumbling stomach reminded me I hadn't eaten.

I had to walk through the ruined streets for a long way until I found a trolley line that was still intact. As I stood waiting to board, I realized I didn't have a token. I hadn't thought to bring money or a purse as I had rushed out of the hospital to climb into the ambulance. The conductor looked at me and seemed to take in my disheveled condition.

"You been helping out?" he asked. I could only nod. He gestured for me to climb aboard and he let me ride without paying the fare. I made it home and then to the hospital in time to report for my shift. A news vendor was hawking papers in front of the entrance and I paused to read the headlines. The Nazis were gloating, of course, that the Americans had missed the factory and destroyed a Belgian town. They listed the grim statistics in huge font: thousands had been injured. Nearly ninety were still missing. More than nine hundred people had died so far, including two hundred children. Four schools had been hit. Out of the 3,700 homes in the village of Mortsel, more than 3,400 had been destroyed or heavily damaged.

Later, when it was time for my lunch break, I went into the hospital chapel and knelt on the carpeted kneeler as I had been taught to do. There had been many, many times when I'd been angry with God for everything that my family was suffering. Times when it had been impossible to pray. But today I needed to thank God for sparing Ruthie. A simple school outing to the forest had saved her. Maybe a miracle would save Sam and my parents, too.

I looked up at the man being tortured to death on the crucifix. A Jewish man named Jesus. And I thanked God that this Jewish man's followers were helping us.

17

Peggy

JULY 1946

Three days after Donna told me about the job at the pharmacy, I dressed in my Sunday best and walked into town to apply for it. My anxiety mushroomed as I got closer to the store until I could feel the pressure building in my chest, squeezing my lungs. I hadn't reacted this way when I'd applied at the IBM factory, but then I had been just one among hundreds of women. I didn't know any of the others and they hadn't known me. And I had wanted to help win the war.

A chime sounded when I opened the door. Joanie Edmonds stood behind the counter, straightening a display of Life Savers. She cocked her head to the side in her perky way and smiled her perfect smile. "May I help you, miss?"

Was it possible that she didn't recognize me? I couldn't remember the last time we'd seen each other. Probably not since high school. I usually shopped in neighboring villages to avoid meeting people from town. "I heard you're looking for someone to work here," I said. "I'm Peggy Serrano." Joanie stared at me, her smile frozen as if she couldn't put the familiar name and the unfamiliar face together. I nearly turned around and bolted from the store. Then her eyes widened and she suddenly seemed to recognize the "dog girl" behind the adult facade.

"Oh! Right! *Peggy!* Of course. I'll get you an application." She disappeared into the back. I drew a deep breath and took a moment to look around. The ceiling seemed close enough to touch, the neon lights humming and glowing with an unnatural bluish light. Display shelves crowded together, jam-packed with items like Pepto-Bismol and aspirin and Alka-Seltzer. Two barefoot boys stood beside a rack of magazines near the front window, thumbing through the comic books. I glimpsed Mr. Edmonds behind the window of his raised office, wearing a white jacket and dark-rimmed glasses as he filled prescriptions. A teenage couple sat on swiveling stools at the soda fountain, gazing into each other's eyes and sipping from the same malted milk through two straws.

My panic soared. I couldn't spend eight hours a day trapped in here, smiling at customers and making ice cream sodas. I was used to the outdoors, with open spaces and views of the mountains. When I had worked for Pop, I never stayed in his office a moment longer than I had to. And the only reason I could work inside the IBM plant all day was because I had wanted to help win the war.

Joanie returned with the application and a pen. "You can sit at the soda fountain and fill it out if you want to, *Peggy*." She emphasized my name as if to let me know that she recognized me now. I wondered if she was going to bark and howl at me like she used to do.

My hand shook as I took the application from her. "Thanks. I'll fill it out at home and bring it back."

My hands were still shaking when I got home. I fixed myself a glass of Kool-Aid and sat in the backyard with Buster to read through the application. They wanted to know about my education and my work experience, and I was supposed to list three people as references. I had gotten no further than filling in my name and birth date when Joe came around from the garage in his coveralls, a bottle of beer in his hand.

"I'm taking a little break," he said, lifting the bottle. He tapped it against my glass of Kool-Aid as if we were toasting and sat down on the apartment steps. He purchased his own six-packs of beer now and drank it warm rather than trying to limp up and down the steps to our refrigerator every time he wanted one. "Hey, they drink their beer warm over in Europe," he had explained. "You get used to it." Joe still worked in the garage with Pop even though he must have enough money for gas by now. Every day I wondered when he would take off and if I would ever see him again.

"Hey, what you got there?" he asked.

"It's an application for the job at the pharmacy."

"You don't sound too excited about it."

"I'm not. I'm no good around people, Joe. I've been alone too long. And I hate the idea of being cooped up inside that lousy store all day."

"Then why are you doing it?"

"I need a job. A full-time one. Donna wants me to move out so she can have the apartment and Pop all to herself."

He shook his head, staring down at his feet. "She doesn't treat you right."

"Pop is on her side. He says it's time I moved out on my own, and I know he's right. I'm not a kid anymore." I needed to change the subject before I got teary. I didn't want Joe's pity. "By the way, you're still planning to go to Mitch O'Hara's memorial service on Sunday, right? Jimmy's father is getting him out of the hospital for the day. Frank Cishek and Chaplain Bill will be there, and I think a few more of your old buddies, too."

"Yeah, sure." Joe didn't sound very enthusiastic. I watched him drain the bottle in two more gulps.

"You knew Mitch, didn't you?"

"Heck of a nice guy. He didn't deserve what he got."

"I'm really hoping that honoring him and taking time to grieve for him will help Jimmy somehow. Maybe he'll start responding to people again or at least tell us what's causing his nightmares. When we talked with Jimmy's doctor at the VA the other day, he told us they're doing surgery on veterans' brains now, supposedly to cure their battle fatigue—"

Joe sprang to his feet, interrupting me. "Don't let them do that to Jim! I've seen some of those guys who had their brains cut in half."

"A lobotomy?"

"Yeah. The guys who had it done shuffled around as if they were sleepwalking! I didn't know any of them before the war, but it seemed pretty clear to me that there was nothing left of them now. Jim would be better off dead! Don't let them do it!"

The idea that Jimmy would be in a daze for the rest of his life made me shiver. My heart went out to the men who'd had the surgery. And to their families. "Jimmy's father spoke right up and told the doctor that he'd never allow it. But Dr. Morgan seemed to think it was the only way Jimmy would ever be able to come home again. I know how much you hated it there in the hospital and I can't stand the thought of him—"

"Hey, it's time to get him out of there. If I can get better on my own, Jim can, too."

But was Joe really getting better? He drank too much, he still had nightmares, he rode around the country aimlessly on his motorcycle, and his future seemed as pointless as mine. I remembered Dr. Greenberg saying that his job and his family kept him moving forward, and I realized that I'd never asked Joe about his family or what he'd done before the war. Did he have any dreams for his future back then?

"What did you do before the war, Joe?" I was staring out at the weeds and junked cars when I asked the question, but Joe took so long to reply that I turned to him in alarm. "Did I ask the wrong thing? I'm sorry. It's none of my business—"

"No, that's okay," he said quietly. Buster was leaning against Joe with his head in Joe's lap. I waited, and when Joe finally replied, he spoke so softly I barely heard him. "I was a firefighter."

A firefighter. It took a moment for me to digest what losing his leg had meant to Joe. No wonder he hadn't resumed his job. No wonder he was wandering aimlessly. He had every right in the world to be angry. "Oh, Joe. I'm so sorry."

"It's all I ever wanted to be, you know?" He twisted the empty bottle in his hands and I wondered if he was going to hurl it as hard and as far as he could. "I was eight years old the first time I visited the fire station. I had an uncle who was a firefighter. He let me stand on the ladder truck for a second, and I knew that's what I wanted to be. Hey, I know a lot of kids say that, but I really meant it. I signed on right after high school and served for nearly four years until I enlisted."

I waited a moment, then asked, "What did you love about it, Joe?" I hoped it would help if he talked about it, yet I didn't want to hurt him.

"The adrenaline rush, of course," he said with a crooked grin. "The challenge of it. You never know what to expect. Each fire is different, no two are the same, and you never know what you'll find when you get there. You learn as you go, until you finally get an instinct for what the fire is going to do and how to beat it."

I struggled to say something comforting or to suggest a similar line of work and offer him hope, but I couldn't think of a single job that would be the same.

"It was like being in the Army in a lot of ways, you know?" he continued. "The other men become your brothers, your family. You eat together, sleep, cook, and shoot the breeze, share the same quarters for a twelve-hour shift. You get to know them like you know yourself. You have to so you'll be ready to work together and fight fires. You get so you trust these guys with your life, and they're trusting you with theirs. You'd risk your life for any of them."

He paused, still twisting the bottle. I waited the way Jimmy used to do when he listened to me, not wanting to intrude on Joe's thoughts with worthless words. "I went from working at the fire station, straight into basic training, and bonded with the guys in my company, you know? Jim and Mitch and Frank and Dave." He gave a little laugh. "All the way across the Atlantic on a troop transport, jammed into bunks . . . Then the day came when we landed in France. It was a shock, let me tell you, when the bullets started flying and you realize that someone is trying to kill you. As a firefighter, you always know that a fire flare or a collapsing building could kill you, too. But it's the brotherhood that gives you the courage to keep going, you know? You don't want to let them down."

"And you've lost all of that," I murmured. "The brotherhood of soldiers and firefighters."

"Yeah."

I could see that he wanted more beer but his was empty—as empty as his life must seem after the war. He had nothing to return home to. I wondered if he'd found a sense of purpose for a time by working with me and Chaplain Bill and the others to help Jimmy. Still, it must be hard to remember the camaraderie they'd shared and hear their advice about moving forward into the future. I remembered how upset Joe had become when I had talked to Jimmy about returning to the clinic and working as a veterinarian. Joe got drunk to erase the past that had taken away his future. No wonder he had nightmares of the moment he'd lost his leg. It was the moment he had lost himself.

"I'm so sorry, Joe," I said again.

"When you're good at something, and you enjoy it—like you with that horse the other day—you ought to be allowed to do it." He pulled himself to his feet and sighed. "Guess I'll get cleaned up and take off this evening." He was going to go out drinking, and it was my fault for stirring his memories and his sorrow.

I stood as well. "May I come with you tonight? You offered to take me once before and—"

"I don't want your pity."

"That's not why—"

"Yes, it is. Another time, maybe." He walked back to the garage. An hour later I heard his motorcycle roar away. I shuddered to think that he would try to re-create the adrenaline rush of fighting fires by driving too fast on our curving mountain roads.

On Sunday, I rode to the veterans' hospital with Mr. and Mrs. Barnett, but instead of visiting Jimmy, we checked him out of the hospital for Mitch O'Hara's memorial service. Mr. Barnett had phoned ahead and told them to make sure Jimmy was dressed and ready to go. Jimmy seemed confused as we led him through the corridors and out the front door. He halted in the parking lot and looked around at the river and distant mountains as if he'd never seen them before. I heard him draw a deep breath. The air smelled of newly mown grass.

"I know this might be hard for you, Jim," Mr. Barnett said as we drove. "But we're taking you to a memorial service for your friend Mitch O'Hara." Jimmy was riding in the front seat beside his father, so I couldn't see his face when he learned where we were going. His father waited a moment before continuing. "It's being held in his hometown, and Mitch's family will be there. You went home with Mitch a couple of times when you were roommates at Cornell, remember?" Again, he left space for Jimmy to comment, but he didn't. "Mitch is buried in Belgium, in the Ardennes American Cemetery. I'm told that many of the soldiers and airmen who are buried there also died in the Battle of the Bulge, like he did. Your company chaplain, Reverend Ashburn, made all of the arrangements for the service."

"And your friends Joe Fiore and Frank Cishek are meeting us there, too," I added, "along with some of your other Army buddies."

We all stood outside on the ferry deck as we crossed the Hudson, the summer sun warm on our backs, a fish-scented breeze ruffling our hair. It would take a little over three hours to get to Mitch's small hometown outside of Binghamton. Mr. Barnett offered Jimmy a road map and asked if he wanted to help navigate, but he shook his head. The mountain air was cool and we rolled down the car windows and inhaled the aroma of pine as we drove through the Catskill Mountains. I could never get enough of those glorious mountains.

Mr. Barnett talked about his work at the clinic to help pass the time and shared how I had delivered Persephone's foal. "She did a great job, Jim. I was proud of her." I had brought along the photo album and a few of the latest letters from Jimmy's friends, and I read parts of them aloud to him. We talked about all manner of things as if Jimmy was part of the conversation, but he barely spoke a word. I missed the sound of his voice and his warm laughter. I bet his parents did, too.

Mitch's family and boyhood friends filled the churchyard. Joe was chatting with a bunch of Army buddies when we arrived, and they came over to greet Jimmy with handshakes and good-natured thumps on his back. Some of them had driven a long way to come, and I was especially surprised to see Dr. Greenberg there from New Jersey. I was overjoyed when Jimmy began talking with them. It was exactly what I'd hoped for. I had brought my camera and extra rolls of film, so I snapped a lot of pictures of their reunion.

We went inside when the service began, sang a hymn that had been one of Mitch's favorites. Chaplain Bill prayed. Several of the men, including Joe and Frank Cishek, gave eulogies and shared their memories of Mitch. I wished I could have watched Jimmy's reaction, but he was sitting farther down the pew from me, and I didn't want to lean forward to stare at him. Chaplain Bill spoke last, talking about Mitch and explaining to Mitch's family how his Army friends had taken up a collection to fund a college scholarship in his name at his high school. I wondered if that was why Joe had been hanging around, working for Pop.

Chaplain Bill prayed again, then told us he wanted to say a few final words. "I know we're all asking why Mitch O'Hara had to die. The simple answer—as a very wise friend of Mitch's used to remind me—is that all of Mitch's days were written in God's book before one of them came to be. We can't understand it now, but one day we'll understand God's reasons, and we'll be amazed and comforted. In the meantime, I want to remind us all that death isn't the end. This life on earth isn't all that there is. We've been promised eternal life, resurrection life. We experience sorrow in parting for now, but the Bible says that one day the earth will be made new. This planet that we were created to inhabit will be a place without tears and without wars. We'll exchange these broken bodies for brand-new ones, bodies that we'll inhabit forever, bodies that will never grow old or die. People often ask me what I think this renewed earth will be like, and I tell them to imagine the very best moments they've experienced in this life, laughing with friends and loved ones like Mitch, enjoying the beauty of creation, eating the richest food. Moments like those will be ours for eternity. We'll walk with God as Adam and Eve once did and be united with our Savior forever." He paused to wipe his eyes, unashamed. "Until that day, yes, we mourn for Mitch. We miss him. But for now, we must go on our way, living all the days that God has numbered for us in His book. We must live in faith and hope, trusting the goodness of our heavenly Father's plan."

Chaplain Bill's words stirred me. As we all made our way to the fellowship hall, where the church ladies had prepared a light meal, I wished I knew what plans God had written in His book for me.

We ate ham buns and strawberry Jell-O and homemade chocolate cake. Then it was time to head home. I wished Jimmy didn't have to return to the hospital. Joe lingered to talk to his friends as if drawing life from them, but just as we were getting ready to leave, he pulled Mr. Barnett aside. They talked for a few minutes, and I saw them glance over at me. Or maybe they were looking at Jimmy, standing nearby with his mother, her arm linked through his. I wondered if Joe was telling him about his own experiences at the veterans' hospital.

Mr. Barnett surprised me when he asked Jimmy to sit in the back seat with his mother on the way home and asked me to sit up front with him. The afternoon sun was behind us but it wouldn't set until late on these long, summer days. Tomorrow was Monday. I couldn't put off applying for the job at the pharmacy any longer. I needed to ask Mr. Barnett if I could give his name as a reference. I had to tell him that if I got the job, I could no longer work for him. I was gathering up my courage to do that when he said, "So, Peggy. Your friend Joe tells me you're looking for a job. I was wondering if you would you like to work for me full-time." I looked over at Mr. Barnett in surprise, my mouth hanging open. I didn't want to burst into tears but I couldn't help it. He chuckled in his gentle way and patted my knee. "I'll take that as a yes. I would have asked you to work full-time for me ages ago, but I knew you also managed your father's office and I didn't want to steal you away from him."

"I don't work for Pop anymore," I said, wiping my eyes. "His girlfriend, Donna, quit her job at the Crow Bar, and she's doing his books now."

"That's what Joe said. You are more than capable of being my assistant, Peggy. You've done all manner of tasks for me over the years with remarkable skill. Delivering Persephone's foal was an impressive accomplishment. I have no doubt that you could be a fine veterinarian if you decided to pursue it one day."

I couldn't absorb that much praise. And when Jimmy leaned forward from the back seat and said, "You'll do a great job, Peggety," I started bawling all over again. Mrs. Barnett reached over my seat and squeezed my shoulder.

"I would love the job!" I said, blowing my nose. "I can start tomorrow! Or right now! But are you sure you want me? You know how awkward I am around people. I have trouble talking to strangers sometimes."

"I've never thought that of you, Peggy," Mr. B. said. "You're quiet, but I would never consider you awkward. I know you can handle this job. Especially since most of my clients already know you, and you know them and their animals. I've needed more help for some time, but I've been putting it off, hoping things would work out and that Jim . . . Well, it seems like that's going to take a little longer now. But even when he's ready to join me in our practice, we'll still need a good veterinary assistant. In fact, with two working veterinarians, we'll need you even more."

It was an answer to all my prayers. And it was much more than a job. I now had a future doing work that I loved. If only we could take Jimmy home with us, then my life would be just about perfect. But the strain of watching him day and night so he wouldn't try to kill himself again would be too much for his parents.

I tore up the pharmacy application when I got home and hugged Buster. "It's going to be okay," I told him. "I'll start looking for a place for us to live." I wanted to thank Joe, but I wasn't surprised when he didn't return home after the memorial service.

I went to work at the clinic the next morning, and Mr. Barnett showed me some of the tasks I would be doing from now on, like keeping patients' records and sterilizing glass syringes and needles. A local farmer brought in his dog who had tangled with a porcupine, and Mr. Barnett showed me how to remove the quills from the poor dog's snout. We talked about Jimmy as we worked, and he agreed that it had been an encouraging sign when Jimmy had chatted with his friends yesterday.

"Keep doing what you're doing with all the letters from his buddies, Peggy. I think it's working."

I went home for lunch at noon and found Joe in the garage with Pop. "I have a job!" I announced. "A full-time one! And I have you to thank for it, Joe."

"At the drugstore?" Pop asked.

"Forget the drugstore," I said. "Mr. Barnett hired me to work at the clinic full-time. I'm now his veterinary assistant." Nothing could dent my happiness, not even Donna, who marched out of the office as if headed into battle.

"Did I hear right?" she asked. "You gave up the chance for a nice, respectable job at the drugstore for . . . for *that*?" She gestured toward the clinic across the street.

"Gladly!"

"You've been his servant long enough, Peggy, doing all his dirty work."

"I love what I do."

"You love shoveling horse manure?"

"I do more than that. I delivered a foal the other day. And it was a difficult birth."

"Can't you see how those people have used you all these years?"

"No. That's not what I see at all." She would never understand, so there was no point in trying to explain it to her. "I'll be moving out as soon as I find a place," I said. I turned away with Buster at my heels and headed toward the apartment to fix lunch. From now on, I would pack my lunch in the morning and eat it among friends. I was almost to the stairs when I heard Joe calling my name.

"Peggy! Wait up!" I halted so he could catch up with me. "Hey, don't listen to that old bat. You do what your heart tells you to do, okay?"

"Thanks, Joe," I said, smiling. "And thanks for talking to Mr. Barnett for me. You're my hero!" He laughed as I gave him a hug.

"Hey, it was nothing. Remember how you asked what I liked about being a firefighter? Well, the best part of all was rescuing people."

18

Gisela

A month after Mortsel was destroyed, I received a letter from the nursing school in Antwerp. I held my breath as I tore open the envelope. Inside was a handwritten note from Sister Veronica.

> *Dear Gisela,*
>
> *I'm afraid I have difficult news. I contacted Father Damien, the priest from the parish near your parents' apartment, and asked him to try to find the answers to your questions. He talked to your former landlord, who relayed some of the tragic news. I'm very sorry to tell you that your father was too ill to go into hiding or to survive deportation to a labor camp. Your mother wouldn't leave his side. Before the Nazis raided the building to take everyone away, your parents chose to die together, rather than allow the Nazis to take their lives. I am so very sorry. You will be in my prayers.*
>
> *Sister Veronica*

I felt too stunned to cry. It didn't seem real. How could I accept such terrible news? And how would I ever tell Ruthie? Why hadn't Sam helped them or insisted that my mother escape? It wasn't like Sam to allow this to happen—unless something had happened to him as well. I closed my eyes and finally let my tears fall, remembering how hopeful we had all felt as we'd stood on the deck of the *St. Louis* in the tropical heat, gazing at Havana in the distance. We'd ridden high on that wave of hope, but like a ship in a storm-tossed sea, our hope had sunk when the *St. Louis* had been forced to return to Europe. Hope had risen again when we'd landed in Belgium, then sunk when the Nazis invaded. Now I was drowning in a tidal wave of grief. I vowed never to allow my hopes to rise again.

Of course, I knew I had to go on living. Unless I wanted to give up like my parents or let despair send me overboard like Max Loewe, I had to continue getting out of bed every morning and putting one foot in front of the other. If Sister Veronica had told me that Sam had been taken away on the transports or had died with the Resistance fighters, I would have had no reason to continue living. But she hadn't. She had said nothing at all about Sam. And I still had Ruthie.

* * *

Months passed, and then one day I was surprised to realize that nearly a year had slipped by since I'd last seen Ruthie. I had been mailing a letter to her every week, hoping Sister Marie was giving them to her, never knowing if she had. Then in the spring of 1944, I received a note from Sister Marie, asking me to come to the orphanage. I remembered how thin and fragile Ruthie had looked and I feared the worst. I went as soon as I could.

Mortsel was still in ruins. The horror of that day came rushing back to me as I walked through what remained of the town. There had been bombing raids near other Belgian cities and towns since then, and we'd treated many civilian casualties in our hospital. But nothing had been as disastrous as the bombing of that village last April.

"Your sister is fine, Miss Maes," Sister Marie said before I could ask. "Please don't concern yourself. I asked you here to let you know that she has moved out of the orphanage. She's sixteen now and too old to remain in our care."

"You . . . you kicked her out?" I imagined my fragile sister all alone in a world at war, and I couldn't breathe.

"Not at all. When our wards come of age, we find jobs and safe lodging for them on the outside. That's what we've done for Ruth Anne."

"Where? What kind of job? Not in a factory—it could be bombed!"

"She has been placed with a family and lives in their home. Ruth Anne was always very gentle and caring toward the younger children when she lived here, and she was easy to place as an au pair. It's a large family with seven children, so she will be a welcome help to the parents in return for her room and board."

"They won't work her like a slave, will they?"

"We screen all of our placements very carefully."

"Do they know she's Jewish?"

"No one knows, Miss Maes. Ruth Anne has learned to blend in as a devout Catholic girl."

The image of Ruthie as a devout Catholic girl startled and upset me. We had both been forced to blend in for our own survival, but I wanted to picture Ruthie sitting at our family's Passover seder, not sitting in a church. She had always been so proud, as the youngest child, to ask the traditional questions every year— *"What makes this Passover night different from all other nights?"* Her sweet voice should be singing *"Dayenu,"* not hymns.

"I need my sister's address so I can write to her," I said. Sister Marie sighed as she opened a drawer in her cabinet and pulled out a bundle of letters, tied with a ribbon. She set them on her desk. They were my letters, the ones I'd written to Ruthie. "You had no right!" I shouted.

Sister Marie held up her hand to silence me. "Ruth Anne read them every week, Miss Maes. I allowed her to come into my office and take as long as she liked with them. But it was too risky to let her keep them in her room. The war has produced a lot of hungry, desperate people who are willing to do anything to survive, including betraying an innocent soul." She returned the bundle to her drawer and closed it. "And now I'm afraid your letters must stop altogether."

"But I need to know where she is! How will I ever find her when the war ends?"

"We keep excellent records here. You can always come to us."

I had to trust her. I had no choice. Just as I was trusting Sister Veronica to tell Sam where I was when he returned for me.

* * *

In June, the long-awaited Allied landing finally took place. Everyone in Belgium heard the good news in spite of the Nazis' efforts to suppress it. Our rescue was closer than ever before, on the beaches and in the villages of France. We noticed an increase in air activity overhead, with convoys of planes flying bombing missions and the Luftwaffe fighting back with artillery and antiaircraft guns and rockets. The war was all around us, closing in on us, on land and in the air. Civilian casualties multiplied. We were all aware that any one of us could become a casualty at any time. We prayed that the Allies would liberate us with lightning speed, as swiftly as the Nazis had overrun us.

I concentrated on my work, letting it fill my days and occupy my mind. I was assigned to the women's ward one morning when the supervisor called all of the nurses aside to introduce us to the newest member of our staff. It was Lina Renard from my nursing classes. I quickly ducked my head, remembering how she had held up my sweater with the yellow star on it, hoping Lina wouldn't recognize me. Lina had always been different from the other girls, and there had been rumors that the reason she could still get silk stockings while the rest of us couldn't was because her father was a Nazi sympathizer. No one knew if it was true. I felt very uneasy seeing her again, but we all welcomed her to Hospital Sint-Augustinus and continued with our work.

I was stripping one of the beds later that morning when Lina strode up to me. "I thought I recognized you. You're Gisela Wolff. Why did the matron call you by a different name?"

"I-I go by Ella Maes now."

"But why?"

If I had been able to think more quickly, I could have lied and said Maes was my married name and Ella was short for Gisela, but her question took me by surprise. And in that moment of hesitation, I saw her eyes widen with comprehension.

"I remember now! You're Jewish! You had a yellow star on your sweater." I glanced around, hoping no one had overheard her. "You used to come to school with those two other Jewish girls. What were their names? And your accent. It isn't really Swiss, is it?"

I pulled Lina off to the side, my heart racing out of control. "If you know I'm Jewish," I said quietly, "then you know why I moved away and changed my name. No one else here knows the truth, Lina. It would help me a lot if you didn't tell anyone. And please, call me Ella now." She gave me a phony smile in return. She didn't promise to keep my secret.

Lina had never liked me. I avoided her as much as I could after that, hoping she would forget all about me. I was relieved when she was assigned to the night shift so we never worked together. I managed to push her from my mind.

* * *

One Friday morning in July, I arrived at work and was checking my patient's vital signs when I noticed that her IV bottle was empty. It should have been exchanged for a new one by her last attending nurse. I checked the clipboard to see if the doctor's orders had changed. They hadn't. The patient's treatment was overdue. It was a sloppy, dangerous mistake. And Lina Renard had been the attending nurse.

I debated whether or not to tell the head nurse or to simply cover up Lina's mistake. But I debated too long. The head nurse must have seen me standing there, trying to decide what to do, and she approached. "Is something wrong, Nurse Maes?"

I had to tell her. She stormed off to confront Lina, who was still filling out reports before going home. Everyone on the floor could hear the matron chastising her for her mistake.

I thought Lina had gone home after things quieted down, but she strode back onto the ward with her coat on, looking for me. "You always thought you were better than everyone else, didn't you? Just like all the other filthy Jews."

My heart raced. "I didn't report you, Lina, I swear. I was about to change the IV bottle myself when the supervisor came over and—"

"You expect me to believe that? You were always too good to hang around with us or go to a dance now and then or have a laugh. No, you were too busy kissing Sister Veronica's ring and trying to impress our teachers with your *hard* work. You graduated head of the class—la-di-da! And I see that you're still kissing rings and thinking you're better than everyone else."

"I wasn't going to report you, Lina—"

"Jew!" She spit on the front of my uniform, then turned and walked away.

My shift had just begun, so I had to finish. I was sick with dread all day. I hurried back to my room as soon as the long afternoon finally ended. I needed to write to Sister Veronica immediately. She needed to help me transfer to a different hospital, change my name again, find a new place to hide. But a letter would take too long. I needed to act now. It was too close to curfew to risk leaving today, but I would pack my things tonight and take the first train to Antwerp tomorrow morning and never look back.

I was leaving the rooming house with my suitcase as soon as the curfew ended the next day when I noticed two men standing by the curb out front. Their uniforms bore the twin lightning bolts of the dreaded SS.

My heart thrashed against my ribs. Should I turn around and hurry back inside as if I'd forgotten something? Should I bolt and run through the back lanes and try to hide somewhere? Or should I pretend to ignore them and walk calmly past them? I didn't have a chance to do any of those things. As soon as the men saw me, they started walking toward me.

One of them held out his hand. "Identification, please." I fumbled for it in my bag with trembling fingers and nearly dropped it. The officer looked it over and said, "You must come with us." He spoke in German. They each gripped one of my arms and we started walking in the direction of the train station. I couldn't draw a deep breath. My body felt like it belonged to someone else, refusing my command to break free and run. They propelled me all the way to the train station, and we boarded a train. The other passengers averted their eyes as the men shoved me into a seat between them. I knew there was no point in praying. The train was headed south, to the city of Mechelen and the deportation prison where all of Belgium's other Jews had been taken. We arrived much too soon. The transit camp couldn't have been a secret in Belgium because the former military barracks sat in a popu-lated area of Mechelen, close to the train station and a major rail hub. Surely people had noticed the boxcars filled with Jews who were being transported east to labor camps week after week. They must have heard the rumors that they were being sent to Nazi-occupied countries like Poland and Czechoslovakia.

The huge three-story brick building had been built in a square with an open plaza in the center. A transport truck with a canvas roof arrived in the plaza at the same time that I did, and I watched men, women, and children spilling out of the back of it, clinging to their suitcases and to each other. They were Jews. Like me. I scanned their faces for a familiar one—Sam's or one of his brothers' or his mother's—hoping I wouldn't see them. Hoping they weren't here, that they never had been here.

The prison officials spoke in German as they processed the new arrivals. I overheard them saying most of these people were bound for a labor camp called Auschwitz in Poland. When my turn came, they seemed to know all about me, that I was a German Jew and that I was a nurse. I would be sent to Buchenwald, they decided, where nurses were needed for the medical experiments Nazi doctors were conducting there. They said all of these things to each other, not to me. I might have been invisible. I didn't know anything about Auschwitz, but I knew from Vati's descriptions what I would face in Buchenwald.

*　*　*

I spent a week in Mechelen, crowded together with too many other women in a cramped cell. Animals were treated better than we were. I could see a river from the window of our cell and smell it when we were forced to assemble outside in the plaza for a few minutes each day. I tried to remember what Sam looked like and what it had felt like to be held in his arms, but I couldn't. It seemed like only a dream I'd once had.

Then the day came when I was taken down to the enclosed plaza and loaded into the back of a truck with dozens of others. After a short drive, we reached the railroad station where armed SS officers with snarling dogs herded us into a wooden boxcar. It quickly filled to capacity with prisoners, but the soldiers shoved even more prisoners inside until we could barely move or breathe. I was one of the very few women. The bolt slammed shut with a terrible sound as we were locked inside. Hours passed until the train began to move. We had no food. It was just as well. The stench of filth inside the boxcar made me too nauseated to eat. There was one bucket of water for all of us to share, another bucket to use as a toilet. I thought of my gentle, elegant mother, and for the first time, I was grateful that my parents had chosen the path they had. They wouldn't have to endure this.

The journey took several days, measured only by the slivers of sunlight or darkness that were visible between the boards of the boxcar. My mind wandered into dark places as I remembered and grieved for everything we had lost. I recalled how we'd emptied our apartment, whittling away our precious furnishings and possessions to raise money for our escape. Now I had no possessions at all—and I hadn't escaped. My faith had been pared to the bone as well. I had grown up reading the tale of Queen Esther every Purim and how the wicked Haman, like

Hitler, made plans to exterminate every Jew in the world. Yet God had intervened. We had been saved. Jews around the world also celebrated God's miraculous delivery from slavery every year at Passover, and we remembered how the Red Sea had parted and we'd been set free. Had those stories been mere fairy tales? Where was our deliverance now?

I thought about how life could turn on a hinge of fate. If Vati hadn't run out to save the Torah scrolls on Kristallnacht, he wouldn't have been arrested and sent to Buchenwald. He wouldn't have become ill with tuberculosis. He and Mutti might have escaped together instead of dying together. If the *St. Louis* had been allowed to dock in Havana and if the Cubans hadn't rejected our landing permits, my family and Sam's would be living safely in Cuba. If the United States had offered us refuge or if we had been accepted by the English representative instead of the Belgian one, we might all be alive and still together. And if Lina Renard had gone to work at a different hospital or if she had remembered to attach the patient's IV bottle or if she'd never seen the yellow star on my sweater, I wouldn't be on this train on my way to Buchenwald. There had been so many chances for fate to take a different path, but it hadn't. The Nazis had chased my family and me across an ocean and back, and they'd captured me at last.

We arrived in Buchenwald on a warm August morning, just after dawn. A breeze raised the layer of gritty gray ash that seemed to have settled on every surface and swirled it into the air like snow. The stench of decay and burning flesh that hovered above the massive camp overwhelmed me. I was herded together with the other women and made to strip naked. They shaved my head and tattooed a number on my arm. I was given a striped uniform several sizes too large for me and assigned to a barracks that already overflowed with women. I was the envy of all the others when I was put to work in the camp infirmary instead of in one of the camp workshops. But the others didn't know what went on in that infirmary.

I soon learned that the Nazi doctors were testing their experimental vaccines on prisoners, vaccines that were supposed to prevent contagious diseases such as typhus, typhoid, cholera, and diphtheria. Our patients usually became gravely ill. I did what I could to ease their suffering, but most of them died horribly. Sam had once said there was a reason why I had become a nurse, but surely this couldn't be it.

"You're wondering if you're going to survive, aren't you?" a nurse named Ada asked me one afternoon about a month after I had arrived. Four of our patients had died that day, and Ada, myself, and another nurse named Lotti had all stepped outside the infirmary for a moment as we waited for the cart that would carry the bodies to the crematorium. By then, I had been in this place long enough to know what went on behind Buchenwald's walls and gates and barbed wire fences. "Everyone wonders the same thing when they first arrive," Ada said.

"And will we?" I asked. "Will we survive?"

"That depends. Do you want to? Do you really want to keep on living if the people you love are all dead?"

I still had Ruthie. And maybe Sam.

"Do you want to live in a world where people treat their fellow human beings the way we're treated here?"

I knew there were kind people in the world like Sister Veronica, people who had risked their lives to hide us. And Allied soldiers were fighting and dying to set us free. "The Allies have landed in France," I told Ada. "And the Soviets are winning battles in the east. Everyone says that the Nazis are losing the war."

"So you still have hope? That's good. That's what you'll need to survive this place. Hope."

"That and luck," Lotti added. "If we don't starve to death, we could die like our patients from typhus or dysentery or pneumonia. Who knows what else the doctors have cooked up to kill us with?"

"Or maybe one of the guards will decide to shoot you one day because you make him mad," Ada said. "Or because he felt like shooting someone."

"Don't scare the poor girl," Lotti said. "It's hard enough to survive when you're not shaking in your shoes every day."

Sam and I had promised to find each other. I had promised Ruthie I would come back for her. Those were reasons enough. "I want to survive," I told Ada and Lotti. "No matter what."

19

Peggy

JULY 1946

I was so excited about working all day with Mr. Barnett that I was awake with the chickens the next morning. Mrs. Barnett kept a few in her backyard coop so she would always have fresh eggs, and her rooster faithfully serenaded the dawn. Mr. B. and I spent all morning at two different dairy farms, testing their cows for tuberculosis. We enjoyed riding around the countryside together and didn't need to talk much in order to be content. When we got back to the clinic, Buster was sitting on the Barnetts' back steps waiting for me. He greeted me like a long-lost friend. I quickly apologized to Mr. Barnett.

"I'm so sorry that he came over here. I'll take him back to our yard."

"Let him be," he said. "He seems happy sitting there."

"Come on inside and have some lunch, Peggy," Mrs. Barnett called to me.

"Oh, you don't have to feed me. I packed myself a baloney and cheese sandwich."

"Well, sit down and eat it with us anyway. I already poured you a lemonade. And I have something I want to show you afterwards." She insisted that I sit at her kitchen table, which I didn't mind doing at all. Her kitchen was clean and tidy and always smelled like something good. Today it smelled like strawberries. Eight jars of fresh, homemade jam were cooling on her stovetop. I heard one of the lids give a satisfying pop as it sealed. Ever since Donna started cooking for Pop, our kitchen had smelled like cigarettes and burnt toast. My feet stuck to the floor when I walked through it on the way to my bedroom. It had never, ever smelled like strawberry jam.

"I'm going to borrow Peggy for a few minutes," Mrs. Barnett told her husband after we ate. "She'll return to work in a bit." She led me into their parlor and opened a cloth carpetbag that held her knitting. "I haven't been doing any knitting since last winter, and I happened to come across this bag today when I was vacuuming. Look what I found inside." She showed me a slim packet of letters in airmail envelopes. I recognized Jimmy's handwriting on them. "This was the last batch of letters Jimmy sent home to us. I kept them in my knitting bag so I would remember to pray for those poor souls while I was knitting."

"The wounded soldiers?"

"No, the survivors in those terrible concentration camps. Remember how Jimmy wrote and told us he was helping in a hospital there?"

I had forgotten, but the letters reminded me now. I opened the first one and read it out loud.

"Dear Mom and Dad,

I'm sorry that I haven't written in a while, but I haven't been able to talk about what's happening over here. Even now, I don't think I can put it into words—and for your sakes, I'm not sure I should try.

As our forces penetrated deeper into Germany, we liberated a Nazi concentration camp. The immediate need was so great that they asked all medical personnel to suspend our regular work and help set up a hospital to care for the survivors. Nothing in my life could have prepared me for what I've encountered here. I wasn't the only soldier who wept at what we saw. These are people! Human beings! Yet they have been beaten and starved and worked to the point of death. Now they are walking skeletons with skin. I don't know how they can still be alive.

I find it impossible to understand the evil and depravity that led to this. The horror of it paralyzed me at first, but when I saw how badly they needed our help, I went to work. I've heard that our soldiers are finding more and more of these concentration camps all over eastern Europe. They were built to kill hundreds of thousands of innocent people. The vast majority of them were Jewish. The press has been called in to document these war crimes, so you'll be seeing photographs in the newspapers. They won't begin to portray the horror. Or the overwhelming stench of death and decay.

Sorry for the rush, but I need to get back to work.

Love,
Jim"

Mrs. Barnett's eyes glistened with tears when I finished. "When they started printing photographs of those camps and the gas chambers in the newspapers," she said, "they moved me to tears. In fact, Gordon wouldn't let me see any more of them after the first few. He said they were the stuff of nightmares. I couldn't imagine our Jimmy having to witness such inhumanity in person. I prayed for him every day, but most of my prayers were for those poor people who had endured so much. Imagine, being torn from your home and taken to a place like that to suffer and die."

"I can't. It's unimaginable. My heart aches for them." The mention of being torn from their homes reminded me that I needed to find a new home for myself and Buster. But my situation was nothing compared to what millions of people in Europe had suffered. I needed to remember that so I wouldn't be tempted to feel sorry for myself.

Jimmy had written a few more letters after that first one, but they were very short. The last one said:

I don't have much time to write but I wanted to let you know
I'm okay. I'm still working at the concentration camp where we're
nursing thousands of poor souls back to life. What will become
of these survivors afterwards is another question. I haven't had
a chance to celebrate V-E Day yet, but I'm glad that victory has
finally come. I know a lot of soldiers who are hoping to go home
soon. Their work is done but my friend and fellow medic Art
Davis and I are committed to postponing our discharge and staying
for as long as we're needed. Our work is far from finished.

As soon as Jimmy mentioned his friend's name, my pulse sped up. "We need to write to Chaplain Bill right away and ask him to get Art Davis's address," I told Mrs. Barnett. "Art was probably one of the last people Jimmy worked with before he was discharged. Maybe he can tell us who Gisela is and what happened to Jimmy."

Mrs. B. shared my excitement. "A letter will take too long. Use our telephone, dear. Do you have the chaplain's phone number?"

"I do. But a long-distance call to Connecticut will be expensive."

"It doesn't matter. Let's call him right away."

I retrieved the number and called Bill at his church, giving him Art Davis's name. He promised to call back as soon as he got Art's address.

Later that afternoon, I was still grieving for all those people in the death camps as I applied a poultice to Pedro's front leg. I had noticed that the horse had a slight limp, and when I'd mentioned it to Mr. Barnett, he'd diagnosed a shin splint. He showed me how to palpate Pedro's front leg and find the hot spot and the lump.

"Good call, Peggy," he told me. "I think you caught it in time, before it could do permanent damage."

I had just finished the treatment Mr. B. had prescribed and was wrapping Pedro's leg when I heard footsteps crunching on the gravel driveway outside the stable. I looked up, surprised to see Joe standing in the doorway. Buster, who had been keeping me company outside the stall, went over to greet him, tail wagging.

"You going to deliver another baby horse?" Joe asked.

"This horse's name is Pedro," I said, laughing, "and *he* definitely isn't pregnant. He's gone lame."

"How about that. Pedro has a bum leg just like us, Tripod." He scratched the dog's ears. Joe looked as though he wanted to tell me something but didn't know how to begin. I took a guess.

"You're taking off again, aren't you? Is that what you've come to tell me?"

He sighed. "I have a hankering to see the ocean. Thought I'd drive down there, you know?" Mitch O'Hara's memorial service had been hard on Joe, but I still hated to see him go. I had gotten used to having him around.

"I'm glad you didn't leave without saying goodbye," I said, swallowing a lump in my throat. "Will you—I mean, do you think you'll be coming back this way ever again?"

"I don't know. I don't have any plans . . . just . . . you know."

"You've been a huge help to me, Joe. And to Jimmy, too. I don't want to tie you down here, but Jimmy's mother found some more of his letters and we discovered another name to contact. Someone he worked with when they liberated a concentration camp."

"Jim was there? In those camps?"

"Yes. We could tell from his letters that it was a horrifying experience. Maybe it's one of the reasons he became so depressed. We're going to try to contact his friend, and if he doesn't live too far away, maybe we can visit him. But I'm no good with people, Joe, and you are. I could really use your help."

He rewarded me with a grin. "I'll be glad to help. I'll just go and stick my five remaining toes in the ocean, and then I'll be back."

"Thanks." He could probably tell how relieved I was. He had started to limp away when I called to him. "Joe?" He turned around to face me.

"Don't get into any trouble, okay? And be careful driving. No speeding."
He laughed and gave me a salute.

*　*　*

A week and a half later on a sunny Saturday morning, I climbed onto the
back of Joe's motorcycle to ride to Bennington, Vermont, to talk with
Art Davis. It was the longest trip I'd taken on his motorcycle so far, but
one of the prettiest. Vermont's Green Mountains took my breath away,
rolling into the distance like a rumpled green carpet. Bennington was
the kind of picturesque hometown that every GI must have longed to
return home to. But I felt as though every bone and organ in my body
had been jiggled out of place by the time we arrived. My ears were still
ringing when Art came out of his house to greet us. He was probably
thirty, a tall, lanky, down-to-earth New Englander with a pretty, pregnant wife. Art was a high school science teacher and volunteer firefighter,
so he and Joe hit it off right away as we sat talking on his front porch.
But Art grew very serious and closed his eyes as if he was in pain when
I told him about Jimmy's breakdown in a little more detail than I had
on the phone.

"We're hoping you can tell us about your time with Jim, and how
you adjusted to civilian life afterwards, so we can help Jimmy get better."

Art drew a deep breath as if about to plunge into cold water. "I'm
sorry to hear about Jim but to tell you the truth, I'm not surprised. Anyone who was there at that camp and saw the things we did . . . I admit
there are days when I still have a hard time with it. I think Jim was even
more deeply affected than I was. Having the love and support of my
wife made all the difference, I think. It was like she was able to show me
that there's still some good in this world and some hope for the future.
I know Jim wasn't married—are you his girlfriend?"

"Just a friend."

"It helps to have good friends. I had only known Jim for a few
months by the time the camp was liberated in April of '45, but it felt
like we'd known each other all our lives because of everything we went

through. Experiencing the carnage of warfare and seeing so many young men gravely wounded and dying . . . that would give any sane man reason enough to want to check out of this world. But then we came to Buchenwald." He paused and I saw him struggling with his emotions.

"Even now, it's hard for me to talk about. You don't want to remember, but the memory is seared into your brain and your heart, and it's impossible to forget. We don't dare to forget!" He paused, and when he spoke again, his voice sounded raw. "I won't describe it for you because it's beyond description. Jim and I were both deeply shaken to see the things that evil men are capable of doing to their fellow human beings. Jim fell to his knees and wept, right there on the road. I wanted to do the same, but all of these skeletons were shuffling toward us, some of them kneeling down to try to kiss our feet, so I pulled him up again. We had to get to work, doing what we could for them. It was the only way to keep from breaking down ourselves." Tears filled Art's eyes but he didn't try to wipe them.

"We eventually set up a hospital in the former SS barracks and attended to the survivors who were closest to death. Jim would look each person in the eye, and he would ask their name. He would remember them all, too, and call everyone by name whenever he took care of them. They had been treated like animals for so long, Jim said, that he wanted to let them know they were still living people with names and a soul. He said we needed to restore their dignity and humanity as much as we needed to restore their bodies."

My tears started falling at Art's description of Buchenwald. It was so easy to picture the Jimmy I knew so well, offering warmth and compassion in such a terrible place. "That must have been heartbreaking," I murmured.

"The people who revived, who were resurrected from the dead almost, were the ones who kept us going. They were so grateful. There was a language barrier because the survivors had been transported to the camp from countries all over Europe—France, the Netherlands, Belgium. But compassion speaks all languages."

"Do you know if there was a woman Jimmy was close to?" I asked. "A nurse or maybe a patient?"

He thought for a moment. "There weren't any Army nurses. The nurses who had been working with us before we liberated Buchenwald had to be transferred someplace else. Seeing such misery and human suffering would have been too much for them. It was hard enough on us men, and we'd already seen a lot during the war. But there were a handful of Jewish physicians and nurses who had been prisoners in the camp. They had suffered like everyone else, yet as soon as they regained their strength, they insisted on working alongside us. One of those nurses spoke a couple of languages, including English. She was a big help to us."

I pulled Gisela's picture from my bag and showed it to Art. "Might she be one of them? We found this picture in Jimmy's pack. It says on the back that her name is Gisela. And it looks like she's wearing a nurse's uniform."

Art studied it carefully. "I don't know. She might have been. You have to understand how emaciated and close to death these survivors were. Their heads had been shaved. Hundreds of them died in the weeks after we arrived, in spite of our best efforts to save them. We were just too late. When the liberating armies first arrived, some of the soldiers mistakenly fed their rations to the survivors, but their bodies simply couldn't handle food and it ended up killing them. It's hard to deny food to a starving man, but we had to proceed slowly and feed some of them intravenously. The soldiers meant well and they wanted to do something to help, so we let them donate blood for transfusions."

"Do you know what happened to any of those Jewish nurses who'd been in the camp?"

"The first thing most of the survivors wanted to do after they recovered was find their loved ones. They didn't want to imagine that they were the only one in their family who had survived. Organizations started springing up to try to reunite all of these survivors and help them return to their homes—or what was left of their homes."

"How would you even begin such an enormous task?"

"I don't know. It was overwhelming. They posted lists of names, of the dead as well as the living, and the survivors checked and rechecked them every day. As soon as our patients were well enough to leave, they usually moved to a displaced persons' camp if they had nowhere else to go. The authorities were trying to get everyone back to the cities and nations where they had lived before the war, but I can understand why many of them refused to go back. Anti-Semitism didn't end with the war." He shook his head as if unable to comprehend such a thing. "Jim spent his free time helping his patients get in touch with various Jewish agencies or the Red Cross. By the time we left Buchenwald, I was starting to feel a glimmer of hope for the future. But Jim? In his mind, he had unfinished work to do. He wanted to put everything back together again, as if the world were a giant jigsaw puzzle with all the pieces scattered, and it was up to him to fix it. I kept telling him it was an impossible task, but he was driven. And it started taking a toll on him."

Art's wife came out with a tray of sandwiches and some colas, and our conversation drifted to other subjects. I could tell that Joe would have preferred a beer—or two. We ate lunch on the front porch, watching kids riding bikes, skipping rope, and playing hopscotch on the sidewalk. We would have to be on our way soon. We had a long drive ahead of us to get home.

"I thought of one more question, Art, if you don't mind," I said as we were finishing lunch. "Did Jimmy ever talk with you about God or his faith?"

I could see Art searching his memory. "Not that I can recall. Why?"

"Because all the other men who served with Jim—like Joe, here—said that Jimmy talked a lot about what he believed and was always inspiring others and even praying with them. I just wondered if he still did that when you knew him."

Art slowly shook his head. "I never heard him mention God, and Jim and I worked together pretty closely. Buchenwald was a very dark place. God seemed very far away." My heart squeezed. That didn't sound like the Jimmy I knew. "Now that I think about it, Jim got so depressed after working there for a few months that Major Cleveland, our CO, made him take a week's leave. Eventually we were both transferred out. I don't know where Jim ended up after that. Sorry."

I wrote down the commander's name, Major Mike Cleveland, so Chaplain Bill could try to get in touch with him. Art had given us some important information about when and why Jimmy had begun to change, and I could see that liberating Buchenwald had obviously had a profound effect on Jimmy. The fact that he hadn't talked about his faith or prayed with his patients while working there was upsetting. Jimmy had wanted to put all the broken pieces back together again, and it must have devastated him when he couldn't.

Before we left, Art gave me a letter to give to Jimmy. "If I can get away after the baby is born," he said, "I'll try to drive down to visit him."

I thanked Art for his willingness to open some very painful wounds for his friend and took his photograph for Jimmy's scrapbook. Art walked with us to the street and paused a moment to admire Joe's motorcycle. Then he turned to Joe.

"I couldn't help noticing your leg," he said. "Were you wounded in combat?"

"Yeah, in France. Jim was one of the medics who saved my life."

Art rested his hand on Joe's shoulder. "You paid a huge price, my friend. But when you get back home again, make sure you look at some of the photographs and news footage from the concentration camps. I won't lie—they're hard to stomach. But if you ever start to wonder if your sacrifice was worth it, the record of what went on in those camps will help you remember why we fought. Your sacrifice meant the difference between life and death for those survivors. You rescued a multitude of people—along with the generations of children who will be born to them someday. You are their hero."

20

Gisela

It was hard to keep track of what day or month it was in Buchenwald. The only way we knew that the year was now 1945 was because we heard a few of the guards toasting the New Year one bitterly cold winter night. We had nothing to celebrate. Everyone was dying. The little bit of food that we ate went straight through us.

"Still hanging on to hope?" Ada would ask me from time to time. The vaccine experiments had been halted, and there were rumors that all the female prisoners, including the nurses, would be moved to a satellite camp soon.

"Yes, I still have hope," I replied. And my hope sometimes came through very strange means. When thousands of exhausted, dying prisoners arrived in Buchenwald after the New Year, we learned through camp gossip that these prisoners had been forced to march here from a concentration camp in Poland called Auschwitz. The Nazis had evacuated them because the Soviet Army was approaching, closing in on Berlin from the east.

The Nazis quickly set up what they called the "little camp" inside

Buchenwald, housing these newcomers in tents and a windowless horse stable. There was only one latrine for thousands of men, no water, no heat, and little food. We were glad that the Allies were inching closer, but it didn't change the fact that we were all starving to death. Corpses littered the ground, piling up faster than they could be taken away. Gritty ash fell on us every day, turning the snow gray, but the crematorium still couldn't keep up with the demand. Prisoners continued to be used as slave labor in the nearby stone quarry or were forced to work twelve-hour shifts in the munitions plant. It was our job in the infirmary to keep as many of them alive as we could so they could continue to be worked to death.

Spring arrived, but the only difference was that fewer of us froze to death. We were still starving. When we learned that thousands of prisoners were now going to be evacuated from Buchenwald, we knew it could mean only one thing—Allied troops must be approaching from the west. The Nazis were being squeezed from both directions. I had learned of an underground Resistance group operating inside Buchenwald, and those brave souls did whatever they could to hinder the Nazis' plans and delay our evacuation. Weak as we were from hunger and illness, most of us wouldn't have survived a forced march.

But even as the Allied armies marched closer, so did the angel of death. I wondered which of the two would reach me first. Ada, Lotti, and I, along with most of the women in our barracks, fell ill with fevers and dysentery. Our bodies were too weak to fight off illness, too weak to stand in line for our meager food rations, too weak to move the bodies of the women who had died during the night out of our overcrowded bunks. Hope came in the form of artillery fire, which we could hear in the distance. It meant help was coming closer. When the sun set each day, I would remember what Sam and I used to say to each other, and I would whisper, "We're another day closer." I could only hope that help didn't arrive too late.

My fever soared. One minute I was shivering; the next I was burning up. My fitful sleep was haunted by nightmares of torture and death, yet each time I awoke, I discovered that the nightmares were real. I was still a prisoner. I was still in Buchenwald. I still wanted to survive, but I was slowly forgetting the reason why. At least death would bring relief.

I wasn't sure how many days I lay on my bunk, delirious and dying, before I became aware of shouting outside. I thought I heard the word *Americans*. Someone was shouting that the Americans were here. I didn't know whether to rejoice or not. Were these the same Americans who had called out to us from the Coast Guard cutter off the coast of Florida, telling us to go away, saying we weren't wanted? Or the same Americans who had clumsily dropped tons of bombs on innocent civilians in Mortsel? I wanted to ask these Americans if they were really going to help us this time or turn their backs on us again.

I summoned my strength and managed to roll over and drop from my bunk to the floor. I could see blue sky beyond the open door, but I knew I wouldn't be able to walk. I crawled instead, pulling my way forward, holding on to whatever I could grasp, until I was outside. The commotion was louder now—voices and shouts and the sound of motor vehicles. I had managed to drag myself only a few feet forward in the dirt before I collapsed, facedown. I heard footsteps approaching, then a man's voice above me saying, "Looks like we got here just in time." The man crouched in the dust and gently rolled me over. I opened my eyes and looked up.

Sam! It was Sam!

I smiled and whispered his name. He was still as handsome as a film star with hair the color of honey and eyes the same greenish-blue as the ocean. I remembered the first time we met, just as the *St. Louis* began to steam out of the harbor in Hamburg. I had heard a voice saying, *"Right on time,"* and I'd turned to see a young man about my age standing behind me, studying his pocket watch. *"Germans are always on time,"* he'd said. He'd closed the lid and returned the watch to his pant pocket, then smiled and held out his hand. *"I'm Sam Shapiro."* And now Sam was bending over me and reaching for my hand again, not to shake it but to feel for my pulse.

"Sam," I whispered again.

"What's your name?" he asked me in English. Sam and I used to practice speaking English on board the ship. We had taken English lessons together in Antwerp.

I smiled up at him. Sam knew my name but I whispered it anyway. "Gisela."

"I'm Jim," he said. "And I'm going to take good care of you, Gisela."

＊　　＊　　＊

I was one of the lucky ones. My body responded to the food and medicine I received. Maybe it was because I had been in Buchenwald less than a year, while others had been there for a lifetime, laboring in the quarries. But when my fever broke and I was able to sit up by myself for the first time, I saw a Nazi guard tower and strings of barbed wire outside the window. Tears filled my eyes as I sank down in bed again. I was still in Buchenwald. This hospital and the care I'd received had been only a dream. Soon I would awaken to the nightmare that my life had become.

"Are you all right, Gisela? Is something wrong?" I opened my eyes and saw the soldier who had first rescued me. The soldier I had mistaken for Sam. I thought I remembered him feeding me in my feverish dreams, giving me medicine and kind, tender care. His face had often been the first one I saw when I startled awake from a nightmare. Even so, I was disappointed to realize that he wasn't Sam after all. I rose up on my elbows again and looked around at the rows of beds crowded together, filled with hundreds of patients like me. Many had IV bottles dangling from stands by their cots.

"Where am I?" I asked.

"In the hospital. I'm an American soldier, and we set up this hospital after we liberated the camp." He had replied in English but his words were clear and easy to understand.

"So I am still in Buchenwald?" I asked, also in English.

"Yes, but you're no longer a prisoner. We turned the former SS barracks into a hospital for now. We believe you have typhoid fever but you're getting better, Gisela. I'm so glad."

"How long have I been sick?"

"We arrived at this camp almost a month ago. And I have more good news for you. The Nazis have surrendered. Hitler killed himself. The war is over."

"Is that really true?"

"Yes. It's really true." I closed my eyes as they filled with tears. "You'll be strong enough to leave this place pretty soon, Gisela. You're a real fighter. I admire your courage."

He had called me by my real name, not Ella Maes and not by the number tattooed on my arm. "How did you know my name?" I asked.

"You told it to me on the day I arrived. My name is Jim, by the way. Jim Barnett. I'm a medic in the US Army. Are you hungry? We'd like it if you tried to eat every few hours. Not much, just a little bit at a time." I told him I would try, and he let me feed myself for the first time since I'd been rescued, urging me to go slowly. "Your body needs to get used to food again."

In the days that followed, Jim slowly brought me back to life as surely as if he had transfused the blood from his own arm into mine. The food and medicine healed my ravaged body, but his gentle touch and soft voice healed my soul after years of bitter abuse. "Do you feel like getting up and maybe taking a few steps?" he asked one morning. "I can help you."

I agreed, knowing I would need to recover my strength if I hoped to leave Buchenwald and search for Sam and Ruthie. As far as I knew, they were the only loved ones I had left, and they gave me a reason to go on living. Jim slowly helped me to my feet, pausing until the dizziness passed and I found my balance. He wrapped his arm around my waist to steady me as I started walking again. I wondered if he was repulsed to be gripping a living skeleton. We reached the end of the row of beds, and I stopped for a moment to rest and catch my breath before turning back. There was a small window there that looked out at the bright spring day. Buchenwald meant "beech grove," and the trees on the little hill beyond the barracks had new green leaves. I looked only at the trees—another sign of hope—and not at the barbed wire or the sprawling ugliness of the camp below. Death had been a daily presence in Buchenwald. The sight of it and the stench of it had filled every wretched inch of the camp. Now, like the new green leaves on the trees beyond the guard tower, life was reclaiming me and my fellow prisoners.

"You seem to understand English very well, Gisela," Jim said as I hobbled back to my bed. "Where are you from?"

"I grew up in Berlin and lived in Belgium before I was brought here. I learned English because my family hoped to immigrate to the United States."

"Would you be willing to help us communicate with our other patients when you're feeling stronger?"

"Yes, of course. I would be glad to help." He and the other medics and doctors would tell me what they wanted to say, and I would try to translate it into German or Flemish. The fact that I had nurse's training helped.

When I was able to move around on my own fairly well, I glimpsed my reflection in a window one day and was appalled by what I saw. My hair had grown back in ragged patches after being shaved off. Festering sores covered my pale, colorless skin from lice and flea bites and malnutrition. I could have counted all my bones, like the diagrams of skeletons we'd studied in anatomy class. Would Sam still love me if he saw me? Even if I had been strong enough to search for him, I didn't want him to see me this way.

Little by little, my strength returned and I was released from the camp hospital. But there were still so many thousands of people to care for. I had told Jim and the others that I was a licensed nurse, and now I asked if I could stay and help take care of the other patients and translate for them.

"You would be willing to stay in this terrible place when you have a chance to leave?" Jim asked in amazement.

"It's the least I can do. Besides, I have no home to return to and no money to get there even if I did have the strength to travel."

Major Cleveland, who was in charge of all the hospital facilities, agreed.

"But please take it slow and easy," Jim said. "You can start by helping just a little bit every day." I took patients' vital signs, adjusted IV tubes, gave sponge baths, and hand-fed people too weak to feed themselves. I talked with them and listened to their stories. The SS barracks was filled with the most desperate cases, but many thousands in the camp outside still had urgent needs for nursing care, too. Jim moved a cot into what had been the barracks' pantry and I slept there when I wasn't working. The work I did in the following weeks helped restore me to wholeness. At last, I had found the reason for my becoming a nurse.

The stronger I grew, the more restless I became to find Sam and Ruthie. I had already begun searching while I was still a patient, helped by various Jewish relief agencies and the Red Cross. They had set up tracing services in the camp to help former prisoners find their loved ones. I had added my name to the lists of the living, and whenever a new list was printed, I searched it for Sam's and Ruthie's names. There were also endless lists of the dead. Hope and fear wrestled in my heart every time I read through those names. I was reading the list of the dead from Auschwitz one day when I saw Sam's name. My heart stopped. But this Sam Shapiro had been from Austria and was sixty-seven years old when he died. I must have looked pale when I finished reading because Jim hurried over to me and asked, "Are you all right, Gisela?"

"I had a bad scare. I found my fiancé's name on a list from Auschwitz, but it wasn't him after all."

"Let's step outside for some air and you can tell me about him." We walked out of the barracks and all the way to the open gate so I wouldn't feel so trapped behind the walls and barbed wire. Jim and I had become friends by then, and I knew I could tell him anything. He had a gift for being still and listening to people, and sometimes it seemed as though he could see into our very souls. An Army vehicle was parked outside the wall and we sat down on the bumper together. "What's your fiancé's name?" Jim asked.

"Sam Shapiro."

"I think you called out his name a few times when you were delirious. Is he also from Berlin?"

"We met on board a luxury steamship, the *St. Louis*, that was supposed to take us to safety in Cuba. But something went wrong and the
Cuban government refused to accept our landing permits. We sailed
around the Atlantic Ocean for a month, searching for someplace to land,
trying to find a friendly nation that would offer us refuge."

"I remember when that happened," Jim said. "I followed the story
in the newspaper for days. I even wrote a letter to President Roosevelt,
begging him to let the passengers land in the United States. When the
ship had to return to Europe, the newspapers led us to believe there'd
been a happy ending to the story. Everyone had found refuge outside
of Germany."

"That's true; we were given refuge, but it wasn't a happy ending.
Most of us ended up in either France, the Netherlands, or Belgium,
countries that eventually fell to the Nazis. Only the passengers who'd
gone to Great Britain were able to stay out of their hands."

"That's what makes me so furious about all the death and destruction
I've witnessed over here. And now in this terrible place—which I'm told
is just one of many camps. None of this had to happen! It was our own
indifference and prejudice that caused this. Stories circulated, telling
about what was happening over here, how the Jews were being persecuted. There were even people who'd escaped and who tried to tell the
world the truth about the so-called labor camps. But people in America
didn't want to hear it. They thought the war was none of our business.
Yes, the Nazis are responsible for this. But so are ordinary people like me
who decided to look the other way."

Jim had balled his hands into fists, and I took one of them between
my own, unfolding his fingers and rubbing them to soothe away his tension. My hands looked frail and skeletal compared to his brawny ones.

"I'm sorry," he said with a sigh. "I didn't mean to go off that way. You
were telling me about Sam."

"Sam felt everything very deeply, like you do. You remind me of him. You even resemble him a little bit. I thought you were him at first. We promised to find each other after the war ended but it seems like an impossible task at the moment. There must be millions of displaced people, refugees like me with no place to go. Aside from reading the lists every day, I don't even know where to begin."

"When did you see him last?"

"Right after I finished nursing school in 1942. We were still living in Antwerp. When the Nazis started rounding up Jews to deport us to the camps, Sam got me a forged identity card under a new name. The Catholic sisters helped me move to a different town and get a job at a different hospital. The last I knew, Sam was still in Belgium, working with the Resistance. But that was three years ago."

"I'll do whatever I can to help you, Gisela. Just let me know what you need me to do."

"Thank you. You're a good friend, Jim." I started to rise, thinking I should get back to work, but he made me stay.

"What about your other family members? Tell me about them."

"I have a younger sister, Ruthie. The Christians in Belgium let her hide in one of their orphanages. I was only able to see her once, and that was two years ago. Later, the nuns told me that she'd been placed with a family as an au pair after she turned sixteen. I don't know where she is or . . . or if she's still safe or . . . or if the Nazis found out that she's Jewish . . ."

My voice broke and it was a moment before I could continue. Jim held my hand as he listened, a gesture of warmth that had been missing in my life.

"I want to go back to Antwerp and search for her and Sam, but I know I'm not strong enough yet. As far as I know, they're the only family I have left. Before I was betrayed by a girl I knew in nursing school, I found out that my parents had both died when the transports began. I was devastated. But at least I know they were spared from this hellish place. I want to find out if Sam and Ruthie are alive, and yet I'm terrified to learn the truth. I dread reading the lists of the people who've died. As long as I don't see their names, they are still alive to me."

"I'm so sorry, Gisela," he murmured. A moment later he asked, "Did you have any other family members?"

"One of Vati's brothers, Uncle Aaron, fled to Cuba with his family. Another brother, Uncle Hermann, fled to Ecuador. I assume they're still safe, but I would hardly know them anymore after all these years. Mutti's brother and his family moved to Paris with my grandmother before the war. I haven't seen their names on a list . . . yet."

I closed my eyes to shut out the present as I remembered how our family used to gather together for holidays and birthdays and other special occasions. Our apartment in Berlin would overflow with aunts and uncles and cousins, and our table would overflow with food. I remembered how soft and warm Oma's arms were when she held me close. I remembered the sweetness of her perfume—and suddenly my sorrow threatened to drown me. I needed to talk about something else.

"Why do you stay here and do this?" I asked Jim. "I overheard Major Cleveland saying the other day that you and some of the other medics had volunteered to stay here. He said you could rejoin your unit anytime."

"What else could I possibly do that would be more important than this?" Jim replied.

"But I can tell that the work wears you down. I don't think I've ever seen you smile." Nor did he seem to sleep or eat as he worked tirelessly to save his patients. Jim shrugged but didn't reply. "Do you have a family back home? A wife or a girlfriend?" I asked.

"I have lots of friends, but there's no one special to return home to. If my parents saw this place, they would understand why I need to stay here." Jim seemed to be weighing his thoughts as if deciding whether or not to say more. When he finally spoke, his voice was soft but I heard the passion behind his words. "I saw a lot of good men die by the time we fought our way here from France. Some very good friends, men I'd known since basic training, were killed and wounded, including my college roommate. There was nothing I could do for them except try to stop the bleeding, give them morphine, and get them to an aid station so they could be evacuated to a field hospital away from the front lines. But death is everywhere here, and I want to defeat it. I want to win for once. The patient I was carrying to the hospital, just before you, died in my arms. I was determined not to let that happen to you. When I picked you up on that first day, you smiled. I saw that you had the will to fight to survive, so I wanted to save you. I wouldn't let death take away such a beautiful person. And I want to help all of the others dig down deep and find that same will to live."

I ran my fingers over my patchy hair and turned away, embarrassed to be called beautiful when I knew I wasn't.

* * *

Two days later, I read a list of Jews transported from Paris who had perished at Auschwitz. On it were my aunt's and uncle's names. My cousins' names. My grandmother's name. I couldn't handle this terrible news all alone, so I staggered to the ward where Jim was working, blinded by tears and grief. He looked up when I spoke his name and hurried over to the doorway to let me fall into his arms, weeping.

"They all died a year ago," I told him when I was able to stop sobbing. "But they were alive in my mind and in my heart until the moment I saw their names." I was trembling with emotion, and I felt a tremor in Jim's arms as he held me. It was as if he was absorbing some of my grief and helping me bear the terrible weight of it. "I don't want to be the only one left," I wept. "What will I do with all the memories of my family? I can't carry them alone."

"Maybe your sister—"

"But what if she isn't, Jim? What if I am all alone?"

His arms tightened around me, holding me together. "You'll never be alone, Gisela. I'm your friend. You know that, don't you?"

I looked up at him and saw that his eyes were wet with tears. "Yes. I do know it," I said. "And I'm very grateful."

21

Peggy

I wasn't surprised when Joe went out drinking on Saturday night after we returned home from visiting Art Davis. Dredging up memories of the war was always hard on him, yet I also knew that Art's words had touched him. Everything Joe and I had done for these past few weeks had been to help Jimmy, and now I longed to help Joe put his life back together, too. I knew nothing about his life in Ohio, only that he'd worked as a firefighter. I needed to learn more.

After Pop and Donna left the apartment to join Joe at a bar in Newburgh, I decided to sneak downstairs to the office and search through Joe's saddlebags to see what I could find. Maybe there would be a home address and I could write to Joe's family and tell them where he was and how he'd been helping me. I let myself into Pop's office, where I'd worked for so many years. Buster halted at the door and wouldn't come inside, as if afraid that Donna would jump out and yell at him. It was Donna's office now and stank of her cigarettes and the unpleasant air freshener she used to try to cover up the smell. I looked around and could see that she had reorganized the office. I told myself I didn't care.

Joe's bags lay open on the floor. His things were already in disarray, so even with a little rummaging, he probably wouldn't notice that I had riffled through them. Close to the top of his pack, I found something that surprised me—a packet of letters written by someone named Barbara Symanski. The mailing addresses and the dates on the postmarks told me that she'd sent the letters to Joe during the war. I remembered him mentioning a girlfriend who had traveled to Washington, DC, to visit him in the VA hospital. I couldn't recall anything else except that they had broken up because of his drinking. The fact that Joe still kept her letters and even carried them on his travels told me that he still cared for her. I wondered if Barbara Symanski still loved him. I would be crossing a line if I read the letters, but I copied down her return address, determined to contact Barbara and find out more.

I woke up later that night when Joe had one of his nightmares. Buster and I hurried downstairs to wake him. We talked for a while until Joe stopped trembling, but I lacked the courage to ask him about Barbara. The stars were fading in the east when I finally returned upstairs to sleep for a few more hours before church.

I didn't have to think of clever small talk when I saw Paul Dixon after the Sunday service. He was still gushing praise and thanking me for helping Persephone. "I hope you'll come out and see her new little filly. She's a real beauty. It was a shame that you and your boyfriend needed to hurry off again after all your hard work."

My boyfriend? It took me a moment to remember that I had ridden out to the farm on Joe's motorcycle. "Oh, you mean Joe? No, Joe isn't my boyfriend. I-I just needed a ride because Donna, my stepmother— well, Donna isn't really my stepmother—but she took my car and . . ." I stopped. I was babbling, still weary from being awake half the night. "Thank you. I would love to see Persephone's filly. What's her name?"

"Her owner named her Tyche after the Greek goddess of fortune. Her sire is named Best Chance and of course Persephone is a Greek goddess, too. It's clever, don't you think?" I nodded, afraid to open my mouth and babble nonsense again. "Tyche is as shy as her mother, so I may need your help with her, Peggy. You seem to speak their language."

"That's because I'm shy myself."

"Not with me, I hope."

"No." I dared to meet his gaze and noticed for the first time that his eyes were as blue as the summer sky. Things got awkward after that, so I promised to visit Persephone and Tyche and wished Paul a good day. When I returned home, Joe's motorcycle was gone. I went into Pop's office to see if his saddlebags were there, but they were gone, too. He'd left a note for me on the daybed.

I don't think I can go to the VA with you today, Peggy. Sorry for not saying goodbye, but I need to take off. I always wanted to see Niagara Falls. Maybe I'll stop back in a week or so. Thanks for everything.

Joe

I rode to the VA hospital with Jimmy's parents after lunch and told them about my trip to Vermont to see Art Davis. "From what I can gather, the change in Jimmy came between the winter of 1944 when Mitch O'Hara died, and the spring of 1945 when his Army unit liberated Buchenwald," I said. "Art Davis didn't remember Jimmy ever praying or talking about his faith in the concentration camp. And it seems to me that he would need to call on God more than ever and pray for those suffering people in order to work in a place like that. It's almost like he got so overwhelmed or so mad at God that he stopped talking to Him."

"You're a very wise young lady, Peggy," Mr. Barnett said. "I think you may be close to figuring out this mystery."

"I've always loved your tender, compassionate heart," Mrs. Barnett added. We were standing on the ferry deck as we crossed the river with the bright summer sun shining down on us. She linked her arm through mine and leaned against me. "I've seen your kind heart in the way that you care for the animals at the clinic but most of all in the way that you've been working so hard to help our son."

"That's what's missing in the treatment he's getting across the river," Mr. B. said. "Compassion."

"I know you haven't had an easy life," Mrs. Barnett continued. "You lost your mother at such a young age. But I've watched you grow in faith over the years and I've seen how you've allowed God to use your suffering to become a loving person. You've always been like a daughter to me."

Her words felt like a blessing and they made me want to bawl my eyes out. I didn't know what to say in return, so I hugged her tightly. Did she really think of me as her daughter? I had longed to have Mrs. Barnett for a mother ever since the day she gave me the bubble bath, but whenever I spent time with her, I would hear Pop's voice in my mind, telling me not to be a pest. I rode the rest of the way to the hospital savoring her words and the warmth of her hug.

We found Jim slumped in a chair in the common room, and he seemed wearier than usual. I wondered if his nightmares were still keeping him from sleeping well. Joe was always afraid to go back to sleep after an especially bad nightmare. More letters from Jimmy's Army buddies had arrived in the mail, so I showed him the photographs they'd sent and I read parts of their letters out loud. His mother sat beside him and talked about home as they looked at the album I'd made.

"You have so many friends, Jimmy, and we all miss you so much," she said. "We hope you'll be able to come home with us soon."

We were encouraged when he actually talked to us a little bit, speaking in simple sentences, even though his voice was a dull monotone not at all like his own. The visit seemed to be going well until I took out Jimmy's Bible and tried to read one of his underlined verses out loud. "Stop!" he said. He grabbed the book from my hands, closing it. His reaction shook me.

"I'm sorry," I murmured. "I'm so sorry." I bent to pick up the braided straw bookmark, which had fluttered to the floor. Mr. Barnett suggested we all go outside and walk around the grounds, but I knew I had ruined the day. I tried to apologize to his parents on the ride home.

"No, I'm glad it happened," Mr. Barnett said. "It shows that you were right, the root of Jim's problem might be a crisis of faith."

"But if Jimmy has lost his faith, what can we do about it?" I asked.

"I'm not sure. Maybe Jim's chaplain friend can help us out."

I wanted to leave the sadness of the VA hospital behind me as we recrossed the river, but I couldn't help carrying some of it with me to the other side.

We made a long-distance call to Chaplain Bill when we returned home and asked him to please find an address for Major Mike Cleveland, the man Art Davis had told us about. I quickly told Bill how Jimmy had reacted when I'd tried to read the Bible, and he promised to help us figure out what that meant. "I'll try to get over for a visit one of these Sundays," he promised. There was nothing more we could do except wait.

I worked at the clinic all day Monday, going with Mr. Barnett on his call to a dairy farm and then stopping at Blue Fence Farms so we could check on Persephone and Tyche. I felt less awkward chatting with Paul Dixon out on the farm than I did when trying to be polite among the Sunday morning crowd. I fell in love with gentle Tyche immediately.

When we returned to the clinic, Buster was waiting outside the farmhouse. He had followed me across the street when I'd left Pop's apartment in the morning, and I'd had to haul him home. Now he was back again. I could have tied him up behind the garage, but I was afraid he would bark and howl all day if I did.

"Let him stay here, Peggy," Mr. Barnett said when he saw me grabbing Buster's collar to drag him back across the street. "He's not hurting anything. I think it's nice to have a friendly dog to welcome people to the clinic. Besides," he said, his voice going soft, "he reminds me that healing miracles can happen."

When Buster and I finally walked home late that afternoon, Pop called to me from the garage before I had a chance to go upstairs to the apartment. I was afraid he was going to ask me where Joe was and say something about how unreliable he was for disappearing all the time, but Pop surprised me with a question. "You still want a used car?"

"Um, yes."

He closed the hood of the car he'd been working on and picked up a rag to wipe grease off his hands. "How much you thinking to spend?"

"I don't know. I have a little saved up from working at IBM, but I don't want to use all of it."

"Well, I found a car," he said, tossing the rag into the work sink. "A 1939 Ford Deluxe. Runs real good. But Donna says she'd like to have it."

I lifted my arms and let them drop again. I had no idea how to respond or why he was telling me this. It was getting harder and harder not to resent Donna. "So what are you saying?" I finally asked.

"Give me fifty dollars for her old car and we'll call it even."

"*Her* old car? You mean the car I used to drive before Donna quit working at the Crow Bar and started using it all the time? *That* car?"

"Right." Pop didn't seem to notice my sarcasm or see the irony in asking me to pay him for a car that had practically been mine. "Donna says that car stinks from hauling your dog all over the countryside."

I exhaled and counted to ten. "Fine. The bank is closed for the day, but I'll go there tomorrow on my lunch hour and withdraw fifty dollars." I hurried away before I said something I shouldn't. Pop might not have realized how much he hurt me when he took Donna's side against me. It was time for me to move out of the apartment before the two of them broke my heart for good. I could do it now that I had a car and a full-time job.

I walked to the bank on my lunch break the following day and withdrew one hundred dollars. I would give half of it to Pop for the car and use the other half to find a place to live. A widow named Mrs. Jenkins who attended my church operated a guesthouse on the other side of town, a roomy Victorian home with a tower and lead glass windows. She didn't have regular boarders, just weekend visitors who came up from New York City to spend time in the mountains. I walked there after going to the bank, hoping she would let me board until I could find a permanent place. Mrs. Jenkins didn't ask any questions as she showed me a large room on the second floor facing Main Street. The simple space was plain but clean, with twin beds and a dresser and a shared bathroom down the hall with a large tub.

"There's no one staying here at the moment," she said, "so you'll have the place to yourself. But I'm expecting people from the city this weekend." I gave her enough money to stay for a week, including my evening meals, and told her I would be back later with my things. I paid Pop fifty dollars before returning to work, and the old car was mine. Since Buster was already making himself at home at the Barnetts' house, I summoned my courage to ask if I could board him in the clinic's kennels at night.

"Pop's girlfriend hates him," I explained. "I know he'll be happier here, since she doesn't want him around, and then I won't have to worry about him crossing the road all the time."

"Of course, Peggy," Mr. Barnett said. "Is . . . um . . . everything all right?" I could tell by his concerned expression that he didn't understand what had changed back home. I wasn't sure I did, either. After all, Donna had moved in with us more than four years ago.

"I don't think it will be for very long," I said quickly. "I'm planning to find a place of my own now that I have a full-time job."

"Buster is welcome for as long as you need. And let me know if I can help in any way."

Buster followed me home to Pop's apartment after work, unaware that it would be for the last time. He came up to my bedroom with me and watched as I packed a suitcase with enough clothes for a week and stuffed everything else that I owned into grocery bags. They could stay in the trunk of my car for now. Donna saw me making trips up and down the stairs with the bags and loading them into my car, but she didn't say a word. When my bedroom was empty, I took Buster across the street to feed him his dinner and lock him inside the kennel. We were both brokenhearted. I couldn't remember ever being apart from him overnight. And he had never been locked inside a cage before.

"I'm sorry, Buster. I'm so sorry," I said as I knelt and hugged him.

"This is only temporary. I'll find us a place to live—I promise." I heard him whine as I hurried away and tried with all my heart not to hate Donna. A desert began to grow inside me as I drove across town to my lonely room in the guesthouse. Grief howled through my heart like a savage wind. I hadn't felt this bad since Mama and our baby died. It was one thing to leave home voluntarily and quite another to be pushed out of the only home I'd ever known. I felt unloved. Unworthy of love.

"I kept your dinner warm in the oven, dear," Mrs. Jenkins said when I arrived. "I hope you like chicken and dumplings."

"Yes, thank you so much." I had no appetite, but she'd gone to so much trouble. I ate at her kitchen table while she bustled around, washing dishes and scouring the sink with Dutch cleanser. I knew that the polite thing to do would be to make conversation but I felt too desolate to try.

"You're welcome to use the parlor anytime, to read or listen to the radio, if you'd like," she told me.

"Thank you. But I think I'll just get settled in my room for the night." I wondered if I would be able to sleep.

I set Mama's crucifix on the bureau as I filled the empty drawers with my things. The little wooden cross brought back another memory of Jimmy, and for a moment, it was as if he had come to sit alongside me and console me in my grief. *It doesn't matter what other people think of you, Peggety; the important truth is what God thinks. And you are His daughter. His beloved child.*

On the day that he'd spoken those words, I had taken the path from the road down to the river to be alone, upset by something that had happened at school. But Jimmy was already sitting on a rock beside the river, tossing pebbles into the water. I quickly turned back, thinking he probably wanted to be alone, too. But Buster bounded over to him with his crazy, three-legged gallop, and gave me away.

"Hey, don't go," Jimmy had called. "Come sit for a while." I wiped my tears on my sleeve and tried to keep my head lowered so he wouldn't see that I'd been crying. But Jimmy knew. He always knew. "What's wrong, Peggety?" he asked after we'd sat there for a while. I was a freshman in high school at the time and Jimmy must have been home from college for the weekend. The war hadn't started yet.

I swallowed a sob and told him how there was a sock hop at the school that night, and the other girls had been whispering and giggling all day about what they were going to wear and which boys they hoped to dance with. A bunch of these girls were also having a pajama party afterwards, and it sounded like so much fun—but of course they would never invite someone like me. "They make me feel so worthless. Like there's something wrong with me. That I'm not like everyone else."

We sat side by side for the next hour while Jimmy patiently explained that I had been made in God's image. I had value and worth in His eyes. God loved me with a passionate love that made Him grieve when I was mistreated. He had stroked Buster's head and said, "The fierce, protective love that you feel for Buster is only a fraction of the love God feels for you. You don't care that Buster isn't like other dogs, do you?"

"No," I'd said, shaking my head.

"If you ever doubt God's love for you, Peggety, just look at the cross. It will always remind you of how much He loves you. He hates to watch you suffer. He would never allow it unless He had a reason for it."

Jimmy's words hadn't changed my situation but they had changed me. I needed to remind myself of them now, alone in the echoing guesthouse. I thought about the passage in Isaiah that had become one of my favorites. *"Can a mother forget her nursing child? Can she feel no love for the child she has borne? But even if that were possible, I would not forget you! See, I have written your name on the palms of my hands."*

"You are God's beloved child," Jimmy had said. I wished there was a way that I could remind him of his own words. I wanted so badly to help him get well. I needed to stop feeling sorry for myself and think about helping him. And helping Joe, too. I had packed stationery and envelopes in my suitcase, planning to write a letter to Joe's girlfriend, Barbara Symanski. I got them out now, thinking of what I could say. I rehearsed everything in my mind, then pulled out a sheet of stationery and wrote:

Dear Miss Symanski . . . I stopped. Exchanging letters took much too long. I didn't know how much longer Joe would keep coming around before he took off for good. I needed to telephone Barbara instead.

The August evening was warm, the summer sky still light, so I gathered up all of the loose change I could find and walked through town to the corner store to cash some dollar bills. Then I closed myself inside the public telephone booth that stood outside the store and called directory assistance in Youngstown, Ohio. The operator told me that the phone number for Barbara's address was listed under a Henry Symanski. I wrote down the number, then said a little prayer and dialed the long-distance operator. She told me the amount, and I plunked coins into the slot as fast as I could. I could have made the call person-to-person for a little more money, but I decided to take a chance on reaching Barbara. A man answered the phone.

"May I please speak to Barbara Symanski?" I asked, my voice trembling.

I heard him shouting, "Hey, Barbie! Telephone," and my heart sped up. I had never done anything this bold or crazy before. What in the world would she think of this busybody from New York calling her on a Tuesday night? I didn't have time to worry about it.

"Hello, this is Barb," she said a few moments later.

"Um, hi. My name is Peggy Serrano. I-I met a friend of yours, Joe Fiore, and—"

"Joe? Do you know where Joe is? Is he all right?" I guessed by the way she nearly shouted the questions into the phone that Barbara still cared for him.

"Yes. Yes, he's fine. He's here in New York State."

"Thank God!" I heard her sigh. "What's he doing there? Where's he staying? Do you know when he's coming home?"

"Well, Joe came here about a month and a half ago to visit my friend Jimmy Barnett, who he knew from the Army. But when he found out that Jimmy is in the VA hospital with battle fatigue, Joe decided to stick around and help Jimmy's family and me try to get him better again. Joe has been coming and going ever since, staying in my pop's car repair shop and even working for Pop when he needs a little money. Joe has been a real godsend to us." I had poured out my story quickly, aware of how much each minute was costing me. I could only hope my hurried explanation made sense to her.

"Oh, I've been so worried about him!" Barbara said when I paused. "Joe has battle fatigue, too. I tried to help him when he came home from the hospital, but he got mad at me and everyone else and took off on his motorcycle. You say he's better now?"

"Well, not exactly. He still has nightmares about the war, which he tries to forget by drinking too much. He's still a bit of a lost soul. That's why I decided to call you. Joe carries all your letters around with him—that's how I got your name and address—so he must still care about you."

"I love him. I'll do anything to help him!"

"Great! Joe has become a good friend. We've been contacting some of his old Army buddies, and they've been offering some good advice about how to leave the war behind and move forward. Joe has been listening to everything they've said. I know he can't be a firefighter anymore, but I think with a little help, he could figure out what to do next. Many of his friends told us how important their wife or girlfriend was in their recovery—"

"I tried so hard. But Joe just got mad and accused me of nagging."

"I understand. Joe puts up a tough front. I also know that helping his friend Jimmy has made him feel like he's doing something useful. I think he might have learned a few things about himself, too, along the way. He's starting to see that he isn't alone, that other soldiers are also having a hard time. Maybe he'll let you help him now, after hearing his buddies' advice and traveling around a bit. At least, I hope so. Joe is a great guy and he deserves to be happy again. I want to help him and I wanted to talk to you since you know him better."

"I would do anything for Joe. Did he say when he's coming home?"

"No. But I just had a crazy idea that maybe—" The operator

interrupted, asking for more money. I scrambled to deposit another handful of coins, then asked, "Are you still there, Barbara?"

"Yes, I'm here. You said you had a crazy idea?"

"Well, what if you took a Greyhound bus out here to be where Joe is? You could stay with me. Joe might get mad at us for meddling, but at least he would see how much you still love him."

She was quiet for a moment. "Goodness. That is a crazy idea. But I love Joe so much—at least I loved the 'old' Joe, the man I knew before he went off to war."

"He's still a great guy—I can tell. It's been really hard for him to talk about the war, but he's determined to rescue Jimmy. And he rescued me, too, by helping me get a job that I love. That's another reason why I want to help him."

I heard the phone beep, warning me that I had one minute left before I would need to put in more money. "My time is almost up again—"

"Give me your address and phone number," Barbara said quickly. "I'll think about it and get back to you. You said your name is Peggy?"

"Yes, Peggy Serrano." I gave her my information and the telephone number at the clinic moments before my time was up.

"Thank you so much for calling!" I heard Barbara say before we were cut off.

I walked back to the guesthouse, looking up at the millions of stars and thanking God that He loved me. And thanking God that my friend Joe had a woman who loved him.

22

Gisela

Izaak had become one of my favorite patients. He was young, only six-teen years old. Too young to even shave or grow a beard. He had been near death when Jim found him in the "little camp" among the prisoners who had been forced to march to Buchenwald from Auschwitz. He was a Polish Jew, captured while fighting with the partisans. Izaak always had a smile for me, even when he was in pain. I helped him read through the lists of names every day, searching for his family and for fifteen-year-old Rivka, the rabbi's daughter, whom he'd loved since he was a boy. But then Izaak's condition worsened, complicated by an infection after los-ing his toes to frostbite. The doctors did everything they could, but they couldn't save him. Jim and I were at his bedside when he died.

Many of our patients had died in spite of everything we did to save them, but this loss was too much for Jim. Everyone in the barracks could hear him weeping. It was as if Izaak's death had unleashed the floodgates of his grief, and he wept for every person who had died in Buchenwald. I did my best to console Jim, but I was grieving for young Izaak, too. Later that afternoon, the major in charge of the camp sent for Jim.

"Come with me, Gisela," Jim begged. "He's probably having me transferred, and I need your help to convince him to let me stay."

I looked at Jim's gray face and red-rimmed eyes and said, "Maybe you should get away from this awful place for a while."

He shook his head. "There's still work to do here."

I went with him.

The major was using the same office in the former barracks that the SS had used, and even though all the swastikas and other insignias had been removed, the place still made me uneasy. It reminded me of how powerless I and all the people I loved had been—and still were, for that matter. I was dependent on others for my food and shelter and even for restoring my health. Jim had talked Major Cleveland into allowing me to work here, as if he knew that the work would help restore my dignity. Now I pushed aside my queasiness to help Jim in return.

"I'm worried about you, Corporal Barnett," Major Cleveland said.

"I'm sorry for breaking down, sir. It won't happen again."

The major banged his fist on his desk. "It *should* happen again, Corporal! Every one of us should be weeping rivers of tears over what went on in this camp! That said, I believe it's time I transferred you back to your unit."

"Please don't do that, sir," I said. "Every patient in the hospital heard the corporal weeping today. Do you have any idea how long it has been since a Jew heard someone weeping for him? We've been despised, spat upon, degraded in every way. Jim showed us that we're still worthy of someone's tears."

The major leaned back in his chair and sighed. "Is that what you want, Corporal? Do you want to stay?"

"Yes, sir."

"Very well. But you still need to take a break from this place." He removed a pen from its marble holder and started writing on one of the papers in front of him. "I'm issuing you a seven-day leave and ordering you to take it."

Jim lifted his hands. "Where would I go, sir?"

"That's up to you. Anywhere! As long as it's out of this godforsaken place."

Jim stared at the floor without replying. I couldn't guess what was going through his mind, but when he finally spoke, I wasn't surprised to learn that he'd been thinking of others, not himself. "Nurse Wolff has been working just as hard as me, Major, and I know that she's anxious to search for her loved ones in Belgium. With your permission and with your help, I would like to spend my leave escorting Gisela to Antwerp, along with any other Belgians who want to go. A military escort, of sorts."

"As long as you take time to rest, Corporal."

"I'll make sure of it, sir," I said.

"Very well. I believe the trip can be arranged."

We left the major's office with the papers we would need. I would be leaving the camp for the first time, and with memories of Nazi persecution still haunting me, I was glad that I wasn't making the journey alone. My friend Jim, who would wear his US Army uniform, was committed to helping me search for Sam and Ruthie. I was both excited and terrified.

Jewish relief agencies and the Red Cross supplied clothes and shoes to former prisoners like me, and they also provided food for our trip. Together with a group of nine recovered prisoners who also wanted to make the journey, we boarded an Army vehicle for the ride to the train station in Weimar.

"We learned about the city of Weimar in school," I told Jim as we waited there in the train station. "It was the home of Johann von Goethe, one of Germany's treasured authors. But after what happened nearby in Buchenwald, I wonder if the city will ever seem noble again."

"In the first weeks after the surrender," Jim said, "when you were still very ill in the hospital, our Army forced the citizens of Weimar to take a tour of Buchenwald. We wanted them to see for themselves the dirty little secret they had allowed to happen in their backyard."

"How did they react?"

"They seemed shocked. Many claimed they didn't know what was happening there, but I think they chose not to know. In my mind, that makes them just as guilty."

*　　*　　*

The train trip across Germany to Belgium, with all of the transfers and delays and layovers, took three times as long as it would have before the war. Jim's uniform and official papers paved our way through a lot of confusion and red tape, especially since the other survivors and I didn't have any identification to show at the borders. We ate our Red Cross rations and dozed on and off in train stations and in passenger cars, slumped against each other. None of us complained, remembering the wretched journey that had brought us to Buchenwald. Gazing from the train window, we sometimes saw fields and villages that seemed untouched by the war. But there were many more scenes, especially in cities like Frankfurt and Cologne, where the ruin and destruction seemed so complete that I couldn't imagine how Europe could ever be rebuilt. We passed countless abandoned Army vehicles and military sites with twisted wreckage of tanks and artillery. Soldiers from the liberating armies seemed as ever present as the Nazis had been.

At last we got off the train in Antwerp and were met by representatives from the Jewish relief agency. They took me and the others to a temporary hostel for displaced persons where we would have a warm meal and could spend the night. I registered my name with them and asked for their help in finding Uncle Aaron and Sam's father in Havana. They promised to contact their branch in Cuba. I also gave them what information I had about Uncle Hermann in Ecuador.

I didn't know where Jim went, but he returned for me in the morning, and we sat down in a little café in the city center to drink coffee and make plans. The brew smelled wonderful, but I ordered hot milk, not daring to drink coffee yet. I gazed out at the bustling square, remembering how lovely it had looked when I'd seen it for the first time with Sam—how many years ago?

Jim saw me staring into the distance and said, "I hope you're think-ing of a pleasant memory."

"Yes, pleasant, but also painful." I paused, blowing on the milk to cool it. "I was remembering how Sam and I used to explore Antwerp's coffee shops together when we first arrived in Belgium. Back then, no one cared that we were Jewish. We were so young and hopeful—" I stopped. My tears would start falling if I said more.

Jim gently brought me back to the present. "Where would you like to search for Sam first?" My memories of Sam flew off like startled sparrows.

"I need to see Sister Veronica at the nursing school. She offered to relay messages for us. If Sam is searching for me, that's where he'll begin." We finished our beverages and hopped on the same trolley line that I'd used to travel to school. Classes were in session when we arrived, and everything looked the same: the nuns in their black habits, their dan-gling crosses swinging as they walked; the young, eager-looking nursing students hurrying through the halls in their uniforms. It was as if I had never left, and I wondered how that could be. I had lived a lifetime since graduating three years ago.

"May I please speak with Sister Veronica?" I asked the nun in the outer office. "I'm one of her former students, Gisela Wolff."

"I'm so sorry," she said softly. "But Sister Veronica passed away shortly before liberation." I had to sit down. It was another loss, another friend gone forever. "Are you all right?" the nun asked.

"Just shocked. And sad."

"Would you like to speak with Sister Mary Margaret? She's in charge now."

I stood and entered the office where Sister Veronica had always wel-comed and encouraged me, and I recognized Sister Mary Margaret right away. She had traveled on the train with Ruthie and me when we'd fled Antwerp, and had given us prayer books and rosary beads. She knew who I was, too.

"Gisela! Welcome back!" She hurried from behind her desk and drew me into her embrace. "We were told you'd been arrested. I can't even imagine all that you've suffered!" I could only nod. "Please, have a seat. Tell me what I can do for you, dear."

I sank down gratefully, my knees trembling with fear and hope as I prepared to ask about Sam. "Before I went into hiding at Hospital Sint-Augustinus, Sister Veronica offered to relay messages between me and my fiancé, Sam Shapiro. She knew my false name, Ella Maes, and where I was working and hiding. You did, too, of course."

"Yes, I remember. We've prayed for you every day, Gisela, which is why I'm so thrilled to see you."

"Has . . . has my fiancé come looking for me? He must be trying to find me. Has he left any messages?" I held my breath in anticipation and dread.

"I'm afraid not. I'm so sorry."

I closed my eyes as the darkness that had nearly suffocated me in Buchenwald threatened to swallow me alive. Thoughts of finding Sam had been my only ray of light. But Sam hadn't come. He hadn't left any messages for me. I dared to offer up a prayer, my first in a very long time. *Please don't let him be dead. Please help us find each other.*

When I was in control again, I asked, "When was Antwerp liberated?"

"In December of last year. Brussels was liberated a few months earlier."

I was speechless. Antwerp had been freed from Nazi domination just four months after I had been arrested. Four months! What cruel twist of fate had put Lina Renard in the same hospital with me, to betray me, when I might have been free all this time? It seemed absurd that the Nazis would continue to conduct their transports to the death camps even as they were losing the war. And even more absurd to think that if it weren't for Lina Renard's betrayal, I would have been free since last December. The news raised another, more terrifying question: if Belgium had been free for so long, why hadn't Sam come here to search for me? I was certain he would have—if he had been able to.

"May I ask what your plans are now, Gisela?" Sister Mary Margaret asked, interrupting my thoughts.

"I-I don't know. I'm still trying to find all the people I love."

"I wish you success and God's blessings. If you ever need work, please know that we will be very happy to find a place for you at our hospital." She copied down Jim's military address to contact me, and I thanked her for her kindness.

"I guess that didn't go well," Jim said when I came out of the office. I was wiping tears that I hadn't realized were falling.

"She was very kind. But she hasn't heard from Sam."

"Come on," he said, taking my arm. "Let's not give up just yet. Do you want to try the apartment building where your families used to live?"

"No," I said quickly. I couldn't face those memories yet. My parents had died in that apartment. "I want to find my sister, Ruthie," I said.

We rode the trolley back to the central train station, then took another train to Mortsel. As Jim and I walked through the still-ruined village to the Catholic orphanage, I told him about the terrible day that the Americans had mistakenly bombed an innocent town. How four schools had been struck and hundreds of children and civilians had died.

Jim looked so devastated by the story that I was sorry for telling him. "It wasn't your fault," I told him, but he didn't seem to hear me.

We reached the orphanage, and it appeared to house even more children than before. I wondered what would happen to the Jewish children they'd been hiding if their parents had perished in the camps. "I'm very glad to see you, Miss Maes!" Sister Marie said when she greeted me. I could tell by her smile that she was sincere. "Your sister, Ruth Anne, is living with the same family as the last time you were here, working as their au pair." Sister Marie told us it wasn't far and gave us directions. I would have run all the way to see Ruthie if I had been able, overjoyed to know that she was still alive and well.

"I can only hope that my sister will forgive me," I told Jim as we walked. "Ruthie begged me not to leave her alone in the orphanage. And after Mortsel was bombed, she begged me to take her with me. She was so afraid to stay there, so afraid there would be another bombing."

"But if you'd done what she'd asked, she would have ended up in Buchenwald, too."

I knew Jim was right. But I couldn't forget how frightened Ruthie had been, how she had clung to me, crying and pleading.

My knees nearly buckled when I saw the house—a large three-story brick home in a neighborhood of wealthy homes. The windows were open on this hot summer day, and I could hear children's laughter and voices coming from inside.

"Are you going to be all right?" Jim asked. I nodded. "Then unless you need me, I think it would be better if I gave you some time alone with your sister. I'll take a walk and come back in a little while."

I watched him go, then took a deep breath and rang the bell. I could hear scurrying inside, and a minute later, the front door opened. For a moment, I couldn't speak. The young woman before me looked exactly like Mutti in the old photographs of her as a young woman—slender and delicate, with raven-dark hair. It was like seeing Mutti's ghost, except that Ruthie had Vati's dark, mournful eyes. She was wearing the pearl necklace from our great-grandmother that I had given her.

"Ruthie," I breathed. "Ruthie, it's me—Gisela."

"Gisela?" She swayed a bit and had to lean against the doorframe. "Is it really you?" She looked as though she wanted to hug me but was afraid. I stepped forward and pulled her into my arms. I never wanted to let her go. My sister! My beloved sister was alive and warm and real!

"Yes! Yes, it's really me," I told her. "And now we're together again at last!" Two small children had come to the door with Ruthie, and I heard the excitement in Ruthie's voice as she told them in Flemish that I was her sister. I breathed a sigh of relief.

"But why are we standing on the doorstep?" she said, flustered. "Come inside and I'll fix tea and we can talk." She shooed away the children, telling them to be good and go to their mother. Then she led me down a long hallway to the kitchen in the rear. I noticed a crucifix on the wall and a small statue of the Virgin Mary in an alcove.

"What happened to you, Gisela? Are you all right?" she asked as she filled a kettle with water.

"I've been a prisoner in the same camp as Vati."

She froze. "Buchenwald?"

"Yes. But I'm all right now." We didn't talk as Ruthie finished making the tea. I dreaded telling her about Vati and Mutti.

It was only after the tea was poured and she was seated at the table across from me that she asked, "Have you found Vati and Mutti?" My eyes filled with tears, giving her my answer before I spoke. "Oh no. No," she murmured.

I reached for her hand. "They died together, Ruthie. In our apartment. Before the Nazis had a chance to come for them."

"Vati was already dying when I left," she said. "He knew the truth, and he told me that he wasn't afraid."

"Mutti wouldn't leave him. They stayed together. I watched hundreds of people die in Buchenwald and on the trains that took us there. They all died horrible deaths, Ruthie. In some of the camps, like Auschwitz, the men and women were separated as soon as they arrived and either killed in gas chambers right away or worked to death as slaves. It was merciful that Mutti and Vati were never taken. And that they died together." We held hands as our tears fell.

"What about Sam and his family?" she asked.

"I haven't been able to find him yet. A friend came to Antwerp with me to help me find you and search for him." I was almost afraid to ask Ruthie my next question but I summoned my courage. "How has it been for you here? Do they treat you well? Have you been happy?"

"I am very fond of the Peeters family and they of me. We've had food shortages, of course, and not enough fuel last winter. But they're good people and they've been good to me. They say I'm like a daughter to them."

"Do they know that you're Jewish?"

"Mrs. Peeters guessed, so I told her the truth. When the newspapers started showing pictures of the concentration camps and saying what happened there, she said I would always be welcome to live here if I learned that my family was gone. It's been months since Belgium was liberated, and when I didn't hear from you or anyone else, I thought that everyone was dead and I was all alone." She pulled out a linen hand-kerchief to wipe her eyes.

"I'm glad you've been happy here," I said. I wondered if it would be hard for Ruthie to tear herself away from them since they'd become her new family.

"What are you going to do now, Gisela?"

The vastness of my unknown future left me hollow inside, especially if I had to face it without Sam. "I'm not sure. The war may be over but everything is still in chaos. I need to find Sam so we can decide what to do together. I've contacted the Jewish Joint Committee in Havana to try to find Uncle Aaron. If he's still in Cuba, maybe we can go live with him."

"Is that what you want to do? Move to Cuba? It was so hot there. And they didn't want us. Remember?"

"I don't know what else we can do. I saw Mutti's family and Oma's name on a list of casualties from Auschwitz." I gave her a moment to digest the news. "I only know that I want to be with you and Sam. The rest is still . . ." I lifted my hands and let them drop again.

"Where are you living now?"

"Nowhere. I was a patient in the American hospital in Buchenwald at first; then they let me work there until I was strong enough to come and search for you. If you come back with me, we'll probably need to live in a displaced persons camp until I hear from Sam or Uncle Aaron. It won't be much of a life, and we'll be starting all over again, but at least we'll be together."

Ruthie hesitated as if she was trying to imagine herself there. "Would it be all right—I mean, may I stay here until you find Sam?" she asked. "I know Mrs. Peeters will let me stay and work for her." It had been five years since I'd left home to board at the nursing school, five years since Ruthie and I had lived together as sisters. We were almost strangers after so much time and separation. She had a home here and a life of her own. I had nothing.

"Yes, of course you may stay. I'm glad you're safe and that you're happy here."

"And if you decide to go to Cuba? Would I have to go, too?"

My heart squeezed. "No," I replied. "You're my sister and I love you, but you're old enough to make your own decisions. You're a young woman now, Ruthie. And you're so pretty. I was your age when I met Sam, remember? I'll bet the young men are already flocking around you, am I right?"

She looked down at her hands and blushed a little. "There is someone I like at church. He isn't my boyfriend or anything, but we talk sometimes."

Her words struck me hard. She was talking about a Christian boy at a church, not a Jewish boy from the synagogue. "Are you still going to church and pretending to be Catholic?"

Ruthie shrugged. "I don't have to now that the war is over. But I still go with the family."

I told myself it didn't matter. Aside from my silent prayer in Sister Mary Margaret's office earlier today, I hadn't called on the God of my childhood in a very long time. I wasn't even sure I still believed in Him. "I think you should stay here until I find Sam; then we can all figure out what to do next."

We finished our tea and said goodbye. It was what I'd been doing for as long as I could remember—saying goodbye.

Jim was waiting for me outside. I saw him studying me as if to see if I was all right, so I managed a quick smile. "Ruthie is fine. She's happy here. We decided that she should stay here until . . . well, until we have someplace to go."

"Give it more time, Gisela. Everything is still in chaos after the war. The way forward will be clearer once things settle down."

"Yes, and once I find Sam."

"Shall we go back to Antwerp?" Jim asked. "I can see you're getting tired."

"Not yet. I would like to go to the rooming house where I lived before I was arrested. I didn't have very many belongings, but maybe some of them are still there."

The rooming house also seemed unchanged, and for a horrible moment, I relived the panic I'd felt on the morning that I'd seen two SS officers waiting out front for me. But the owner remembered me and was very kind. "One of the other nurses saw you being taken away and . . . well, when you didn't come back, we guessed what might have happened. I packed up all of your belongings, hoping you would return for them. They're up in the attic."

Jim climbed the ladder to the attic and retrieved the box, then sat beside me in the lounge while I sifted through it. My clothes were too large for me, but they might fit once I gained back the weight I'd lost. I would no longer need the prayer book and rosary beads Sister Mary Margaret had given me. Jim spotted the photograph my roommate's father had taken of me on graduation day and pulled it from the box. I was glad he could see that I hadn't always looked this way.

"I was going to give that picture to Sam but I never got a chance—" Suddenly the grief that had been slowly filling my heart all day caught up with me. Grief for Sister Veronica. For Sam. For the village of Mortsel. For my sister, Ruthie. And for all of my lost years. I covered my face with my hands and wept. Jim wrapped his arms around me and let me cry.

"Sam would have come looking for me if he could," I sobbed. "We promised each other!"

"We won't give up until we find him."

"And Ruthie . . . she's all the family I have left, but I feel like she was lost to me a long time ago. Nothing will ever be the same as it was before Kristallnacht . . . before Hitler and the Nazis . . . when we lived in Berlin with our aunts and uncles and cousins and grandparents . . ."

"You're right, Gisela," Jim murmured after a moment. "I'm afraid it can never be the same. But I'll help you any way I can."

Jim made me eat something before we took the train back to the hostel in Antwerp. "We've done enough for today," he said. "Try to get some rest."

I did manage to sleep, but I awoke before dawn, thinking about Sam. I remembered what he'd told me about his plans to hide his mother and brothers. "We have to go to the Hotel Centraal," I told Jim when he came for me after breakfast. "The owner was in the Resistance. He helped Sam find hiding places for his mother and brothers."

We found the modest hotel easily enough, but it seemed to take forever for my request to speak with the owner to make its way from the front desk to his office. When it finally did, Lukas Wouters welcomed Jim and me warmly. He was a tall, stately gentleman in his seventies with white hair and old-fashioned side-whiskers—not at all how I had pictured a Resistance fighter. The fact that someone his age would risk his life and his livelihood to fight the Nazis gave me a deep respect for him. But I was desperate to find Sam, so I blurted out my question before we'd barely been seated. "I'm looking for Sam Shapiro, my fiancé. Do you know what happened to him or his family?"

He nodded, but it seemed ominous that his smile had vanished. "Sam's mother, Mrs. Shapiro, hid in my family's home under a false name, posing as our maid. She remained safe with us for the duration of the war. We found hiding places for her two sons on two different farms in the countryside. Their fair coloring helped keep them safe, and the three of them were reunited after Belgium was liberated."

"What about her oldest son, Sam?"

"Yes, Sam."

My heart pounded wildly as Mr. Wouters paused.

"Sam was very active with the underground, which is how we met. He arranged for his family and for countless other Jews to go into hiding, providing false IDs and so forth. He and the others also rescued downed Allied airmen and helped them escape back to England, mostly through Spain. In the winter of 1943, Sam came to me and said that he'd decided to go to England with one of the rescued RAF crews and join the British Army. I thought it was much too dangerous. I told him the Resistance needed him here, but he was determined to fight."

"And have you heard from him?" My heart was pounding so hard that my chest hurt.

"Well, we learned through coded radio signals that he and the crew made it back to England. But after that—nothing."

My hope plummeted. Nothing? For a year and a half? "Is . . . is Mrs. Shapiro still with you?"

Mr. Wouters shook his head. "As soon as Belgium was liberated and communication became possible again, she sent a telegram to her husband in Cuba. He had acquired valid landing permits, and he'd arranged for her and their sons to join him by steamship as soon as the war ended."

"So they're gone?"

"They sailed more than a month ago. I promised to send them a cable if I heard from Sam."

"May I have their address in Cuba?"

"Certainly. I'll have my assistant get it for you. And where can I reach you, Miss Wolff, if I hear news of Sam?"

"I'll give you my APO address," Jim said. "You can reach Gisela through me for now."

"If you ever need anything, Miss Wolff—anything at all—please don't hesitate to ask."

I was so demoralized as we left the hotel that I wanted to sit down on the curb and cry. I had no idea where to go or what to do next.

"Listen," Jim said as we walked, "we know that Sam made it to England, right? And if he did join the British Army, they'll have a record of it. We'll contact them and ask for his service record."

"Do you know how to do that?" I asked.

"I'll figure it out."

There was only one place left for me to visit in Antwerp—our old apartment building. Maybe the landlord had stored some of Mutti and Vati's belongings. As we approached the building, so many memories came flooding back—not only good memories of Sam and me and our families, but also heart-pounding memories of the Antwerp pogrom. Even if I did stay in Belgium, and Sister Mary Margaret found a nursing job for me at the hospital, I would never feel truly safe or at home here. I would always see Nazi sympathizers roaming the streets, burning and looting. I would see SS officers waiting for me outside every building. And I would always wonder if the nurse working alongside me was like Lina Renard, hating me because I'm Jewish. The Nazis might have been defeated, but the hatred and cowardice that allowed them to come to power would merely go underground for now.

But if I didn't live in Belgium or in Germany, where would I live?

I was still pondering these thoughts when the landlord came to the door and welcomed us inside. He seemed impressed, as everyone had been, by Jim in his uniform. My spirits revived when he showed us a box of personal items that Vati had asked him to store for Ruthie and me. My parents' wedding rings were in there. And Mutti's photo album. We hadn't brought very much with us on the *St. Louis*, but Mutti had refused to leave the photographs behind. I would always have pictures of my family to remember them by.

"What now?" Jim asked as we left with the precious keepsakes. Once again, he had given his own address in case Sam returned or the landlord wanted to contact me.

I halted in the middle of the sidewalk. "I have no place to go," I said. Thunder rumbled in the distance, and I thought it was artillery at first, forgetting that the war was over.

Jim gazed up at the threatening sky, dark with rain clouds. "Return to Germany with me, Gisela, if you can bear it. You've been such an enormous help. There's still a lot of work you can do in the hospital and the displaced persons camps while we wait to hear back from the British authorities about Sam."

I considered it for a moment, then nodded. What else could I do? Jim was the only friend I had. He had promised not to give up until we found out what had happened to Sam. And I didn't know how I would ever face the news alone if it turned out to be bad.

23

Peggy

Buster trotted along beside me as I walked to the corner store after work
to buy a newspaper. We both preferred to walk along the river on the
other side of town, but this had become our new routine. I would carry
the paper to the nearby park and sit on a bench, circling all the available
apartments for rent while Buster sniffed in the bushes and barked at the
squirrels. Squealing children climbed on the monkey bars and swung on
the creaking swings nearby. If I found any prospects, Buster and I would
walk to the pay phone with a roll of coins from the bank and I'd call all
the promising ones. Today, there were no new listings.

"It's beginning to look like you'll be in a kennel and I'll be living in
Mrs. Jenkins's guesthouse indefinitely," I told Buster when he returned
to my side. He was bored with the park and eager to be on our way. But
I took another moment to scan the news headlines first. I had taken an
interest in the plight of the displaced persons in Europe after reading
Jimmy's letters and talking with Art Davis about the camp survivors.
Some survivors had begun crowding onto decrepit ships in an attempt

to reach Palestine, but the British government refused to allow them sanctuary there. In today's news, a ship named *Mataroa* had sailed from Marseille, France, to the port of Haifa with more than 1,200 homeless men, women, and children on board. The British Navy had intercepted it, and the refugees, many of whom had survived Nazi concentration camps, were now being detained in British internment camps on the island of Cyprus. It seemed so cruel and heartless. I hoped Jimmy would never read this news. After working so hard to save the concentration camp survivors, it would break his heart.

I finished reading and refolded the paper. The tragedy of the *Mataroa* reminded me of the newspaper clippings that Jimmy had saved, telling the story of the homeless refugees aboard the *St. Louis* before the war. I understood a little about how it felt to be homeless and unwanted, but I didn't dare feel sorry for myself if I compared my life with theirs.

Buster and I walked to the guesthouse afterwards, and I tied him to Mrs. Jenkins's clothesline pole while I went inside to eat my supper. "I still haven't been able to find an apartment for my dog and myself," I told her. We sat across from each other at the kitchen table, eating fried chicken and mashed potatoes and green beans from her garden. "I'll need to rent the room for another week, if that's okay."

"That's fine with me, dear," she replied. I wondered if she was glad to have me for company or if I was a bother. After eating, I walked back to the clinic with Buster to feed him his dinner and lock him inside his kennel for the night.

"I'm so sorry, old friend," I said as I hugged him good night. "It looks like you'll have to stay here for another week. But I'll be back first thing in the morning."

I was up and dressed shortly after dawn to keep my promise. "You're here early," Mr. Barnett said when he saw me releasing Buster. "Have you had breakfast?" I hadn't, but I hesitated to reply, not wanting to be a bother. He read my hesitation accurately. "Come inside, then. We're just about to eat. I already have a job for you today." Mrs. Barnett quickly fried two more eggs, gathered from her coop that morning, and sliced more bread for toast. I sipped her fresh coffee, eager to hear what task Mr. Barnett had for me.

"You remember the new trainer, Paul Dixon, out at Blue Fence Farms? He called and asked if you'd be willing to come out and help with Persephone and her foal."

"Has something happened to them?"

"Not at all. But they're both very skittish, and he'd like your help. You can take my truck."

"I'm not going to drive your brand-new truck," I said, laughing. "I'll drive my own car. But thanks for being willing to trust me with it." It seemed like an enormous gift.

I hurried through my morning chores after breakfast, then went across the street with Buster trotting behind me to fetch my car. I left it parked outside Pop's garage most of the time and walked everywhere.

Pop saw me and called to me from the open door of his garage. "Where have you been hiding? Donna said you moved out." I had left a week ago. Was Pop just noticing? "You find a place to rent?"

"Not yet, but I'm looking for one. Listen, I have to get going. Mr. Barnett has a job for me out at Blue Fence Farms. I'll see you later." I said the words automatically, even though they weren't true anymore. Buster leaped into the car the moment I opened the door, so I decided to take him with me. The morning was still cool, and I could park in the shade and roll all the windows down for him.

One of the stable boys directed me to the corral where Persephone and her foal were grazing. Paul was already there, and a friendly grin spread across his tanned face as I approached. "Morning, Peggy. Thanks for coming out."

"I'm happy to help." We went into the corral through the gate and watched the two horses for a moment. "She's such a beautiful mare, isn't she?" I said. "And Tyche is a little beauty, too."

"Mmm. I'm not supposed to play favorites, but Persephone is pretty special. So is her filly. I'm hoping you'll help me win their trust. I've trained a lot of horses over the years, but these two have been pretty shy about making friends with me." I loved the slow, easy way Paul talked and the way he pronounced *I'm* and *I've* like *Ah'm* and *Ah've*. It made me smile.

"I would be happy to help," I said. He had brought along a cut-up apple, and I held out the pieces as I called to Persephone. She ambled over with Tyche at her side. I murmured softly to her as I fed her the apple slices and showed Paul her favorite spots to be scratched and petted. Within half an hour, Paul had made friends with both horses.

"Thanks, Peggy," he said when we'd run out of apples. "I think she's gonna trust me from now on."

"You're welcome." He seemed nervous all of a sudden, and that made me nervous, too. "Well, I guess I should get going," I said.

He walked with me as I headed back to my car. "Say, Peggy, I've been wondering . . . would you like to go on a picnic or something with me on Sunday afternoon?"

I halted in my tracks and stared up at him, my mouth hanging open. I couldn't believe it! I had never been asked out on a date in my life! If that's what this really was. "I . . . I . . . I . . ." It was all I could manage to say. The smile went out of his eyes. He'd misunderstood my hesitation. "Yes!" I quickly blurted. "Yes, I would! But I can't go on Sunday because that's the only day I can visit my friend in the hospital."

We had reached my car and Buster was hanging halfway out the window, tongue lolling, tail thumping against the back seat as he greeted Paul and me. I let him out, and Paul crouched beside him. "Who's this?" he asked, patting Buster's head.

"My dog, Buster." I laughed as Buster licked apple juice from Paul's hand, then swiped his hot tongue across Paul's cheek in thanks. "I think he likes you."

"What happened to his leg?"

"He got hit by a car but Mr. Barnett saved his life. That's how I started working at the clinic—to pay him back for the operation. Listen, about the picnic, if we can find another day for it, I would love to go with you."

"How about after work on Saturday?"

"Okay."

"Do you know any good places around here for a sunset picnic?"

"Um . . . I think I know one," I said, even though I had never gone on a sunset picnic in my life, let alone on a date. My heart was singing so loudly I was sure Paul could hear it.

"Tell me where you live," he said, "and I'll pick you up."

My happiness popped like a balloon. What would he think if he knew I didn't have a home and that I carried everything I owned in paper bags in the trunk of my car? He would probably form the same opinion of me that everyone else in town had. "Um . . . it would be easier if I drove out here for you," I said. "The place I have in mind is up there." I pointed to the mountain. "And I'm in the other direction. If you're living in the trainer's cottage, I know where that is."

"Okay, then." His smile had returned. "How about six o'clock? I'll pack the picnic. And you can bring Buster if you want."

I drove home smiling. It was all too good to be true. The "dog girl" had a date for the first time in her life—and Paul even liked my three-legged dog.

I parked the car by Pop's garage and was about to hurry back to the clinic when Pop called to me from the open garage door. "Hey, Peg! Donna wants to see you in her office." I bristled at the reference to *her* office, then reminded myself that if Donna hadn't taken over, I wouldn't be working full-time at a job I loved. And I probably wouldn't have delivered Persephone's foal or become friends with Paul. I strode into *her* office, determined that nothing she said would destroy my good mood.

"You wanted to see me?" I asked.

"A letter came for you yesterday. I guess you haven't filled out a change of address at the post office yet."

I opened my mouth to tell her that it had only been a week since I'd moved out and that I rarely got any mail to begin with. But I closed it again. None of that mattered. The letter was from Barbara Symanski.

Dear Peggy,

Ever since we talked, I haven't been able to stop thinking about Joe. I've decided that I want to accept your kind offer and come out to New York and do whatever I can to help him and let him know that I love him. I checked the Greyhound bus schedule, and I'm willing to make the trip out there from Youngstown whenever the time is right. I can change buses in New York City, then take another one north. According to the route maps, it looks like New Paltz is the bus station that's closest to you. Just give me a call the next time that Joe comes, and I can be there in about twelve or thirteen hours. Thanks again, and let's pray that our plan works.

Your friend,
Barbara

I returned to the clinic with another reason to dance. If only I knew when Joe would be back.

The afternoon mail at the clinic brought bills and payment checks and more accounting work for me to do, but it also brought more letters and photographs from Jimmy's Army friends. I carried them into the house to show to his mother.

She was washing a batch of tomatoes from her garden that she planned to can, but she dried her hands and sat down at the table with me to read them. The letters made her smile. "I can certainly see how well-loved Jim was," she told me. The photograph album was bulging.

A letter from Chaplain Bill contained a short note and the address for Major Mike Cleveland. "Oh no," I groaned. "Jimmy's commanding officer at Buchenwald is stationed at Fort Bragg, North Carolina, now. I won't be able to talk with him in person."

"We could try to track him down by telephone," she said.

"Your long-distance bill must be high already." I knew how much my calls at the phone booth were costing me.

She smiled as if we were conspirators. "When Gordon saw last month's bill, he said it looked like the national war debt. But he agreed that it's worth every penny if it helps Jim. Leave this address with me and I'll look into it." We were nearly finished with the letters when the telephone rang. Mrs. Barnett went into the front hallway to answer it. "That was the veterans' hospital," she said when she returned. "Dr. Morgan would like to speak with us on Thursday morning."

"I hope it's good news this time." I was in such a pleasant mood that I believed anything was possible.

"I hope so, too. Will you come with us again, Peggy?"

"Of course."

Mr. Barnett was called out later to stitch up a cow who had torn her udder on barbed wire, and I was happy to go with him. It was a simple procedure, he said, but I watched everything he did in fascination. "How did your visit to Blue Fence Farms go this morning?" he asked as we worked.

I told him how Mr. Dixon had made friends with Persephone and Tyche, but I was too shy to tell him that Paul had also been making friends with me. Every time I thought about Saturday's picnic, my stomach fluttered like a nest of baby birds. I smiled when I thought about his sky-blue eyes and Kentucky drawl. But at the same time, I agonized over what I should wear and what we would talk about and how I could ever show my face out at Blue Fence Farms again if the date turned out to be a disaster.

* * *

On Thursday morning, the Barnetts and I were nervous yet hopeful as we drove to the hospital. Along the way, we rehearsed everything we wanted to tell the doctor and prayed that he would have good news for us in return.

"We've seen several encouraging signs in these past few weeks," Mr. Barnett told Dr. Morgan as we took our seats. The doctor was already lighting a cigarette. "Jim has been talking to us a bit more, and he responded very well to seeing his old friends when we took him to the memorial service. It seemed like the trip and the day away from the hospital did him good, and we—"

Dr. Morgan brushed away his words with a wave of his cigarette before Mr. B. could finish. "Anecdotal reports are fine in their context, but we haven't documented any clinical signs of improvement from either the insulin treatments or the recent electroshock therapy. Nightmares continue to disrupt his sleep. He has no appetite and is losing weight. He won't participate in sports or other activities, and he remains silent in our group therapy sessions."

I heard Mr. Barnett sigh. "So what's next?" I shifted in my chair, prepared to stand up and object if Dr. Morgan mentioned the water torture treatment that Joe had described.

"I plan to suspend the shock therapy for a week to give his brain a chance to adapt before attempting private therapy sessions. But in order for me to understand him better and make progress with his therapy, I'll need you to describe any traumatic incidents from his childhood that might be at the root of his neurosis."

Mr. and Mrs. Barnett looked at each other. They had to be even more frustrated than I was. "We're very willing to talk about Jim's childhood," Mr. Barnett said slowly. "But I really don't see how it will help. I believe he had a very happy childhood."

"He's our only child and is dearly loved," Mrs. Barnett added. "By us and by his grandparents, when they were alive."

"Yes," her husband continued, "and while their deaths were sad for all of us, they weren't what I'd call traumatic. Jim worked alongside me in my veterinary practice, so he was realistic about the natural process of death. He was studying veterinary medicine at Cornell when he enlisted."

"He was popular in school," Mrs. Barnett said. "He had a lot of friends; he got good grades. He played sports and went on dates."

"There were a few typical boyhood incidents and scrapes. The usual teenage stuff."

"But we never had to worry about him for a moment."

Dr. Morgan looked as though he didn't believe a word they were saying. He gestured to me. "And who are you? Sister? Girlfriend?" I was so startled that I couldn't speak.

Mrs. Barnett reached for my hand. "Peggy has been a friend of ours and Jimmy's for many years."

The doctor leaned forward in his chair. He appeared angry. "Look, I can't help Corporal Barnett unless someone is willing to be perfectly honest with me."

The fact that he had practically accused the Barnetts of lying helped me find my tongue. "Everything they just said is the God's honest truth. Jimmy was happy before the war. But I've been reading the letters he sent home from overseas and talking with his Army buddies about his experiences as a medic, and I think he saw a lot of tragic things during the war. Jimmy's Army unit liberated a Nazi concentration camp. He kept working there after the war ended, and one of his friends said Jimmy got so depressed that he needed to take a week's leave. I think Jimmy needs to talk about those memories. They must be a terrible burden to carry around."

"Was this friend a medical professional?"

"He was an Army medic, like Jimmy."

The doctor shook his head as he tapped the ash from his cigarette. "I believe I explained once before that wartime experiences merely exacerbate underlying childhood trauma."

"How could any trauma be worse than witnessing what happened in those death camps?" Mr. Barnett said. "Have you seen the pictures and read the reports? I know my son, and witnessing what went on there must have broken his heart. I fought in the first war and saw a lot of horrors, yet it nearly broke my heart just to read about the camps."

The doctor extinguished the first cigarette and pulled out a second one. "Let me try to explain this to you the same way we present it to our patients. For many soldiers, combat stress puts them in a heightened state of alert, like a cat that reacts physically when threatened by a dog—hackles raised, claws extended, adrenaline pumping in readiness to fight or flee. They've been conditioned to react this way by events in their childhood and the stress of warfare keeps them in this heightened state even after the threat is gone. The goal of the insulin and electrotherapies is to shock patients out of this state. Their bodies must learn to relax and return to normal."

The doctor paused to take a puff of his new cigarette and I had to stifle the urge to say, *"Baloney! Jimmy isn't a startled cat!"*

"Corporal Barnett's condition is an extreme example of this," the doctor continued. "His reaction to the perceived threat was to shut off all outside stimuli until he became nearly catatonic. Perhaps he reacted similarly but on a smaller scale during childhood, retreating to his room, refusing to communicate, becoming moody and withdrawn."

Mrs. Barnett looked at her husband. "Jimmy was never like that, was he, Gordon?"

"Not that I can recall. Listen, Doctor—"

"Your regular visits have likely prevented him from having a complete shutdown, which is good—"

"Then why not let us visit more often?" I asked.

The doctor exhaled smoke, then adopted an overly patient tone, as if forced to explain these things to children. "It has been two and a half months since his suicide attempt. Twelve weeks. Yet his depression persists. Unless we get to the root of it, I'm afraid we're looking at long-term hospitalization."

"Then we'll take him home," Mrs. Barnett said. "Let's take him home, Gordon, please? We'll hire a nurse to watch him and—"

"You'll be risking a second suicide attempt if you discharge him. The alternative is to consent to psychosurgery."

"Out of the question," Mr. Barnett said. "I will never consent to a lobotomy."

"I believe it's your best option at this point," the doctor said. "The surgery has been performed successfully in VA hospitals all across the country—"

"Not on my son."

"As you wish. In the meantime, if you truly want to help him, I urge you to reexamine his childhood from his point of view and let me know what you discover."

* * *

I was outside in the corral on Friday afternoon, exercising Pedro, who was recovering nicely from his shin splints, when I heard the familiar rumble of Joe's motorcycle coming down the road. Buster must have heard it, too, because he rose from his shady spot on the Barnetts' back porch and trotted to the driveway to stare across the road. I ducked out of the corral and hurried over. Sure enough, Joe was parking his motorcycle in front of Pop's garage. Buster looked up at me and barked as if to ask, *"What are we waiting for?"* We jogged across the road to greet him. Buster gave Joe a full, doggy welcome, leaping against his chest and wagging his tail like a flag on the Fourth of July.

"Welcome back, Joe," I said.

"Thanks. Hey, it looks like Tripod really missed me."

"I did, too. How long can you stay?" My mind was already racing to think of a way to keep him here until Barbara arrived.

"Well, I was hoping I could work in the garage again, you know?" Joe looked sheepish. "I kinda got carried away a few nights ago and . . . Well, you don't need to hear about all that. But anyway, I'm a little low on cash."

Perfect! "You'll have to ask Pop about working, but I hope you'll at least stay through the weekend. Listen, I have to finish my chores, Joe, but I'll leave Buster here with you until later."

I was putting Pedro in his stall when I remembered that I didn't live in Pop's apartment anymore. I would have to go back and explain it to Joe. But first, I raced to the telephone booth in town and called Barbara Symanski.

"I have the bus schedule right here," she said after my breathless explanation. "Let's see. If I hop on the next bus . . . and change in New York City . . . I can arrive at the station in New Paltz tomorrow night at . . . it looks like 6:25. Will that work?"

I stifled a groan. I was supposed to pick up Paul for our picnic at six. Who knew if he would ever ask me out again if I canceled? Yet this might be my very last chance to help Joe. He had done so much to help Jimmy and me. "Yes, that will be great," I said, wincing. "I'll tell Joe that I have a surprise for him, and I'll bring him with me to the bus station. I guess we'll see you tomorrow."

I pulled out the directory that was chained inside the booth and looked up the number for Blue Fence Farms. It rang and rang on the other end but no one answered. The office must have closed for the day. I would have to try to reach Paul tomorrow. In the meantime, I had to make sure Joe didn't go anywhere. And that he stayed sober on Saturday. I raced back to the garage and found him laughing and already drinking a beer with Pop, who seemed quick to forgive Joe's wanderings.

"May I have a word with you in private, Joe?" I asked. We stepped outside. "Listen, I don't live here anymore, but I'm sure Pop will let you stay."

"He already said he doesn't mind. He told me you're on your own now, hey?"

"I am—thanks to you for putting in a good word for me with Mr. Barnett. Listen, I could really use your help with an errand tomorrow night around six thirty. Do you think you'll be free then?"

"Sure. What do you need me to do?"

"I have to pick something up in New Paltz." He waited as if expecting to hear more. "I'll explain everything tomorrow. Thanks, Joe."

I arranged with Mrs. Jenkins for Barbara to stay in the guesthouse with me on Saturday night, and I was back at the phone booth first thing on Saturday morning, calling Blue Fence Farms. "Mr. Dixon left early this morning to take a horse up to the raceway in Saratoga," the manager said.

"When do you expect him to return?"

"Not until later this afternoon. Maybe around four. You want him to call you back?"

Call me back? I was in a telephone booth. I lived in a rooming house.

I couldn't expect Donna to take a phone message for me, and I didn't feel right about giving out the Barnetts' telephone number. But that's what I ended up doing. I had Saturdays off, but I went to the clinic in the afternoon and did a little paperwork, just so I would be near the telephone when Paul called. He didn't.

I glanced at the clock, willing it to slow down. I was running out of time. I waited until four thirty, then called the farm again. "He still isn't back," the manager said. "You want to leave a message?" It didn't seem right to cancel our date by leaving a message, so I decided to drive out to Blue Fence Farms and wait to tell him in person. Or if he still wasn't back, I would slide a note under the door of his cottage.

I hurried across the street and checked to make sure that Joe was still there, working with Pop. "I'll be back for you in an hour or so, okay, Joe? You won't forget, will you?"

Buster and I jumped into my car and I drove out to the farm, imagining Barbara enduring the long, tiring bus ride from Ohio. She must be going through a mixture of emotions, feeling anxious and hopeful and fearful and excited and very eager to hold the man she loved in her arms again. But thinking about her and Joe and my part in this plan gave me a sick, queasy feeling in my stomach. What if calling Barbara had been a terrible mistake? Added to that, my anxiety about facing Paul made me sick with nerves.

Paul still wasn't back. "You're the veterinarian's assistant, right?" the manager asked.

"Um . . . yes. Peggy Serrano. Could you please tell Mr. Dixon I was here looking for him? I-I'll have to leave a note for him under his door." It seemed like a cowardly way out. And he wouldn't learn about the cancellation until the last minute. What if he'd already purchased the food for the picnic? I took my notebook out of my bag and scribbled a note.

Dear Paul,

I'm so sorry, but I have to reschedule our picnic for another time. Someone needs my help, and she's coming all the way from

*Ohio by bus, and I need to pick her up at the station tonight. I'm
so disappointed, Paul. I hope you will forgive me.*

Peggy

Joe and Pop were drinking beer when I returned. Joe had cleaned
himself up and seemed in good spirits. He drained the bottle and asked,
"How long are you going to keep me in suspense before you tell me
what we're doing?"

"It only takes twenty minutes to drive to New Paltz. I think you can
wait that long."

"Are we taking my motorcycle?"

"No, we'll need to go in my car." Buster leaped inside when Joe
opened the door. "Um . . . it may not be a good idea to bring Buster," I
said. I had no idea how Barbara felt about dogs.

"Aw, he can come along, can't he?" It wasn't really a question. Buster
and Joe had already settled into their seats. I got in and started toward
New Paltz.

Of course, the bus was late. Joe kept checking his watch as if eager for
a night out on the town, and I paced back and forth in front of the shiny,
bullet-shaped diner that doubled as a bus station. I thought I might have
to tell him my secret before he throttled me, but the bus arrived in the
nick of time. Only one person stepped off.

"Barbie?" Joe breathed when he saw her. "Barbie! Hey! It's really
you!" She dropped her bag and ran into his arms, just like people did
in the movies.

"Hey, did you arrange all this?" Joe asked me with a grin.

"She did!" Barbara said. "Thank you, Peggy. You're wonderful! It's so
nice to finally meet you."

I had no idea what to do next. I figured they must want to be alone.
Barbara solved my dilemma by gesturing to the diner. "Could we get a
bite to eat? I ate the ham sandwich I packed hours ago. I'm starving!"

"Sure," Joe said but he looked like he was eating a banquet just by
gazing at her.

"I'll wait out here," I said, but Barbara wouldn't hear of it. I tied Buster up near the car, then went in and sat in the booth across from Barbara and Joe and ordered a cola, wondering if Paul had gotten my note and if he was angry with me for standing him up. Meanwhile, Barbara did most of the talking, telling Joe about her bus ride and filling him in on the news from back home. I didn't know how she would manage to eat with only one hand, but Joe finally let go of hers long enough for them to eat their hamburgers.

"I've arranged for you to stay here tonight," I told her when we passed the guesthouse on the way into town. "I'll take your bag there for you." I dropped the two lovebirds off at Pop's garage and heard them making plans to leave again on Joe's motorcycle. I didn't blame them. It was only eight thirty on a balmy Saturday evening. I put Buster in his kennel and returned to the guesthouse, contented yet feeling strangely empty inside as I wondered what my picnic with Paul would have been like.

I tossed in bed all night, looking at the glowing hands of my alarm clock and listening for Barbara to come home. The sun was just appearing when I finally heard Joe's motorcycle outside. I hurried down to the back door to let her in, hoping we wouldn't awaken Mrs. Jenkins or the couple from New Jersey who were renting one of her other rooms.

"Sorry," Barb whispered as we hurried upstairs to my room. "Oh, I have so much to tell you, Peggy!" We sat on our twin beds, talking like two old friends as she told me about her night. Joe had taken her up to the lookout to see the stars, and they had stayed up there all night, talking and planning their future. Joe hadn't even needed a drink.

"He has changed so much in these past few months, thanks to you," Barbara said.

"To me? I haven't done anything."

"Yes, you have! Joe told me how you've been trying to help his friend Jim and talking to all his old Army buddies. Joe has been listening to all the advice they gave, and it really helped him. He was so hard on himself in the past because of his shell shock. He said he felt like a coward and a failure for not shaking it off. It really helped him to know that all the others had trouble getting over it, too. He said his friend Jim still struggled, and Joe had always admired him so much."

"I'm glad," I said. I remembered what Dr. Morgan had said about long-term hospitalization and wished his buddies' advice had helped Jimmy, too.

"Joe said that a lot of the men talked about how their wives or girl-friends helped them, but he thought it was all over for us. He thought he had ruined everything and that I didn't love him anymore. He said when I stepped off the bus, he felt like the sun was shining for the first time in months." She wiped her eyes and said, "How can I ever thank you, Peggy?"

"Just be happy," I said. "And take good care of each other."

I wondered if I would ever find someone to share my life with, the good times as well as the hard times. Something shifted in my heart, and for a brief moment I saw Donna and Pop in the light of Barbara and Joe's love. They deserved a new start, too. In an apartment all to themselves.

"So what's next?" I asked Barbara.

"We're going to get some sleep," she said, laughing. "Joe went back to your father's garage for a few hours and I'm going to try to nap here. Then we're leaving for Ohio together this afternoon."

"On his motorcycle? All that way?"

She laughed again. "I'm not letting him out of my sight or out of my arms ever again!"

* * *

I had plenty of time to get dressed and go to church, but I was too cow-ardly to face Paul Dixon. Instead, I bought the Sunday paper and sat in the park with Buster, searching for an apartment until it was time to ride to the hospital with the Barnetts.

"May I ask you something, Peggy?" Mr. Barnett said as we drove the now-familiar route to the ferry crossing over the Hudson River. "And you can tell me it's none of my business if you want to. I'll understand."

"You can ask me anything." I tried not to sound too hesitant.

"I ran into Paul Dixon at church this morning and he was looking for you. He asked me if I knew how to get in touch with you. I didn't know what to say."

"We've been worried about you," Mrs. Barnett added. "We've seen you walking to the clinic from town every morning, and you're boarding Buster with us . . . Is everything all right?"

"Um . . . yes . . . ," I managed.

"But where are you living?" Mr. Barnett asked. "Not with your father, I gather. Are you sure you're okay?"

It was going to be hard to explain it without bawling, but I cleared my throat and summoned my bravest voice. "Well, Pop and Donna thought it was high time I moved out on my own—and they're right, of course. I'm a grown woman, after all. I've been looking for a place that will let me keep Buster, but I haven't had any luck yet. I'm boarding at Mrs. Jenkins's guesthouse in the meantime."

The Barnetts looked at each other across the front seat. Then Mrs. Barnett turned around to face me. "You should have said something, Peggy. We would love it if you and Buster stayed with us. Gordon and I just rattle around in that great big house, and I know you would be good company for us."

I couldn't face her. I looked out at the distant mountains instead. "Pop is always telling me I shouldn't bother you. He says I'm being a pest for spending so much time over at your house."

"Oh, Peggy," she laughed. "What a silly thing to worry about. We have plenty of empty bedrooms upstairs, and you are more than welcome to use one of them."

24

Gisela

On a rainy day in August, I packed the few belongings I owned and climbed into the back of an Army vehicle with a dozen other Buchenwald survivors. Our lives were about to change once again. My new home would be in a displaced persons' camp in Bensheim, Germany, on the edge of the Odenwald Mountains. Jim and most of the medical team from Buchenwald had been transferred to an Army hospital in Frankfurt, thirty miles away, and they were helping me and the others relocate. Jim promised to visit me whenever he had free time.

I was glad to finally leave Buchenwald. The Allies had divided Germany among themselves, and the concentration camp was now located in the Soviet occupation zone. So was the section of Berlin where my family's home had once been. The new DP camp in Bensheim was in the American sector, and the nearly one thousand people who lived there with me were all fellow Jews who had somehow survived the Nazis. After an emissary from President Truman had toured the DP camps, the Americans had decided that the needs of displaced Jews were very different from those of other war refugees because we had no homes to return to. The Jewish communities all over Europe where we'd once lived had been destroyed, our homes and businesses confiscated. We were reluctant to return to countries where we would be an unwelcome minority again, so for now, we were placed by ourselves in camps like this one in Bensheim and given a measure of independence to govern ourselves. We were liberated but still not free. Together we faced an unknown, uncertain future.

It didn't take long for me to settle into my new barracks and adjust to a new routine. The camp was clean and orderly, the food nourishing. As I got to know the other women who were part of my new life, I learned that most of us had lost our entire families. All of us were without homes. All of us still grieved our many losses. There was some small comfort in knowing that my life wasn't unique. The people who shared my new barracks and ate and worked alongside me understood my loneliness and grief. They shared my rootlessness. As we talked during mealtimes and in the evening hours before bed, the questions that seemed to haunt all of our thoughts were "Why did I survive?" and "What should I do next?"

One thing I did have in this new camp was an address. I could get mail from Ruthie and the Jewish agency that was helping me search for my uncles without using Jim's military address. Sam could find me here.

A few days after settling in, I was assigned to work with the doctors in the camp clinic and the small thirty-bed hospital, helping hundreds of other survivors who were still recovering from the ravages of illness and starvation. My work was satisfying and offered me a reason to keep living until, hopefully, the day would arrive when I would feel alive again.

* * *

"How are you doing, Gisela?" Jim asked about a month after I arrived in Bensheim. "And don't smile and put on a good face. I want to know the truth." He had brought medical supplies from Frankfurt, and he and I sat outside on the bumper of his vehicle with the view of the mountains in front of us. They seemed to be the only permanent feature in my life right now.

"I have good days and bad days. I miss my family. I miss Sam. I miss looking forward to the future we'd planned together. We would talk about it every night and we'd say, 'We're another day closer.'"

Jim took my hands in his, holding them tightly for a long moment. We had always been comfortable with long silences between us, but today I sensed a tension in Jim and feared he had bad news to share. "Gisela, I need you to be strong right now," he finally said. His voice trembled. "And I know that you are strong and very courageous or you wouldn't have survived everything that you've been through."

"You have news of Sam, don't you?" I continued to stare at the mountains, unwilling to see the truth in his eyes.

"Yes."

I stopped breathing, waiting to hear more as my heart thrashed like a wounded animal against my ribs. "Is he dead?"

"We don't know for sure." He drew a breath. "I finally heard from the British Army and learned that Sam enlisted in what was called the Jewish Brigade, made up of Jewish soldiers. Nearly all of the other men had been born in Palestine, so it was unusual that they allowed him to join. They trained in Egypt, then served with the British Eighth Army in Italy. They fought in two important offensives this past March, then faced a German parachute division in early April. After the last battle, Sam was listed as missing in action."

He gave me a moment to absorb the news, as if waiting for me to breathe again. I couldn't. A blanket of grief had settled on my chest, suffocating me. "I'm so sorry, Gisela," he said.

"But there's still hope?" I asked. I pulled my hand free so I could wipe my tears.

Jim sighed and shrugged. "I delayed telling you while I waited for a more definite answer because it seemed cruel to leave you suspended between hope and grief. But my contact at the British consulate still doesn't have an answer for me."

I knew what that meant. "They haven't found his body, have they?"

"No. But it's also possible that he may have been taken prisoner. We can hope for the best."

"But I should expect the worst. The Nazis surrendered in April. Surely all of the prisoners of war have been exchanged by now."

"I'm so sorry," he said again. "I asked for the name and address of Sam's brigade commander. I thought it might help you and Sam's family if you could talk to someone he trained with and fought alongside, someone who could provide more details about his disappearance. The commander has returned to Palestine, but I'll let you know as soon as I get his address."

"Thank you."

Jim paused again, but this time I could tell that much of his tension had uncoiled. "I have more news that's a little better, I think," he said. "Your former landlord in Antwerp contacted me because he has heard from Sam's parents. They were finally allowed to immigrate to the United States from Cuba. I have their new address in Miami, Florida." Jim handed me a piece of paper.

I stared at it, picturing the coast of Florida as we had seen it from the deck of the *St. Louis*. "They're finally together again," I murmured. "And they made it to United States. I'm so happy for them."

"Would you like me to write to his parents and—?"

"No, I'll do it." I heard voices from inside the clinic and turned to look at the screen door. "I should get back to work." I rose slowly to my feet.

Jim stood as well. "I don't think you should go back to work. You need time to take in this news. I'll ask them to let you have the rest of the afternoon off."

I shook my head, edging toward the door. "My work is a distraction—"

"No, Gisela." Jim held my shoulders, stopping me. "Stay here while I go inside to tell them. I'll be right back."

We spent the rest of the afternoon wandering around the grounds together as my weary heart absorbed this terrible blow. Sometimes we talked, but most of the time we remained silent. I sensed a deep sadness in Jim, a raw wound that wasn't healing. Even though we had become close friends, I didn't know what had caused it. For now, helping me seemed to help him.

"Are you sure you're going to be all right?" he asked when it was time for him to go.

"Yes, I think so. Thank you, Jim." He gave me a long hug before leaving.

Strangely, I didn't cry, even after I returned to my barracks alone. Sam was missing. He might be dead, but he also might be alive. Until I knew for certain, I would keep him alive in my heart.

In the meantime, I wrote to Ruthie and also to Sam's parents with the news. Sam's mother and brothers had been like family to us when we'd lived in Antwerp, and my joy when I heard back from them was bittersweet. They were starting a new life in the United States. But where was Sam? And where was home for me?

* * *

As summer came to an end, there was a stirring of activity in the camp as we prepared for the high holy days. Rosh Hashanah celebrated the creation of the world and the beginning of a new year, and every one of us was embarking on a new beginning. Yom Kippur came in mid-September. It was the holiest day of the year, a day for repentance and seeking forgiveness from God and each other. Sam used to approach these holy days with great reverence when we lived in Antwerp, fasting and praying with Vati and the other men in the synagogue on Yom Kippur. The rituals might offer comfort to the others here in camp, but I couldn't pray to a God I no longer believed in. Sukkot fell at the end of September, and there was great excitement as the men worked to build the outdoor sukkah where we would eat our meals. I remembered the tiny sukkah that Vati used to build on the balcony of our apartment in Berlin. In rainy weather we would put on our coats and laugh as we shivered through our meals. It seemed like a lifetime ago.

I was tending my patients in the camp hospital on the first day of Sukkot when a messenger arrived from the office, saying I had a visitor. The messenger was from Romania and we couldn't communicate very well, so I hurried up to the office alongside her, wondering who it could be. My racing heart hoped it was Sam. I was stunned to see that it was Ruthie.

My sister stood inside the tiny office looking lost and forlorn. Two tattered suitcases rested on the floor beside her. I cried out with joy and threw my arms around her. She hugged me tightly in return.

"Ruthie! Are you all right?" I asked when I finally pulled back to look at her. "How . . . ? Why . . . ? What are you doing here? What happened?"

"Nothing happened."

"Why didn't you tell me you were coming?"

"I was afraid you'd tell me not to."

"Oh, Ruthie. I would never turn you away. I've missed you so much! But you lived in such a nice home in Belgium and it was so beautiful there. And as you can see . . ." I gestured to the rustic office and bleak compound beyond the open door. "I have nothing here."

"I changed my mind about staying in Antwerp. I want to be with you."

My heart soared. "Then from now on, we'll stay together. Always." I hugged her again, hoping she wouldn't regret her decision. I was thrilled to have my sister with me, someone who was my own flesh and blood. Someone who had known and loved the people I'd known. Someone who could help me keep their memories alive. But I had nothing to offer my dear sister except my love. It would have to be enough for now.

The office clerks watched our tearful reunion and volunteered to go to the hospital to explain why I wouldn't be returning. The afternoon had been a slow one, and I knew that the other nurse on duty could easily cover for me. Every person in the camp understood the exquisite joy of being reunited with a lost loved one. It was what they all dreamed of for themselves.

I carried one of Ruthie's suitcases as I walked with her to my barracks, listening as she explained how the Jewish agency had helped her travel to Bensheim. "They're working very hard to reunite families and return us to our home countries, so they were happy to help me," she said.

"And I'm happy that you're here. Nearly a thousand people live in this camp, but still, I've been very lonely." I found blankets and an empty cot for her in my barracks and we stood on opposite sides of it to arrange the sheets. I couldn't stop staring at her. She reminded me so much of Mutti, dark-haired and slender and graceful. And I still saw Vati every time I looked into her dark, sorrowful eyes. "Are you hungry? Have you eaten?" I asked after we'd stowed her things.

"No, Mrs. Peeters's cook packed a huge sack of food for my trip, enough to eat for days."

"Then, come. I know a place where we can sit in the shade and catch up." I had discovered the spot behind the toolshed, beneath one of the camp's few trees, by accident. It had become my favorite place to go. I could turn my back on the starkness of the DP camp and lean against the wall of the shed and gaze up at the mountains, visible through the leaves. The trees had begun to change color with the cooler fall weather, some of them as bright as flames. I dreaded the winter season when everything would look as stark and empty as death. Maybe winter would be more bearable with Ruthie here.

We sat side by side, and I listened as she talked for a few more minutes before I finally dared to ask the question I'd been longing to ask since the moment I saw her in the office. I approached it slowly, guessing that the reason she was here might be a painful one. "It must have been very hard for you to leave Mrs. Peeters and the children. You said they treated you like part of the family."

"Yes. I'll miss them," she said softly.

"Then . . . why, Ruthie?"

"Because . . ." She exhaled. "Because after the war . . . when people found out I was Jewish . . . everything changed." I sensed by her halting voice and by the hurt I saw in her eyes that she had never expressed her reasons out loud until now. She was explaining them to herself as much as to me. "My friends all treated me differently when they found out the truth. They acted as if I had changed all of a sudden. Some of them seemed mad at me because I wasn't the person I had pretended to be . . . as if I'd been lying to them. Well, I suppose I had been lying in a way." I waited while she paused. "And there was a boy I liked at church, and he liked me. His parents told Mrs. Peeters that they didn't want us to be together, even for a simple walk in the park, until I was baptized and confirmed in the Catholic church."

"I'm so sorry, Ruthie," I said, trying to soothe the hurt. "But you can't really blame them, can you? Vati would have discouraged you from befriending a boy who wasn't Jewish."

"I know. But it made me realize that all the time I'd been hiding with them and trying to blend in, I was fooling myself if I thought I belonged there. I was an imposter. Even worse, if I did stay there and I joined their church, I would be a traitor. That wasn't the life Mutti and Vati would have wanted for me. Everything our family has suffered all these years has been because we're Jewish. I didn't want to live the rest of my life pretending to be somebody I'm not."

I didn't know what to say. But Ruthie's words and the difficult choice she had made jolted me out of the numbing lethargy I'd felt ever since arriving at this camp. For her sake as well as for my own, I couldn't sit by passively and wait until the world decided what to do with us. I needed to start trying to find a home and a future for the two of us.

That very evening, the first night of Sukkot, I made an effort to join in the festivities along with Ruthie and the others. But the celebration brought painful memories of Sam when I remembered how our families had celebrated Shavuot on board the *St. Louis*. Sam and I had danced until the early morning hours and had glimpsed the Bahamas' lighthouse before dawn, a beacon of hope on the horizon. I had known Sam for so few years, yet memories of him permeated everything I did.

* * *

Jim came to visit at the end of the week, and I was excited to introduce Ruthie to him. My sister had always been shy and still was, but Jim was such a kind person that it didn't take long for her to warm to him. "We're still celebrating Sukkot," I told him. "I hope you can stay and eat with us. It's a blessing to invite guests to share our sukkah." I was pleased when he agreed. He sat across the outdoor table from Ruthie and me at dinner that evening.

"Tell me about this celebration," he said after the plates of food were passed.

"The Torah commands us to build booths where we're supposed to eat and even sleep if the weather allows. It's a harvest celebration every fall."

"Like American Thanksgiving?"

"I guess so. The rustic booths are supposed to remind us of how we wandered in the desert with Moses for forty years."

"This roof doesn't look like it will be much help if it rains," he said, pointing above us. "Is it unfinished?"

"It's supposed to be open to the sky. The idea is that God is our covering, watching over us as He did in the desert for forty years. No one here seems to see the irony that we're still wandering and homeless. Or that God hasn't been watching over us very well." Ruthie turned to give me a questioning look, and I was sorry I had spoken my thoughts out loud. "Don't mind me," I said. "Sometimes I speak without thinking. Let's talk about other things."

I was glad when some musicians took out their instruments after dinner and began to play, lightening the mood. A group of young people Ruthie's age came over to ask her to join them. My sister seemed reluctant. "Please come, Ruthie. Yaakov is going to tell us all about Palestine."

"Yes, why don't you join them," I urged. "You don't have to stay long but at least try to make friends. Jim and I will be right here when you come back." We watched her go. Two of the girls linked arms with her on either side as if they weren't going to let her get away.

"It looks like she's in good hands," Jim said when we heard the girls laughing.

"She's seventeen and should be having fun, laughing with her friends and meeting boys. I was about her age when I met Sam." People were leaving the table to gather around the band. Some of them started dancing. "Someone told me the other day that we have to forget the past before we can build new lives. That's what many people here are doing. There is so much frenzied activity here, as if they believe it's their duty to live every day to the fullest and to be happy, even without a home or a secure future. They're starting schools, organizing plays and other cultural activities. Couples who've just met are already planning their weddings. It's as if they need to make up for lost time."

"Isn't that a good thing? To get a fresh start?"

"I don't know. It seems like it's too soon. The Nazis killed their families, so it's almost an act of defiance to start new ones. They want to hurry up and have children so that our Jewish race will continue to exist. The younger survivors are being enticed to dream of immigrating to Palestine. David Ben-Gurion, the leader of the Jewish community there, has been visiting DP camps to rally support for a Jewish state. Zionism is very strong here."

"Is that realistic? I thought the British government is restricting immigration."

"They are." I watched as more and more people joined the lively dance, laughing as they moved to the music. Nothing in me felt like dancing. "Sam used to attend Zionist meetings in Antwerp and he talked about moving to Palestine. He wanted his brothers to go there as students, to escape, but his mother wouldn't let them. We close the Passover celebration every year by saying, 'Next year in Jerusalem,' but it's still a distant dream."

"It's interesting that Sam chose to join the Jewish Brigade instead of a regular British Army unit. Maybe he hoped that if he served in the British Army, they would let him immigrate there afterwards."

"He once asked me if I would move to Palestine with him after the war."

"Would you?"

"Back then, I think I promised to move to the ends of the earth with him as long as we were together. I would never have the courage to go to Palestine now, by myself. I'm not sure it's something Ruthie would agree to, either." I looked around to see where Ruthie was and saw her standing with the other girls next to the band. She had her back to me so I couldn't see her face. "Jim, I'm determined to find a home for Ruthie, but it seems like things are moving so slowly. There are millions of displaced people like us in camps all over Europe. It's going to take forever to find everyone a place to live and a new job and housing. They're saying we could be living here for years."

"If you had a choice, where would you go?"

"I don't know. Someplace that doesn't remind me every day of the people we've loved and lost. Someplace where I'm not haunted by memories of pogroms. I'm still waiting for the Jewish agency to track down Uncle Hermann in Ecuador or Uncle Aaron in Cuba. We lost contact with them during the war. I suppose we could live with one of them if we find them. And if they're willing to have us."

"Have you asked Ruthie where she would like to live if she had a choice?"

"No. She probably doesn't know where 'home' is any more than I do." I shivered as a cool breeze blew down from the mountains, rustling the branches of the sukkah. The flimsy structure offered scant shelter. "I know it's selfish of me to make Ruthie wait here with me until I hear about Sam. I need to lay aside my sorrow for her sake. She deserves a new beginning. She gave up a secure life in Belgium to be with me."

"I'll do whatever I can to help you get settled in the place you and Ruthie choose. Just let me know where that is."

"Thanks, Jim. You're a good friend."

I couldn't stop thinking about Jim's question. Where would I choose to live? Where would Ruthie? As my sister and I got ready for bed later that night, I decided to ask her. "If you had a choice, Ruthie, where would you settle down when we finally leave this camp?"

"I don't know."

The festivities hadn't lifted her spirits any more than they had mine, and I felt bad about that. I didn't want my gloom to weigh her down. "I was offered a job in the hospital in Belgium where I used to work," I told her. "Maybe we could find a place to live in Antwerp, in a community with other Jews. Would you want to return there if we were together?"

"I have a lot of bad memories from Belgium. First the pogrom, then Vati getting sick, then the bombs in Mortsel." She didn't add the years she'd spent alone in the orphanage or the rejection she'd experienced in the last few months, but I wondered if she was remembering them, too. "Living there wouldn't be the same without Vati and Mutti," she finished. "But I'll go there if you want to."

"No, I feel the same way you do."

She climbed into her bed, which was now next to mine, and I couldn't see her expression in the dim light. She was quiet as if giving my question more thought. "The only place where we could really start over again is in America," she finally said. "We could put all of the sad memories behind us there."

"I think you may be right." Even though America seemed very far away and a daunting destination to try to reach. "If you're sure, Ruthie, I will move heaven and earth to get us there."

"Yes," she said after another long moment. "I'm sure. It's where Mutti and Vati wanted us to live."

"Good. I'll ask Jim to help us find out about our visas and if we're still on the waiting list. But just so you know, they're telling everyone that it could take as much as three years to immigrate to America. Can you stand living here for that long?"

"I guess so."

But I already knew that even one year in this place was too long. We weren't exactly prisoners, but it often felt like it. I worried that my sister was already starting to die inside. It happened when you lost hope.

I wrote to Jim the next day, telling him what Ruthie had decided and asking for his help. Two weeks later, he returned to the DP camp with bad news.

"You and Ruthie will need to apply for immigration all over again because you no longer have your father as your means of support in the United States. I also checked to see if your nursing degree could be transferred, and it can't. You would need a degree from an American nursing school in order to work." Jim could tell that I took this news hard.

"Walk with me," he said. "I always think better when I'm walking." It was midday and the DP camp was alive with activity. I greeted people I knew as Jim and I walked past them, but I was still trying to absorb his bad news about immigrating.

"My other news is that I'm being demobilized and sent home in mid-January," Jim said. "Nearly everyone else in my unit has already been discharged, but I signed on to stay longer to work at the hospital. Now my time is up again."

"That should make you happy, Jim. Why aren't you smiling?" In fact, I couldn't recall ever seeing him smile.

"Can I be honest with you?" We had been walking slowly but he halted near the main gate and faced me. The only word that could describe his expression was *tormented*. "I don't think I can bear to return home, Gisela. Everything there will be the same and I'm not the same person I was before the war."

"Tell me who you were before the war."

He gave a humorless laugh. "A naive country boy who lived in a world that made sense. A fool who had faith in the goodness of God and in humanity. I was going to be a veterinarian like my father, live in the town where I grew up. I had started studying to do that in college. But then I was deployed to France, and as the bombs exploded around me, my world blew up along with them. None of what I had believed was real. When I went to war, I saw real life for the first time and more death and human suffering than I ever could have imagined."

The ragged bitterness I heard in his voice surprised me. I turned to look at him and it was like seeing a stranger. I had been so involved with my own problems, so worried about my sister that I hadn't noticed how thin and haunted-looking Jim had become these past weeks. He had been my rock ever since he'd saved me at Buchenwald. Now he seemed to be crumbling like a tower of sand before my eyes. He stared past the gate as he continued talking, his eyes shining with tears.

"I tried to keep pretending at first. I babbled Bible verses and told my friends that God must have a reason why their arms and legs had been blown off. They needed to trust Him, I said. I wanted desperately to keep believing in God, believing that He would miraculously intervene and put an end to the evil and show us how to make sense of it all. Then my best friend died in Bastogne. And a young Belgian nurse named Renée Lemaire who had volunteered to work in our aid station was also killed. She had been planning her wedding, and she didn't even have to be there, helping us. The more I watched people suffer and die, the harder it was to pray. Thousands of innocent civilians were dying. Elderly people. Women and children . . . But the moment I stepped through Buchenwald's gates, I stopped praying altogether."

His voice trembled with emotion as he struggled to continue. "That was when I saw the truth about the unchecked evil in this world and man's inhumanity to his fellow man. And I saw God's indifference to it all." He wiped his eyes with his fist. "I'm sorry if I'm insulting your faith in God—"

"You aren't, Jim. I'm Jewish by birth but I no longer believe." My own bitterness rose in my throat like bile. "The God I learned about in the Torah wouldn't have turned His back and allowed this to happen. Vati used to believe the same thing you did—that God had a reason for everything that happens. But there can't be a reason for Buchenwald and Auschwitz. The people who suffered and died there must have prayed. I know that my parents prayed. But all of those prayers went unanswered. Millions of what the Torah calls God's chosen people were brutally murdered. And the God I once believed in looked the other way."

Jim wiped his eyes again. "I was taught to believe in a God of love and compassion," he said. "A God who is also our Savior. The God I once worshiped couldn't have let millions of innocent people be slaughtered without mercy. The only conclusion I can come to is that He was a childish illusion, a fairy tale, like Santa Claus. And that the Bible was all lies. But even if I'm wrong and God does exist, I have nothing to say to Him."

We turned away from the gate and started walking slowly back toward the barracks. His words chilled me. I longed for the right words to help him but I had none to give. "You need to leave this place and go home, Jim. Your family must miss you terribly."

"My parents are people of faith. I don't know how to tell them that I don't believe in God anymore. It wouldn't be fair of me to destroy their faith by questioning it and talking about my doubts. I can't shake off the darkness that I've experienced over here, and I don't want to bring that darkness home with me. I love them too much to contaminate their idyllic world with the world of my nightmares. I'll go home for a visit and see them briefly, but I don't want to stay there and poison them."

I didn't know what to say. I stopped walking and wrapped my arms around him and hugged him tightly. I needed the embrace as much as he did.

"In the meantime," he said when we pulled apart again, "I'm running out of time here, and your visa process is moving too slowly. I feel like my work here is still unfinished. I can't stand the thought of leaving you and Ruthie here."

"It's not your responsibility, Jim. We're not your responsibility."

"But you are! I care about you, Gisela. I care about what will happen to you and your sister. It's hard for me to go home to a comfortable life in America and leave you in this place. I can't bear it that there are still millions of suffering people like you who have no place to go. My work as a medic, then in Buchenwald, and now helping you is the only thing that keeps me sane."

"But it's time for you to rest and regain your own strength—"

"I can't abandon you with no place to go and no family to turn to.

I have to help you get to America. I want to make sure you and Ruthie are taken care of."

I wanted that, too. My hope of finding Sam alive was fading every day. Jim and I weren't in love, but I felt safe with him. He had helped me, and now I wanted to help him in return but I didn't know how. "Don't you think that once you're home with your family, you'll see things differently?" I asked.

Jim stared into the distance as if he hadn't heard me. Worry wrinkles creased his troubled eyes. Several minutes passed. Then he looked at me again.

"Gisela, I think I know of a way for you and Ruthie to get to America . . . if you're willing to trust me."

25

Peggy

AUGUST 1946

I couldn't stop smiling as I unpacked my belongings in one of Mrs. Barnett's spare bedrooms on Monday. The room was pretty and feminine with pink rosebuds on the wallpaper, ruffled organza curtains on the windows, and white chenille spreads on the twin beds. I kept thinking that I must be dreaming. If I was, I hoped I never woke up. I decided to wait before telling Pop and Donna where I was living, afraid they would spoil my happiness by accusing me of pestering Mr. and Mrs. Barnett. I simply wanted to enjoy my new job and my new home for a little while before thinking too far into the future. I hadn't even slept one night in this room, but I already felt like I had a real home, with people who cared about me.

The only dark cloud in my sunny new world was my concern for Jimmy. His empty bedroom down the hall was a continual reminder that he was lost to us. Sometimes I thought it might have been easier for his mother and father if he had died in the war instead of losing him to this living death. But I refused to give up hope that he would recover.

On my first evening with the Barnetts, I was sitting in the living room with them, listening to Jack Benny on the radio, when the telephone rang. Mr. Barnett went to answer it, and I figured one of his animal patients might need him—and me. He was smiling when he returned. "It's for you, Peggy. Paul Dixon asked to speak with you, but it has nothing to do with Blue Fence Farms."

"H-how did he know I was here?"

"I told him earlier today," Mr. Barnett said with a wink.

I had been laughing at Jack Benny's jokes a moment ago, but my mood sobered quickly. What must he think of me? How could I ever tell him how sorry I was? I picked up the receiver and started stammering my apology, but he wouldn't let me finish.

"It's okay, Peggy. I'm calling to let you know that I understand. I'm not mad."

"Then can we go on our picnic tomorrow night after we both finish work so I can tell you the whole story?" I was making a date with him! I couldn't believe I was being so bold. But if Barbara Symanski could take a bold step, then so could I.

"I would like that," Paul replied. "In fact, our picnic lunch is still in my refrigerator."

The Barnetts could probably hear my sigh of relief all the way in the living room. "Good. I'll pick you up at six, just like we'd planned." My hands were shaking when I hung up the phone. But I was happy. Nervous, but happy.

Nothing got in the way of our picnic this time. We drove up into the mountains and I parked my car near the trailhead, then led Paul and Buster down a short path to a spot that I loved, overlooking Lake Minnewaska. I spread the picnic blanket Mrs. Barnett had loaned me on a huge, flat boulder and we sat down to eat. The summer evening was perfect, the lake as still as glass below us, the warm air scented with pine. Paul opened a brown paper sack. "I bought sandwiches and potato salad at the deli in town. Dill pickles, too. I hope that's okay."

"It's perfect."

He apologized for forgetting paper plates, but I just smiled as we dug into the same container of potato salad with our forks. Buster lay between us, his head resting on Paul's knee.

"Your dog is very friendly, isn't he?"

"He's hoping you'll feed him if he cozies up to you. He already knows that I won't share my dinner with him." I took a long drink from my bottle of soda and swallowed. I couldn't delay my apology any longer. "Listen, Paul. I need to tell you why I broke our date."

"You don't owe me an explanation, Peggy."

"Well, I still want to tell you because it's a good story with a happy ending. And it might help you understand me a little better. But I need to start at the beginning, so here goes." I drew a deep breath as if about to dive into the cool lake. "Mr. Barnett's son, Jimmy, is my oldest friend. He's never been my boyfriend or anything like that, more like a big brother. The apartment where I grew up is across the street from the clinic, and it was Jimmy's idea to try to save Buster after he got hit by a car. His father didn't think Buster would live, but . . . Anyway, I'm getting off track. Jimmy came home from the war with battle fatigue. He's in the veterans' hospital after he tried to kill himself."

"I heard about Mr. Barnett's son from the farm manager. It's a real shame."

"The only day we can visit him is on Sunday. That's why I go running off right after church instead of taking time to visit with you properly."

"I understand."

"So . . . the guy who drove me to the farm on his motorcycle the day Tyche was born is one of Jimmy's Army buddies. Joe has battle fatigue too, but he helped me contact Jimmy's friends to try to figure out what happened to make him so depressed, and Joe became my friend, too. He had broken up with his girlfriend back home in Ohio, and I wanted to help him, so I snooped in his bag one day and found his girlfriend's address. I called her, and she hopped on a Greyhound bus and rode all the way from Ohio to tell Joe that she still loves him. I had to pick her up at the bus station as a surprise for Joe at the same time that we were supposed to have our picnic. But the story has a happy ending because they got back together and went home to Ohio to work things out."

I felt like I had been rambling but Paul was grinning when I finished. "That is a great story. You have a good heart, Peggy. That's why Persephone and Tyche trust you. Horses are very good judges of character, you know."

"Thank you for giving our picnic another chance and—" He burst into laughter, interrupting me. "What's so funny?"

"I like you, Peggy. And I'm not the kind of guy who gives up when there's something I really want. I would have asked you out a second time. And probably a third, if you made excuses. And if that motorcycle guy had been your boyfriend, he would have been in for a fight."

I couldn't believe what I was hearing. This was too good to be true. Once again, I was afraid that I was dreaming, and I didn't want to wake up. I stared at Paul, my mouth hanging open in surprise. He laughed again. "So what are some other things we can do around here when we aren't working?"

"Um . . . do you like to walk in the woods? There are hiking trails and carriage roads that go up to Mohonk Mountain House. It's a beautiful, famous hotel that has had lots of famous guests. It's much too expensive for anybody I know to stay there, but there are miles of trails on the Mohonk Preserve. We could go up to the ice caves or Awosting Falls or Sam's Point or Gertie's Nose."

"You're making up those names."

"I'm not!" I said, laughing. "They're real places. With beautiful views."

"I got myself into trouble trying to pronounce the name of these mountains we're sitting in, so I just gave up."

"All newcomers make that mistake. They aren't pronounced like they're spelled—Shawangunk. You just say *Shongum*."

"I think I can manage that."

"They have mountains where you're from in Kentucky, don't they? Do you miss your home and your family back there?"

"In a way. Yes, we have mountains. I grew up in the ones in eastern Kentucky. Coal mining country. To be honest, my family is very poor. They were glad I was able to move out of there. I started out as a stable boy on a place a lot like Blue Fence Farms. I worked my way up and discovered that I loved working with horses. And I was pretty good at it. After I got out of the Navy, I started looking for a job. The fella I trained under back home put in a good word for me, and now I'm here."

"What did you do in the Navy?"

"I was a radio operator on a destroyer in the Pacific. I don't talk about those years very much."

"I understand. All of Jimmy's buddies feel the same way."

"I haven't lived here very long, but I already love it. I've made some great new friends this summer, including a very pretty gal to take on picnics." He looked at me and I felt my cheeks turning pink. We talked and laughed as we finished our food, then gathered up the trash and the blanket. We needed to walk back through the woods to the car before it got too dark. I hated for the evening to end but we both had to work tomorrow.

"See you soon," Paul said when I dropped him off at his cottage.

I hoped so. Boy, did I hope so!

"It looks like you had fun," Mrs. Barnett said when I returned home. "It's so nice to see you smiling."

"Am I smiling?" I pressed my hands to my cheeks. They felt warm, as if they were glowing with happiness.

"Yes," she said with a chuckle. "Why don't you tell me all about your picnic. Gordon says he's a nice young man."

"He is!" Mrs. Barnett had made lemonade, and we sat in rocking chairs on the front porch as fireflies flickered in the bushes and more and more stars filled the sky. She asked me what I liked about Paul, and as I told her, I thought, *This must be what it's like to have a mother to talk to and to share secrets with.* I could confide in Mrs. Barnett and ask her advice about men and dating and all the other mysteries that lay ahead. I couldn't remember ever feeling happier.

Two days later, when Mr. Barnett and I arrived home for lunch after our morning rounds, Mrs. Barnett had good news. "I've been calling all over Fort Bragg for days, trying to track down Major Cleveland. I've been leaving messages, having my calls transferred, talking to government receptionists and secretaries—and running up the long-distance charges, Gordon. I'm sorry."

"That's all right. I believe it's worth it. What did you find out?"

"Nothing, yet. But I finally managed to arrange a time to telephone Major Cleveland in his office. They promised he would be waiting for my call."

"Is this the man who was Jim's commanding officer at the concentration camp?"

"Yes."

"I think maybe we should all listen in on that call."

Mr. Barnett had planned to place the call himself, but there was an emergency on Windover Farm the next morning, so it was left to me and Mrs. Barnett to speak with the major. We held the receiver between us, listening together.

"I understand that you're calling about Corporal Jim Barnett," Major Cleveland said after we'd exchanged greetings.

"Yes, we're his family," I replied. "Jimmy suffered a breakdown after he returned home. He's in the veterans' hospital."

"I'm very sorry to hear that. How can I help?"

"We've been talking with his Army buddies and the other doctors and medics he worked with, trying to figure out what caused his breakdown so we can help him get well. From what we've learned, he began to change near the end of the war, especially after working in Buchenwald. Anything you can tell us about his time there might help."

"I see. Well, I didn't know Jim before we were assigned to the camp, so I can't make any comparisons. But I can tell you that Buchenwald changed everyone who worked there. It was the stuff of nightmares." There was a long pause as if the major was gathering himself. He cleared his throat. "I was concerned about Corporal Barnett after the first few weeks. Mind you, he was an excellent medic. I believe he would make a fine doctor. But I could see that the work was getting to him. I made him take a seven-day leave at one point after he lost a young patient and took his death very hard. But he went right back to work after he returned."

"We're also wondering about a nurse he may have worked with over there. We found a photograph in his bag of a woman wearing a nurse's uniform."

"The only female nurse we worked with at Buchenwald was a young Jewish woman who had been a prisoner there. She did some translation work for us and later helped care for the other patients after she recovered sufficiently."

"Do you remember her name? Was it Gisela?"

"It might have been. I'm sorry, but I have a hard time remembering names. Later that summer, the Soviets took over Buchenwald because it was in their occupation zone. Jim and I and most of the others were transferred to Frankfurt. I know that he continued to work closely with the Jewish relief agencies and he volunteered in a displaced persons camp nearby. I think the woman he married was from that DP camp."

Married?

Static crackled along the telephone line. His words stunned me. I thought I must have misunderstood, but Mrs. Barnett gasped and covered her heart, so she must have heard him, too.

"What did you say?" I finally breathed. "Jimmy . . . Jimmy got *married*?"

"He filled out all the paperwork that the Army requires for an American soldier to marry a foreign bride and bring her to the United States. I signed everything for him myself. I even helped him postpone his discharge so he could wade through all the red tape."

"H-he never told us—his family, I mean. About getting married. And he didn't have a wife with him when he arrived home."

"I don't know what to tell you. Maybe it didn't work out. I wish I knew more, but I don't. I'm sorry."

"You've been a big help just the same. Thank you for your time."

I hung up the phone. Mrs. Barnett and I stared at each other in disbelief for what felt like an eternity. My heart was racing, and I could tell by Mrs. Barnett's expression that she was as shocked as I was. It felt like we'd walked into the movie theater near the end of the film and had no idea what was going on.

"What do you suppose happened to her?" she murmured.

I could only shake my head. We still hadn't moved away from the telephone stand in the hallway when Mr. Barnett's truck pulled into the driveway. The screen door in the kitchen squealed open, then banged shut again. "Martha?" he called.

"In here."

"Did I miss the telephone call?" he asked as he hurried toward us.

"You'll never believe it, Gordon, never in a million years. Jimmy got married!"

"What?"

"We just spoke to the major and he told us that Jimmy married a woman from one of the displaced persons camps when he was over in Germany."

"Really? Our Jim?"

"That's what he said."

"Well, where is she? What happened to her?" He gestured around the foyer as if she might be hiding behind the coatrack.

"The major didn't know. He couldn't tell us anything else. Oh, Gordon, do you think this might have something to do with why Jimmy—? I mean, if she died . . ."

"It might. Especially when you add it to all of the other things he went through—fighting the war, watching his friends die, liberating the concentration camp."

"There should be more records somewhere, shouldn't there?" I said when I finally recovered enough to speak. "The Army must know if and when he got married and what happened after that. We could write to Washington and . . . and . . ." I stopped. Following another long paper trail and sifting through a mountain of government red tape seemed much too daunting at the moment. I sagged against the wall in the hallway. "Oh, poor Jimmy," I mumbled.

"Do you suppose she's the woman in the photograph?" Mrs. Barnett asked.

"She has to be," I replied. "She signed the picture 'Love, Gisela.' If something happened to her, it must have broken Jimmy's heart."

"There wasn't anything else in his bags about this marriage?" Mr. Barnett asked. "No papers or government forms or letters?"

"Just the photograph," I said. "But I'll go through everything again with a fine-tooth comb now that we know what we're looking for."

Mr. Barnett pulled a handkerchief from his pocket and mopped his brow. "Those first weeks that Jim was home, he acted so strangely, remember? I wouldn't be surprised if he destroyed all the evidence."

"But he didn't destroy her picture," I said. "That must mean something."

"I don't understand why he didn't tell us about her," Mrs. Barnett said. "He didn't say anything in his letters about meeting someone, much less marrying her. We've always been a close family. You would think . . ." She shook her head.

"Jim's a grown man, Martha. Not a little boy. Whatever happened, it must have been something he felt he couldn't talk about."

"Should we bring Gisela's picture with us to the hospital and see how he reacts?" Mrs. Barnett asked.

"No, we'd better not," I said, even though this was none of my business. "If we're shocked by this, imagine how he must feel. I think we should search through all of his things again. Maybe there's something we missed."

But there wasn't. After turning every drawer upside down and searching every corner of Jimmy's room and closet, the only loose end I found that had no explanation was the address in Brooklyn that Jimmy had printed in the back of his Bible. We couldn't ask directory assistance for a telephone number because there was no name, just the street address. The mystery ate away at me. I couldn't get it out of my mind.

"I want to go to that address in Brooklyn tomorrow and see what I find," I told the Barnetts at dinner on Saturday night.

"Do you want one of us to come with you?" Mr. Barnett asked.

Part of me did. In the past, I had relied on Joe to go with me and help break the ice. He had navigated our way to all the places we'd visited and bolstered my courage. But maybe it was time I grew up and learned to speak for myself. "No, I think it's more important for you to visit Jimmy tomorrow," I said. "The trip to Brooklyn could end up being a complete waste of time. But can you help me figure out how to get there? I've never driven to New York City before."

"It would be easier to take the train," Mr. Barnett said. "We can drop you off at the station in Beacon on our way to the hospital, and the train will take you right down to Grand Central station. They can give you information about which bus to take to Brooklyn. Or maybe you can take a taxi from there. I have a city map here someplace." He stood and rummaged through the kitchen junk drawer. "Don't worry. We'll help you get there."

The train I boarded the next day followed the winding Hudson River south to the city. Stunning views of the water and the mountains filled the windows of my passenger car. In one wide section of the river near Croton, I saw the Mothball Fleet—row after row of huge gray Navy vessels left over from the war. Dozens of them, lined up like toy ships with no place to go. They were a vivid reminder of the immense effort that had gone into winning the war. And now it was over. I wondered how many young men there were like Jimmy and Joe who hadn't been able to put aside the war and rest peacefully like those ships at anchor.

I was too nervous to enjoy the trip. My biggest fear was of getting lost. I had never gone to New York City alone before. Yet I knew this was something I had to do. Pop and Donna had finally helped me see that it was time for me to grow up and move forward with my life. I also knew that I needed to learn to trust God to help me, not Joe or Jimmy or anyone else.

Grand Central station was so overwhelming that I nearly turned around and got on the first train home. I took deep breaths and wandered through the vast space, following the signs until I ended up at an information booth. I must have looked lost and frightened because the woman in the booth took pity on my stammering explanation of where I needed to go and said, "Listen, honey. This is what you need to do. It's not hard."

And it wasn't. A city bus took me down to the southern tip of Manhattan and across the Brooklyn Bridge. I watched for my stop in Brooklyn Heights, then got off and consulted my map to walk the rest of the way. I only got mixed up once, but the iconic bridge looming in the background over the East River helped me find my way again.

The Brooklyn Heights neighborhood was like a foreign country to me. For one thing, the streets bustled with people—not at all like a quiet Sunday afternoon back home. We had blue laws in our town, so stores and banks and restaurants had to be closed on Sunday. But all these stores were open and doing a very brisk business. So busy, in fact, that I kept bumping into people as I walked along, trying to read the house numbers and find the correct address. Most of the women wore longish dresses or skirts and covered their heads with scarves. Bearded men in white shirts and dark suits had skullcaps on their heads. I tried not to stare at the small boys I passed wearing long, dangling ringlets in front of their ears.

I found the address at last, printed above the door of a corner bakery. I went inside, making a bell attached to the door jingle. The aroma of fresh bread made my stomach rumble, reminding me that I had been too nervous to eat very much that morning. A woman in a white apron stood behind the counter with her back to me, arranging loaves of bread on the shelves. She turned and asked, "May I help you?"

It was Gisela.

26

Gisela

"May I help you?" I asked a second time. The pretty young woman who stood on the other side of the counter looked shaken. The color had drained from her face. She swayed a little as if she might faint and quickly leaned against the counter. "Miss? Are you all right?" My instinct was to rush around to the other side and help her to a chair, but before I could move, she spoke my name, barely above a whisper.

"Gisela. It's really you, isn't it?"

"Do I know you? Have we met?" I tried to place her but couldn't. She reached into her bag with shaking hands and pulled out a photograph. My photograph. The one my friend's father had taken of me on graduation day. The one I had wanted to give to Sam.

"Where did you get that?" I breathed. I was sure I had never met this woman before.

"I-I'm a friend of Jimmy Barnett. This photograph was in his backpack."

When she spoke Jim's name, the strength drained from my legs. I remembered his kind face, his gentle concern for me. And I remembered my confusion and fear for him when he'd vanished from my life. He had abandoned Ruthie and me and simply disappeared. Maybe this stranger could tell me why. "Where is Jim? Has something happened to him?"

"Can we . . . ? Is there someplace we can sit down and talk?"

I nodded. My head felt like it was spinning and it looked as though hers was, too. "Come this way," I said. She followed me through the back rooms of the bakery to Uncle Aaron's apartment behind the store. My aunt was in the kitchen, and I asked her to take over in the bakery for me. "I'll explain later," I said, handing her my apron. Ruthie had been helping my aunt peel potatoes, and I asked her to bring us some water. The stranger and I sat down at the kitchen table across from each other.

"I'm so sorry," the woman said. "I didn't mean to upset you. My name is Peggy Serrano. I've known Jimmy all of my life, and . . . and is it really true that he married you? Are you really his wife?"

"In a way. He helped me get to America as his war bride, but . . . where is he? What happened to him? I've been waiting to hear from him all this time. I thought he must have abandoned us."

"Jimmy had a breakdown. He came home from the war so depressed that he tried to kill himself."

"No!" I groped for words. "I-I knew he was heartsick after everything he'd seen, but I never imagined . . . I thought . . . I thought that once he returned home, he'd be happy and . . ." I stopped, recalling what he'd said about not wanting to live in a world with so much evil, not wanting to spread the shadow of his darkness over his parents. Maybe I should have done more to help him, but I lived beneath the same suffocating cloud. Finding a home for Ruthie and waiting to hear for certain about Sam were the only things that kept me going most days.

"Jimmy has been in the veterans' hospital since the end of May," Peggy continued. "None of the treatments they've done have helped. We've been trying to find out what happened to make him so depressed, and it seems like it was a whole bunch of grief that just kept piling up on him—the terrible war and losing his friends and then working in Buchenwald. When his commanding officer told us that Jimmy had gotten married, we couldn't believe it. We assumed she might be the woman in the photograph, but Jimmy came home alone. He never said anything about being married. I found this address in his Bible, so I took a chance and came here. Please, if you can tell me anything else—we need to help Jimmy."

My head was swimming. I took a gulp of water and set the glass on the table as I searched for a place to begin. "Jim saved my life. Twice. The first time was when he nursed me back to health in Buchenwald. I'm Jewish, and I was a prisoner there for nearly a year. The second time was when he helped my sister, Ruthie, and me come to America. It was going to take three years to immigrate the usual way. That meant three long years in the displaced persons camp. Jim said that if he and I got married, I could come here as his war bride. We took out a license but the marriage was only on paper. We care for each other, but Jim knows I'm in love with someone else. He's been helping me search for Sam."

"So you came over on a bride ship? Without Jimmy?"

"Yes. Jim had to travel home on a troop ship and then go to Fort Bragg to be discharged. Ruthie and I were supposed to stay with Jim's family, but just before we left Germany, the Jewish agency found out that my uncle Aaron was living here in Brooklyn. We'd been searching for him. I sent my uncle a telegram, and he said to come here, that he would be waiting for Ruthie and me when our ship docked in New York. Jim was happy that we had found our uncle. He told us to go to Brooklyn and wait for him." I looked down at the table, unable to stop my tears. "He said he would come for us but he never did. He left us without a word of explanation."

The kitchen was quiet for a moment. Then Ruthie spoke behind me, her voice soft and hesitant. "Jim didn't leave us, Gisela. He came here."

I whirled around to face her. "What? When?"

She backed up a step to lean against the sink. "Jim came here just like he promised, but you weren't here. Uncle Aaron sent him away."

"What are you talking about? Why didn't you tell me?"

Ruthie wouldn't meet my gaze. "I wanted to tell you, but Uncle

Aaron made me promise I wouldn't. He said there was no point in upsetting you."

"Why would it upset me? I've been waiting for him to come."

Uncle Aaron came in through the back door just then, and I scrambled to my feet to confront him. "Is it true that my friend Jim came to see me here? And you sent him away?"

"Of course I sent him away. I told him you had only used him to get to America, and now that you're here, you didn't need his help anymore. You're Jewish and you belong here, with your family, with other Jews."

We had been talking rapidly in German, and I could see that Peggy was confused. I quickly explained what my uncle had said, then turned back to my sister. "You heard all of this? And you never told me?"

She looked frightened. "I-I thought it was true and that you really did feel that way. I thought you told Uncle Aaron to say those things. Besides, I know you love Sam and you're still hoping he's alive. And . . . and I didn't want to move again. We have a home here."

"What did Jim say? How did he react?"

"It was like . . . like he was shocked. Like he couldn't believe it. He said you needed him, and Uncle Aaron said no, you didn't need him anymore—"

"I told him to hand over the marriage papers so I could have it annulled," Uncle Aaron interrupted. "That was your intent, wasn't it? The marriage was a fake. I told him to go home. The war is over and it isn't his job to save you or take care of you. I told him this was what you wanted."

"Jim wanted to see you one more time," Ruthie said, "but Uncle Aaron said—"

"I told him you didn't want to see him. That it was better this way."

I didn't know what to say or do or where to turn. Learning what Uncle Aaron had done devastated me, just as his words must have devastated Jim. I remembered Jim saying his work as a medic and helping me were the only things keeping him sane. If he believed I had used him and then was rejecting him . . . it must have pushed him over the edge.

"Uncle Aaron, how could you?" I turned away, too furious to face him. "I should have known Jim wouldn't walk away without saying goodbye," I told Ruthie. "He wasn't like that. He wouldn't have deserted me without a word of explanation. Not after going through so much to make sure I got here. But I didn't have his family's address. I had no idea how to get in touch with him."

Uncle Aaron grew angry at this. "You don't need to get in touch with him. I forbid it! So many of our people died, Gisela. And you decide to marry a Gentile? Have children with him? Then what? Raise them as Christians? I can't allow that. You owe it to your father and mother, and to all of the other people who died, to remain a Jew. To rebuild our people."

"Why didn't God save us from the Nazis if He was so worried about our people?" I shouted. "He had plenty of chances to do it. All those years when we were being persecuted, I kept waiting for the Red Sea to part, waiting for Pharaoh's horsemen and chariots to drown, Jericho's walls to crumble. But He didn't do it!"

"Who are we to understand God's ways?" he replied.

"That's not an answer! It's a worthless excuse!" I was furious with my uncle and furious with myself for believing Jim could have deserted me. But I couldn't waste time yelling. I suddenly knew what I needed to do. "I want to go back with you, Peggy, and help you take care of Jim. Is that possible? I'm a nurse. Jim and I understand each other."

"He's still in the hospital."

"Then we must get him out of there. We'll help him. You and me. Is there a place where I can stay? With you, maybe?"

"Yes, with me and Jimmy's parents. They would love to meet you. I'm sure they'll let you stay."

"Are you Jim's girlfriend?" She was pretty enough to be. And she seemed to have his gentle spirit.

"Just a friend. I've known Jimmy for a long time."

I turned to my uncle, still furious with him. "I can't help in the bakery anymore," I told him in German. "I'm leaving with Peggy."

"Just like that? You are running off—who knows where? With this stranger?"

"Jim helped me when I needed it, and now he needs my help. You understand, don't you, Ruthie?" I asked, turning to my sister.

"Are you mad at me?" she asked.

"No, not at all," I said, pulling her into my arms. "But you know Jim. You know I need to straighten this out and help him."

"Are you going to stay there? Stay married to him?"

I smoothed her dark hair from her face. "We were never really husband and wife. But he's hurting, and it's partly my fault, and I need to help him find a reason to live." I went into the crowded bedroom that Ruthie and I shared with our cousins and quickly packed my bag.

When I came back, Uncle Aaron handed me a letter. "This came for you a while back. I think it's from him. I didn't open it."

I swallowed my outrage as I tore open the envelope and pulled out the note, reminding myself that my aunt and uncle had been kind to take Ruthie and me into their home. They had agreed to support us when they had so very little of their own. The note was from Jim:

> *Dear Gisela,*
>
> *I finally received the name and address of Sam's commanding officer in the Jewish Brigade. You can reach him at the enclosed address in Palestine. I hope he can tell you more about Sam and his time in the service.*
>
> *Your uncle told me about your decision to be free from me and our "marriage," and I want you to know that I understand and will respect it. I wish you all the best in your new life in America.*
>
> *Your friend always,*
> *Jim Barnett*

We were about to leave when Peggy said, "If you still have the papers saying that you're his wife, you should bring them. You'll able to make decisions about his medical treatment along with his parents."

Peggy called Jim's parents from Grand Central station, and they were waiting for us when we arrived at the end of our journey. Jim and his father had the same tall, angular build. They stood and moved and walked alike and had the same broad hands. His mother's gray-green eyes were the same color as Jim's, the color of the sea. She pulled me into her arms for a long embrace, loving me without question. Jim had poured out that same love on everyone in Buchenwald. I melted into her arms. We climbed into their car and crossed the river on a ferry. Peggy told my story to Jim's parents on the ride home.

Home. We arrived at the home where Jim grew up a short time later. The dog who greeted me, wagging his entire hindquarters along with his tail, looked like he was smiling up at me. Jim's mother opened her refrigerator and spread a banquet of food on the table for Peggy and me. I hoped she understood how overwhelming it was and why I could put only a few things on my plate. I wanted to rush to the hospital immediately but night had fallen.

"What time can we see Jim tomorrow?" I asked.

His mother shook her head. "Visiting hours are only on Sundays. We'll have to wait another week to visit him again."

"But why should we wait? We're the people who care about him. We're his family, and I am a nurse. Jim needs to come home."

"I agree," Jim's father said. He slapped his hand on the table for emphasis. "The doctors had their chance to help him. We'll go to the hospital tomorrow and bring him home."

We talked and talked until it was very late. Jim's mother showed me to a lovely bedroom of my own on the second floor. I halted in the doorway. "Is something wrong?" she asked.

It took me a moment to put my feelings into words. "There's nobody else in it. I'm not used to sleeping all alone." For as long as I could remember I had shared a room with someone—first with Ruthie, then with my roommates at nursing school, then jammed in with countless others in Buchenwald and the DP camp. I had slept alone in the tiny pantry in the former SS barracks for a few months, but there had been other people and lots of activity just outside my door. Except for the sound of insects beyond the open windows, this room was deathly quiet.

"You can stay with me, in my room," Peggy said. "It has two beds." I accepted her offer with great relief.

I washed in the sparkling bathroom, put on my pajamas, and climbed into bed. Peggy got into her bed and switched off the light. "I'm so excited you're here, Gisela, and that you want to help Jimmy. Gosh, I don't know how I'll ever fall asleep! I've been hoping we could bring him home from the hospital for the longest time."

There was something very comforting about talking to my new friend in the dark in this cozy room. Only a few hours ago, I had been in the bustling city, miles from this peaceful place, working in the bakery and trying to adjust to my new life in America. I hadn't known that Peggy even existed. But she had quickly become my friend, just as Jimmy had in Buchenwald.

"I'm still very sorry for the way everything happened," I said. "It was cruel of my uncle to send Jim away. I could tell that he was depressed when we were still in Germany, but I thought he would be all right once he got home." And yet Jim had told me about the overwhelming darkness he'd felt. I could see why he hadn't wanted to bring that darkness home to these lovely people.

"We've been talking to Jimmy's Army buddies and following his journey through the war," Peggy said. "Jimmy loved God and had a very strong faith when he left home. Even in the beginning when he first went overseas, he was always reading his Bible and encouraging everyone. But later on, he stopped. As the war went on, I think he may have lost his faith in a loving God."

"He did. Jim told me he did."

"That's awful!"

"He talked about the terrible darkness he felt. Maybe he tried to kill himself in order to escape from it."

"If that's true, then we have to find a way to bring him back into the light. Back to his faith in God."

I didn't reply. I didn't know the way back. I lived beneath the same shadow myself, with only a tiny spark of light. Everything I'd been doing for the past few months—traveling to New York City, getting reacquainted with my uncle and his family, helping Ruthie feel settled and at home—those things had kept the light burning dimly in my heart. And the work Jim did in Buchenwald had kept his darkness away for a time. But when he'd arrived home, when my uncle told him I didn't want his help, the darkness must have finally overwhelmed him. I longed to help him as badly as Peggy did, but I didn't know how.

"I have a scrapbook filled with pictures of his friends," Peggy continued. "And all the letters they sent, saying how much he helped them. If we can show Jimmy how much everyone loves him, maybe he'll start believing that God loves him, too."

I hoped she was right. But it would take much more than that to convince me that there was a God who loved me. I lay awake for most of the night and had a headache when I got up in the morning. Peggy's bed was empty. She'd told me that she had to rise early to do her chores at the animal clinic. Jimmy's father was just hanging up the phone in the front hallway when I came downstairs for breakfast.

"It's settled," he told us as we ate. "I talked to Dr. Morgan and told him we would be arriving later today to bring Jim home. Of course, he protested. He says Jim's discharge will be against medical advice. I told him we didn't care, and they should have him ready to leave when we got there at noon."

I didn't recognize Jim when I first saw him, sitting on an ugly chair in the hospital foyer. He was thin and haggard-looking, and his clothes hung on him as if they belonged to someone else. Peggy had warned me that he rarely spoke, so I was surprised when he struggled to his feet and said, "Gisela? What are you doing here?"

I hugged him tightly, not caring how many people stared at us. "My uncle lied to you, Jim. I never said all those things he told you. I never would have sent you away. I had no idea that you came to Brooklyn to find me until Peggy came to my uncle's apartment yesterday. We've both been believing a lie, Jim."

Peggy held one of his hands and I held the other as we walked out of the hospital. The view from the parking lot of the shining river and distant mountains was so beautiful that I stopped to savor it for a moment. I made Jim stop and look at it, too. Later, we stood at the rail together on the ferry ride across the Hudson River and I thought of my time with Sam on board the *St. Louis*. Sam and Jim would have liked each other. Sam would be grateful to Jim for saving my life.

Jim's father and Peggy left for their afternoon rounds when we arrived home. I helped Jim's mother pick the late-summer peas in her garden, then Jim and I sat talking with her on the front porch while she shelled them. Peggy's dog refused to leave Jim's side, sitting contentedly at his feet. The rhythmic creak of the rocking chairs and the pinging of the plump peas as they fell into the pot were soothing, as I told Jim's mother about my long journey from Berlin to America. It was the first time I was able to talk about any of the things that I had endured, even to my aunt and uncle. Somehow the weight of the past seemed lighter after sharing it with her.

"My uncle Aaron just gave me your letter yesterday," I told Jim, "with the address of Sam's commanding officer in Palestine. I need to write to him." His mother gave me stationery and an airmail envelope. I walked to the post office to mail it with Jim and Peggy and Buster after Peggy finished work. The tiny village was quiet and a little shabby-looking. The American flags that hung from the porches of many of the homes barely rippled beneath the warm afternoon sun. It was so peaceful here compared to the city. I wished I had brought Ruthie with me.

Peggy had a letter to mail, too. "It's a note to Jimmy's friend Chaplain Bill," she whispered to me. "I told him Jimmy is home and that he should come for a visit."

Jim remained quiet and distant all day, so unlike the warm, soft-spoken man I knew. At bedtime, when he went outside with his father to shut the barn doors and close the chicken coop, his mother took Peggy and me aside. "Jim had terrible nightmares before he went into the hospital," she said. "He would wake up screaming and trembling. Gordon thinks we shouldn't leave him alone at night. He thought maybe we could take turns watching over him. I'll stay with him tonight and—"

"No, Mrs. Barnett," I said. "I am Jim's wife. I will stay with him tonight. And every night until he's well."

We would be companions in the darkness, watching for the dawn.

*   *   *

I slept so lightly that I heard Jim moaning in his sleep and was able to awaken him from his nightmare before he cried out. He sat up in bed and leaned against the headboard, his eyes wide-open as he stared into the night. It would be a while before dawn. "Sorry I woke you," he said.

"I was already half-awake. I don't sleep very soundly." I understood his reluctance to go back to sleep and return to the world of troubling dreams.

Jim's bed was too narrow to hold two people, so we had carried in the extra mattress from Peggy's room to make a bed on the floor. Jim and I had disagreed over which one of us would sleep in the bed, so Peggy had settled it by flipping a coin. "You can swap places on laundry day," she'd said. I was glad that I'd won the floor. I rose now and rolled up the shades on both bedroom windows so we could watch for the dawn. Then I sat cross-legged on my mattress looking up at Jim.

"What do you see in your nightmares?" I asked. He shook his head, reluctant to reply. "Jim, I saw the same things you did during the war. I helped care for bombing victims in Mortsel. And I wasn't just a nurse in Buchenwald; I lived there. I understand why you can't talk about these things with your parents, but you can talk about them with me."

"Then you'll relive them, too."

"I already do. Every day and every night. I wonder, sometimes, if they will ever go away. But when we sat on your porch yesterday, and I told my story to your mother . . . I can't explain why, but it did seem to help. I think if we keep holding all the poison inside us, it will kill us.

An infected wound has to be lanced and cleansed or it will never heal. That's a very painful process, but you know how necessary it is."

He was silent for so long I didn't think he was going to talk to me. But finally he sighed and said, "I dream I'm in the camp. Or sometimes on a battlefield. People are screaming and suffering. Begging me to help them. I try, but it's like they're underwater or something, and I can't get to them. I'm helpless. I try so hard but . . ."

I knelt and took his hand. He squeezed mine in return before releasing it. "I have nightmares, too," I said when I'd settled on my mattress again. "Most often, I dream that I'm back on the ship, and there are Nazis everywhere I turn. I'm running through all of the corridors and decks and looking inside staterooms, searching and searching for Sam so he can help me find the way out, but I can't find him." A breeze from the open window made the curtains rise and fall as if they were breathing. "Nightmares lose some of their power when you tell them out loud. Ruthie taught me that in the DP camp when I had bad dreams. We have to start talking about the things that haunt us, Jim. I believe you can be honest with your family about losing your faith. They already know you've been through hell, and they want to help you so badly. Peggy showed me the scrapbook she made with photos and stories from all of your friends."

"Peggety is a sweet girl."

"She is. When we were traveling up here on the train, she told me how hard she has been fighting for you."

He didn't reply. There was a question I needed to ask but I was afraid to hear his answer. It took a few moments for me to summon my courage. "Why did you try to kill yourself, Jim? Tell me the truth. Is it my fault in any way? Because if it is, I don't know how I can ever tell you how sorry I am—"

"It's not your fault." He sighed, and I sensed that he was searching for words. It was as if he hadn't spoken for so long that he'd forgotten how. I reached for his hand and waited. "Do you remember what all those towns and cities looked like after they were bombed?" he asked. "How the people wept and mourned with blank eyes and silent screams? The war left me as ruined as those villages and those people. Yet I had to keep going because I was needed. Injured people needed my help. You needed my help. When I came home and was no longer needed, I couldn't keep the darkness away anymore."

He looked at me in the dim light as if asking if I understood. I did, and yet I didn't. I squeezed his hand, shaking my head.

"On Decoration Day," he continued, "there was a ceremony at the church down the road. I heard the bells tolling for all the fallen soldiers. The rifles firing. I should have died with them. I already felt dead inside. I had no reason to keep on living. And it was the only way to stop the memories and the nightmares."

"I'm so sorry," I murmured. I waited again, then asked, "So do you still want to end your life, or do you want to live?"

He seemed to take his time, pondering my question. "I'm having a hard time seeing the point of life," he finally replied.

"I understand. In these last few years, life has seemed very short and difficult and pointless to me, too. We both watched a lot of people die. Most of them didn't have a choice. But if they had, I think most of them would have chosen to live. I know you had friends who died."

"My best friend. Mitch."

"Ruthie and I lost our parents." I swallowed the knot that always rose in my throat when I thought of them. "And one of the things that kept me going in the camp—and even today—is thinking about what they would say if they were able to speak to me from the grave. That's why I accepted your offer to get married and come to America, because I knew that Vati and Mutti would be shouting at me to stop grieving and get out of that DP camp and live! After the pogrom in Antwerp, they wouldn't let me cower in fear in our apartment and stop living. They insisted that I continue my nursing studies. So . . . what would your friend Mitch tell you?"

"I get it," he said a little angrily. "You're right. Mitch would punch me and tell me to get on with it. But where do I start?"

"What I learned is that you simply get out of bed in the morning. You get dressed. You eat. Then you do the work in front of you that day. That's what I did in Buchenwald and in the DP camp and in my uncle's apartment in New York. You just keep living until you feel alive again."

"Do you feel alive, Gisela?"

"Not yet. But I'm closer than I was when you carried me to the hospital in Buchenwald. I'll get there someday. And so will you."

27

Peggy

"I'm taking Buster for a walk before I start work," I told Jimmy after breakfast. "Want to come with me?" He hesitated as if searching for an excuse. "Please?" I added.

"You should go," Gisela told him. "I'll help your mother with the dishes."

I was glad he agreed and that we were going alone. I had something in my pocket that I wanted to give him. I hooked Buster's leash to his collar and we headed down the road out of town. The morning air was cool with a hint of fall, the kind of day that made me want to skip like a schoolgirl. I set Buster free when we reached the bridge, and we took the footpath down to the river. We sat on a large, flat stone by the water's edge while Buster sniffed and explored in the bushes and waded into the rock-strewn river to drink.

"This has always been one of my favorite places to come," I said with a sigh. "And yours, too, I think. It's so peaceful here. And so pretty with the river singing and the mountains standing there like old friends.

This seems like a much better place to try to get well than the veterans' hospital."

"It is."

"I'm sorry they put you through all those treatments. And I'm sorrier still that none of them seemed to work."

"I didn't care."

Jimmy's voice sounded flat and emotionless, not at all like the warm, rich voice I remembered. I could tell that he didn't want to talk, but I decided I would make him do it anyway. "Gisela told me you don't believe in God anymore, and I'm sorry to hear it. If I'd been through everything you and Gisela have, maybe I would feel that way, too. I don't think any less of you for it. And you won't change my mind about what I believe. But if I'm still your friend, will you at least share your thoughts with me again, the way you used to do?"

"I . . . I can try."

I had hoped that the simple beauty and peacefulness of the setting would put him at ease, but he still seemed nervous and fidgety, as if his skin didn't fit him anymore. The only thing that seemed to soothe his restlessness was Buster, who flopped down beside him, damp and muddy from his romp in the river. Jimmy stroked his wet fur and scratched behind his huge ears until Buster practically sighed with contentment.

"I remember sitting here with you one day and bawling my eyes out," I said, "because the kids at school made me feel so ugly and worthless. But you convinced me that God loved me with a passionate love and that He was sad when I was mistreated. So what I need to ask is . . . if there isn't a God, does that mean I'm not loved after all? Were the kids in town right when they called me names?"

"It's complicated, Peggety." He sighed.

"Please try to explain it to me. You were always so good at explaining things so I could understand them." I waited, listening to a blue jay's song in the treetops above us.

Finally Jimmy replied. "Millions of people suffered and died. The God I believed in couldn't have turned His back on them." This time I heard a hint of anger in his voice, and I was glad. At least he was show-ing emotion.

"You told me that whenever I doubted God's love, I should look at the cross. You said it would always remind me of His love. So here—I want you to have this." I pulled my mother's crucifix from my jacket pocket and handed it to him. "You were right; it does remind me. Because I can see how much Jesus suffered. And it seemed like God had turned His back on Jesus, too. Remember? He asked, 'Why have You abandoned me?'"

Jimmy nodded. He was holding the crucifix lightly as if it might burn his fingers.

"Everybody wanted Jesus to be a king who would march into town and get rid of all the bad guys," I continued. "We wish He would swoop down and fix everything for us, too. Instead, Jesus suffered and died— and made it possible for all of us to become God's children. That means there isn't just one Son to fix all the things that are broken in the world, but a whole bunch of us who are willing to suffer like He did to show God's love—even to the evil people in this world. Didn't Jesus say we're supposed to take up our cross and follow Him?"

I waited for him to reply but he didn't. "God didn't turn His back and let all those people die, Jimmy—we did. People like you and me. When Gisela and her family were on that ship and they needed a place of refuge, everyone turned his back. The truth is, a lot of people don't like Jews, and they didn't want them in our country. You tried to help. I saw the letter you wrote to President Roosevelt. But too many other people just read the newspaper article and tossed it aside. What if every Christian had written a letter to the president, offering to take one of those families on that ship home with them?"

I let him think about my words for a minute or maybe argue with me, but he didn't. "I knew I could always come to you, Jimmy, when the kids were bullying me. But no one else ever stuck up for me. Pop said I should ignore them, and even my teachers looked the other way. I think God is counting on us to speak up, whether it's one girl being called names or a whole group of people who are being persecuted."

He glanced at me and I saw a flash of anger in his eyes. I worried that he was angry with me but he finally spoke. "There's a town just down the road from Buchenwald. The people who lived there claimed they had no idea what was happening in that camp."

"See? That's what I mean. The war and everything else that happened is because of what people chose, not God. He put us in charge of the earth. We're responsible for it and for each other. Even before America entered the war, there were reports of what the Nazis were doing to the Jews, yet no one did a thing. God doesn't control us like puppets and make us do what we should. Ever since Adam and Eve, He lets us live with our own choices. The people wanted Hitler as their leader and they got him. Americans chose to turn our backs on Hitler's evil until one day it was out of control. If we learn anything at all from this horrible war, it's that followers of Jesus need to speak up and to act."

"Some did," Jimmy said. "There were Christians in Belgium who risked their lives to help Gisela and her family."

"Thank God for them. And for you and all of your Army buddies, too, who went to war to defeat evil."

I noticed that he was holding the cross a little tighter in his hands, running his thumb over the smooth wood. "When did you become so wise, Peggety?" he asked.

"Don't you know?" I said, laughing. "I learned everything from you." He looked at me and smiled faintly.

On the way home, Buster meandered and sniffed and explored in all the bushes as usual. We were walking along the other side of the road this time, and at one point he seemed to find one scent more interesting than the others. He strained and pulled on his leash, refusing to obey me. My arms got tired of tugging, so I handed the leash to Jimmy. "Can you control him? I can't imagine what he's after."

"I'll go see." Jimmy jumped across the ditch and followed Buster into the underbrush. A moment later he halted and crouched down. "Peggety!" he called. "Come here!"

The bundle of bones and matted fur lying in the weeds was a dog. I thought it must be dead but I saw it move when Buster licked its muzzle. He tried to lick one of the deep cuts on the dog's belly but Jimmy held him back. He ran his gentle fingers over the dog's body. "Her injuries aren't new. The blood has clotted."

"Do you suppose she got hit by a car?"

"Looks like it. But either she's been here for a while, or she was abused and neglected beforehand. Look how thin she is." The dog had longish fur and floppy ears, like she might be part cocker spaniel. Jimmy felt her neck for a collar but there was none. Only a noose of rope that had chafed her neck raw before it had broken, leaving a short piece attached. Her eyes were infected and caked nearly shut. "We need to help her," Jimmy said. He slid his hands beneath the dog and lifted her into his arms. The dog gave a soft whine. "She's as light as a feather."

We hurried home and went straight into the clinic. Jimmy laid the dog on the examining table and studied her wounds more carefully while I hustled around, turning on lights and preparing a tray with antiseptic and sutures and bandages and all the other things he would need. "Do you know where my dad went?" he asked.

"He had animals to see on three different farms. He said not to expect him before lunch."

"We'll have to take care of her ourselves."

We gave her an anesthetic so Jimmy could cleanse her cuts and abrasions and stitch them closed. He carefully disinfected the deep wound on her belly, worried about peritonitis. One of her front legs was broken, but it was a clean break and could be splinted. As he continued to examine and tend her, he suddenly looked up at me in surprise. "She's pregnant, Peggety! It's a wonder she didn't miscarry after being this badly injured." He held a stethoscope to her chest. "Her heart sounds pretty weak, but her puppies' hearts are still beating. I hear at least two of them." For some reason that news made me smile and tear up at the same time.

I lost all track of time while we worked, with Jimmy suturing and me handing him all the things he needed. When we finally finished and I stepped back, I saw Buster sitting in the doorway as if guarding it. His leash was still attached. I went over to pet him. "Good boy, Buster. You saved this dog's life." I heard a chuckle and turned, amazed to see Jimmy smiling. "What?" I asked.

"I used to tell stories to the injured men in the field hospitals about Buster the three-legged dog. I made him into a hero, like Lassie, in the movie, you know? Today he lived up to his legend."

I laughed and gave Jimmy a hug. He was talking! And smiling! And working as a veterinarian again. He had once saved Buster's life, and now Buster and this little dog might help save his.

* * *

The little stray was still alive and even eating a bit of food two days later. "I couldn't have stitched her up any better myself," Mr. Barnett had said when he'd seen Jimmy's work. Gisela, Jimmy, and I all took care of the little animal, which we'd named Lucky. I had just finished helping Jimmy change Lucky's dressings one afternoon when we heard a car pull up. I looked out the window to see if we had another patient and was happy to see Chaplain Bill getting out of his car.

We all went into Mrs. Barnett's kitchen, and after drinking coffee and chatting for a while, Mr. Barnett pulled me aside and whispered, "Take Bill and Jimmy away somewhere so they can talk. I'll handle office hours by myself."

It took a bit of convincing, but at last, Jimmy and I climbed into Bill's car and drove toward the mountains. I directed Bill up the winding road past the hairpin turn to the lookout on top. "You really get a broader view of things from up here, don't you?" Bill said after we'd stepped from the car.

"It's one of my favorite places," I said. I brushed my hair from my eyes, tangled by the glorious mountain breezes. We enjoyed the view in silence for a few moments before Bill turned to Jimmy.

"I have to be honest and admit it, Jim—my faith was badly shaken by what we went through. In fact, I wrote a letter of resignation to my church board. I felt I had to give up the pastorate because of all my doubts and uncertainties. Your friend Peggy here helped me find my way back." Bill and Jimmy both turned to me. I didn't know what to say. I felt surprised and embarrassed more than anything else by his kind words. Bill continued: "I would like to explain to you what I finally figured out—and feel free to interrupt and argue and add your own two cents, Jim, the way you used to do. I always enjoyed discussing theology with you."

Jimmy gave a curt nod and stepped over the guardrail so he could sit down on it. Bill and I did the same. The day was warm, and the broad valley stretched in front of us with row after row of mountains lining up on the distant horizon. The pastures of Blue Fence Farms looked like tiny green squares below us.

"I don't think you and I ever questioned God very much before we went away to war," Bill said. "We were a little too certain about what we believed, as if we had God all figured out. But over in France, it became harder and harder to reconcile God's goodness with what we were experiencing. If He was loving and all-powerful, why did He allow such suffering? Was He powerless to stop it? It was as if those bombs blew up our belief system when it clashed with reality. Of course, the spiritual realm is invisible. God's actions behind the scenes are invisible. So all we had to rely on was what we were seeing. But our enemy wasn't just the Nazis. Satan's ploy is to spread evil throughout the world and let it drive a wedge between us and God. His evil is most painful and most dangerous when it seems purposeless to us. When we can't see how God can possibly bring anything good from it."

Bill paused as we watched a hawk soar through the sky below us, its broad wings outstretched as it rode the wind. "It was something Peggy said to me that led me to the book of Job," he continued. "Job wanted to know why God had made him suffer so horribly. Instead of giving His reasons, God asked Job a series of unanswerable questions, like 'Where does light come from, and where does darkness go?' and 'Does the rain have a father?' The answers are beyond Job's understanding. Besides, Job doesn't need to know because he isn't in charge of the darkness or the weather—God is. God never did tell Job the reason for his suffering. Job just had to trust that God was at work."

"But Job was only one man," Jimmy said. "This time, millions of innocent people suffered!" Again, I heard the anger in his voice. But at least he was listening to Bill and talking to him.

"I know," Bill replied. "And for now, we are left without answers for what the Nazis did. But Job didn't turn away from God in spite of not receiving any answers. The only light we'll ever have in this dark world comes from God. If we turn away from Him, we're left with darkness and despair."

"Is it any wonder I turned away? I didn't see much light on the battlefield, did you? And you weren't there when Buchenwald's gates were opened."

"No. I wasn't. But can I tell you something, Jim? And forgive me if I sound harsh, but you always tried to handle everything yourself. When we were all offered a week's leave from the battlefront, you wouldn't take it. You exhausted yourself as you went about playing God, trying to save as many lives as you could because you didn't think God was doing a very good job of it. You were angry with Him, so you tried to be a medic on your own strength instead of asking for His help. Is it any wonder you burned out? You kept saying that all of our days are written in His book, but you seemed determined to rewrite that book your own way. If God wasn't going to act and straighten everything out, then you would do it yourself." He waited as if expecting an argument. Jimmy was staring down at his feet. "Does anything I'm saying make sense to you?" Bill asked.

"I . . . I'll have to think about it," he said softly. I heard a rumble of distant thunder and turned to look behind us. The sky was darkening as an afternoon thunderstorm approached. It wouldn't be much longer before we got drenched.

Bill pulled a folded piece of paper from his shirt pocket and handed it to Jimmy. "In the meantime," he said, "I want you to carry this with you and pull it out and read it at least once a day—no, don't read it now. Wait until you're by yourself. I watched you put a lot of splints on broken bones so they could heal. You applied tourniquets above deep wounds so the bleeding would stop. Use these verses in the same way, Jim. Apply them to your broken heart and wounded spirit until time and God do their healing work."

I was curious to know what the verses were but I didn't ask. We stood and made our way back to the car. The first spitting drops of rain had started to fall. Thunder rumbled and echoed between the mountains, louder now. I loved that majestic sound. *"The angels in heaven are rearranging their furniture,"* my mama used to say when I was small.

"You know," Bill said before we climbed into the car, "the cross made no sense to Jesus' disciples the day after it happened. Jesus' brutal death seemed senseless. That's where we are right now. The war is over but we're living in those days between the cross and the empty tomb. I can't explain why millions of people suffered and died. But I do know that death never has the final word. Easter Sunday brings life in all its triumph. We just need to trust and wait a little longer, Jim. God is at work. We will see His redemption and restoration one day."

✳   ✳   ✳

A few days before Labor Day, we were sitting around the supper table when Jimmy's mother announced that she would like to celebrate that day with a picnic. "We'll have hamburgers and hot dogs and potato salad," she said. "And play horseshoes on the lawn like we used to—remember? I think we need to give summer one last hurrah before it comes to an end. Jimmy, maybe you could invite your Army friend—what was his name? The one who lives in Milford?"

"You mean Frank Cishek?" I asked. "That's a great idea."

"And how about if we invite the new horse trainer from Blue Fence Farms?" Mr. Barnett said. He looked at me and winked when he said it.

"I would like that," I said, blushing. "A lot!"

"Good. We have to go out there tomorrow to check on a couple of their horses. We'll ask him then."

"Peggy, please feel free to invite your father and his girlfriend," Mrs. Barnett added.

"Okay. I will." I had been avoiding going over to see Pop, but this would give me a good excuse to go. It was still light outside after we finished washing the dishes, so I summoned my nerve and walked across the street.

"Where have you been hiding out?" Pop asked. I found him in the garage, tinkering with a car engine. "We haven't heard a peep from you."

"I'm sorry. Jimmy finally came home from the hospital, so things have been busy over at the Barnetts' house. I . . . I'm living with them for now." Pop looked up from his work. He frowned but didn't say anything. "I'm looking for an apartment," I said quickly. "I won't be living there forever. But it's hard to find a place that will let me keep Buster."

"You're not making a pest of yourself, are you?"

"They invited me to stay."

"You make sure you ask them. Tell them I want to know."

Donna came out of Pop's office just then, a cigarette in one hand and a letter in the other. "This came for you. I didn't know where to forward it."

"Oh. I'm sorry. I meant to go to the post office and change my address, but I guess I forgot." I looked down at the envelope. It was from Barbara Symanski. I could hardly wait to rip it open. "Listen, Donna, the Barnetts are having a Labor Day picnic and they invited you and Pop to come."

"Tell them thanks but we have no business over there." Donna nudged Pop's ribs, then gestured to me. "Tell her our news, as long as she's here."

Pop cleared his throat. "Yeah . . . well . . . Donna and I are tying the knot. On her birthday. September 10."

"Congratulations!" I said. "That's great news."

"Nothing big," Donna said. "Just down at the city hall in Newburgh."

"But we want you there," Pop said. "To stand up with us."

I was stunned. But pleased. It took me a moment to reply. "I-I . . . of course I'll come. Thank you."

I tore open Barbara's letter as I hurried across the street again, then sank down on the back porch steps to read it.

Dear Peggy,

The leaves are changing colors, the schools will be opening soon, and I'm getting ready to start teaching my kindergarten class in a few days. But I wanted to thank you again for helping Joe and me and to tell you what's been happening here in Ohio. Joe still has good days and bad days, but he knows he can always come to me whenever he needs to. I've been learning to be more patient and understanding with him and not to push him too hard or too quickly. He's drinking a lot less than he did before, and I'm glad for that. We've both had to accept that he may never completely get over the awful experiences he had in the war. We're trying to take one day at a time, and we're committed to moving forward together.

He still doesn't have a full-time job, but his friends at the fire station are helping him look for one. There's a chance that with some training he might become a fire safety inspector or an arson investigator. He likes the idea of solving fiery crimes. In the meantime, he has been doing free car repairs for families at church who are down on their luck. He says your pop taught him a lot when he worked for him. And he says to give Tripod a good scratch behind the ears for him.

Joe and I will always be grateful to you for all your help, Peggy. Maybe we'll ride out to visit you again next summer. Until then, I wish you well in all that you do.

Your friend,
Barbara

I was still sitting on the back steps, watching the fireflies and slapping mosquitoes, when Mrs. Barnett approached after closing her chicken coop for the night. "I invited Pop and Donna, but they already have plans," I told her. I thought about what Pop had said about being a pest, and his words still unsettled me. I had to know the truth. "Can I ask you a question, Mrs. B.?"

"Sure, honey."

"Pop wanted me to ask you . . . he wants to know if you're sure I'm not being a pest?"

She sat down beside me on the step and wrapped her arm around my waist. "Dear, sweet Peggy," she said, leaning against me. "I thought you knew by now how much you mean to Gordon and me. But maybe it's high time we told you. You've been a wonderful companion and helper for Gordon, sharing his love of animals and the work that he does. He told me just the other day that he would be lost without you. But you're so much more than that to both of us. You filled an empty place in our lives when Jimmy went off to war, and you've stood with us all these months as we've tried to get help for him. You've become a daughter to us in every way. The love we share with you is very special to us. We aren't trying to take the place of your parents. Pop will always be your father. But you're part of our family now, and you don't ever need to think of yourself as anything else."

I was still wiping my eyes and hugging Mrs. B. when Gisela came to the screen door behind us. "Come inside! Hurry! Lucky is having her puppies!"

We stood and followed her into the kitchen, where Jimmy had made a bed for Lucky in a cardboard box. Mrs. Barnett and I had our arms around each other as we watched the miracle of birth in silence. I saw it often as Mr. Barnett's assistant but I never grew tired of seeing a new life emerge. I watched Jimmy's face as he crouched beside his dog, waiting for the first little wet puppy. He had tears in his eyes and a faint smile on his face. I thought of Chaplain Bill's words. Death never had the last word—life would always triumph.

28

Gisela

Jim's mother hummed softly as we washed the dishes together after breakfast. She always seemed so cheerful, and I loved working alongside her. For the moment, we were alone. Peggy had left to work in the clinic with Jim's father, and Jim was taking Lucky for a short walk outside. Two weeks had passed since I had come from New York City with Peggy to help Jim. Two weeks since I had mailed the letter to the commander of the Jewish Brigade in Palestine, asking for more information about Sam's disappearance. And two weeks since Jim had come home from the hospital. I could already see his spirits lifting a bit, as if every morning he was choosing to live. Peggy had wisely enlisted the help of his Army friends in his recovery, and Jim had enjoyed spending time with his former chaplain and with his friend Frank on Labor Day. Now his devotion to Lucky and her two pups was giving him a purpose.

The kitchen door squealed open and Jim came inside, cradling Lucky and carrying a small, yellow envelope. "Western Union just delivered this telegram. It's for you, Gisela."

I took the envelope from him, my heart pounding with dread and hope. I was afraid to open it. Jimmy settled Lucky in her box with her mewling puppies and came to stand beside me.

"Do you want me to read it first?" he asked.

"Would you?"

He took it from me and opened the flap. I watched his face for clues while he read it. "I think it's good news," he finally said, looking up at me. "It's from Sam's former Army commander in Palestine." He handed it back to me.

```
Captain Aaron Cohen can answer questions
about Samuel Shapiro. Jewish Benevolent
Association, E. 69th St., NY, NY
```

We telephoned the Benevolent Association right away and learned that Captain Cohen was visiting from Palestine. We made an appointment to see him, my heart swirling with a mixture of emotions. He might be able to give me a clearer picture of what had happened to Sam. He might have been one of the last people to see him alive. But was I ready to learn the truth?

Jim insisted on coming with me to my appointment. It seemed like a good sign that he was interested in making the trip to New York City with me. We walked through a dreary, misty rain to the address on Sixty-Ninth Street, and my knees felt shaky as I went up the steps and rang the doorbell.

Captain Cohen himself welcomed us inside. "Shalom! I am Aaron Cohen. So nice to meet you. Please, come this way." He had the same, slightly nasal accent as the Jews from Palestine who had come to the DP camp to talk about Zionism. I was surprised that he was so young, probably no more than thirty. He led us to a small reception room, and a young woman brought a tray with tea. I was too nervous to drink it.

"Thank you for seeing us on such short notice, Captain," I said as I sat down beside Jim on the love seat.

"Yes, of course. How can I help?"

"I received this telegram from your brigade commander," I said, passing it to him. "I understand you served with Sam Shapiro in the Jewish Brigade."

"Yes. And you are . . . a relative? A girlfriend?"

"I'm his fiancée. Sam and I met on board the *St. Louis* and fell in love. We would have been married if not for the war. The last time I saw him was in 1942 in Belgium. He was working for the underground, and he got false IDs for my sister and me so we could go into hiding. My friend Jim traced him after that," I said, gesturing to him. "He learned that Sam had escaped to England and joined your Jewish Brigade. Any information you can give me on how he became missing in action would—"

"Has no one told you?"

"Told me what? I don't know anything—"

"Sam is alive!"

I stopped breathing. I wanted to believe his words but I didn't dare. My entire body began to tremble. "He—he's alive?"

"Yes! I'm sorry for not telling you right away, but I thought you knew."

"Oh, thank God! Thank God!" I cried. Jim held me tightly, letting me sob against his shoulder. No one spoke for a long moment, as if giving me space to weep and rejoice and bring Sam back to life in my heart. "You're certain he's alive?" I finally asked as I let go of Jim and dried my eyes on his handkerchief. "H-how do you know?"

"The refugee ship he was piloting was intercepted by the British Navy, and everyone on board was taken to Cyprus. That's where he is, Miss Wolff—in a detention camp on Cyprus."

I pressed the handkerchief against my eyes and wept some more. His words were finally sinking in. Sam, my beloved Sam, was alive!

"Please, take a drink of tea, Miss Wolff, and allow me to tell you the whole story." He handed me one of the cups. It rattled against the saucer as I took it from him and lifted it to my lips. I felt it go all the way down, calming my stomach, settling me.

"I trained with Sam in Egypt and fought beside him in Italy," the captain began. "By the time the war came to an end, we had moved into northeastern Italy and were encountering survivors from the concentration camps. Our brigade worked in a displaced persons camp to care for the refugees and help as many as we could escape to Palestine. We eventually acquired the use of a modest fishing boat, and since Sam knew a bit about navigation, he offered to help pilot it to Palestine with some 150 refugees on board. In order for Sam to do that, our commander sent a report to the British military that Sam was missing in action. Sam knew that his family was safe and that Antwerp had been liberated. He hadn't listed anyone as next of kin, so he hoped you wouldn't be wrongly notified that he was missing. He mailed a letter to the gentleman who was hiding his mother and brothers, telling them what he was doing."

"His letter never arrived."

Captain Cohen's face fell. "Oh no. That is very unfortunate. And it has caused a great deal of pain, I am sure. I am so sorry."

"It's not your fault. So what happened?"

"Sam's ship smuggled the refugees past the British patrols during the night, and they landed safely on a deserted beach north of Tel Aviv. It seemed easy, and because they had been so successful, they decided to make a second run with more people. And then a third. But his ship was intercepted by British patrols the third time. Sam and the others were taken to a detention camp on Cyprus."

"Aren't they allowed to send mail from there?" Jim asked.

"I assume so. But does Sam know where to find you after all this time?"

"Probably not," I said. "Is there a way I can contact him?"

"I will give you the address of the Jewish relief agency that is working on the island. They'll track him down and make sure he gets your letter."

It was too good to be true. I covered my face and wept again.

"Are you all right, Gisela?" Jim asked.

"Yes. Yes! Just stunned and . . . and overwhelmed!"

"Sam is a big supporter of a Jewish homeland in Palestine. Did you know?" the captain asked.

"He used to go to Zionist meetings in Antwerp."

"Aren't the British restricting immigration at the moment?" Jim asked.

"They are. But the detention camps on Cyprus are fueling international outrage. The British are asking the United Nations to send observers to Palestine to advise them what to do. I realize that it is impossible to see any sane reason for what the Nazis did to us. But if the doors to Palestine are flung open because of it, and if the Jewish people are able to return to our homeland after two thousand years, future generations will see this terrible trial as the hand of God."

"No!" I cried out. "The sacrifice was much too great! Millions of us were murdered!"

Captain Cohen leaned toward me, resting his arms on his thighs. "Let me ask you this, Miss Wolff. You have lost family members, yes? Your parents, perhaps?" I nodded and stared at him through my tears. "If you could ask them if they would be willing to give up their lives to make sure you and your children and grandchildren had a homeland, a place where no one could ever persecute you or make you leave again, what do you think they would say?"

I closed my eyes as my tears fell, remembering how hard Vati had worked to get our visas and landing permits for Cuba. He and Mutti had sold all of their possessions so we could be free from persecution. They'd been so relieved when we boarded the *St. Louis*, believing we were sailing to safety. They had made sure that Ruthie and I had hiding places in Belgium before they died. They had wanted us to survive. To be safe from pogroms and persecution. From wandering and homelessness, from concentration camps and DP camps. They wouldn't want us to experience the pain of being unwanted and rejected ever again. But I couldn't give Captain Cohen's question a simple reply. There wasn't one.

"The world witnessed the tragedy of your voyage on the *St. Louis*, Miss Wolff. And now it is being repeated with the refugee ships. People were appalled by the photographs of the concentration camps. And now they are seeing photographs of women and children living behind barbed wire once again, on Cyprus. A terrible war has been fought and won, yet nothing has changed for us. Outrage is growing. Many are ready to say to the pharaohs of this world, 'Let my people go!' I believe the Red Sea is going to part."

"We're still hated," I said. "We would be fools to believe that anti-Semitism died with the Nazis."

"We are a people set apart from everyone else because we have been given the Torah, in which God speaks to humanity. It teaches that every person has dignity and value because we are made in His image. It gives the world morals and values, a conscience. That is why we are hated. If they can be rid of us, they can silence God's voice. Whether it is Haman or Hitler or Pharaoh drowning Jewish babies in the Nile, there will always be someone who is desperate to silence us and to silence God. Right now, we stand like the prophet Ezekiel, staring at a valley of dry, dead, lifeless bones. But God isn't finished. Hitler doesn't get the last word. God does. In the prophet's vision, God fused those dead bones back together and breathed His own breath into them—and they lived! That is what I believe He is about to do."

The captain had given me more than good news—he had given me hope. I didn't feel the cold or the raindrops or the water soaking through the soles of my shoes as Jim and I retraced our steps to Grand Central station in the drizzling rain. I was giddy with joy, laughing one minute and sobbing tears of happiness the next. We took a bus from the station to Uncle Aaron's apartment, and I started crying all over again as I told Ruthie and my family the wonderful news about Sam.

"So are you coming back here to live now?" Uncle Aaron asked.

"No, I want to return upstate with Jim."

"You don't have to do that—" Jim began.

"I know I don't have to, but I want to. I feel hope again for the first time in a very long time. I'm not leaving you until you see the light of hope, too."

"But only to visit," Jim said. "Your uncle is right. You belong with your family and your people. And soon with Sam."

"Captain Cohen believes that someday we will be allowed to return to our homeland in Palestine," I told my uncle.

"Never," he said, shaking his head. "That is never going to happen. It's impossible."

His words sounded loud and harsh and very final in the tiny kitchen. But then Jim spoke, his voice strong and sure. "Isn't the God of the Torah a God who can do the impossible?" he asked.

I looked at him in surprise. He had once told me that he no longer believed in God. At the time, neither had I. But I had learned of a miracle today, and it made me dare to believe again. Perhaps it had made Jim believe, too.

* * *

September was a beautiful month to be living in the countryside in upstate New York. The leaves on the trees changed to an artist's palette of glorious colors—red, orange, yellow, rust, amber. I wrote a letter to Sam as soon as Jim and I returned from New York City and sent it to him by airmail through the relief agency on Cyprus. A month later I received Sam's reply:

Dear Gisela,

The war is over and we are both alive, and no one can ever tear us apart again! Now I know there is a God of mercy and grace and love because I have been praying that you are still alive, praying we would find each other again—and He has answered my prayers. What joy I felt when I received your letter! I'm surprised you didn't hear my shout of happiness all the way across the ocean in New York! We will have to be patient and wait a little longer, but now that I'm able to contact my parents in America, they can sponsor my immigration. The paperwork may take several months, but then I will be allowed to leave this detention camp for good and come to be with you.

But listen, my love. I am convinced more than ever that our

*real home, our children's home, will be in the land of our ancestors.
God is breathing new life into the precious souls of those who died
in the camps in order to bring about the rebirth of our Promised
Land. None of our fellow Jews will ever have to wander the world
without a home, being rejected by the nations the way we were on
the St. Louis. The prophet Zechariah gave us this glimpse of what
God is doing:*

*"This is what the Lord of Heaven's Armies says: You can be sure
that I will rescue my people from the east and from the west. I will
bring them home again to live safely in Jerusalem. They will be my
people, and I will be faithful and just toward them as their God."*

*Those words are our hope. I believe they will come true in our
lifetime and that you and I will be part of it. For now, we must
place our trust in God, who has kept us this far and who will bring
us together once again.*

We're another day closer!

All my love, all my life,
Sam

EPILOGUE

Gisela

MAY 1947

I stood with Uncle Aaron at the Port Authority Passenger Ship Terminal in Manhattan, clinging to his arm as I waited for Sam's ship to dock. The sea air tasted salty on my lips and smelled strongly of fish. Seagulls whirled above my head, calling to each other. I had been dressed and ready to leave our apartment since dawn. "We don't need to go so early," my uncle had said when I'd coaxed him to hurry. "It will take time for the ship to be towed into port and dock at the pier. Then the gangway will have to be secured before the passengers are finally allowed off."

"Please, Uncle Aaron. I want to be there from the moment Sam's ship comes into view. I need to see it land! The *St. Louis* wandered the Atlantic for more than a month, waiting to be allowed to dock. And Sam's refugee ship wasn't allowed to land in Palestine, either. I need to see his voyage completed at last, in America."

The dock was already crowded with people when we arrived. I spotted Sam's ship off in the distance being slowly guided into the port. My heart began beating so fast I feared it would wear itself out.

I had returned to New York City to live with Ruthie and my uncle at the end of September last year, in time to celebrate Yom Kippur and Sukkot with my family. Sam and I wrote to each other throughout his long immigration process, declaring our love and planning our future. With Sam's father settled and working in Miami, his parents were able to sponsor Sam's application to reunify their family. Jim's and my marriage in name only had been annulled, so Sam and I would be able to marry right away at my uncle's synagogue in Brooklyn. Then we would travel by train to Miami to see Sam's parents. After that, we weren't sure what the next step would be, but we would be making it together. Sam talked about Palestine a lot in his letters. He was convinced that God would make it possible for us to return to our Promised Land. Sam believed it would be soon.

I watched his ship move up the Hudson River toward us at a snail's pace. The long, slow wait seemed endless. At last, the ship was close enough for me to see people lining its rails, waving enthusiastically at the waiting crowd on the pier. One of them might be Sam. But there were too many of them and they were still too far away to be recognizable. The sudden blast of the ship's horn made me jump and yelp and grip my uncle's arm. We both laughed.

At last, the ship was secured, the gangway put in place, the ship's hatch opened. Passengers flooded from the ship into their families' waiting arms. I barely felt the crowd buffeting me or heard the noise and babble of languages as I kept my gaze glued to the doorway. Would I even recognize Sam after so much time? My appearance certainly had changed in the past five years. And I was a different woman on the inside, as well. I had been sixteen years old and Sam had been eighteen when we'd met. Now we were adults. Everything we'd endured had transformed us into different people. Sam had fought a world war. I had survived Buchenwald.

But I needn't have worried. I recognized Sam immediately, even from a distance. I knew him by his honey-gold hair and by the way he moved as he strode forward. I drew a sharp breath and held it at the sight of him, gazing at him in joy and wonder. In my darkest moments, I had thought I would never see him again. Tears filled my eyes. Sam seemed to pause and slow his steps, scanning the huge crowd for me. I released my uncle's arm and pushed my way toward him, calling, "Sam! Sam, I'm here!" I knew he couldn't possibly hear my voice above the noise, but I shouted anyway. "Sam!"

But he did hear me. He turned his head in my direction. "Gisela!" he shouted.

For a glorious moment our gazes locked. Then we began running toward each other, elbowing people aside. At last! At last, we were in each other's arms, clinging tightly to each other, kissing and weeping for joy. Sam was the same. We were the same. We were two people in love who were meant to be one. We had been cruelly torn apart, and now we were together once again. A song of praise to God rose up in my heart as I thanked Him for this moment. For Sam. For my life.

*　*　*

Peggy

JUNE 1947

This beautiful June day was going to be the happiest one of my life. Today I would marry the man I loved and become Mrs. Paul Dixon. But I wanted to begin the morning the way Jimmy and I usually did— fastening leashes to Lucky and Buster to take them for their morning walk.

"How do you feel, Peggety?" Jimmy asked as the dogs tugged us down the road. "Are you nervous?"

"No. I'm excited! You've seen the trainer's cottage on Blue Fence Farms, haven't you? I can hardly believe that Paul and I and Buster get to live there. I'll wake up to my favorite view of the mountains every day and see the long-legged thoroughbreds and their foals grazing in the pasture right outside my window. Best of all, I get to wake up with the man I love."

"I'm happy for both of you. Paul is a fine man."

"And I get to keep working with you and your father, too."

"You're very good at your job, Peggety."

Jimmy strolled along with one hand in his pocket, and I was reminded of something I had long been curious about. "Can I ask you a question?"

"Sure."

"I've always wondered. What was written on that paper Chaplain Bill gave you to carry in your pocket? I remember that he told you to use it like a splint for your broken spirit."

Jimmy stopped walking and reached into his shirt pocket, then handed me the wrinkled, tattered page. "I still carry it and read it every day."

I unfolded it and read the words Chaplain Bill had printed:

I am convinced that nothing can ever separate us from God's love. Neither death nor life, neither angels nor demons, neither our fears for today nor our worries about tomorrow—not even the powers of hell can separate us from God's love. No power in the sky above or in the earth below—indeed, nothing in all creation will ever be able to separate us from the love of God that is revealed in Christ Jesus our Lord.

Romans 8:38-39

I smiled as I handed it back. Jimmy smiled, too. He had been taking things slowly for the past ten months, working with his father and me part of the time, and finishing his Bachelor of Science degree, a few courses at a time, at the nearby state college in New Paltz.

"It's so good of Chaplain Bill to drive all the way here today to perform the ceremony for Paul and me," I said. "Especially since his own church has been growing so fast. He's a very busy man these days."

"And a very good friend." We had reached the bridge, and the dogs pulled us forward again, eager to trot down the footpath to the river. We took off their leashes and let them run.

Paul and I would be married in our little white church in town today, the one with the arched windows and towering steeple that pointed to heaven. We would serve cake and punch for our guests on the church lawn after the simple ceremony. The spring day promised to be a beautiful one.

"I didn't know much about love growing up," I told Jimmy. "The most important lessons I ever learned about it came from you."

"From me?"

"Yes. From your friendship and acceptance and all the loving things you did for me—like the time you brought your girlfriend over to cut my hair and donate her used clothes. You also pointed me to the source of love. I think I would have grown up to be a very different person if you and your parents hadn't been part of my life. I wouldn't have been able to return Paul's love. And I wouldn't have known God's love. I owe you a huge debt."

"Well, if that's true, then you've paid it back many times over, Peggety. I was in a very dark place a year ago, and you came along with your little candle and kept shining it into my darkness. You got all my friends to shine their lights, too. And you found Gisela for me. The shadows still haunt me some days, but the way forward is getting brighter all the time. Thank you for not giving up on me, Peggety."

We hugged, and I thought of the verse, "The light shines in the darkness, and the darkness can never extinguish it."

We whistled for Buster and Lucky, and they came splashing out of the river. Jimmy and I stood back and laughed as our dogs shook off the muddy water. Then I set off for home, walking beside my best friend, eager to begin my future as Paul's wife.

Turn the page for
a sneak peek

DON'T MISS
LYNN AUSTIN'S
NEXT BOOK

COMING IN 2023

Watch for it in stores and online

NEW YORK CITY, 1899

Adelaide Stanhope sat at her father's gravesite, as still and upright as the surrounding tombstones. The enormous Stanhope obelisk loomed nearby, marking the place where her grandfather, great-grandfather, and now her father had been laid to rest. Grandmother Junietta Stanhope's hand, gloved in black lace, lay limp and fragile in her own as the service droned on. Adelaide grasped so few of the clergyman's words that they might well have been in another language—*eternity . . . dust . . . life . . . rest.* The scent of roses and lilies, piled prodigiously on her father's coffin and heaped in profusion around it, drifted to her on the breeze. The heady fragrance seemed misplaced. It usually accompanied one of Mother's grand dinner parties or balls, filling their New York mansion or summer home in Newport with their perfume. Adelaide closed her eyes, picturing Father in his tuxedo and starched, white shirtfront, Mother reigning beside him in a dazzling gown and ropes of pearls as they greeted guests in their vast, flower-filled foyer.

She opened her eyes again and glanced at her grandmother's face, clouded by a veil of black netting. For a parent to lose a child at any age was a tragedy, especially an only child, an only son. Yet Grandmother's eyes and wrinkled cheeks were dry. She sat stoically unbowed as if carved from wax like the figures Adelaide had seen in Madame Tussaud's museum in London last year. Adelaide's own eyes were dry as well, not only because a proper lady never mourned in public, but because her father, Arthur Benton Stanhope III, was a distant figure to her, a giant in New York's business world who had spent most of Adelaide's life in boardrooms and business meetings before his unexpected death. As his third and final child, she had been a disappointment to him from the day of her birth. A third daughter.

The minister closed his book with an *amen*. A sigh escaped before Adelaide could capture it, and she glanced around discreetly, hoping no one had heard. They hadn't. She was accustomed to being ignored, but perhaps that wouldn't be true much longer. With her two older sisters successfully married—one to a British duke, no less—Adelaide, at age nineteen, would be next.

She stood when her mother did and helped her grandmother to her feet. "Are you all right, Mimi Junie?" she whispered, using the affectionate name from her girlhood.

"Yes, child." Grandmother gripped her silver-headed cane with one hand and Adelaide's arm with the other. They shuffled forward to drop more roses onto the smothered coffin. Before moving on, Grandmother Junietta paused to stare at one of the floral arrangements. The ribboned banner read *Beloved Son*. "My son . . . ," she murmured. "My son."

Mimi's thoughts sometimes slipped between decades, and occasionally back to her girlhood, so it would have been a blessing if she didn't comprehend her loss. Her words proved that she had.

"Yes, Mimi Junie. He was your son and my father. I'm so very sorry . . . Come, our ride is waiting."

Grandmother didn't move. She looked up from the flowers and scanned the crowd of black-cloaked mourners as if searching for someone. "Is my other son here?" she asked. "Did he come today?"

Adelaide's skin prickled. "I'm not sure who you mean, Mimi."

"Where is my other son?" Her hand fluttered as if trying to stir a pot of dusty memories and draw out a name. "You know . . ."

Adelaide swallowed. "You don't have another son, Mimi. Only my father. He was your only child."

Grandmother stared at Adelaide for a long moment, then shook her head. "No, he wasn't." She scanned the crowd again. "I was hoping he would come today. I would so love to see him." She gazed into the distance again before allowing Adelaide to lead her to the waiting carriage. Grandmother was obviously confused.

They climbed into the carriage and rode in dignified silence. Yet Mimi Junie's puzzling words had shaken Adelaide, eroding her composure. Had Mimi lost a son through miscarriage or stillbirth or an early death? Wouldn't there be a marker in the family cemetery plot if she had? And she would hardly expect a dead son to attend Father's funeral, would she?

The questions niggled into Adelaide's thoughts as she sat with Mimi in Mother's enormous dining room for the funeral luncheon, accepting condolences from streams of people. After a long, wearying hour, Grandmother had had enough. Adelaide helped her to her room and settled her in a chair by the window, overlooking the garden. But before leaving, Adelaide had to ask.

"Mimi Junie . . . ," she said, crouching in front of her. "At the funeral you mentioned another son."

"Did I?" She stared into her lap, idly pulling off her lace gloves.

"Yes. And it was the first time I'd ever heard of him. Can you tell me more about him?"

Grandmother dropped the gloves and gathered Adelaide's hands in hers, holding them with surprising strength. She met Adelaide's gaze, her eyes bright with intelligence, brimming with love.

"You're named after me, Adelaide Junietta Stanhope."

"Yes, I—"

"What plans are they making for you, Addy?"

"What do you mean?"

"Have they chosen a husband for you? Decided your future?"

The change in topics confused her, but she answered dutifully. "Mother said she has several gentlemen in mind, but with Father gone so suddenly, I suppose a period of mourning must be observed before—"

"You don't have to do things their way, you know. You can live the way ordinary people do. Love a man of your own choosing. But it will require courage."

"I-I don't understand."

"It's your life, not theirs. Your father can't stop you now. Do you have the courage it takes to do that, Addy?"

Her heart picked up speed. She couldn't reply. Might Mimi's questions have something to do with a mysterious second son after all? But no, Adelaide's beloved Mimi Junie—the upright, formidable grande dame of New York society—would never live a secret, scandalous life, much less urge her granddaughter to live one.

Would she?

There was a soft knock on the door and a maid entered with a tea tray. The silver teapot was small, and the tray held only one cup and saucer. "Your mother would like you to return to your guests downstairs, Miss Adelaide," the maid said. There would be no more questions or revelations today.

Grandmother squeezed Adelaide's hands tightly before releasing them. "Give me a kiss before you go, Addy dear," she said.

Adelaide did as she was told. She always did as she was told.

A NOTE FROM
THE AUTHOR

When I began researching *Long Way Home* and the stories of veterans returning from World War II, I learned some startling facts. Veterans Affairs experts estimate that one out of every twenty soldiers returning from that war suffered from what is now recognized as post-traumatic stress disorder, or PTSD. At the time, it was called combat fatigue, shell shock, or war neurosis. The field of psychiatry was in its infancy, still largely influenced by the writings of Sigmund Freud, and PTSD wasn't officially recognized by the American Psychiatric Association until 1980—after seeing it in veterans of the Vietnam War in the 1970s. As a result, the treatments available after WWII were limited to those I've described in the novel: electroshock, insulin therapy, water therapy, and surgical lobotomy, which was performed on a startling number of suffering veterans.

My portrayal of the chain-smoking doctor and his comparison of shell-shocked veterans to a startled cat were taken from a series of documentary films made by the US government during that era. While some WWII veterans suffered as severely as my character Jim Barnett, millions more of our fathers and grandfathers returned from the war and courageously went on with their lives, never talking about their experiences, while suffering from the effects of PTSD. These heroes of the war fought two battles, first against the enemy, then against the trauma they'd endured because of it. Looking back, I now recognize some mild symptoms in my own dad, who joined the Navy at age eighteen and fought in the Philippines. I wanted this novel to honor him and his fellow veterans for their courage in taking their long journey home.

While millions of soldiers were returning home at the war's end, millions of Jews who'd survived the Holocaust were still a long way from finding a new home. I wanted to honor them along with the brave citizens who risked their lives to help them hide and survive. In Belgium in particular, many Catholic priests and nuns aided in their rescue. One month before the establishment of the State of Israel on May 14, 1948, there were still 165,000 Jewish displaced persons in Germany alone. Many survivors went from concentration camps to displaced persons camps to internment camps on Cyprus before finally being allowed to immigrate to Israel—truly a long way home. The last displaced persons camp in Germany wasn't closed until 1957.

The story of the *St. Louis*'s tragic voyage is true. Aside from the survivors who were allowed into England, most of the more than nine hundred passengers ended up in countries that were later occupied by the Nazis.

I pray that this book will help us view the sacrifices of the soldiers who fight for peace and freedom in a new light, as well as look with compassion upon the innocent refugees whose lives are disrupted by the horrors of war.

ACKNOWLEDGMENTS

Once again, I have to humbly admit that I couldn't have written this book without the help of my family, my friends, and my publishing team at Tyndale House. My husband, Ken, who has been my loving partner for fifty-one years now, continues to be my biggest helper and cheerleader. Our dear friends Jane Rubietta, Cleo Lampos, Ed and Cathy Pruim, Paul and Jacki Kleinheksel, and my sweet sister Peggy Hach faithfully join him in cheering me on when I get discouraged. Many thanks to my brother-in-law Lee Hach and his rescue dog, Franny, for inspiring Buster.

I'm grateful for the advice and expertise of Jolee Wennersten, DVM, whose veterinary wisdom and love for her animal patients helped me create my characters and their work with animals. My friend Cindy Golden added her work experiences in an animal shelter. Her husband, Ted Golden, a retired fire chief, gave me valuable insight into my character Joe Fiore, who'd been a firefighter before the war.

As always, my collaboration with my agent, Natasha Kern; my assistant, Christine Bierma; and my team at Tyndale House has made this a better book. Karen Watson, Stephanie Broene, Kathy Olson, Andrea Garcia, Andrea Martin, and Katie Dodillet, I love celebrating with you at Zoom parties each time one of my books is launched.

DISCUSSION QUESTIONS

1. This novel includes two stories, which start out happening a few years apart and then converge near the end of the book. Did you find one story line more compelling than the other, or did they both hold your interest? Did you like the way they intertwined?

2. Peggy's father and his live-in girlfriend don't treat her very well. Why do you think that is? Is there anything that might excuse or justify their behavior? Is there anything different you think Peggy should have done in response?

3. Sam and Gisela meet and fall in love when they are quite young, then they are separated for many years and through many tragedies. Yet their love endures. Does that seem realistic under the circumstances, or is it just a storybook ending?

4. How does Joe try to address his PTSD? Which parts of his self-treatment are effective, and which are destructive? How does Barbara's reaction help him? What kind of a future do you envision for the two of them?

5. Peggy finds satisfaction—and makes some new friends—in her project to remind Jim of all the good things he's accomplished. Why is that rewarding for her?

6. The fate of the *St. Louis* and its passengers is taken from actual historical records. Why did Cuba and the US refuse to let the passengers come ashore? What parallel situations are we seeing in today's headlines?

7. Peggy has a hard time feeling loved and accepted. What is it about her background that contributes to this? What helps her overcome this uncertainty and accept first the Barnetts' love and eventually Paul's?

8. Buster, "the famous three-legged dog," has a significant role to play, both in the stories Jim told about him and in the way he connects with Jim when Peggy and Joe smuggle him in to visit. How have pets or other animals been important in your life?

9. Gisela and her fellow refugees experienced great kindness from Christians in Belgium. Did this part of the story surprise you?

10. How did you feel about the doctor's attempts to "cure" Jim of his battle fatigue (what we now refer to as PTSD)? In what ways has the treatment of mental illness improved since the 1940s? Where is there still room for improvement?

11. Are there veterans in your family, past or present, who have suffered from PTSD? If you or a loved one has dealt with this kind of trauma, what can you share about your experiences that might help someone who is going through something similar?

12. The Barnetts place a lot of faith in Jimmy's doctor, even though—by today's standards—they probably shouldn't have. In contrast, today we find many people dismissing expert medical opinions. Where is the middle ground? How should we evaluate the advice of experts when it goes against our instincts?

13. The theme of home is a recurring one in this book. How do each of the main characters find their "long way home"? What does

home mean to you? Have there been times in your life when you struggled to find or make a home for yourself?

14. Chaplain Bill gives Jim a Bible passage (Romans 8:38-39) to think about. In what ways does it help him? Is there a particular passage from the Bible that has been especially meaningful to you during a difficult time in your life?

ABOUT THE AUTHOR

 Lynn Austin has sold more than one and a half million copies of her books worldwide. A former teacher who now writes and speaks full-time, she has won eight Christy Awards for her historical fiction and was one of the first inductees into the Christy Award Hall of Fame. One of her novels, *Hidden Places*, was made into a Hallmark Channel Original Movie. Lynn and her husband have three grown children and make their home in western Michigan. Visit her online at lynnaustin.org.

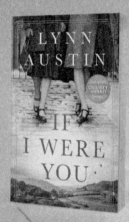  

CONNECT WITH LYNN ONLINE AT

lynnaustin.org

OR FOLLOW HER ON:

f facebook.com/LynnAustinBooks

y @LynnNAustin

g Lynn Austin

By purchasing this book from Tyndale, you have
helped us meet the spiritual and physical needs of
people all around the world.